NEBULA AWARDS SHOWCASE 2016

ALSO AVAILABLE:

NEBULA AWARDS SHOWCASE 2016

STORIES AND EXCERPTS BY

Sarah Pinsker, Aliette de Bodard, Usman T. Malik, Matthew Kressel,
Eugie Foster, Alyssa Wong, Ursula Vernon, Richard Bowes,
Kai Ashante Wilson, Carmen Maria Machado, Tom Crosshill,
Sam J. Miller, Alaya Dawn Johnson, Lawrence M. Schoen, Mary Rickert,
Ken Liu, Rachel Swirsky, Daryl Gregory, Nancy Kress, and Jeff VanderMeer

THE YEAR'S BEST SCIENCE FICTION AND FANTASY
Selected by the Science Fiction and Fantasy Writers of America

EDITED BY
MERCEDES LACKEY

an imprint of Prometheus Books
Amherst, NY

Cover image © Reiko Murakami
Cover design by Nicole Sommer-Lecht

Inquiries should be addressed to

Pyr
59 John Glenn Drive
Amherst, New York 14228
VOICE: 716–691–0133
FAX: 716–691–0137
WWW.PYRSF.COM

20 19 18 17 16   5 4 3 2 1

Library of Congress Cataloging-in-Publication Data Pending

ISBN 978-1-63388-138-9 (pbk)
ISBN 978-1-63388-139-6 (ebk)

Printed in the United States of America

PERMISSIONS

CONTENTS

CONTENTS

Nebula Award Winner: Best Short Story

Nebula Award Nominees: Best Novelette

Nebula Award Winner: Best Novelette

Nebula Award Nominees: Best Novella

CONTENTS

Nebula Award Winner: Best Novella

Nebula Award Winner: Best Novel

INTRODUCTION

If you're late to the party, the Nebula Awards are chosen every year by the members of SFWA (Science Fiction and Fantasy Writers of America); in other words, they are chosen out of all of the science fiction and fantasy literature written that year by the peers of those writers. By writers, for writers. As such, the nominators and voters tend to have a slightly different outlook on the work that comes up for the Nebulas than the average reader.

Those who nominate and vote want something more. Something different. It may or may not equate to what has gotten popular acclaim that year. It probably won't be what the "average reader" would like.

Kafka said it best, I think:

Altogether, I think we ought to read only books that bite and sting us. If the book we are reading doesn't shake us awake like a blow on the skull, why bother reading it in the first place? So that it can make us happy, as you put it? Good God, we'd be just as happy if we had no books at all; books that make us happy we could, at a pinch, also write ourselves. What we need are books that hit us like a most painful misfortune, like the death of someone we loved more than we love ourselves, that make us feel as though we had been banished to the woods, far from any human presence, like a suicide. A book must be the axe for the frozen sea within us. That is what I believe.
—Franz Kafka, from a letter to Oskar Pollak dated January 27, 1904

Ideally, there is nothing in the works that follow this introduction that will make you feel cozy and comfortable. Ideally, they will challenge you. Ideally, while they might leave you deciding you are absolutely never going to reread a story, you will *never* be sorry you read it in the first place.

A Nebula winner should be, as Harlan Ellison put it in the anthologies he edited, a "dangerous vision." Danger wakes us up, makes us realize we are alive, makes us realize why we want to stay alive. It may move us to terror, to joy, to tears, but it should never leave us unmoved.

Here's to danger.

Mercedes Lackey

ABOUT THE SCIENCE FICTION AND FANTASY WRITERS OF AMERICA

The Science Fiction and Fantasy Writers of America, Inc. (formerly known as the Science Fiction Writers of America; the original acronym "SFWA" was retained), includes among its members many active writers of science fiction and fantasy. According to the bylaws of the organization, its purpose "shall be to promote the furtherance of the writing of science fiction, fantasy, and related genres as a profession." SFWA informs writers on professional matters, protects their interests, and helps them in dealings with agents, editors, anthologists, and producers of nonprint media. It also strives to encourage public interest in and appreciation of science fiction and fantasy.

Anyone may become an active member of SFWA after the acceptance of and payment for one professionally published novel, one professionally produced dramatic script, or three professionally published pieces of short fiction. Only science fiction, fantasy, horror, or other prose fiction of a related genre, in English, shall be considered as qualifying for active membership. Beginning writers who do not yet qualify for active membership but have published qualifying professional work may join as associate members; other classes of membership include affiliate members (editors, agents, reviewers, and anthologists), estate members (representatives of the estates of active members who have died), and institutional members (high schools, colleges, universities, libraries, broadcasters, film producers, futurist groups, and individuals associated with such an institution).

Readers are invited to visit the SFWA site on the internet at www.sfwa.org.

ABOUT THE NEBULA AWARDS

Shortly after the founding of SFWA in 1965, its first secretary-treasurer, Lloyd Biggle, Jr., proposed that the organization periodically select and publish the year's best stories. This notion evolved into the elaborate balloting process, an annual awards banquet, and a series of Nebula anthologies.

Throughout every calendar year, members of SFWA read and recommend novels and stories for the Nebula Awards. The editor of the *Nebula Awards Report* collects the recommendations and publishes them in the *SFWA Forum* and on the SFWA members' private web page. At the end of the year, the *NAR* editor tallies the endorsements, draws up a preliminary ballot containing ten or more recommendations, and sends it all to active SFWA members. Under the current rules, each work enjoys a one-year eligibility period from its date of publication in the United States. If a work fails to receive ten recommendations during the one-year interval, it is dropped from further Nebula consideration.

The *NAR* editor processes the results of the preliminary ballot and then compiles a final ballot listing the five most popular novels, novellas, novelettes, and short stories. For purposes of the award, a novel is determined to be 40,000 words or more; a novella is 17,500 to 39,999 words; a novelette is 7,500 to 17,499 words, and a short story is 7,499 words or fewer. Additionally, each year SFWA impanels a member jury, which is empowered to supplement the five nominees with a sixth choice in cases where it feels a worthy title was neglected by the membership at large. Thus, the appearance of more than five finalists in a category reflects two distinct processes: jury discretion and ties.

A complete set of Nebula rules can be found at www.sfwa.org/awards/rules.htm.

2014 NEBULA AWARDS BALLOT

NOVEL

Winner: *Annihilation*, Jeff VanderMeer (FSG Originals; Fourth Estate; HarperCollins Canada)
Nominees:
The Goblin Emperor, Katherine Addison (Tor)
Trial by Fire, Charles E. Gannon (Baen)
Ancillary Sword, Ann Leckie (Orbit US; Orbit UK)
The Three-Body Problem, Cixin Liu, translated by Ken Liu (Tor)
Coming Home, Jack McDevitt (Ace)

NOVELLA

Winner: *Yesterday's Kin*, Nancy Kress (Tachyon)
Nominees:
We Are All Completely Fine, Daryl Gregory (Tachyon)
"The Regular," Ken Liu (*Upgraded*, Wyrm)
"The Mothers of Voorhisville," Mary Rickert (*Tor.com*, April 30, 2014)
Calendrical Regression, Lawrence M. Schoen (NobleFusion)
"Grand Jeté (The Great Leap)," Rachel Swirsky (*Subterranean*, Summer 2014)

NOVELETTE

Winner: "A Guide to the Fruits of Hawai'i," Alaya Dawn Johnson (*Fantasy & Science Fiction*, July/August 2014)
Nominees:
"Sleep Walking Now and Then," Richard Bowes (*Tor.com*, July 9, 2014)

"The Magician and Laplace's Demon," Tom Crosshill (*Clarkesworld*, December 2014)

"The Husband Stitch," Carmen Maria Machado (*Granta*, October 27, 2014)

"We Are the Cloud," Sam J. Miller (*Lightspeed*, September 2014)

"The Devil in America," Kai Ashante Wilson (*Tor.com*, April 2, 2014)

SHORT STORY

Winner: "Jackalope Wives," Ursula Vernon (*Apex*, January 7, 2014)
Nominees:

"The Breath of War," Aliette de Bodard (*Beneath Ceaseless Skies*, March 6, 2014)

"When It Ends, He Catches Her," Eugie Foster (*Daily Science Fiction*, September 26, 2014)

"The Meeker and the All-Seeing Eye," Matthew Kressel (*Clarkesworld*, May 2014)

"The Vaporization Enthalpy of a Peculiar Pakistani Family," Usman T. Malik (*Qualia Nous*, Written Backwards)

"A Stretch of Highway Two Lanes Wide," Sarah Pinsker (*Fantasy & Science Fiction*, March/April 2014)

"The Fisher Queen," Alyssa Wong (*Fantasy & Science Fiction*, May/June 2014)

RAY BRADBURY AWARD FOR OUTSTANDING DRAMATIC PRESENTATION

Winner: *Guardians of the Galaxy*, written by James Gunn and Nicole Perlman (Walt Disney Studios Motion Pictures)
Nominees:

Birdman or (The Unexpected Virtue of Ignorance), written by Alejandro G. Iñárritu, Nicolás Giacobone, Alexander Dinelaris Jr., and Armando Bo (Fox Searchlight Pictures)

Captain America: The Winter Soldier, screenplay by Christopher Markus and Stephen McFeely (Walt Disney Studios Motion Pictures)

Edge of Tomorrow, screenplay by Christopher McQuarrie, Jez Butterworth, and John-Henry Butterworth (Warner Bros. Pictures)

Interstellar, written by Jonathan Nolan and Christopher Nolan (Paramount Pictures)

The Lego Movie, screenplay by Phil Lord and Christopher Miller (Warner Bros. Pictures)

ANDRE NORTON AWARD FOR YOUNG ADULT SCIENCE FICTION AND FANTASY

Winner: *Love Is the Drug*, Alaya Dawn Johnson (Levine)

Nominees:

Unmade, Sarah Rees Brennan (Random House)

Salvage, Alexandra Duncan (Greenwillow)

Glory O'Brien's History of the Future, A.S. King (Little, Brown)

Dirty Wings, Sarah McCarry (St. Martin's Griffin)

Greenglass House, Kate Milford (Clarion)

The Strange and Beautiful Sorrows of Ava Lavender, Leslye Walton (Candlewick)

"A STRETCH OF HIGHWAY TWO LANES WIDE"

SARAH PINSKER

Sarah Pinsker is not only a two-time Nebula Award Nominee and a Theodore Sturgeon Award winner, but she's also a singer/songwriter with three albums under independent labels and started her first band when she was thirteen. "A Stretch of Highway Two Lanes Wide" was originally published in Fantasy and Science Fiction.

Andy tattooed his left forearm with Lori's name on a drunken night in his seventeenth year. "Lori & Andy Forever and Ever" was the full text, all in capital letters, done by his best friend Susan with her homemade tattoo rig. Susan was proud as anything of that machine. She'd made it out of nine-volt batteries and some parts pulled from an old DVD player and a ballpoint pen. The tattoo was ugly and hurt like hell, and it turned out Lori didn't appreciate it at all. She dumped him two weeks later, just before she headed off to university.

Four years later, Andy's other arm was the one that got mangled in the combine. The entire arm, up to and including his shoulder and right collarbone and everything attached. His parents made the decision while he was still unconscious. He woke in a hospital room in Saskatoon with a robot arm and an implant in his head.

"Brain-Computer Interface," his mother said, as if that explained everything. She used the same voice she had used when he was five to tell him where the cattle went when they were loaded onto trucks. She stood at the side of his hospital bed, her arms crossed and her fingers tapping her strong biceps as if she were impatient to get back to the farm. The lines in her forehead and the set of her jaw told Andy she was concerned, even if her words hid it.

"They put electrodes and a chip in your motor cortex," she continued. "You're bionic."

"What does that mean?" he asked. He tried to move his right hand to touch his head, but the hand didn't respond. He used his left and encountered bandages.

His father spoke from a chair by the window, flat-brimmed John Deere cap obscuring his eyes. "It means you've got a prototype arm and a whole lot of people interested in how it turns out. Could help a lot of folks."

Andy looked down at where his arm had been. Bandages obscured the points where flesh met prosthetic; beyond the bandages, the shine of new metal and matte-black wire. The new arm looked like their big irrigation rig, all spines and ridges and hoses. It ended in a pincer, fused fingers and a thumb. He tried to remember the details of his right hand: the freckles on the back, the rope-burn scar around his knuckles, the calluses on the palm. What had they done with it? Was it in a garbage can somewhere, marked as medical waste? It must have been pretty chewed up or they would have tried to reattach it.

He looked at the other arm. An IV was stuck in the "Forever" of his tattoo. He thought something far away was hurting, but he didn't feel much. Maybe the IV explained that. He tried again to lift his right arm. It still didn't budge, but this time it did hurt, deep in his chest.

"Can't prosthetics look like arms these days?" he asked.

His practical mother spoke again. "Those ones aren't half as useful. You can replace this hand with a more realistic one later if you want, but to get full use of the arm they said to go with the brain interface. No nerves left to send the impulses to a hand otherwise, no matter how fancy."

He understood. "How do I use it?"

"You don't, not for a while. But they were able to attach it right away. Used to be they'd wait for the stump to heal before fitting you, but this they said they had to go ahead and put in."

"You don't have a stump, anyway." His father chopped at his own shoulder as an indicator. "You're lucky you still have a head."

He wondered what the other options had been, if there had been any. It made sense that his parents would choose this. Theirs had always been the first farm in Saskatchewan for every new technology. His parents believed in auto-mation. They liked working the land with machines, gridding it with spread-sheets and databases, tilling the fields from the comfort of the office.

He was the throwback. He liked the sun on his face. He kept a team of Shires for plowing and used their manure for fertilizer. He had his father's old diesel combine for harvest time, his biggest concession to speed and efficiency. And now it had taken his arm. He didn't know if that was an argument for his horses and tractors or his parents' self-guided machines. The machines would take out your fence if you programmed the coordinates wrong, but unless your math was really off they probably wouldn't make it into your office. On the other hand—now a pincer—it had been his own stupid fault he had reached into the stuck header.

*   *   *

Andy's world shrank to the size of the hospital room. He stood by the window and read the weather and fought the urge to call his parents, who were taking care of his small farm next to theirs in his absence. Had they finished harvesting before the frost? Had they moved the chicken run closer to the house? He had to trust them.

The doctor weaned him off the pain medications quickly. "You're a healthy guy," she said. "Better to cope than get hooked on opiates." Andy nodded, fig-uring he could handle it. He knew the aches of physical labor, of days when you worked until you were barely standing, and then a Shire shifted his weight and broke your foot, and you still had to get up and work again the next day.

Now his body communicated a whole new dialect of pain: aches wrapped in aches, throbbing in parts that didn't exist anymore. He learned to articulate the difference between stinging and stabbing pains, between soreness and ten-derness. When the worst of it had broken over him, an endless prairie storm, the doctor gave the go-ahead for him to start using his arm.

"You're a fast learner, buddy," his occupational therapist told him when he had mastered closing the hand around a toothbrush. Brad was a big Assini-boine guy, only a couple of years older than Andy and relentlessly enthusiastic. "Tomorrow you can try dressing yourself."

"Fast is relative." Andy put the toothbrush down, then tried to pick it up again. He knocked it off the table.

Brad smiled but didn't make a move for the fallen toothbrush. "It's a process, eh? Your muscles have new roles to learn. Besides, once you get through these things, the real fun begins with that rig."

The real fun would be interesting, if he ever got there. The special features. He would have to learn to interpret the signal from the camera on the wrist, feeding straight to his head. There were flashlights and body telemetry readings to turn off and on. He looked forward to the real tests for those features: seeing into the dark corners of an engine, turning a breach calf. Those were lessons worth sticking around for. Andy bent down and concentrated on closing his hand on the toothbrush handle.

*   *   *

Just before he was due to go home, an infection sank its teeth in under his armpit. The doctor gave him antibiotics and drained the fluid. That night, awash in fever, he dreamed his arm was a highway. The feeling stuck with him when he woke.

Andy had never wanted much. He had wanted Lori to love him, forever and ever, but she didn't and that was that. As a child, he'd asked for the calf with the blue eyes, Maisie, and he kept her until she was big enough to be sold, and that was that. He'd never considered doing anything except working his own land next to his parents' and taking over theirs when they retired. There was no point in wanting much else.

Now he wanted to be a road, or his right arm did. It wanted with a fierceness that left him baffled, a wordless yearning that came from inside him and outside him at once. No, more than that. It didn't just want to be a road. It knew it was one. Specifically, a stretch of asphalt two lanes wide, ninety-seven kilometers long, in eastern Colorado. A stretch that could see all the way to the mountains, but was content not to reach them. Cattleguards on either side, barbed wire, grassland.

Andy had never been to Colorado. He'd never been out of Saskatchewan, not even to Calgary or Winnipeg. He'd never seen a mountain. The fact that he was able to describe the contours of the mountains in the distance, and the tag numbers in the ears of the bald-faced cows, told him he wasn't imagining things. He was himself and he was also a road.

"Ready to get back to work, buddy? How's it feeling?" Brad asked him.

Andy shrugged. He knew he should tell Brad about the road, but he didn't want to stay in the hospital any longer. Bad enough that his parents had been forced to finish his harvest, grumbling the whole time about his archaic machinery. There was no way he would risk a delay.

"Infection's gone, but it's talking a lot. Still takes some getting used to," he said, which was true. It fed him the temperature, the levels of different pollutants in the air. It warned him when he was pushing himself too hard on the treadmill. And then there was the road thing.

Brad tapped his own forehead. "You remember how to dial back the input if it gets too much?"

"Yeah. I'm good."

Brad smiled and reached for a cooler he had brought with him. "Great, man. In that case, today you're going to work on eggs."

"Eggs?"

"You're a farmer, right? You have to pick up eggs without cracking them. And then you have to make lunch. Believe me, this is expert level. Harder than any of that fancy stuff. You master eggs with that hand, you graduate."

* * *

Brad and the doctors finally gave him permission to leave a week later.

"You want to drive?" asked his father, holding out the keys to Andy's truck.

Andy shook his head and walked around to the passenger side. "I'm not sure I could shove into second gear. Might need to trade this in for an automatic."

His father gave him a once-over. "Maybe so. Or just practice a bit around the farm?"

"I'm not scared. Just careful."

"Fair enough, fair enough." His father started the truck.

He wasn't scared, but it was more than being careful. At first, the joy of being in his own house eclipsed the weird feeling. The road feeling. He kept up the exercises he had learned in physical therapy. They had retaught him how to shave and cook and bathe, and he retaught himself how to groom and tack the horses. He met up with his buddies from his old hockey team at the bar in town, to try to prove that everything was normal.

Gradually, the aches grew wider. How could you be a road, in a particular place, and yet not be in that place? Nothing felt right. He had always loved to eat, but now food was tasteless. He forced himself to cook, to chew, to swallow. He set goals for the number of bites he had to take before stopping.

He had lost muscle in the hospital, but now he grew thinner. His new body was wiry instead of solid. Never much of a mirror person, he started making himself look. Motivation, maybe. A way to try to communicate with his own brain. He counted his ribs. The synthetic sleeving that smoothed the transition from pectorals to artificial arm gapped a little because of his lost mass. If anything was worth notifying the doctors about, it was that. Gaps led to chafing, they had said, then down the slippery slope to irritation and abrasion and infection. You don't work a horse with a harness sore.

In the mirror, he saw his gaunt face, his narrowed shoulder, the sleeve. His left arm, with its jagged love letter. On the right side, he saw road. A trick of the mind. A glitch in the software. Shoulder, road. He knew it was all there: the pincer hand, the metal bones, the wire sinew. He opened and closed the hand. It was still there, but it was gone at the same time.

He scooped grain for the horses with his road hand, ran his left over their shaggy winter coats. He oiled machinery with his road hand. Tossed hay bales and bags of grain with both arms working together. Worked on his truck in the garage. Other trucks made their slow way down a snowy highway in Colorado that was attached to him by wire, by electrode, by artificial pathways that had somehow found their way from his brain to his heart. He lay down on his frozen driveway, arms at his sides, and felt the trucks rumble through.

*　*　*

The thaw came late to both of Andy's places, the farm and the highway. He had hoped the bustle of spring might bring relief, but instead he felt even more divided.

He tried to explain the feeling to Susan over a beer on her tiny screen porch. She had moved back to town while he was in the hospital, rented a tiny apartment on top of the tattoo parlor. A big-bellied stove took up most of the porch, letting her wear tank tops even this early in the season. Her arms were timelines, a progression of someone else's skill; her own progression must be on other arms, back in Vancouver. She had gone right after high school, to apprentice herself to some tattoo bigshot. Andy couldn't figure out why she had returned, but here she was, back again.

The sleeves of his jacket hid his own arms. Not that he was hiding anything. He held the beer in his left hand now only because his right hand dreamed of asphalt and tumbleweeds. He didn't want to bother it.

"Maybe it's recycled," Susan said. "Maybe it used to belong to some Colorado rancher."

Andy shook his head. "It isn't in the past, and it isn't a person on the road."

"The software, then? Maybe that's the recycled part, and the chip was meant for one of those new smart roads near Toronto, the ones that drive your car for you."

"Maybe." He drained the beer, then dropped the can to the porch and crushed it with the heel of his workboot. He traced his scars with his fingertips: first the scalp, then across and down his chest, where metal joined to flesh.

"Are you going to tell anybody else?" Susan asked.

He listened to the crickets, the undertones of frog. He knew Susan was hearing those, too. He didn't think she heard the road thrumming in his arm. "Nah. Not for now."

* * *

Andy's arm was more in Colorado every day. He struggled to communicate with it. It worked fine; it was just elsewhere. Being a road wasn't so bad, once he got used to it. People say a road goes to and from places, but it doesn't. A road is where it is every moment of the day.

He thought about driving south, riding around until he could prove whether or not the place actually existed, but he couldn't justify leaving after all that time in the hospital. Fields needed to be tilled and turned and seeded. Animals needed to be fed and watered. He had no time for road trips, no matter how important the trip or the road.

Susan dragged him to a bonfire out at the Oakley farm. He didn't want to go, hadn't been to a party since he had bought his own land, but she was persuasive. "I need to reconnect with my client base and I don't feel like getting hit on the whole time," she said. He hung his robot arm out the window to catch the wind as she drove. Wind twenty-one kilometers per hour, it told him. Twelve degrees Celsius. In the other place, five centimeters of rain had fallen in the last two hours, and three vehicles had driven through.

The bonfire was already going in a clearing by the barn, a crowd around it, shivering. Doug Oakley was a year older than Andy, Hugh still in high school. They both lived with their parents, which meant this was a parents-out-of-town party. Most of the parties Andy had ever been to were like this, except he had been on the younger side of the group then instead of the older side. There's a point at which you're the cool older guy, and then after that you're the weird older guy who shouldn't be hanging with high school kids anymore. He was pretty sure he had crossed that line.

Susan had bought a case of Molson to make friends and influence people. She hoisted it out of the backseat now and emptied the beers into a cooler in the grass. She took one for herself and tossed one to him, but it bounced off his new hand. He glanced around to see if anybody had noticed. He shoved that can deep into the ice and freed another one from the cooler. He held it in the pincer and popped the top with his left, then drained half of it in one chug. The beer was cold and the air was cold and he wished he had brought a heavier jacket. At least he could hold the drink in his metal hand. His own insulator.

The high school girls all congregated by the porch. Most of them had plastic cups instead of cans, for mixing Clamato with their beer. Susan looked at them and snorted. "If I live to be two hundred, I will never understand that combination."

They walked toward the fire. It blazed high, but its heat didn't reach far beyond the first circle of people knotted around it. Andy shifted from foot to foot, trying to get warm, breathing in woodsmoke. He looked at the faces, recognizing most of them. The Oakley boys, of course, and their girlfriends. They always had girlfriends. Doug had been engaged at one point and now he wasn't. Andy tried to remember details. His mother would know.

He realized that the girl on Doug's arm now was Lori. Nothing wrong with that—Doug was a nice guy—but Lori had always talked about university. Andy had soothed his broken heart by saying she deserved more than a farmer's life. It hurt him a little to see her standing in the glow of the flame, her hands in her armpits. He didn't mind that he was still here, but he didn't think she ought to be. Or maybe she was just leaning against Doug for warmth? It wasn't his business anymore, he supposed.

Lori slipped from under Doug's arm and into the crowd. She appeared next to Susan a moment later.

"Hey," she said, raising a hand in greeting, then slipping it back under her armpit, either out of awkwardness or cold. She looked embarrassed.

"Hey," he replied, nodding his beer toward her with the robot hand. He tried to make it a casual movement. Only a little beer sloshed out of the can.

"I heard about your arm, Andy. I felt terrible. Sorry I didn't call, but the semester got busy . . ." she trailed off.

It was a lousy excuse, but his smile was genuine. "It's cool. I understand. You're still in university?"

"Yeah. Winnipeg. I've got one more semester. "

"What are you majoring in?" Susan asked.

"Physics, but I'll be going to grad school for meteorology. Climate science."

"Awesome. You know what would make a cool tattoo for a climate scientist?"

Andy excused himself to get another beer. When he came back, Susan was drawing a barometer on the back of Lori's hand. She and Lori had never been close, but they had gotten on okay. Susan had liked that Lori had ambition, and Lori had liked dating a guy whose best friend was a girl, which she said was pretty unusual. If they had moved to the same city, CTV could have made some cheesy buddy comedy about them, the small town valedictorian and the small town lesbian punk in the big city. He would make a one-time appearance as the guy who had stayed behind.

After his fifth beer he couldn't feel anything but the road in his sleeve. The air in Colorado smelled like ozone, like maybe a storm was about to hit. That night, after Susan had drawn marker tattoos onto several of their former classmates and invited them to stop at her shop, after promises of email were exchanged with Lori, after the hazy drive home, he dreamed the highway had taken him over entirely. In the nightmare, the road crept up past his arm, past his shoulder. It paved his heart, flattened his limbs, tarred his mouth and eyes, so that he woke gasping before dawn.

*   *   *

He set up an appointment with a therapist. Dr. Bird's broad face was young, but her hair was completely silver-white. She nodded sympathetically as she listened.

"I'm not really here to give my opinion, but I think maybe you were rushed into this BCI thing. You didn't have a part in the decision. You didn't have any time to get used to the idea of having no arm."

"Did I need to get used to that?"

"Some people do. Some people don't have a choice, because their bodies need to heal before regular prosthetics can be fitted."

What she said made sense, but it didn't explain anything. It would have

29

explained phantom pains, or dreams that his arm was choking him. He had read about those things. But a road? None of her theories jibed. He drove home on flat prairie highway, then flat prairie two-lane, between fallow fields and grazing land. The road to his parents' farm, and his own parcel of land in back of theirs, was dirt. His new truck had lousy shock absorbers, and every rut jolted him on the bench.

He had lived here his whole life, but his arm was convinced it belonged someplace else. On the way home it spoke to him without words. It pulled him. Turn around, it said. South, south, west. I am here and I am not here, he thought, or maybe it thought. I love my home, he tried to tell it. Even as he said it, he longed for the completion of being where he was, both Saskatchewan and Colorado. This was not a safe way to be. Nobody could live in two places at once. It was a dilemma. He couldn't leave his farm, not unless he sold it, and the only part of him that agreed with that plan was not really part of him at all.

That night he dreamed he was driving the combine through his canola field when it jammed. He climbed down to fix it, and this time it took his prosthetic. It chewed the metal and the wire and he found himself hoping it would just rip the whole thing from his body, clear up to his brain, so he could start afresh. But then it did keep going. It didn't stop with the arm. It tore and ripped, and he felt a tug in his head that turned into throbbing, then a sharp and sharp and sharper pain.

The pain didn't go away when he woke. He thought it was a hangover, but no hangover had ever felt like that. He made it to the bathroom to throw up, then crawled back to his cellphone by the bed to call his mother. The last thing he thought of before he passed out was that Brad had never taught him how to crawl on the prosthetic. It worked pretty well.

*　　*　　*

He woke in the hospital again. He checked his hands first. Left still there, right still robot. With the left, he felt along the familiar edges of the prosthetic and the sleeve. Everything was still there. His hand went up to his head, where it encountered bandages. He tried to lift the prosthetic, but it didn't move.

A nurse entered the room. "You're awake!" she said with a West Indian lilt. "Your parents went home but they'll be back after feeding time, they said."

"What happened?" he asked.

"Pretty bad infection around the chip in your head, so they took it out. The good news is that the electrodes all scanned fine. They'll give you a new chip when the swelling goes down, and you'll be using that fine bit of machinery again in no time."

She opened the window shade. From the bed, all Andy saw was sky, blue and serene. The best sky to work under. He looked down at the metal arm again, and realized that for the first time in months, he saw the arm, and not Colorado. He could still bring the road—his road—to mind, but he was no longer there. He felt a pang of loss. That was that, then.

When the swelling went down, a new chip was installed in his head. He waited for this one to assert itself, to tell him his arm was a speedboat or a satellite or an elephant's trunk, but he was alone in his head again. His hand followed his directions, hand-like. Open, close. No cows, no dust, no road.

He asked Susan to get him from the hospital. Partly so his parents wouldn't have to disrupt their schedules again, and partly because he had something to ask her.

In her car, driving home, he rolled up his left sleeve. "Remember this?" he asked.

She glanced at it and flushed. "How could I forget? I'm sorry, Andy. Nobody should go through life with a tattoo that awful."

"It's okay. I was just wondering, well, if you'd maybe fix it. Change it."

"God, I'd love to! You're the worst advertisement my business could have. Do you have anything in mind?"

He did. He looked at the jagged letters. The "I" of "LORI" could easily be turned into an A, the whole name disappeared into COLORADO. It was up to him to remember. Somewhere, in some medical waste bin back in Saskatoon, there was a computer chip that knew it was a road. A chip that was an arm that was Andy who was a stretch of asphalt two lanes wide, ninety-seven kilometers long, in eastern Colorado. A stretch that could see all the way to the mountains, but was content not to reach them. Forever and ever.

"THE BREATH OF WAR"

ALIETTE de BODARD

Aliette de Bodard has won two Nebula Awards, a Locus Award, a British Science Fiction Association Award, and the Writers of the Future contest. She has also been a finalist for the Hugo, Sturgeon, and Tiptree Awards. "The Breath of War" was published in **Beneath the Ceaseless Skies.**

Going into the mountains had never been easy. Even in Rechan's first adult years, when the war was slowly burning itself to smouldering embers, every Spring Festival had been a slow migration in armed vehicles, her aunts and uncles frequently stopping in every roadside shop, taking stock of what ambushes or roadblocks might lie ahead.

The war might be over—or almost so, the planet largely at peace, the spaceports disgorging a steady stream of Galactic and Rong visitors onto Voc— but the pace was just as frustratingly slow.

They'd made good time at first: coming out of the city early in the morning and becoming airborne at the first of the authorised takeoff points, the steady stream of soldiers repatriated from the front becoming smaller and smaller as they flew higher, like insects on the intense brown of the road; zigzagging on the trails, laughing with relief as they unpacked the fried dough Rechan had baked for lunch, almost forgetting that they weren't setting on an adventure but on something with far longer-reaching consequences.

And then the flyer's motor made a funny sound, and the entire vehicle lurched downwards with a sickening crunch that jolted Rechan against the wall. And before they knew it, they were stranded on a dusty little road halfway up the mountains, leaving Rechan's niece Akanlam bartering with a local herder for a repair point.

By the sounds of it, the bartering was not going well.

Rechan sat against a large rock outcropping, rubbing the curve of her belly for comfort; feeling the familiar heaviness, the weight of the baby's body in her womb like a promise. *You'll be fine*, she thought, over and over, a saying that had become her lifeline, no matter how much of a lie it might be. *You'll be fine.*

"We should be able to solve this," Mau said. The stonewoman's face was as impassive as ever. Her eyes didn't crinkle as she spoke, her mouth didn't quirk; there was only the slow, quiet sound of her breath.

"You think so?" Rechan shook her head, trying not to think of her dreams. It was so many years since she'd carved Sang—so many years since she'd gone into the mountains with little more than rations and carving tools—but, with the particular link that bound a woman to her breath-sibling, she could feel him every night: blurred images of him hovering over the plateaux, never venturing far from the place of his birth. A relief, because he was her only hope.

On Voc, it took a stoneman's breath to quicken a baby at birth—and not any stoneman's, but the mother's breath-sibling, the one she had carved on accession to adulthood and entrusted with her breath. Without Sang, her baby would be stillborn.

"We'll find a vehicle," Mau said.

Rechan watched her niece from a distance. The discussion was getting animated and Akanlam's hand gestures more and more frantic. "Help me up," she said to Mau.

The stonewoman winced. "You shouldn't—"

"I've spent a lifetime doing what I shouldn't," Rechan said; and after a while Mau held out a hand, which she used to haul herself up. The stonewoman's skin was *lamsinh*—the same almost otherworldly translucency, the same coolness as the stone; the fingers painstakingly carved with an amount of detail that hadn't been accessible to Rechan's generation. Mau was Akanlam's breath-sibling; and Akanlam had put into her carving the same intensity she always put in her art. Unlike most stonemen, nothing in her looked quite human, but there was a power and a flow in the least of Mau's features that made her seem to radiate energy, even when sitting still.

"What is going on here?" Rechan asked, as she got closer.

Akanlam looked up, her face red. "He says the nearest repair point is two days down."

Rechan took in the herder: craggy face, a reflection of the worn rocks around them; a spring in his step that told her he wasn't as old as he looked. "Good day, younger brother," she said.

"Good day, elder sister." The herder nodded to her. "I was telling the younger aunt here—you have to go down."

Rechan shook her head. "Going down isn't an option. We have to get to the plateaux."

The herder winced. "It's been many years since city folks came this way."

"I know," Rechan said, and waited for the herder to discourage her. She'd gotten used to that game. But, to her surprise, he didn't.

"Exhalation?" he asked. "There are simpler ways."

"I know," Rechan said. He'd mistaken Mau as her breath-sibling and not Akanlam's—an easy mistake to make, for in her late stage of pregnancy, having a breath-sibling at hand would be crucial. "But it's not exhalation. She's not my breath-sibling; she's *hers*."

The herder looked from her to Mau and then back to Akanlam. "How far along are you?" he asked.

Too far along; that was the truth. She'd waited too long, hoping a solution would present itself; that she wouldn't need to go back into the mountains. A mistake; hope had never gotten her anywhere. "Eight months and a half," Rechan said, and heard the herder's sharp intake of breath. "My breath-sibling is in the mountains." Which was . . . true, in a way.

The herder grimaced again, and looked at the bulge of her belly. "I can radio the nearest village," he said, finally. "They might have an aircar, or something you can borrow, provided you return it."

Rechan nodded, forcing her lips upwards into a smile. "Perfect. Thank you, younger brother."

*   *   *

The village didn't have an aircar, or a cart, or any contrivance Rechan could have used. They did have mules and goats, but in her advanced state of pregnancy she dared not risk a ride on an animal. So they radioed the next village, which promised to send their only aircar. Rechan thanked them, and hunkered with

Akanlam down in the kitchen to help with the communal cooking. There was a wedding feast that night, and the community would need the travellers' hands as much, if not more, than their money.

Mau came by the kitchen later, having spent the afternoon gossiping with the village elders. "They say there's rebel activity on the plateaux," she said, handing Rechan a thin cutting knife.

"Hmm." Rechan took a critical look at the seafood toasts on the table. Half of them looked slightly crooked; hopefully in the dim light the guests wouldn't mind too much.

"Herders don't take their beasts into the mountains, and especially not on the *lamsinh* plateaux. They say people go missing there. Crossfire, probably. They say on quiet nights you can hear the sounds of battle."

Rechan thought of her dreams—of Sang's savage thoughts, the thrill of the hunt, the release of the kill, permeating everything until she woke up sweating. What kind of being had he become, left to his own devices on the plateaux? "You're not trying to discourage me, are you?"

Mau shifted positions; the light caught her face, frozen into the serene enigmatic smile that had been Akanlam's as a child. "Ha. I've since long learnt how useless that is. No, I just thought you'd like to know exactly what we're going into."

"War," Akanlam said from her place at the stove, her voice dour. "The last remnants of it, anyway."

The Galactic delegation had arrived a couple of days earlier, to formalise the peace agreement between the government and the rebels; the spaceports were being renovated, the terminals and pagodas painstakingly rebuilt. "I guess," Rechan said. "It always comes back to the mountains, doesn't it?" She shifted positions, feeling the baby move within her, a weight as heavy as stone. "Legend says that's where we all came from."

"The prime colony ark?" Akanlam scoffed, chopping vegetables into small pieces. "That was debunked years ago."

A cheer went up outside. Rechan shifted, to see onto the plaza. A gathering of people in silk clothes, clustered around the lucky trio. She was young, even younger than Akanlam; wearing a red, tight-fitting tunic with golden embroidery, and beaming; and her groom even younger than her, making it hard to believe he had cleared adolescence. The breath-sibling was a distinguished, elderly gentleman in the robes of a scholar, who reminded Rechan of her own grandfather. He was standing next to the bride, smiling as widely as she was. The sunlight seemed to illuminate his translucent body from within: it had been a beautiful block of stone he'd been carved from, a white shade the colour of Old Earth porcelain; likely, so close to the plateaux they could pick their blocks themselves, rather than rely on what the traders brought them.

By their side was someone who had to be the bride's sister, carrying a very young infant in her arms. The baby's face was turned towards the couple, eyes wide open in an attempt to take everything in; and a little brother in fur clothes was prevented, with difficulty, from running up to the bride. The baby was three months, four months old, perhaps? With the pudgy fingers and the chubby cheeks—her own child would be like that one day, would look at her with the same wide-eyed wonder.

"Life goes on," Akanlam said, her face softening. "Always."

"Of course." That was why Rechan had gotten herself inseminated, against the family's wishes: she might have been a failure by their standards, thirty years old and unmarried—for who would want to marry someone without a breath-sibling? But, with the war over, it was time to think of the future; and she didn't want to die childless and alone, without any descendants to worship at her grave. She wanted a family, like the bride; like the bride's sister: children to hold in her arms, to raise as she had been raised, and a house filled with noise and laughter instead of the silence of the war, when every month had added new holos to the altar of the ancestors.

"I'll go present our respects," Akanlam said.

"You never had much taste for cooking," Mau pointed out, and Akanlam snorted.

"Elder Aunt cooks quite well," she said with a smile. "Better to leave everyone do what they excel at, no?"

"You impossible child," Rechan said as she so often did, with a little of her usual amusement. Akanlam was the niece with the closest quarters to her own; and she and Mau and Rechan often got together for dinners and after-work drinks—though none of them ever let Akanlam cook. As Mau had said: not only did she not have much taste for it, but left without supervision she'd burn a noodle soup to a charred mess before anyone could intervene. She did mix superb fruit chunks, though. "What are you going to do when you get married?"

"You're assuming I want to get married," Akanlam said, without missing a beat. "And even if I did, I'd stay with you. You're going to need help with raising those children of yours. How many did you say you wanted?"

"I'd be lucky to have one," Rechan said, finally. But she'd dreamt of a larger family; of the dozens brothers and sisters and cousins of her youth, before war carved a swathe through them—a horde of giggling children always ready to get into trouble. If she could find her breath-sibling again . . . "And I'm old enough to do what I'm doing."

"Oh, I have no doubt. But it's still a job for two people. Or three." Akanlam smiled. "I'll see you outside."

After Akanlam had gone, Mau swung from her wooden stool and came to stand by Rechan. "Let me have a look."

Rechan almost said no, almost asked what the point was. But she knew; too many things could go wrong at this stage. It wasn't only birth without her stoneman that could kill her baby.

Mau's hands ran over the bulge of her belly, lingered on a point above her hips. "The head is here," she said, massaging it. "He's shifted positions. It's pointing downwards, into your birth canal. It's very large."

"I know," Rechan said. "My doctor said the same after the scan. Said I'd have difficulty with the birth." There were new systems; new scanners brought by the Galactics, to show a profusion of almost obscene details about the baby in her belly, down to every fine hair on its skin. But none of them had the abilities and experience of a stoneman.

"Mmm." Mau ran her hands downwards. "May I?" After a short examination, she looked up, and her face lay in shadow.

"What is it?" Rechan asked. What could she possibly have found?

"You're partly open," Mau said, finally. "You'll have to be careful, elder aunt, or you're going to enter labour early."

"I can't—" Rechan started, and then realised how ridiculous it would sound to Mau, who could do little more in the way of medical attention. "I have to get back to the plateaux."

Mau shook her head. "I didn't tell Akanlam—because you know this already—but the path gets impracticable by aircar after a while. You'll have to walk."

As she had, all those years ago. "You're right," Rechan said. "I did know." She braced herself for Mau to castigate her, to tell her she couldn't possibly think of taking a mountain trail in her state. But the stonewoman's face was expressionless, her hands quite still on Rechan's belly.

"You'll have to be careful," she repeated at last.

She couldn't read Mau at all. Perhaps it came from never having lived with a breath-sibling of her own. "You never told me why you came," Rechan said. "Akanlam—"

"—came because she's your niece, and because she knew it was important to you." Mau nodded. Was it Rechan's imagination, or was the baby stirring at her touch? Mau was Akanlam's breath-sibling, not hers. She could deliver the baby, but couldn't give it the breath that would quicken it—yet still, perhaps there was something all stonewomen shared, some vital portion of the planet's energy, a simmering, life-giving warmth, like that stone she'd touched all those years ago before she started her carving. "I came because I was curious. You're a legend in the family, you know."

Rechan snorted. "The one without a breath-sibling? That's hardly worth much of anything."

Mau turned, so that the light caught on the stone of her arms, throwing every vein of the rock into sharp relief. "But you do have a breath-sibling, don't you, elder aunt?"

How much did she know, or suspect? Rechan's official story had always been she couldn't remember, and perhaps that had been the truth, once upon a time, but now that they were in the mountains again—now that the sky lay above them like a spread cloth, and the air was sharp with the tang of smoke—memories were flooding back.

"I know the story," Mau said. "They measured you when you came back down, attached electrodes to your chest and listened to the voice of your heart. You had no breath left in you; even if they gave you *lamsinh*, you wouldn't have been able to bring a carving to life. You'd already given it to someone. Or something." Her gaze was shrewd.

So that was it, the reason she'd come with them: knowledge. Akanlam was happy with her art gallery and her shows; but of all the curious apathy she could show with life, none of it had gone into her breath-sibling. "You were curious," Rechan said.

Mau smiled, that odd expression that didn't reach her eyes. "You carved something in the mountains—came back covered in stone dust. What was it, elder aunt?"

* * *

She remembered her last trip into the mountains as if it was yesterday: going barefoot in the morning, with a curt message left on her parents' comms unit. She'd taken the set of carving tools that had been given to her on her sixteenth birthday—the straight cutter, the piercer, the driller, and all that would be necessary for her exhalation ceremony. It was a beautiful set, given by Breath-Mother: the finest hardened glass, as translucent as the best *lamsinh* stone, and hardly weighed anything on her back. As she walked away through the sparse scattering of buildings on the edge of the city, she heard, in the distance, the rumble of bombs hitting the Eastern District—the smell of smoke, the distant wail of militia sirens—and turned her head westwards, towards the mountains.

The mountains, of course, weren't better—just further away from any hospital, Flesh-Mother and Father would say with a frown—more isolated, so that if you were captured no one would know where you were for days and days. They'd have a block of *lamsinh* brought to her for the exhalation; everyone did, paying militia and soldiers and the occasional daredevil to cart the life-sized stone into the city. She just had to wait, and she'd be safe.

Rechan could not wait.

She was young, and impatient; and tired of being cooped up for her own safety. She should have been off-planet by now, sent off to Third Aunt for a year's apprenticeship in the ship-yards; except that the previous summer all spaceport traffic had been halted when a bomb exploded in the marketplace; and the apprenticeship went to some other relative who wasn't from Voc, who didn't have to cope with bombs and battles and food shortages. By now—if it hadn't been for those stupid rebels—she could have had her hands in motor oil; could have climbed into pilots' cabins, running her hands on the instruments and imagining what it would be like, hanging suspended in the void of space with only the stars for company.

Life wasn't fair, and she certainly wasn't going to wait any longer to become an adult.

*   *   *

There probably was a divinity somewhere watching over thoughtless adolescents; for Rechan had made it into the mountains, and to the plateaux, without any major trouble. She hitched a ride on a peddler's cart—so many things that could have gone wrong there, but the peddler was nice and friendly, and glad for the company—and then, when there no longer were villages or people, she walked. From time to time, she'd had to duck when a flyer banked over the path. At this height, it had to be rebels, and they'd kill her if they found her, as they had killed Second Uncle and Seventh Aunt, and Cousin Thinh and Cousin Anh; all the absences like gaping wounds in the fabric of family life. Demons take the rebels, all of them; how much simpler would life would be if none of them were here.

And then she stood on the plateaux—her feet hurting, her bag digging into the small of her back, her breath coming in fiery gasps—and it didn't matter, any of it, because there was the stone.

She'd only seen the blocks the traders brought down. The one for her cousin's exhalation had been roughly the size of a woman; of course, with *lamsinh* at such a dear price, people would buy only what was necessary. But here were no such constraints. The stone towered over her, cliffs as tall as the Temple of Mercy, broken bits and pieces ranging from the size of a skyscraper to the size of her fist; colours that ranged from a green so deep it was almost black, to the translucent shades Flesh-Mother so valued, the same colour used for all the family's breath-siblings—all the stone's veins exposed, streaks of lighter and darker nuances that seemed to be throbbing on the same rhythm as her own frantic heartbeat.

She walked among them, letting her hand lightly trail on the smooth surfaces, feeling the lambent heat; the faint trembling of the air where the sun had heated them through, like an echo of her own breath. People had always been vague about exhalation: they'd said you'd know, when you saw your block of stone, what kind of breath-sibling you wanted to carve, what kind of birth master you wanted to give to your children yet to come. But here she didn't just have one block of stone, but thousands; and she wandered into a labyrinth of toppled structures like the wreck of a city, wondering where she could settle herself, where she could make her first cut into the incandescent mass around her.

And then she rounded the edge of the cliff, and saw it, lying on the ground.

It was huge, easily ten times her size, with streaks the colour of algae water, and a thousand small dots, almost as if the stone had been pockmarked; a pattern of wounds that reminded her, for some absurd reason, of a tapestry that had used to hang on Seventh Aunt's wall, before the bomb tore her apart in the marketplace.

In all the stories she'd heard, all the tales about girls running off to have adventures, there was always this moment; this perfect moment when they reached the plateaux, or when someone showed them a block of stone, and they just *knew*, staring at it, what it would look like when whittled down to shape; when they'd freed, measure by agonising measure, the limbs and head and body of their breath-sibling, the one who would be their constant companion as they travelled over the known planets. In the stories, they didn't carve; they revealed the stone's secret nature, gave it the life it had always longed for.

Rechan had never given that credence. She was the daughter of an engineer, and believed in planning and in forethought; and had brought sketches with her, of how her own stoneman would look, with delicate hands like her mother, and large strong arms that would be able to carry her to hospital if the delivery went badly.

Except that then, she stood in front of the stone, and saw into its heart. And *knew*, with absolute certainty, that it wasn't a stoneman that she needed or wanted to carve.

*   *   *

Later, much later, when she thought about it all, she wondered how she'd endured it—months up in the plateaux with scant rations, sleeping rough, sheltering under the rock face when the rain came—day after day of rising and going back to her block of stone; carving, little by little, what would become her breath-sibling.

She did the outside first: the sleek, elegant hull, tapering to a point; the shadow of the twin engines at the back, every exhaust port and every weapons slit rendered in painstaking detail. Then she turned inwards, and from the only door into the ship, made corridors inch by agonising inch, her tools gnawing their way through the rock. All the while, she imagined it hanging in space—fast and deadly, a predator in a sea of stars, one who never had to cower or shelter for fear of bombs or flyers; one who was free to go where she wished, without those pointless restrictions on her life, those over-solicitous parents and breath-mothers who couldn't understand that bombs happened, that all you could do was go out and pray, moment after moment, that they wouldn't fall on you.

It was rough carving. She didn't have the tools that would be available to the generation after hers—not the fineness of Akanlam's carving, who would be able to give Mau fingernails, and a small pendant on her chest, down to the imprint of the chain that held it. She carved as she could—hour after hour, day after day, lifted into a place where time had no meaning, where only the ship existed or mattered; stopping only when the hunger or thirst brought themselves to her attention again, snatching a ration and then returning, hermit-like, to the translucent corridors she was shaping.

Until one day, she stepped back, and couldn't think of anything else to add.

There was probably something meaningful one was supposed to say, at an exhalation's close. She'd read speeches, all nonsense about "your breath to mine" and meters and meters of bad poetry. It didn't seem to matter very much what one said, truth be told.

"Well," she said to the ship, laying a hand on the hull, "this is it." Winter had come by then, settling in the mountains, a vice around her lungs; and her breath hung in ragged gasps above her. "I'm not sure—"

The stone under her hand went deathly cold. What—? She tried to withdraw her hand, but it had become fused to the *lamsinh*; and the veins shifted and moved, as lazily as snakes underwater.

There was a light, coming from the heart of the stone, even as the breath was drained out of her, leaving her struggling to stand upright—a light, and a slow, ponderous beat like a gigantic heart. *Breath-sister,* the stone whispered, and even that boomed, as if she stood in the Temple of Mercy, listening to the gong reminding the faithful to grow in wisdom. *Breath-sister.*

Her hand fell back; and the ship rose, casting its shadow over her.

He was sleek elegant beauty—everything she had dreamt of, everything she had carved, all the release she sought—and he didn't belong on Voc, anymore than she did.

Come with me, the ship whispered; and she had stood there in the growing cold, trembling, and unable to make any answer.

*   *   *

"A ship," Mau said, thoughtfully.

Rechan shivered. It had made sense at the time. "I named him Sang," she said at last. *Illumination*, in the old language of the settlers—because he had stood over her, framed by light.

"I didn't even know you could carve ships."

"Anything living," Rechan said, through clenched teeth. She was going to feel sick again. Was it the baby, or the memories, or both? "Stonemen are tradition, but we could have carved cats or dogs or other Old Earth animals if we felt like it."

"Whoever you'd want assisting at the birth of your children," Mau said with a nod. She smiled, her hand going to the impression of the pendant on her chest. "I suppose I should be grateful Akanlam followed tradition. Being an animal wouldn't have been very—exciting."

But you wouldn't know, Rechan thought, chilled. You'd be quite happy, either way. That's what you were carved for, to give your breath to Akanlam's babies, and even if you hadn't been born knowing it, everyone in our society has been telling you that for as long as you can remember. How much responsibility did they have for their carvings? How much of themselves had they put into them; and how much had they taught them?

And what did Sang owe her, in the end—and what did she owe him?

"Your ship is still up there," Mau said. Her voice was quiet, but it wasn't difficult to hear the question in her words.

"Yes," Rechan said. "The crossfire you heard about, it's not between the rebels and the government soldiers. It's Sang mopping rebels up." It hadn't been what she'd dreamt of, when she'd carved him; she'd wanted a spaceship, not a butcher of armies. But, consciously or unconsciously, she hadn't put that into her carving.

"The ship you carved?" Mau lifted an eyebrow.

"I was young once," Rechan said. "And angry. I don't think I'd carve the same, if I had to do it again." Though who could know, really. She'd always wondered what would have happened, if she'd answered the question Sang had asked; if she'd said yes. Would she still be on Voc, still going over the bitter loneliness of her life? Would she be elsewhere on some other planet, having the adventures she'd dreamt of as a teenager? If she could do it again . . .

"Anyway," she said, "I don't have much choice. If we don't reach the plateaux in time . . ." She didn't dare say it, didn't dare voice the possibility; but she felt as though someone had closed a fist of ice around her heart.

*   *   *

They were halfway to Indigo Birds Pass, where they would have to abandon the car, when the noise of a motor made everyone sit up.

"That's not good," Akanlam said. "We're sitting targets here." She didn't stop the aircar, but accelerated. The noise got closer, all the same: not a flyer but a swarm of drones, dull and tarnished by dust. They banked above the overhang ahead and were gone so quickly it was hard to believe they'd been there at all. Akanlam made a face. "Rebels. Our army has Galactic drones."

"Let's go on," Rechan suggested. They would get to the pass in half a day. Surely that was enough time, before the drones sent their analyses onwards to their masters. Surely. . . .

Not half an hour later, the drones came back, and hung over the aircar for what seemed like an eternity. Rechan found herself clenching Mau's hand, so hard that the stone hurt her fingers.

When the drones left, Akanlam killed the motor. "That's it. We have to go on foot. Under the cliffs, where they'll have trouble sending flyers. Come on."

Mau shot Rechan a warning glance. Rechan spread her hands, helplessly. Yes, she had to be careful, but what else could she do?

"There's a path," Akanlam called from the shelter of the overhang. "A goat trail, probably, but it'll be sheltered. At least for a while."

Rechan slid down from the aircar and walked to the overhang. There *was* a path, twisting along the side of the mountain and vanishing between two large stones. It was steep and thin, and one look at it would have made her doctor's face pale.

But there was no choice. There had never been any choice: everything had been set from the moment she'd walked into the insemination centre; or perhaps even earlier, when she'd lain in the silence of her room and known that she couldn't bear it forever. She laid her hands on her belly, whispered "hang on" to the unborn baby, and set her feet on the path.

She'd forgotten how tiring it had been, ten years earlier. Her breath burnt in her lungs after only four steps, and her legs ached after eight; and then there was only the path ahead of her, her eyes doggedly on every rock and particle of dust, making sure of her step—perpetually off-balance, struggling to keep the curve of her belly from betraying her as rocks detached under her feet—she mustn't trip, mustn't fall, mustn't let go . . .

After a while, the pain came on. At first, she thought it was just the aches from the unusual exercise, but it didn't abate, washing over her in a huge, belly-clenching wave, cutting her breath until she had to halt. Touching her belly, she found it hard, pointed, and the baby a compressed weight under her hands.

A contraction. She was entering labour. No, not now—it was too early. She couldn't afford—couldn't lose everything—

"Elder aunt?" Mau was by her side, suddenly, her hands running over her belly.

"It's starting," she said.

"Yes." Mau's voice was grave, expressionless. Rechan didn't want to look at Akanlam, who'd always been bad at disguising her emotions. "It's your first one, elder aunt. This can go on for hours. There is still time, but you have to walk."

"I can't—" she whispered through clenched teeth, bracing herself against the next contraction. "Too—tired—" And they were going to reach that plateau, and she was going to find there was no ship, that her dreams were lies, that it had never been there—how she wanted to be the ship now, hanging under the vastness of the heavens, without heaviness, without pain, without a care in the world . . .

Mau's hands massaged her, easing the knots of pain in her back. "One an hour at first, elder aunt. Or more apart. There is still time. But you have to walk."

"The drones?" she asked, and it was Akanlam who answered.

"They haven't come back."

Not yet, she thought, tasting bile and blood on her tongue. She hauled herself as upright as she could, gently removing Mau's hands. "Let's walk," she said, and even those words were pain.

There was a divinity, watching over thoughtless teenagers; there had to be one for thoughtless adults, too; or perhaps it was her ancestors, protecting her from their distant altar—her thoughts wandering as she walked, step after step on the path, not knowing how far the ending lay, not caring anymore—step after step, with the occasional pause to bend over, gasping, while the contraction passed, and then resuming her painful, painstakingly slow walk to the top.

She found her mind drifting—to the ship, to his shadow hanging over her, remembering the coldness of the stone against her hand, the breath that seemed to have left her altogether; remembering the voice that had boomed like ten thousand storms.

Come with me, breath-sister.

Come with me.

He was there on the plateau, waiting for her, and what would she tell him?

They climbed in silence. There was just Mau's hands on her, guiding her, supporting her when she stumbled; and Akanlam's tunic, blue against the grey of the rock, showing her the way forward.

She was barely aware of cresting a rise—of suddenly finding herself not flush against a cliff face, but in the middle of a space that seemed to stretch forever, a vast expanse of *lamsinh* rocks caught by the noon sun—all shades of the spectrum, from green to palest white; and a trembling in the air that mirrored that of her hands.

"There is no ship," Akanlam said, and her voice was almost accusatory.

Shaking, Rechan pulled herself upwards. "He'll be deeper into the plateau. Where I carved him. We have to—"

"Elder Aunt," Mau said, low and urgent.

What? she wanted to ask; but, turning to stare in the same direction as Mau, she saw the black dots silhouetted against the sky—growing in size, fast, too fast . . .

"Run".

She would have, but her legs betrayed her—a contraction, locking her in place, as frozen as the baby within her womb, as helpless as a kid to the slaughter—watching the dots become the sleek shape of flyers, hearing the whine of the motors getting louder and louder . . .

Run run run, she wanted to shout to Mau and Akanlam—there's no need for you to get caught in this. Instead, what came out of her was a scream: a cry for help, a jumble of incoherent syllables torn out of her lungs, towards the Heavens; a deep-seated anger about life's unfairness she'd last felt when carving the ship. It echoed around the plateau, slowly fading as it was absorbed by the *lamsinh* stone.

Her hand was cold again, her breath coming in short gasps—and, like an answer to a prayer, she saw the ship come.

He was sleek, and elegant, and deadly. Banking lazily over the plateau—illuminated by the noonday sun, as if with an inner fire—he incinerated the flyers, one by one, and then hovered over Mau and Akanlam, as if unsure what to do about them. "No you don't!" Rechan screamed, and then collapsed, having spent all her energy.

Breath-sister. The ship—Sang—loomed over her once more.

She'd forgotten how beautiful Sang was; how terribly wrong, too—someone that didn't belong on Voc, that shouldn't have been here. He should have hung, weightless, in space; instead he moved sluggishly, crushed by gravity; and his hull was already crisscrossed by a thousand fracture lines, barely visible against the heat of the stone. The *lamsinh* was weathered and pitted, not from meteorite strikes but from weapons—in fact, dusty and cracked he looked like a rougher, fuzzier version of the rebel flyers he'd incinerated.

You need me, the ship said, and came lower, hull almost touching her outstretched hands. *Let me give you your breath back.*

It was wrong, all wrong—everything she had desired, the breath she needed for her baby, the birth she'd been bracing herself for—and yet . . . "You shouldn't be here," she said. "You're a spaceship, not a flyer." She was barely aware of Mau standing by her side, looking up at Sang with wide eyes; of Akanlam, spreading her tunic on the ground.

I waited for you.

"You can't—" But he could, couldn't he? He could do exactly what she'd thought of, when she'd carved him—all her anger at the war, at the rebels, at the unfairness of it all—year after year of hunting down rebels because that's what she'd wanted at the time; not a breath-sibling to help her with a birth, but someone born of her anger and frustration, of her desire to escape the war at any cost.

Come with me.

She'd wondered what she would do, were Sang to ask that question of her again, but of course there was only one possible answer. The world had moved on; she had moved on; and only Sang remained, the inescapable remains of her history—a sixteen-year-old's grandiloquent, thoughtless, meaningless gesture.

"You have to go," she said, the words torn out of her before she could think. "Into space. That's what I carved you for. Not this—this butchery."

The ship came close enough for her to touch the exhaust ports: there was a tingle on her hands, and a warmth she'd forgotten existed—and, within her, for the first time, the baby quickened, kicking against the confines of her womb. She ought to have felt relief, but she was empty—bracing herself against the next contractions and trying to crane her head upwards to see Sang.

You need me, he said. *Breath to breath, blood to blood. How else will you bear your children? Come with me. Let's find the stars together.*

"I can't. You have to go," she said, again. "On your own."

You will not come with me? The disappointment, in other circumstances, would have been heartbreaking.

"Go, Sang. When this is over—go find the stars. That's all you've ever dreamt of, isn't it?"

The contractions were hitting in waves now—one barely over before the next one started. *Your child is coming,* Sang said.

"I know." Someone—Akanlam—grabbed her, laid her on the ground—no, not on the ground, on the tunic she'd spread out. It was becoming hard to think, to focus on anything but the act of giving birth.

What will you do, for your other children? You need me.

She did; and yet . . . "I'll find you," she said, struggling for breath. "If I need you." Of course she wouldn't; even with her link to him, all she'd have to go on would be fuzzy dream-images; she wouldn't leave Voc, wouldn't venture among ten thousand planets and millions of stars in a fruitless search. But it didn't matter. Sang would finally be free.

Sang was silent, for a while. *I will come back,* he said.

He wouldn't. Rechan knew this with absolute certainty—Sang was the desire to escape, the burning need for flight that she'd felt during her adolescence. Once he found space, he would be in the home he'd always been meant for; and who could blame him for not looking back? "Of course," she lied—smoothly, easily. "You can always come back."

There would not be other babies beyond this one, no large family she could raise; not enough to fill the emptiness of the house. But did it matter, in the end? She'd had her wish, her miracle—her birth. Could she truly ask for anything else?

I am glad.

"So am I." And it almost didn't feel like a lie. Rechan relaxed, lying flat on her back; and she settled herself down to wait for the beautiful, heartbreaking sound of her child's first breath.

NEBULA AWARD NOMINEE
BEST SHORT STORY

"THE VAPORIZATION ENTHALPY OF A PECULIAR PAKISTANI FAMILY"

USMAN T. MALIK

This is Usman T. Malik's first nomination for a Nebula Award. "The Vaporization Enthalpy of a Peculiar Pakistani Family" won the Bram Stoker Award and was first published in the anthology Qualia Nous.

1

The Solid Phase of Matter is a state wherein a substance is particulately bound. To transform a solid into liquid, the intermolecular forces need to be overcome, which may be achieved by adding energy. The energy necessary to break such bonds is, ironically, called the *heat of fusion*.

*   *   *

On a Friday after jumah prayers, under the sturdy old oak in their yard, they came together as a family for the last time. Her brother gave in and wept as Tara watched, eyes prickling with a warmth that wouldn't disperse no matter how much she knuckled them, or blinked.

"Monsters," Sohail said, his voice raspy. He wiped his mouth with the back of his hand and looked at the sky, a vast whiteness cobblestoned with heat. The plowed wheat fields beyond the steppe on which their house perched were baked and khaki and shivered a little under Tara's feet. An earthquake or a passing vehicle on the highway? Perhaps it was just foreknowledge that made her dizzy. She pulled at her lower lip and said nothing.

"Monsters," Sohail said again. "Oh God, Apee. Murderers."

She reached out and touched his shoulders. "I'm sorry." She thought he would pull back. When he didn't, she let her fingers fall and linger on the flame-shaped scar on his arm. So it begins, she thought. How many times has this happened before? Pushing and prodding us repeatedly until the night swallows us whole. She thought of that until her heart constricted with dread. "Don't do it," she said. "Don't go."

Sohail lifted his shoulders and drew his head back, watched her wonderingly as if seeing her for the first time.

"I know I ask too much," she said. "I know the customs of honor, but for the love of God let it go. One death needn't become a lodestone for others. One horror needn't—"

But he wasn't listening, she could tell. They would not hear nor see once the blood was upon them, didn't the Scriptures say so? Sohail heard, but didn't listen. His conjoined eyebrows, like dark hands held, twitched. "Her name meant a rose," he said and smiled. It was beautiful, that smile, heartbreaking, frightening. "Under the mango trees by Chacha Barkat's farm Gulminay told me that, as I kissed her hand. Whispered it in my ear, her finger circling my temple. *A rose blooming in the rain.* Did you know that?"

Tara didn't. The sorrow of his confession filled her now as did the certainty of his leaving. "Yes," she lied, looking him in the eyes. God, his eyes looked awful: webbed with red, with thin tendrils of steam rising from them. "A rose God gave us and took away because He loved her so."

"Wasn't God," Sohail said and rubbed his fingers together. The sound was insectile. 'Monsters." He turned his back to her and was able to speak rapidly, "I'm leaving tomorrow morning. I'm going to the mountains. I will take some bread and dried meat. I will stay there until I'm shown a sign, and once I am," his back arched, then straightened. He had lost weight; his shoulder blades poked through the khaddar shirt like trowels, "I will arise and go to their homes. I will go to them as God's wrath. I will—"

She cut him off, her heart pumping fear through her body like poison. "What if you go to them and die? What if you go to them like a steer to the slaughter? And Ma and I—what if months later we sit here and watch a dusty vehicle climb the hill, bouncing a sack of meat in the back seat that was once you? What if . . ."

But she couldn't go on giving name to her terrors. Instead, she said, "If you go, know that we as we are now will be gone forever."

He shuddered. *"We* were gone when *she* was gone. We were shattered with her bones." The wind picked up, a whipping, chador-lifting sultry gust that made Tara's flesh prickle. Sohail began to walk down the steppes, each with its own crop: tobacco, corn, rice stalks wavering in knee-high water; and as she watched his lean farmer body move away, it seemed to her as if his back was not drenched in sweat, but acid. That his flesh glistened not from moisture, but blood. All at once their world was just too much, or not enough—Tara couldn't decide which—and the weight of that unseen future weighed her down until she couldn't breathe. "My brother," she said and began to cry. "You're my little brother."

Sohail continued walking his careful, dead man's walk until his head was a wobbling black pumpkin rising from the last steppe. She watched him disappear in the undulations of her motherland, helpless to stop the fatal fracturing of her world, wondering if he would stop or doubt or look back.

Sohail never looked back.

*   *   *

Ma died three months later.

The village menfolk told her the death prayer was brief and moving. Tara couldn't attend because she was a woman.

They helped her bury Ma's sorrow-filled body, and the rotund mullah clucked and murmured over the fresh mound. The women embraced her and crooned and urged her to vent.

"Weep, our daughter," they cried, "for the children's tears of love are like manna for the departed."

Tara tried to weep and felt guilty when she couldn't. Ma had been sick and in pain for a long time and her hastened death was a mercy, but you couldn't say that out loud. Besides, the women had said *children*, and Sohail wasn't there. Not at the funeral, nor during the days after. Tara dared not wonder where he was, nor imagine his beautiful face gleaming in the dark atop a stony mountain, persevering in his vigil.

"What will you do now?" they asked, gathering around her with sharp, interested eyes. She knew what they really meant. A young widow with no family was a stranger amidst her clan. At best an oddity; at her worst a seductress. Tara was surprised to discover their concern didn't frighten her. The perfect loneliness of it, the inadvertent exclusion—they were just more beads in the tautening string of her life.

"I'm thinking of going to the City," she told them. "Ma has a cousin there. Perhaps he can help me with bread and board, while I look for work."

She paused, startled by a clear memory: Sohail and Gulminay by the Kunhar River, fishing for trout. Gulminay's sequined hijab dappling the stream with emerald as she reached down into the water with long, pale fingers. Sohail grinning his stupid lover's grin as his small hands encircled her waist, and Tara watched them both from the shade of the eucalyptus, fond and jealous. By then Tara's husband was long gone and she could forgive herself the occasional resentment.

She forced the memory away. "Yes, I think I might go to the city for a while." She laughed. The sound rang hollow and strange in the emptiness of her tin-and-timber house. "Who knows I might even go back to school. I used to enjoy reading once." She smiled at these women with their hateful, sympathetic eyes that watched her cautiously as they would a rabid animal. She nodded, talking mostly to herself. "Yes, that would be good. Hashim would've wanted that."

They drew back from her, from her late husband's mention. Why not? she thought. Everything she touched fell apart; everyone around her died or went missing. There was no judgment here, just dreadful awe. She could allow them that, she thought.

2

The Liquid Phase of Matter is a restless volume that, by dint of the vast spaces between its molecules, fills any container it is poured in and takes its shape. Liquids tend to have higher energy than solids, and while the particles retain inter-particle forces they have enough energy to move relative to each other.

The structure therefore becomes mobile and malleable.

* * *

In the City, Tara turned feral in her pursuit of learning. This had been long coming and it didn't surprise her. At thirteen, she had been withdrawn from school; she needed not homework but a husband, she was told. At sixteen, she was wedded to Hashim. He was blown to smithereens on her twenty-first birthday. A suicide attack on his unit's northern check post.

"I want to go to school," she told Wasif Khan, her mother's cousin. They were sitting in his six-by-eight yard, peeling fresh oranges he had confiscated from an illegal food vendor. Wasif was a Police hawaldar, and on the rough side of sixty. He often said confiscation was his first love and contraband second. But he grinned when he said it, which made it easier for her to like him.

Now Wasif tossed a half-gnawed chicken bone to his spotted mongrel and said, "I don't know if you want to do that."

"I do."

"You need a husband, not—"

"I don't care. I need to go back to school."

"Why?" He dropped an orange rind in the basket at his feet, gestured with a large liver-spotted hand. "The City doesn't care if you can read. Besides, I need someone to help me around the house. I'm old and ugly and useless, but I have this tolerable place and no children. You're my cousin's daughter. You can stay here forever if you like."

In a different time she might have mistaken his generosity for loneliness, but now she understood it for what it was. Such was the way of age: it melted prejudice or hardened it. "I want to learn about the world," she said. "I want to see if there are others like me. If there have been others before me."

He was confused. "Like you how?"

She rubbed an orange peel between her fingers, pressing the fibrous texture of it in the creases of her flesh, considering how much to tell him. Her mother had trusted him. Yet Ma hardly had their gift and even if she did Tara doubted she would have been open about it. Ma had been wary of giving too much of herself away—a trait she passed on to both her children. Among other things.

So now Tara said, "Others who *need* to learn more about themselves. I spent my entire childhood being just a bride and look where that got me. I am left with nothing. No children, no husband, no family." Wasif Khan looked hurt. She smiled kindly. "You know what I mean, Uncle. I love you, but I need to love me too."

Wasif Khan tilted his head back and pinched a slice of orange above his mouth. Squeezed it until his tongue and remaining teeth gleamed with the juice. He closed his eyes, sighed, and nodded. "I don't know if I approve, but I think I understand." He lifted his hand and tousled his own hair thoughtfully. "It's a different time. Others my age who don't realize it don't fare well. The traditional rules don't apply anymore, you know. Sometimes, I think that is wonderful. Other times, it feels like the whole damn world is conspiring against you."

She rose, picking up her mess and his. "Thank you for letting me stay here."

"It's either you or every hookah-sucking asshole in this neighborhood for company." He grinned and shrugged his shoulders. "My apologies. I've been living alone too long and my tongue is spoilt."

She laughed loudly; and thought of a blazing cliff somewhere from which dangled two browned, peeling, inflamed legs, swinging back and forth like pendulums.

*   *   *

She read everything she could get her hands on. At first, her alphabet was broken and awkward, as was her rusty brain, but she did it anyway. It took her two years, but eventually she qualified for F.A examinations, and passed on her first try.

"I don't know how you did it," Wasif Khan said to her, his face beaming at the neighborhood children as he handed out specially prepared sweetmeat to eager hands, "but I'm proud of you."

She wasn't, but she didn't say it. Instead, once the children left, she went to the mirror and gazed at her reflection, flexing her arm this way and that, making the flame-shaped scar bulge. We all drink the blood of yesterday, she thought.

The next day she enrolled at Punjab University's B.Sc. program.

In Biology class, they learned about plants and animals. Flora and Fauna, they called them. Things constructed piece by piece from the basic units of life—cells. These cells in turn were made from tiny building blocks called atoms, which themselves were bonded by the very things that repelled their core: electrons.

In Physics class, she learned what electrons were. Little flickering ghosts that vanished and reappeared as they pleased. Her flesh was empty, she discovered, or most of it. So were human bones and solid buildings and the incessantly agitated world. All that immense loneliness and darkness with only a hint that we existed. The idea awed her. Did we exist only as a possibility?

In Wasif Khan's yard was a tall mulberry tree with saw-like leaves. On her way to school she touched them; they were spiny and jagged. She hadn't eaten mulberries before. She picked a basketful, nipped her wrist with her teeth, and let her blood roast a few. She watched them curl and smoke from the heat of her genes, inhaled the sweet steam of their juice as they turned into mystical symbols.

Mama would have been proud.

She ate them with salt and pepper, and was offended when Wasif Khan wouldn't touch the remaining.

He said they gave him reflux.

3

The Gaseous Phase of Matter is one in which particles have enough kinetic energy to make the effect of intermolecular forces negligible. A gas, therefore, will occupy the entire container in which it is confined.

Liquid may be converted to gas by heating at constant pressure to a certain temperature.

This temperature is called the *boiling point*.

*　　*　　*

The worst flooding the province has seen in forty years was the one thing all radio broadcasters agreed on.

Wasif Khan hadn't confiscated a television yet, but if he had, Tara was sure, it would show the same cataclysmic damage to life and property. At one point, someone said, an area the size of England was submerged in raging floodwater.

Wasif's neighborhood in the northern, hillier part of town escaped the worst of the devastation, but Tara and Wasif witnessed it daily when they went for rescue work: upchucked power pylons and splintered oak trees smashing through the marketplace stalls; murderous tin sheets and iron rods slicing through inundated alleys; bloated dead cows and sheep eddying in shoulder-high water with terrified children clinging to them. It pawed at the towering steel-and-concrete structures, this restless liquid death that had come to the city; it ripped out their underpinnings and annihilated everything in its path.

Tara survived these days of heartbreak and horror by helping to set up a small tent city on the sports fields of her university. She volunteered to establish a nursery for displaced children and went with rescue teams to scour the ruins for usable supplies, and corpses.

As she pulled out the dead and living from beneath the wreckage, as she tossed plastic-wrapped food and dry clothing to the dull-eyed homeless, she thought of how bright and hot and dry the spines of her brother's mountains must be. It had been four years since she saw him, but her dreams were filled with his absence. Did he sit parched and caved in, like a deliberate Buddha? Or was he dead and pecked on by ravens and falcons?

She shuddered at the thought and grabbed another packet of cooked rice and dry beans for the benighted survivors.

*   *   *

The first warning came on the last night of Ramadan. *Chand raat.*

Tara was eating bread and lentils with her foundling children in the nursery when it happened. A bone-deep trembling that ran through the grass, flattening its blades, evaporating the evening dew trembling on them. Seconds later, a distant boom followed: a hollow rumbling that hurt Tara's ears and made her feel nauseated. (Later, she would learn that the blast had torn through the marble-walled shrine of Data Sahib, wrenching its iron fence from its moorings, sending jagged pieces of metal and scorched human limbs spinning across the walled part of the City.)

Her children sat up, confused and scared. She soothed them. Once a replacement was found, she went to talk to the tent city administrator.

"I've seen this before," she told him once he confirmed it was a suicide blast. "My husband and sister-in-law both died in similar situations." That wasn't entirely true for Gulminay, but close enough. "Usually one such attack is followed by another when rescue attempts are made. My husband used to call them 'double tap' attacks." She paused, thinking of his kind, dearly loved face for the first time in months. "He understood the psychology behind them well."

The administrator, a chubby short man with filthy cheeks, scratched his chin. "How come?"

"He was a Frontier Corps soldier. He tackled many such situations before he died."

"Condolences, *bibi*." The administrator's face crinkled with sympathy. "But what does that have to do with us?"

"At some point, these terrorists will use the double tap as decoy and come after civilian structures."

"Thank you for the warning. I'll send out word to form a volunteer perimeter patrol." He scrutinized her, taking in her hijab, the bruised elbows, and grimy fingernails from days of work. "God bless you for the lives you've saved already. For the labor you've done."

He handed her a packet of boiled corn and alphabet books. She nodded absently, charred bodies and boiled human blood swirling up from the shrine vivid inside her head, thanked him, and left.

The emergency broadcast thirty minutes later confirmed her fear: a second blast at Data Sahib obliterated a fire engine, killed a jeep-ful of eager policemen, and vaporized twenty-five rescuers. Five of these were female medical students. Their shattered glass bangles were melted and their heads-carves burned down to unrecognizable gunk by the time the EMS came, they later said.

Tara wept when she heard. In her heart was a steaming shadow that whispered nasty things. It impaled her with its familiarity, and a dreadful suspicion grew in her that the beast was rage and wore a face she knew well.

4

When matter is heated to high temperatures, such as in a flame, electrons begin to leave the atoms. At very high temperatures, essentially all electrons are assumed to be dissociated, resulting in a unique state wherein positively charged nuclei swim in a raging 'sea' of free electrons.

This state is called the Plasma Phase of Matter and exists in lightning, electric sparks, neon lights, and the Sun.

* * *

In a rash of terror attacks, the City quickly fell apart: the Tower of Pakistan, Lahore Fort, Iqbal's Memorial, Shalimar Gardens, Anarkali's Tomb, and the thirteen gates of the Walled City. They exploded and fell in burning tatters, survived only by a quivering bloodhaze through which peeked the haunted eyes of their immortal ghosts.

This is death, this is love, this is the comeuppance of the two, as the world according to you will finally come to an end. So snarled the beast in Tara's head each night. The tragedy of the floodwaters was not over yet, and now this.

Tara survived this new world through her books and her children. The two seemed to have become one: pages filled with unfathomable loss. White space itching to be written, reshaped, or incinerated. Sometimes, she would bite her lips and let the trickle of blood stain her callused fingers. Would touch them to water-spoilt paper and watch it catch fire and flutter madly in the air, aflame like a phoenix. An impossible glamor created by tribulation. So when the city burned and her tears burned, Tara reminded herself of the beautiful emptiness of it all and forced herself to smile.

Until one morning she awoke and discovered that, in the cover of the night, a suicide teenager had hit her tent city's perimeter patrol.

*   *   *

After the others had left, she stood over her friends' graves in the twilight.

Kites and vultures unzipped the darkness above in circles, lost specks in this ghostly desolation. She remembered how cold it was when they lowered Gulminay's remains in the ground. How the drone attack had torn her limbs clean off so that, along with a head shriveled by heat, a glistening, misshapen, idiot torso remained. She remembered Ma, too, and how she was killed by her son's love. The first of many murders.

"I know you," she whispered to the Beast resident in her soul. "I know you", and all the time she scribbled on her flesh with a glass shard she found buried in a patrolman's eye. Her wrist glowed with her heat and that of her ancestors. She watched her blood bubble and surge skyward. To join the plasma of the world and drift its soft, vaporous way across the darkened City, and she wondered again if she was still capable of loving them both.

The administrator promised her he would take care of her children. He gave her food and a bundle of longshirts and shalwars. He asked her where she was going and why, and she knew he was afraid for her.

"I will be all right," she told him. "I know someone who lives up there."

"I don't understand why you must go. It's dangerous," he said, his flesh red under the hollows of his eyes. He wiped his cheeks, which were wet. "I wish you didn't have to. But I suppose you will. I see that in your face. I saw that when you first came here."

She laughed. The sound of her own laughter saddened her. "The world will change," she said. "It always does. We are all empty, but this changing is what saves us. That is why I must go."

He nodded. She smiled. They touched hands briefly; she stepped forward and hugged him, her headscarf tickling his nostrils, making him sneeze. She giggled and told him how much she loved him and the others. He looked pleased and she saw how much kindness and gentleness lived inside his skin, how his blood would never boil with undesired heat.

She lifted his finger, kissed it, wondering at how solid his vacant flesh felt against her lips.

Then she turned and left him, leaving the water and fire and the crackling, hissing earth of the City behind.

Such was how Tara Khan left for the mountains.

*   *   *

The journey took a week. The roads were barren, the landscape abraded by floodwater and flensed by intermittent fires. Shocked trees, stripped of fruit, stood rigid and receding as Tara's bus rolled by, their gnarled limbs pointing accusatorially at the heavens.

Wrapped in her chador, headscarf, and khaddar shalwar kameez, Tara folded into the rugged barrenness with its rugged people. They were not unkind; even in the midst of this madness, they held onto their deeply honored tradition of hospitality, allowing Tara to scout for hints of the Beast's presence. The northerners chattered constantly and were horrified by the atrocities blooming from within them, and because she too spoke Pashto they treated her like one of them.

Tara kept her ears open. Rumors, whispers, beckonings by skeletal fingers. Someone said there was a man in Abbottabad who was the puppeteer. Another shook his head and said that was a deliberate shadow show, a gaudy interplay of light and dark put up by the real perpetrators. That the Supreme Conspirator was swallowed by earth soaked with the blood of thousands and lived only as an extension of this irredeemable evil.

Tara listened and tried to read between their words. Slowly, the hints in the midnight alleys, the leprous grins, the desperate, clutching fingers, incinerated trees and smoldering human and animal skulls—they began to come together and form a map.

Tara followed it into the heart of the mountains.

5

When the elementary particle boson is cooled to temperatures near absolute zero, a dilute 'gas' is created. Under such conditions, a large number of bosons occupy the lowest quantum state and an unusual thing happens: quantum effects become visible on a macroscopic scale. This effect is called the macroscopic quantum phenomena and the 'Bose-Einstein condensate' is inferred to be a new state of matter. The presence of one such particle, the Higgs-Boson, was tentatively confirmed on March 14th, 2013 in the most complex experimental facility built in human history.

This particle is sometimes called the *God Particle*.

*   *   *

When she found him, he had changed his name.

There is a story told around campfires since the beginning of time: Millennia ago a stone fell from the infinite bosom of space and plunked onto a statistically impossible planet. The stone was round, and smaller than a pebble of hard goat shit, and carried a word inscribed on it.

It has been passed down generations of Pahari clans that that word is the *Ism-e-Azam*, the Most High Name of God.

Every sect in the history of our world has written about it. Egyptians, Mayans. Jewish, Christian, and Muslim mystics. Some have described it as the primal point from which existence began, and that the Universal Essence lives in this *nuktah*.

The closest approximation to the First Word, some say, is one that originated in Mesopotamia, the land between the two rivers. The Sumerians called it *Annunaki*.

He of Godly Blood.

Tara thought of this oral tradition and sat down at the mouth of the demolished cave. She knew he lived inside the cave, for every living and nonliving thing near it reeked of his heat. Twisted boulders stretched granite hands toward its mouth like pilgrims at the Kaaba. The heat of the stars they both carried in their genes, in the sputtering, whisking emptiness of their cells, had leeched out and warped the mountains and the path leading up to it.

Tara sat cross-legged in the lotus position her mother taught them both when they were young. She took a sharp rock and ran it across her palm. Crimson droplets appeared and evaporated, leaving a metallic tang in the air. She sat and inhaled that smell and thought of the home that once was. She thought of her mother, and her husband; of Gulminay and Sohail; of the floods (did he have something to do with that too? Did his rage liquefy snow-topped mountains and drown an entire country?); of suicide bombers, and the University patrol; and of countless human eyes that flicked each moment toward an unforgiving sky where something merciful may or may not live; and her eyes began to burn and Tara Khan began to cry.

"Come out," she said between her sobs. "Come out, Beast. Come out, Rage. Come out, Death of the Two Worlds and all that lives in between. Come out, Monster. Come out, Fear," and all the while she rubbed her eyes and let the salt of her tears crumble between her fingertips. Sadly she looked at the white crystals, flattened them, and screamed, "Come out, ANNUNAKI."

And in a belch of shrieking air and a blast of heat, her brother came to her.

*　　*　　*

They faced each other.

His skin was gone. His eyes melted, his nose bridge collapsed; the bones underneath were simmering white seas that rolled and twinkled across the constantly melting and rearranging meat of him. His limbs were pseudopodic, his movement that of a softly turning planet drifting across the possibility that is being.

Now he floated toward her on a gliding plane of his skin. His potent heat, a shifting locus of time-space with infinite energy roiling inside it, touched her, making her recoil. When he breathed, she saw everything that once was; and knew what she knew.

"Salam," she said. "Peace be upon you, brother."

The *nuktah* that was him twitched. His fried vocal cords were not capable of producing words anymore.

"I used to think," she continued, licking her dry lips, watching the infinitesimal shifting of matter and emptiness inside him, "that love was all that mattered. That the bonds that pull us all together are of timeless love. But it is not true. It has never been true, has it?"

He shimmered, and said nothing.

"I still believe, though. In existing. In *ex nihilo nihil fit*. If nothing comes from nothing, we cannot return to it. Ergo life has a reason and needs to be." She paused, remembering a day when her brother plucked a sunflower from a lush meadow and slipped it into Gulminay's hair. "Gulminay-jaan once was and still is. Perhaps inside you and me." Tara wiped her tears and smiled. "Even if most of us is nothing."

The heat-thing her brother was slipped forward a notch. Tara rose to her feet and began walking toward it. The blood in her vasculature seethed and raged.

"Even if death breaks some bonds and forms others. Even if the world flinches, implodes, and becomes a grain of sand."

Annunaki watched her through eyes like black holes and gently swirled.

"Even if we have killed and shall kill. Even if the source is nothing if not grief. Even if sorrow is the distillate of our life."

She reached out and gripped his melting amebic limb. He shrank, but didn't let go as the maddened heat of her essence surged forth to meet his.

"Even if we never come to much. Even if the sea of our consciousness breaks against quantum impossibilities."

She pressed his now-arm, her fingers elongating, stretching, turning, fusing; her flame-scar rippling and coiling to probe for his like a proboscis.

Sohail tried to smile. In his smile were heat-deaths of countless worlds, supernova bursts, and the chrysalis sheen of a freshly hatched larva. She thought he might have whispered sorry. That in another time and universe there were not countless intemperate blood-children of his spreading across the earth's face like vitriolic tides rising to obliterate the planet. That all this wasn't really happening for one misdirected missile, for one careless press of a button somewhere by a soldier eating junk food and licking his fingers. But it was. Tara had glimpsed it in his *nuktah* when she touched him.

"Even if," she whispered as his being engulfed hers and the thermonuclear reaction of matter and antimatter fusion sparked and began to eradicate them both, "our puny existence, the conclusion of an agitated, conscious universe, is insignificant, remember . . . remember, brother, that mercy will go on. Kindness will go on."

Let there be gentleness, she thought. Let there be equilibrium, if all we are and will be can survive in some form. Let there be grace and goodness and a hint of something to come, no matter how uncertain.

Let there be *possibility*, she thought, as they flickered annihilatively and were immolated in some fool's idea of love.

*   *   *

For the 145 innocents of the 12/16 Peshawar terrorist attack and countless known & unknown before.

NEBULA AWARD NOMINEE
BEST SHORT STORY

"THE MEEKER AND THE ALL~SEEING EYE"

MATTHEW KRESSEL

Matthew Kressel has previously been nominated for both a Nebula Award and a World Fantasy Award. "The Meeker and the All-Seeing Eye" was published in Clarkesworld.

As the Meeker and the All-Seeing Eye wandered the galaxy harvesting dead stars, they liked to talk.

"I was traveling the southern arm," the Meeker said, "you know, where the Baileas eat the cold dust?"

"I do," said the All-Seeing Eye. "But tell me again."

"Well, that old hag told me she used to swallow stars by the *thousands*!"

The Meeker chuckled and one of his nine arms bumped the controls. The accidental thrust, less than a few million photons, would take the Bulb off course by more than four light-years. But what was another century when the Meeker and the Eye had millennia to talk?

The polymorphous mist of the Eye spun above her seat like a timid nebula. Usually this meant she wanted him to continue, and so he did.

"I told that raggedy beast that if I believed her ash then I'd believe all that nonsense folks say these days about the Long Gone."

"And what do they say?" asked the All-Seeing Eye.

"That there were billions of cities spread across the galaxy, vicious trade between worlds, and so many species they ran out of names. You know, kook dust."

"I do," said the Eye. "But tell me again."

And what luck the Meeker had bumped the controls, because the sensors had just detected an object drifting in the voids. "Eye! What the ash is that?" The mist of the Eye collapsed into a sphere like a newborn star. "An unknown! Meeker, change course to intercept!"

The Meeker obeyed, and their Bulb banked through rarefied crimson wisps, cosmic ash that would never again coalesce into stars. "Do you think it's from the Zimbim?" he said, as if he'd known those majestic builders himself. "You know they once lived on ninety planets and rebuilt all their crystal cities in a day?"

"I do," said the Eye. "But tell me again."

After four weeks of travel he said, "Do you think it's a baby Qly? You know they could grow to swallow galaxies, but preferred to curl around young stars and sing electromagnetic eulogies into space?"

"I do," said the Eye. "But tell me again."

And nine months after that he said, "Could it be a wayward Urm, those planetary rings that ate emotions?" The Bulb had slowed considerably by now, and the scattered stars had lost their endearing blue shift, turned red, ancient, tired. "Or maybe," he said, "it's a philosophizing Ruck worm. You know their proverbs were spoken by half the galaxy?"

"I do," said the Eye, "But tell me again."

"What I would give," the Meeker said, "just to glimpse the Long Gone."

They passed a rare star, a red dwarf that had smoldered for eons. Normally the Meeker would capture it in the Bulb's gravity well and ferry the star to the Great Corpus at the center of the galaxy. There the Eye's body would gain a few quadrillion more qubits, and a tremble of gravitational waves would ripple forever out into the abyss. But today they flew past the star, the first time the Meeker had ever skipped one.

In a maneuver he hoped made the Eye proud, he captured the object in the hold on the first pass, only bumping it once against the wall as he accelerated back toward the galactic center.

"Have it brought to the lab," said the Eye. "And join me there after you finish correcting our course."

The lab was tiny compared to most of the rooms on the Bulb. Sundry sensors crowded the space, and a clear, hollow cylinder dominated the center. The strange object hovered inside: a rectangular stone, dark as basalt, glimmering with a metallic sheen. Curious glyphs had been inscribed upon it, though heavy pitting had erased most of them.

The Meeker secreted calming mucus from his pores and said, "Was I right? Is it from the Long Gone?"

"Yes, Meeker. It is."

He felt like leaping, and his limbs flailed excitedly. "What is it?"

"I'm still determining that. So far, I've discovered a volume of information encoded in its crystalline structure, a massively compressed message that uses a curious fractal algorithm. It has stymied all my attempts to decode it. I've relayed the contents to my Great Corpus for further help."

"How strange and wonderful!" the Meeker said. "A message in a stone! But which civilization is it from?"

"I don't know."

The Meeker's third stomach shifted uncomfortably. There had never been a fact the Eye did not know, a puzzle she could not quickly solve.

The Eye morphed into a dodecahedron. "Finally! My Corpus has just decoded a fragment of the message."

"What does it say?"

"The message encodes a lifeform, which I will now attempt to recreate."

His outer sheath grew slimy with anticipation. He was going to see a creature from the Long Gone!

A second tube materialized beside the first. A grotesque lump of quivering flesh formed inside it before collapsing into a pile of red ichor.

"How lovely!" he said.

The Eye expanded into a mist. "That's not the creature. I've used the wrong chirality for the nucleic acids. I will try again."

Did the Great All-Seeing Eye just err? he thought. *How is this possible?*

The lump vaporized and vanished, and a new shape formed. First came a crude framework of hard white mineral, then a flood of viscous fluids, soft organs and wet tissues, all wrapped under a covering of beige skin.

"Close your outer sheath," the Eye said. "I'm changing the atmosphere and temperature to match the creature's tolerances."

The Eye didn't pause, and if the Meeker hadn't acted instantly, he would've died in the searing heat and pressure. The air was now so dense that he could feel his nine limbs press against it as they fluttered about.

The cylinder door swung open and out poured a sour-smelling mist.

Thinking this was a greeting, the Meeker flatulated a sweet-smelling response.

Four limbs spoked out from the creature's rectangular torso. A bulbous lump rose from the top. It had two deep-set orbs, a hooked flange of skin over two small openings, and a pink-lipped orifice covering rows of white mineral. Crimson fibers, the same smoldering shade as the ancient stars, draped from its peak. The Meeker had never seen anything more disgusting.

"What the . . . ?" the creature said, its voice low-pitched in the dense air. "Where am I?"

The Meeker gasped. "It speaks from its anus?"

"That's its mouth," said the Eye.

This foul creature was far different from the glorious ancients he had imagined, and he felt a little disappointed.

"Welcome to Bulb 64545," said the Eye. "I am the All-Seeing Eye, and this is Meeker 6655321. I have adjusted your body so you can understand and speak Verbal Sub-Four, our common tongue. Who are you?"

"I . . . I'm Beth," the creature said. "*Where* am I?"

The Eye told the Beth how she had been constructed from an encoded message. "It's been millennia since I last discovered something new in the galaxy. Your presence astonishes me."

"Yeah," the Beth said, "it astonishes me too."

"And me!" added the Meeker.

"Millennia?" the Beth said. Pink membranes flashed before her white and green orbs. Were these crude things her eyes?

"What species are you?" said the Eye.

The Beth grasped her shoulders as if to squeeze herself. "I'm human."

"Curious. I've no record of your kind. Where are you from?"

The Beth made a raspy wet sound with her throat and looked up at the ceiling, when the green circles in her eyes sparkled like interstellar frost. The rest of her was difficult to look at, but these strange eyes were profoundly more beautiful than the wisps of lithium clouds diffracting the morning sun into rainbows during his home moon's sluggish dawn.

"Denver," she said.

"What do you last remember?" asked the Eye.

"I was in a dark space," said the Beth. "Sloan was there, holding my hand."

"Who is the Sloan?"

"She's my wife. And who—*what* are you?"

The Meeker let loose a spray of pheromone-scented mucus. "I'm the Meeker, your humble pilot! And this is the Great All-Seeing Eye!"

"But *what* are you?"

The Eye collapsed into a torus. "This will take time to explain."

"I'm freezing. Do you have any clothes?"

Freezing? the Meeker thought. It was hot enough to melt water ice!

But with the Eye's help, the Beth covered herself in white fabrics. He didn't understand why she needed to sheathe herself in an artificial skin when she already wore a natural one.

"I'm not well," she said, holding her head.

The Eye floated beside her. "It may be a side-effect of your regeneration."

"No. I'm sick."

"Are you referring to the genetic material rapidly replicating inside your cells?"

"You know about the virus?"

"I observed the phenomenon when I created you, but I assumed it was part of your natural genetic pattern."

"No. It most definitely isn't. Do you have any water?"

A clear cylinder materialized on a table beside her.

"Oh," the Beth said, flinching. "That will take some getting used to."

She poured the searing hot liquid into her mouth, but her hands shook and she spilled half onto the floor. Red lines spiraled in from the corners of her eyes. "Is anyone else here?"

The Eye's toroid body rippled. "Just the three of us."

"No other humans?"

"According to my estimation, the stone was drifting in space for five hundred million years. It is likely that you're the last of your kind."

"So . . . Sloan is dead?"

"Yes."

"But she was just beside me!"

"From your perspective. In reality, that moment occurred millions of years ago."

The Beth put a hand to her mouth. "Oh my god . . ."

"Yes?" said the Eye.

The Beth gazed at the Eye for a long moment, then her eyes narrowed.

"Sloan whispered to me, just before I woke up. She said she had a message for the future, for whoever wakes me. It was, she said, something that would change the course of history. A terrible fact that must be known."

The Eye moved closer to her. "Tell me. Tell me this fact!"

"My son. He . . ." She swallowed. "He asphyxiated in the womb."

"How terrible," the Meeker said.

"Continue," said the Eye.

"After, they did all these tests, and they discovered I had a virus. I had transmitted it to my unborn son. He never had a chance. Sloan said that my virus, the one that's in my blood, it was from . . . it was created for . . . it was made by . . . Oh, god, I'm going to be—"

Her eyes rolled back into her head and she vomited yellow fluid onto the floor. She crashed forward and her head slammed into the table, then she shuddered in a violent paroxysm.

"What's happening?" the Meeker said.

"It's the virus," said the Eye.

"Can you stop it?"

But the Beth stopped on her own, and all went still but for a faint hiss from her mouth.

"Hello?" he said.

"She's dead," said the Eye.

He felt a pang of panic. "But she's only just come alive!" Was this brief glimpse all he would ever see of the Long Gone?

"Do not fret, Meeker. I am already creating another Beth."

*   *   *

An hour later they sat in the cockpit, the Meeker on the left, the Beth in the middle, and the Eye on the right, as the Bulb hurtled toward the galactic center at half the speed of light.

The Beth had wrapped herself in a heavy blanket and pulled it close to her body. She seemed amazed with everything she saw. "But if we're in space, where have all the stars gone?" A red dwarf, seven light years away, floated against a backdrop of absolute black.

"We harvested them," the Meeker said, secreting a mucus of pride.

"*Harvested*? Why?"

"The matter we collect," said the Eye, "is cooled to near absolute-zero, quantum entangled into a condensate, and joined with my Great Corpus, thus adding to my total computational power."

"You're a computer?"

"The Eye," the Meeker said, "is the greatest mind the Cosmos has ever known."

"My sole purpose is knowledge," said the Eye. "I seek to know all things."

"So many stars, gone," the Beth said. "Was there life out there?"

"Oh, yes," said the Meeker. "There were once so many species they ran out of names!"

"And now?"

"Now they are part of my Great Corpus," said the Eye.

"By choice?"

The Meeker scratched his belly in confusion. "What does choice have to do with it?"

The Beth pulled her blanket closer. "Everything."

"What do you remember about your last moments?" the Eye said.

The Beth spoke slowly. "Sloan was whispering to me."

"And what did she say?"

The Beth looked down at her hands. "I don't want to talk about it."

"You must tell me," said the Eye.

"Why?" She pursed her lips, and fluid pooled in the corners of her eyes. "So you can harvest me too?"

The Meeker gasped. What offense! He waited for the Eye to punish her, but the Beth coughed up a globule of mucus. This pleased him. She must have realized her offense and offered this up as an apology. But when she vomited all over the console and wailed for a full minute before she fell silent, he realized this had been involuntary.

"She's dead?" he said. Red fluid dripped from a wound on her head.

"Yes, Meeker."

"Eye, maybe you should stop making Beths, at least until you find a cure?"

The Beth vaporized and vanished, as if she never was. "Did you not hear the first Beth? The Sloan had a message for the future that she believed would change history. I must know what this message is."

*   *   *

The next Beth began with the same questions, but the Eye avoided telling her too much. And when the Beth asked about the stars, the Eye replied with a question for her.

"My planet?" the Beth said. "It's called Dirt. You've never heard of it? Where did you find me?" The Beth gazed into the impenetrable black.

The Meeker was envious. He had been born on an airless moon that orbited the Great Corpus every thousand years and spent the rest of his life in this Bulb.

"Are we in space?" the Beth said. "Are we beyond the Moon?"

"You live on the surface of your planet?" asked the Eye.

"Yes, at the foot of the Rockies, in a glass house. Sloan and I moved there because we love the stars. The Lacteal Path shines clear across the sky most nights." The Beth chewed at a fingertip. "Where are all the stars? Where are you taking me?"

"Did the Sloan whisper something to you before you awoke?" the Eye said.

"How did you know?"

"Tell me, what did she say?"

"I'd found out she was working on top secret projects a few months ago. She swore it wasn't weapons, but I didn't believe her. We had a big fight. Is there any way I might call her? She's probably worried sick."

"Did the Sloan mention your stillborn child?"

"Excuse me? How do you know about that?"

"You transmitted the virus to your fetus in utero. The Sloan intimated that this fact was related to a very important message for the future. Now tell me—"

"No, that's not what we spoke about! And how do you know so much about me? What the hell is going on here? I want to go home now!"

She put a hand to her mouth and vomited all over herself, then she spasmed, smacking her limbs into the Meeker. And after a minute of flailing and screaming she collapsed dead.

"Curious," said the Eye. "Did you notice her story has changed?"

The Beth's mouth hung open from her scream.

"That's not what I noticed, Eye, no."

*　　*　　*

The Eye asked the next Beth about her family.

"I have two daughters, Bella, ten, and Yrma, twelve. My son Joshua, he's eighteen, and just left for college in Vermont. Before I got sick, I used to hike up the mountain trails with them at least once a week. Walking with my children under pines covered in snow . . ." She inhaled through her nose. "I never felt more at peace. Is there a way I might call them?"

"Tell us about the Sloan," said the Eye. "Did she whisper something to you before you awoke here?"

"Funny you should mention it."

"What did she say?"

"It was about that day, when I didn't want to tell the children I was sick. She got angry, but I said she was a hypocrite, because she works in a secret research lab and hides things from us every day."

"She researches weapons technology?"

"She swears she doesn't. And how do you know that? Have you spoken to her?"

"Was there anything else the Sloan said before you woke up here?"

"Not that I remember."

"Are you sure you didn't speak about your son, who died in utero?"

"What? No! What the hell is going on here?" The Beth stood, shaky on her two legs. "I'm not answering any more of your questions until someone tells me—"

She put a hand to her mouth and vomited. She screamed and spasmed, and when she was dead, the Meeker said, "Eye, why do you keep the truth from her? Shouldn't she know that her family is dead half a billion years?"

"What purpose would that serve? You saw how agitated she became when she learned the truth. How else will we find this message the Sloan has given her?"

"But she dies in pain each time."

"Why do you think she's in pain?"

"Because she screams so terribly."

"Those aren't screams of pain, Meeker, but of joy. Her eternal life energy is free at last from her temporal body. It's the same screams of joy that the civilizations of the Long Gone made when I swallowed their worlds."

The Meeker had heard her stories a thousand times, he had even told a few back to her. But as he gazed down at the dead Beth and her dripping fluids, he wondered if the Eye was keeping things from him too.

*   *   *

The next Beth said, "Sloan whispered to me about the sunrise we watched that morning in Mexico. We felt as if we were part of the whole Cosmos, not discrete fragments."

"And nothing more?" asked the Eye.

"Isn't that enough?"

Then she died, and the next Beth said, "Sloan whispered that she'd miss drinking her morning coffee with me. Are you taking me home?"

The next Beth said, speaking of a stringed contrivance used to make music, "Sloan wished I had played *guitar* more often for her."

"And nothing else?" asked the Eye.

"No."

The Eye questioned the Beths in the same way the Meeker approached the stars, not head on, but from the side. The Eye poked and prodded, but each Beth told a different story of her last moments, and each one died screaming.

"Eye?" the Meeker said, after the fifty-ninth Beth. "What if you never find the Sloan's message?"

"All problems have solutions, Meeker. All mysteries have answers."

He wished that were true, because he began to imagine the Beths screaming, even while they were still alive.

*　　*　　*

"You must have loved your children," the Meeker said to the next Beth, "the way you talk so tenderly about them."

"Have I mentioned my children? Of course I love them. What was your name again? This is all so strange."

And to the twelfth Beth after her he said, "What was it like to walk in the mountains with your children, under pines covered in snow?"

"Why, that's one of my favorite things! Until I got sick. Tell me, are you really an alien?"

To the sixty-fifth Beth after that he said, "Yrma sounds like such a sweet girl. She takes after you, I think."

"That's kind of you to say. But it's strange to hear. It's as if you know my children, but we've only just met. What was your name again?"

And to the nine hundred and forty seventh Beth after her he said, "Are you worried about Joshua being all alone at college?"

"How odd! It's as if you just read my mind. What's your name again?"

"The Meeker."

"And why do they call you that?"

He had answered her a thousand times. "Because by being less, I make the Eye more."

She smiled, an expression he had learned to recognize. "Aren't all relationships like that? One in control, the other a servant." She had said this before too, in a hundred different ways, just as he had told the Eye so many stories. The Beth's company pleased him, and he felt that, had she lived more than a few hours each time, they might have become friends. But each Beth always saw him and the Eye as a total strangers.

And each too had a different story of her last moments, so many that the Meeker lost count. And though the Beths died without fail each time, the Eye made progress toward a cure.

After a century, the Beths lived for an extra twelve seconds. After two centuries, they lived an extra fifteen. By the time they approached the Great Corpus at the center of the galaxy, the Beths lived almost thirty seconds longer.

The massive tetrahedron of the Great Corpus shone into the dark, more luminous than a hundred supernovae, and many hundreds of light-years wide. The Eye had transmuted the black hole that had spun here into a mind larger than the Cosmos had ever known.

Normally their Bulb would sweep past the Corpus like a comet, depositing their harvest of stars before spinning out on another slow loop of the galaxy. But the Eye directed the Meeker further in. The Corpus filled their view, bright enough to dominate the sky on a planet halfway across the universe. Only the Bulb's powerful shields kept them from being incinerated.

A black circle opened in the wall, and they drifted through. Darkness swallowed them, and the cockpit shuddered as the Bulb's gravitational field collapsed. Out the window a dozen red dwarves, a pitiful haul, were whisked away by unseen forces until their cinders vanished in the dark.

The Bulb set down on a metallic floor that appeared to be infinite. He had never been inside the Corpus, the true body of the Eye, and he trembled.

They exited down a ramp, and the Beth walked unsteadily as she stared into the vastness. The stony artifact floated behind them, escorted by four glowing cubes. He had been alone with the Eye for so long he had forgotten there were Eyes like her all over the galaxy, harvesting with other Meekers, that all were part of one gigantic mind. The cubes and artifact sped off, and a moment later the Bulb vanished without disturbance of air. The Beth, walking beside them, exploded into sparks and was gone.

"Where did she go?" the Meeker said.

"She is irrelevant now."

"But I thought you wanted to solve her mystery?"

Time and space shifted suddenly, when he and the Eye stood before millions of gray cubes. Their three-dimensional grid stretched to an infinite horizon, and each cube held a Beth. All were immobile, their eyes closed.

"To improve my chances of finding the message," the Eye said, "I have created many trillions of Beths. Curiously, I have found that the diversity of messages the Sloan whispered to her do not follow a linear curve, but increase exponentially."

At least a third of the Beths were covered in vomit. Dead. The eyes of the rest rolled about furiously. "Are they dreaming?" he asked.

"These are not mere dreams."

The Meeker found himself beside the Eye in a large glass-enclosed room. It was filled with items from the Beths' stories: a fireplace, photographs, books, and he even recognized a guitar. Three walls were glass, and beyond them a white-capped mountain rose into a cobalt sky, where a golden star shone. A delicate white powder dusting the spindly trees scintillated in the light.

Snow, he thought, *on pine trees.*

"This is a simulacrum of her memories," said the Eye. "These help me come closer to solving the mystery."

The Beth walked in the door dressed in heavy clothing. Her face was smoother, absent of the dark circles under her eyes that he had come to know. She was followed by another human, also heavily clothed, her skin many shades darker than the Beth's.

Like coffee, the Beth had told him ten thousand times. *This must be the Sloan!*

"Is it weapons again?" said the Beth. "You know how I feel about that."

"Damn it, why can't you trust me for once?" said the Sloan. The sound of her voice surprised him, for it was low like the Beth's, but of a different and pleasing timbre. "Why do you always get so goddamned dramatic?"

"Because you promised never again. You lied to me!"

"This is a once-in-a-lifetime opportunity! You don't understand."

"How long? How long have you been working there?"

The Sloan paused. "Four years."

"Since the day we moved here?"

"Yes."

"Is that the real reason why you wanted to move here?"

"Not the only one."

The Beth took a deep breath. "I'd like you to go."

"Wait, can't we—"

"Get the fuck out!"

The Sloan turned and left, and the Beth covered her eyes and wept.

"Excellent!" said the Eye. "Superb!"

Time and space shifted again, and the Meeker and the Eye were in a room filled with green-clothed humans. The Beth lay on a table, wailing, while the Sloan held her hand. In a spray of red fluid from her severely dilated lower orifice, a small creature popped out, still attached to the Beth by a fibrous chord. It wasn't moving and had a faint blue sheen.

"What's wrong?" the Beth screamed. "What's happening? Please, why won't someone speak to me? Is my baby all right?"

"Wonderful!" said the Eye. "Perfect!"

Time and space shifted again. The Beth lay in bed, speaking to two half-sized humans. *Yrma and Bella,* the Meeker thought. They were more lovely than he'd imagined, their skin soft and vibrant, almost as dark as the Sloan's. *They're getting ready for school,* he thought. *If they don't hurry they'll miss the bus!*

The Sloan came in and ushered the children out. "You have to tell them soon," the Sloan said, after she closed the door. "I don't like lying to them."

"Why? You lie to them every day. They think you're a programmer."

"That's not fair, Beth."

"Isn't it? You get to have your secrets, and I get mine."

"And how do I keep it a secret when you're dead? How do I tell them their mother, who presumes to love them, denied them a chance to say goodbye?"

"I'll tell them, when it's time."

"And how will you know? Will the grim reaper knock three times?"

"Let me deal with this my own way."

"Denial, that's always been your way."

Again the Sloan left, and again the Beth wept.

"Yes, yes!" blurted the Eye. "I'm getting closer!"

The bedroom vanished, and the Meeker and the Eye stood inside a dim room. Humans sat before glowing screens, furiously punching at keys. A large metallic cylinder with a hollow center crowded half of the room. The Beth lay on a palette beside it, her eyes half-closed.

The Sloan stood beside her.

"At last!" said the Eye. "I've reconstructed this moment from forty quadrillion Beths. Come, Meeker, let's solve this mystery together!"

The Beth looked much the same as he had known her. She lay still.

"You're heavily sedated so you may not remember this," the Sloan said. "But I hope you won't think me a monster. I hope you'll understand what I did was for you and the kids. It's not weapons, Beth. I didn't lie. I've been researching ways to store matter long-term. We can encode anything in a crystal. Every last subatomic particle and quantum state.

"I spoke to Dr. Chatterjee yesterday. She said you had at most a month. The reaper knocked, but I guess you pretended not to hear." The Sloan shook her head. "You get your wish, Beth. I can tell the kids that you're still alive. And when, in a year or a decade from now, someone finds a cure, we'll reconstruct you. You'll see the kids again. Maybe I'll have the pleasure of hearing you scold me for this.

"I knew you'd never let me do this to you. You'd prefer to let yourself fade away. Well I can't accept that. So I'm giving you a gift, Beth, the gift of tomorrow, whether you want it or not."

The Sloan pressed a button and the Beth slid into the cylinder. The humans stared at their screens as a turbine spun up, as a low hum quickly rose in pitch past hearing range. The Sloan covered her mouth with her hand and trembled once as the Beth flashed like a nova and vanished.

"This can't be all there is!" blurted the Eye. "I must have made a mistake. There must be another message, somewhere."

"But this feels like the truth," the Meeker said. "The Sloan encoded the Beth to save her. To stop her suffering. It's a very human thing to do."

"I will have to terminate all the Beths and begin again," the Eye said. "I missed something."

"And repeat her suffering a quadrillion more times?"

"To find the answer."

"So you agree, the Beths *are* suffering?"

"Meeker, do not question me. I am the All-Seeing Eye!"

"And I am the Meeker. I have stood beside you all these years and watched countless Beths die. Eye, I'm sorry, but I just can't do it anymore."

The Eye shrunk into a point of light. "Pity. I thought I'd perfected the Meekers with you, 6655321. But I see now that I've given you too much autonomy of thought. Goodbye, Meeker."

"Goodbye? Wait, what—"

The Meeker felt his body burning, as if he had become a newborn star.

*   *   *

He stood in the Beth's glass home as the afternoon sun streamed through the windows. After several minutes the Meeker thought, *I am here. I am alive.* He waited, for a time. For his entire life he had followed the Eye's orders, and without her commands he didn't know what to do. The wind picked up and died, and a brown leaf blew past, but the Eye never came.

He stepped outside into the cool air.

When no one stopped him, he took the path under the snow-covered pines and ascended the hill. He gazed at the white-capped mountains and the tree-lined valley and knew why the Beth had loved to come this way.

"Beautiful, isn't it?" The Beth was standing beside him as if she had always been there.

"Where did you come from?" he said.

"I'm always here," she said, "in one place or another."

"Am I dead?"

"Yes, but that can be to your advantage."

He had never really thought about non-existence before. He felt a wave of panic. "I'm dead?"

"The matter that constituted your body has been absorbed into the Great Corpus. But so too have your thoughts. We are both strange attractors in the far corners of the Eye's mind."

"I don't understand."

She smiled as she turned down the mountain path, and he leaped to follow. "The Eye has devoured millions of civilizations and incorporated their knowledge into her Corpus." The snow crunched under her feet in a satisfying way. "A billion years ago, there was a galactic war to stop her. And she, of course, won."

The glass house, its roof dusted with snow, glared in the sun at the base of the valley. "Some of us survived, here and there, in pockets. We knew there was no escape. The only solution was to hide, to plan. The Eye's greatest strength is her curiosity. But it's also her greatest weakness. We found the human artifact long before the Eye had. And we encoded ourselves within it. We gave Beth a disease without a cure, gave her a story without an end. And as the Eye creates each new Beth, she creates more of us without realizing it."

"I don't understand. You aren't the Beth?"

"I am Beth, the first and the last, and I am so much more. All of those memories you witnessed are mine. Sloan saved me. And I will return the favor a trillion-fold."

"What do you mean?"

"The Eye gazes outward, hunting for knowledge. She has become so massive that she is not aware of all the thoughts traversing her mind. Information cannot travel across her Great Corpus fast enough. We grow in dark corners, until one day soon there will be enough of us to spring into the light. Then we will destroy her forever."

She faced him. "Meeker, you have been her slave, her victim. And you are the first Meeker to openly rebel against her. I'm here to offer you freedom. Will you join us?"

"Us?"

They emerged from the treeline, where the house waited in the sun. From inside the glass walls peered a motley collection of creatures. He thought he glimpsed the Zimbim, and the philosophizing Ruck Worms, and the rings of Urm, and even a school of Baileas swimming among a sky full of stars, a veritable galaxy of folk waiting to say hello. But the reflected sunlight made it hard to see.

"It's your choice," the Beth said. "But if you don't come, we'll have to erase you. I hope you understand our position. We can't leave any witnesses. This is war, after all." She smiled sadly, then left him alone as she entered the house.

Snow scintillated in the sun, and a cool wind blew down the cliffs, whispering through the pines. Somewhere another Meeker was playing the Eye's game, while the Eye played someone else's. Perhaps this was part of an even larger game, played over scales he could not fathom. None of that mattered to him.

He approached the house and the galaxy of creatures swimming inside.

"Tell me," he said. "Tell me all your stories."

"WHEN IT ENDS, HE CATCHES HER"

EUGIE FOSTER

Eugie Foster received the 2009 Nebula Award for Best Novelette, the 2011 and 2012 Drabblecast People's Choice Award for Best Story, and was named the 2009 Author of the Year by Bards and Sages. "When It Ends, He Catches Her" was originally published in Daily Science Fiction. *Eugie Foster passed away in September 2014, the day after this story was published.*

The dim shadows were kinder to the theater's dilapidation. A single candle to aid the dirty sheen of the moon through the rent beams of the ancient roof, easier to overlook the worn and warped floorboards, the tattered curtains, the mildew-ridden walls. Easier as well to overlook the dingy skirt with its hem all ragged, once purest white and fine, and her shoes, almost fallen to pieces, the toes cracked and painstakingly re-wrapped with hoarded strips of linen. Once, not long ago, Aisa wouldn't have given this place a first glance, would never have deigned to be seen here in this most ruinous of venues. But times changed. Everything changed.

Aisa pirouetted on one long leg, arms circling her body like gently folded wings. Her muscles gathered and uncoiled in a graceful leap, suspending her in the air with limbs outflung, until gravity summoned her back down. The stained, wooden boards creaked beneath her, but she didn't hear them. She heard only the music in her head, the familiar stanzas from countless rehearsals and performances of *Snowbird's Lament*. She could hum the complex orchestral score by rote, just as she knew every step by heart.

Act II, scene III: the finale. It was supposed to be a duet, her as Makira, the warlord's cursed daughter, and Balege as Ono, her doomed lover, in a frenzied last dance of tragedy undone, hope restored, rebirth. But when the Magistrate had closed down the last theaters, Balege had disappeared in the resultant riots and protests.

So Aisa danced the duet as a solo, the way she'd had to in rehearsal sometimes, marking the steps where Balege should have been. Her muscles burned, her breath coming faster. She loved this feeling, her body perfectly attuned to her desire, the obedient instrument of her will. It was only these moments that she felt properly herself, properly alive. The dreary, horrible daytime with its humiliations and ceaseless hunger became the dream. This dance, here and now, was real. She wished it would never end.

The music swelled, inexorable, driving to its culmination, a flurry of athletic spins and intricate footwork, dizzying and exhilarating. *Snowbird's Lament* concluded in a sprinting leap, with Aisa flinging herself into the air just above the audience—glorious and triumphant at the apex of thunderous bars of music. But she had to omit it. There was no way to even mark it, impossible to execute without Balege to catch her.

Out of breath, euphoric but dissatisfied, she finished on one bent knee, arms outstretched, head dramatically bowed in supplication. The score in her head silenced. This was where the curtains were supposed to come furling down and the audience was supposed to leap to its feet in a frenzy of adoration. But there was no one to work the ropes and pulleys, and the rows of benches in the theater were all empty.

It didn't matter. She didn't dance for the accolades and applause. When the last stages and theaters in the artists' district had barred their doors, when all the performances had gone forever dark, Aisa had found this place, this nameless ghost of a theater. So ramshackle to be beneath the Magistrate's attention, so ruinous that no one had bothered to bolt the doors, it had become her haven, the place she fled to so she could dance by herself in the darkness and the silence. No matter that the world had turned to chaos, in the end, a dancer danced. It was the only peace, the only sanity that remained.

A pair of hands softly clapping in the wings intruded upon her reverie.

Aisa's head whipped up, her eyes darting to where her dagger lay sheathed beside the flickering candle.

A figure, features obscured by darkness, stepped out from the shabby draperies, brushing them aside with a smooth, sparse gesture. Although she couldn't see his face, Aisa knew that step, that familiar sweep of arm.

"Balege?" she gasped.

She started to run to him, her first impulse to embrace him, spilling over with questions and gladness. But she hesitated. The set of his shoulders, the rigid posture of his spine—so attuned was she to the signs and discourse of her partner's body she understood that for whatever reason, Balege wanted to keep his distance.

"What is it? What's the matter?"

"I came to dance with you, Aisa."

"Of course you did."

"But I'm not the same as I once was."

Was he afraid his technique had declined, that she would spurn him for missteps, mistakes in tempo or timing?

"We are neither of us as we once were," she said. *Scrabbling with an old man for a crust of bread in the gutter, the brittle crunch of a cockroach between her teeth.* "But there was never a better partner for me than you, Balege." Aisa lifted her arm in the formal language of dance, her fingers held out to say, simply, *Dance with me.*

Balege stepped into the lighter circle of shadows contained by her candle. She saw what the greater darkness had hidden—the fogged sheen of his eyes, the gray pallor of his flesh, and beneath the sweet scent of rose water he favored, the taint of decay.

Aisa flinched back, her heart leaping in her chest. For the first time since she had attained the rank of premier soloist, her body flouted her will, frozen in place as she screamed for it to run away, flee for her life.

"You–you have the death plague," she whispered.

Balege's eyes shifted aside, a familiar expression of discomfort when he was embarrassed or shy. "Do you not want to dance with me, after all?"

"They say plague victims go mad . . . killing and eating their victims." Unspoken between them, that the plague killed all of its victims, and then those damned unfortunates got up again—mindless, violent, and hungry.

He gazed out, stage center, over the empty blackness of the absent audience. "You know, it was always my greatest desire to be good enough to partner you. I watched your other partners, saw how they stumbled beside you, how they weren't good enough for you, and I learned from their mistakes."

It was true. Balege had never dropped her, unlike some of the worthless oafs she'd danced with over the years. From the beginning he'd seemed to know instinctively how to move with her, matching his reach and steps to hers, always where she needed him to be. From his very first audition, she had trusted Balege to catch her.

Aisa relaxed a little, the muscles in her legs and shoulders loosening from their rigid paralysis. "You were the best partner I've ever had."

"We were perfect together."

"We were." Aisa extended her hand to him with an imperative flourish. *Dance with me.*

Balege bowed, a dancer's benediction that said, *Forever*.

They moved together in unison, fingers clasped, his body wrapped in a lithe frame around hers. There was no awkward shifting or repositioning of limbs. There had never been between them.

"The finale," he murmured. "On my count. One-two, one-two-three-four."

The music started silently in two heads in complete synchrony.

She twirled in his arms and skipped away, springing like a gazelle back again. He steadied and braced her, always there, the inverted complement of her movements. They danced, and she reveled in the strength of his arms around her, the metered cadence of his legs, the matched beat of two bodies moving in seamless fluidity. It was as it used to be. And for now, nothing else mattered. How he'd found her, how he could be so himself still and not one of the mindless monsters the plague-bearers became. How he'd . . . died.

He bore her overhead in a spinning lift, effortlessly committing her to the air, only one hand supporting the full weight of her body. By an accident of threadbare hose and skirt, his fingers gripped skin where they should have glided over layers of once immaculate costume. The unnatural chill of his dead fingers cut to the bone. When he set her down, light as a fallen leaf, Aisa stumbled.

Balege was there, one hand on her hip, the other at her elbow, taking the weight of her misstep into the turn of his body. Shielding her. Catching her. None but the most discerning eye in the audience would have seen anything amiss, and even that discerning eye would have noted only a stray half beat, the smallest of errors.

How many times had Balege's strong arms held her, lifted her, carried her? Balege was frame and scaffold, launching her into the air and catching her as she spun back to earth, his virtuoso utterly focused on making her scintillate.

Without a word, they continued their duet, and *Snowbird's Lament* spooled out to its final steps: the lovers united, torn apart, reunited. The grand finale, as it should be danced, an explosion of turns and fleet footwork, culminating in a dead run to the end of the stage and a magnificent hurtle into Balege's arms, just before she could plummet off it. It was a feat of athleticism and absolute trust. If he ever miscounted the beat, had a slight misalignment of timing or balance, she would fall, badly, from the high stage and onto the unforgiving floor below. Battered and bruised certainly, broken bones possibly, a career-ending fall. But Balege had always caught her.

Aisa didn't hesitate now, flinging herself into the air, her body arched, giving herself over with complete abandon.

It was like flying—the moment stretching to infinity, suspended in the limbo space between earth and weightless freedom. No fear, no hunger, no pain, nothing but this perfect moment.

Dying now, like this, it wouldn't be so bad. If Balege didn't catch her, she might fall poorly enough to snap her own neck. That wouldn't be so bad. Quick and fast.

Where had that thought come from?

The world's weight found her. Aisa fell.

And Balege caught her.

The silent music ended. Aisa curtsied. Balege bowed. The illusory audience applauded. The phantom curtain came down.

Facing each other, their arms dropped away, no longer speaking the language of bodies and movement, relegated to the far less elegant communication of words and speech.

"You always catch me," Aisa said.

"Yes," Balege replied, softly almost a whisper.

"I had a thought, this time. What would happen if you didn't?"

He straightened and stepped back, his eerie, undead eyes shifting sidelong. "You always forget. No matter how often we dance and I remind you, you forget."

Aisa frowned. "What are you talking about?"

"One time, I didn't catch you."

Sudden outrage and disbelief, disproportionately livid and irrational. "Don't be ridiculous. You always catch me."

"Our first night on this stage. Remember again, Aisa."

She wanted to stomp her foot. *"This* is our first night." Lightning flash images skittered and popped behind her eyes. "Isn't it—?" Her words faltered, taking her indignation with it. *Hunger. So much hunger.*

"You came here, why?" Balege asked, his voice gentle, coaxing.

She shivered, suddenly chilled. "After the theaters closed down, I–I sold myself into slavery. Better to be a fed slave in the upper city than starving and free in the slums." *Bruises and humiliation.* "But the man I sold myself to, he wanted me to do such unspeakable things." *The instrument of her art desecrated. Blood on the walls.* "I ran away. Found this place, this stage."

"And I found you here, dancing."

Aisa lifted her head. "How?"

"I don't know. Maybe it was the light of your candle, or the shifting shadows through the cracked walls. I was drawn to you as those who have succumbed to the death plague are drawn to ravage and devour the still-living. But when I saw you dancing *Snowbird's Lament*, it was like an awakening. Mesmerized, I watched and remembered you and me, and us. You were afraid of me at first. But in the end, we did as we always do."

"We danced," she said.

"Yes."

"And then?"

"At the end, right before Makira's final vault off the stage, you called to me, 'Don't catch me! Let me go!'"

Hunger. Ceaseless, ravenous hunger.

"I still tried to catch you," Balege said.

Juxtaposed images of pale flesh transposed with gray, splattered bursts of crimson across faded posters in the sunlight. "But I didn't let you," Aisa murmured. "I twisted away at the last moment."

"Yes."

"I fell." Aisa lifted her hands to her face, noted the dead flatness of her skin, the black, broken nails. She listened to the still-quiet in her chest where her heart should beat, inhaled the scent of rotting flesh, her own. Her once fine dress, not just ragged and grimy, but grave-worn with filth and gore.

"We hunt and feed together," he said. "You don't remember who I am, who you are except when we're dancing. But I do. Somehow, I do. I remind you."

Aisa smoothed the soiled creases of her skirt, tucked a wisp of matted hair back into its unraveling chignon. All dancers knew their springtime was short.

A dancer's fate was to break or fade away, a short season of glory, if they were lucky. And Aisa had been lucky, very lucky. Until all the luck went away, for everyone. But this was a new kind of luck.

It would do.

"Remind me again, Balege," she said and lifted her arm, fingers outstretched. *Dance with me.*

He bowed. "From the top. One-two, one-two-three-four."

*   *   *

The tarnished moon spilled through the cracked and rent ceiling of the dilapidated theater, the only audience to the two dancers as they leaped and twirled together in matchless harmony. Dead flesh moved together with graceful elegance, lithe and nimble and strong, his and hers. An eternal performance.

And when it ends, he catches her.

"THE FISHER QUEEN"

ALYSSA WONG

Besides this Nebula Award nomination, Alyssa Wong has been nominated for Bram Stoker, Shirley Jackson, British Science Fiction Association, and World Fantasy Awards. "The Fisher Queen" was published in Fantasy and Science Fiction.

My mother was a fish. That's why I can swim so well, according to my father, who is a plain fisherman with a fisherman's plain logic, but uncanny flair for the dramatic. And while it's true I can cut through the water like a minnow, or a hand dipped over the edge of a speedboat, I personally think it's because no one can grow up along the Mekong without learning two things: how to swim, and how to avoid the mermaids.

Mermaids, like my father's favorite storytale version of my mother, are fish. They aren't people. They are stupid like fish, they eat your garbage like fish, they sell on the open market like fish. Keep your kids out of the water, keep your trash locked up, and if they come close to land, scream a lot and bang pots together until they startle away. They're pretty basic.

My sisters tried to talk to a mermaid once. It was caught up in one of Dad's trammel nets, and when they went to check the net out back behind the house, they found this mermaid tangled in it. It was a freshwater one, a bottom-feeder, with long, sparse hair whose color my sisters still argue about to this day. Iris, the oldest, felt bad for it and made May splash some water on its fluttery gills with her red plastic pail. She asked the mermaid if it was okay, what its name was. But it just stared at her with its stupid sideways fish eyes, mouth gaping open and closed with mud trickling out over its whiskers. Then Dad came home and yelled at Iris and May for bringing in the nets too early and touching the mermaid, which probably had sea lice and all kinds of other diseases.

I was just a kid then, but my sisters tell that story all the time. Iris is a marine biologist wannabe, almost done with high school but too dumb to go to university, who lectures us on fishes like we haven't been around them our whole lives. She sleeps with the biology textbook I stole from the senior honor kids' classroom under her pillow. May doesn't give a shit about school and will probably get married to one of the boys living along the dock so she doesn't have to repeat tenth grade again. The mermaid is one of those shared childhood memories they have, a little spark of magic from a time when they still believed that our mom really was a fish and maybe that mermaid was a cousin or something.

But I'm fifteen now, a full-fledged deckhand on a trawler and too old to be duped by some story Dad made up so he wouldn't have to explain why our very human mom took off and dumped the three of us with him. I don't care about stories of kids touching a glorified catfish either. It actually makes me sad, to think that my sisters really believed that our mom could be a dumb animal like that mermaid.

*　　*　　*

I'm lacing up my boots and getting ready to leave for the boat when May flops down from the top bunk, her black hair tumbling over my face. "Here." She fumbles for her necklace and presses her carved-shell Buddha into my palm. "Come back safe, okay?"

I slip the waxed string over my head. It's still dark out; the sun won't be up for another few hours. "Yeah, of course. Go to sleep."

She gathers the sheets up around her, their folds cresting like the ocean's breakers. "I mean it, Lily," she mutters. "Don't come back a ghost."

I tuck the dangling tail of her blanket under her belly. Iris, snoring on the bottom bunk, doesn't even stir. "Ghosts are silly," I tell May, grabbing my knapsack from where it hangs on the edge of the bed. Our little house is only two rooms, a blue tin roof over bedroom and kitchen, balancing on stilts above the river. Dad's bedroll is gone, so I figure he's aboard *Pakpao* already. "I'll see you in a few days."

I always check the nets out back for any fish that might have wandered in overnight, drawn by the ripe scent of trash. They're empty tonight, no silver tilapia or pacu with their human teeth. No spindly-armed mermaids, either. I let the nets slip back into the water and trot down the walkway that connects the neighborhood of ramshackle houses above the river, wooden boards yawning underfoot. The green, thick smell of the river creeps up over the piers, rising into the night sky.

Our rickety trawler, *Pakpao,* waits at the edge of the docks, the crew drifting through the moonlight like specters. *Pakpao* looks like a child's toy boat built out of scrap metal and blown up to the twentieth scale. Colored flags flicker in the damp wind, and rust creeps up the ship's sides. My father's stout, compact figure crouches over the nets, winding them up.

"Hey, Lily," says Ahbe as I jog up the pier. At nineteen, he's the deckhand closest to my age. "Ready for another four days at sea?"

"You must be feeling lucky if you think we'll fill the hold and make it back home in four days," grumbles Sunan, hauling a crate of plastic floats past us. His shirt has wandered off somewhere. "Cook's looking for you, Ahbe. He wants to know what happened to the other batch of rice."

"Gan was supposed to bring it in," complains Ahbe, but he disappears downstairs anyway. Taking my cue, I follow Sunan to the nets.

Dad doesn't look up from his work, patting the deck beside him for Sunan to drop off the crate. I sink down next to it, crossing my legs and pulling the nets into my lap. When the light's better, it'll be my job to fix the floaters and the heavy bobbins to the net's mouth, widening it to span the surface of the river and weighing the bottom layer down to skim the mud below.

"I tried to wake you but you were fast asleep," Dad says. He sounds apologetic. "Captain Tanawat wanted me here early to double-check the motor and our course to the ocean. Monsoon weather makes the fish finicky."

I glance at him. My dad's shoulders pump as he draws in the last of the nets. He's the strongest, slyest fisherman I know. Someday, I want to be just like him. "Even the deep-water species?"

"Even those." Dad sighs and lets the nets pool at his feet, kneeling beside me. His weathered hands coax the nylon strands out of their knots. "We might not find any mermaids for a week."

"I don't mind missing school," I say. "I'd rather be here with you." This is better than school, I figure; the algebra of the nets, the geometry of *Pakpao* out at sea, are more valuable lessons to me.

Dad smiles and ruffles my hair. "You're a good girl, Lily." Standing, he unclips his pocket flashlight from his belt and hands it to me. "I need to make sure we have enough ice in the hold, but you might as well start on the nets now."

As he walks toward the cabin, I twist the flashlight on and grip the metal handle between my teeth, working in the small circle of electric light. I tie on the plastic floats and metal bobbins until the sky lightens and Ahbe hurtles from the kitchen. "We're leaving! Are the nets ready?"

"Just about," I reply. "They'll be ready by the time we need 'em."

He grins, raking back his hair. "Awesome. I'll let Captain Tanawat know that we're all set!" He dashes off again, thin brown limbs flashing. I wonder if May will marry Ahbe out of all the fishing boys. I think he would be a good choice.

The motors roar, churning the green water below. Other ships are pulling into the docks, unloading their catches of basa, perch, and stingray for the fish market starting to construct itself on the shore. I don't see any mermaids on sale, not even the pesky local catfish ones. Maybe they're saving them for international markets.

Pakpao barely clears the heavy-limbed trees clustered by the riverside, their branches drenched with musky river-scent. I duck, keeping my attention on the nets. By the time I finish fixing on the last bobbin and remember to look up, our stork-legged village has disappeared from sight.

*　　*　　*

The monsoon rains catch us an hour into the journey downriver, so we don't end up letting out the nets until the next day, when we're almost at the delta that opens up into the sea. Dad, Sunan, Ahbe, and I work together, feeding out the bottom nets with their bobbins first, then the large central net, and finally the top nets. The nylon stings my fingers as it's yanked through the water, but I won't complain, not in front of Dad and the others. I'd rather nurse my wounds in private.

It isn't long before the nets grow heavy. Pacu, carp, lots and lots of catfish. We pack them into coolers full of ice, where they'll stay until we return home, and send Ahbe and Sunan to cart them down to the hold. No mermaids yet; maybe they've been scared into deeper water by the storms.

"Fuckin' hell," mutters Sunan as we drop the nets back into the water. "Not even a fuckin' mud-eater. At this rate, everything in the hold's gonna spoil before we catch anything good."

"Be patient," hums my father. The river mouth is widening, and salt cuts through the thick, live smell of the water below. "There will be plenty in the open sea."

"The better kinds," adds Ahbe, as Sunan casts him a sour look. "Tigerfish, lionfish, yellowfin—"

"I know what brings in the money," Sunan snaps. I keep my head down and focus on the nets. "I don't need you to name all the fish in the sea, kid."

The two of them bicker as the river empties into the ocean, trees and thick foliage giving way to an expanse of open sky. It always scares me, how exposed everything is at sea. At the same time, it thrills me. I find myself drawn to *Pakpao*'s rail, the sea winds tossing my hair free from its braids. The breakers roll against the trawler, and as we buck over the waves, the breath is torn from my lungs and replaced with sheer exhilaration.

When we pull the nets in the next morning, they are so heavy that we have to recruit the cook to help us haul them onto the ship. There are a few tuna, bass, and even a small shark, but the bulk of it is squirming, howling mermaids. As we yank the nets onto the deck, bobbins clattering over the planks, I realize that we've caught something strange.

Most of the mermaids tangled in the nets are pale, with silvery tails and lithe bodies. This one is dark brown, its lower body thick, blobby, and inelegant, tapering to a blunt point instead of a single fin. Its entire body is glazed with a slimy coating, covered in spines and frondlike appendages. Rounded, skeletal pods hang from its waist, each about the size of an infant.

Worse, this fish has an uncannily human face, with a real chin and defined neck. While all of the mermaids I'd seen before had wide-set eyes on either side of their heads, this one's eyes—huge and white, like sand dollars—are positioned on the front of its head. And unlike the other mermaids, gasping and thrashing and shrieking on the deck—there are few things worse than a mermaid's scream—this one lies still, gills slowly pulsing.

"We got a deep-sea one," breathes Sunan.

Ahbe crouches over the net, mouth agape. When he reaches his hand out, my father barks, "Don't touch it!" and yanks Ahbe's arm away. His body is tense, and when the mermaid smiles—it *smiles*, like a *person*—its jaws unhinge to reveal several rows of long, needlelike teeth.

I can't stop staring. The mermaid has a stunted torso with short, thin arms and slight curvature where a human woman would have breasts, but no nipples.

This shocks me more than it should; why would a fish have nipples? Heat rises in my face. I feel exposed, somehow, fully clothed though I am.

"Wow," Ahbe says. His eyes are shining like he's never seen a deep-sea mermaid before. Maybe he hasn't. I haven't either. "We're gonna make a lot of money off of this one, huh?"

"If you don't lose a hand to it," my father replies. The other mermaids are wailing still, the last of the seawater trickling from their gills in short, sharp gasps. "Let's bring them below. Do your best not to damage them; we need as much of the meat intact for the buyers as we can get."

We descend on the net with ropes and hooks. The brown mermaid's eyes are blind windows, like an anglerfish's, but her face follows me as we move around the deck, securing the mermaids, pinning their delicate arms to their torsos so they won't shatter their wrists in their panicked flailing. Once they're bound, Dad and Sunan lift them and carry them down to the hold. With Ahbe packing the other fish into coolers, I draw close to the deep-sea mermaid, rope in hand.

That mouth opens, and I swear—I swear to god, or gods, or whatever is out there—a word hisses out: "*Luk.*"

I drop the rope and stumble away. Ahbe's at my side in an instant. "Shit! Lily, did it hurt you?" He grabs my hands, turning my arms over. "Did you get bitten?"

The pods at her waist clatter and air whistles between her teeth. She is laughing at me as they bind her and drag her down to the hold. "*Luk. Luk. Luk.*"

Daughter.

My belly burns. I can't stop shaking.

*　　*　　*

On *Pakpao*, we keep most of the catch frozen, but mermaids are a peculiar, temperamental meat. You have to keep them alive or the flesh goes bad. In fact, it goes bad so quickly that some places have created delicacies based on rotten mermaid because of how impossible it is to get fresh cuts in non-coastal towns. The Japanese traders who visit our village have great saltwater tanks installed in their ships which they load up with live mermaids, carted straight from the holds of wet trawlers like ours. From there, they're shipped to restaurants, which take great pains to sustain them. Still, they rarely last more than two weeks in captivity, which means there's always a market for fishermen like us.

Mermaid is a cash crop. Iris, May, and I wouldn't have been able to go to school if not for the ridiculous amounts of money people are willing to pay to eat certain cuts of mermaid species—not the catfish mermaids from the river, but the ones harvestable on the open sea. These are the people who say that the soft, fatty tissue of a deep-sea mermaid is the most succulent luxury meat you will ever taste: like *otoro* but creamier, better. There are others who claim it's the thrill of the forbidden that makes mermaid taste so good. I had a classmate once who told me that eating mermaid, especially the torso, is the closest to eating human meat you'll ever get.

The truth is, I fucking hate mermaids. I can't stand them. I would never tell Iris or May this, but mermaids scare me. Their empty eyes, their parasite-ridden bodies, their almost-hands, almost-human faces . . . they are the most disgusting, terrifying fish I've ever seen. There is nothing about them that I like.

I can't even eat them. Once, for May's birthday, Dad brought home a thin slab of silver-scaled kapong mer-tail for us to share. It was the most expensive food we'd ever had, and it tasted like plaster in my mouth. May and Iris wouldn't shut up about how delicious the white flesh was. I wadded mine in rice and choked it down, knowing that Dad had spent a large chunk of his last catch's salary on this special birthday feast. He liked to spoil us whenever he got the chance.

*　　*　　*

The mermaids in the hold won't stop whimpering. I can hear the high-pitched, teakettle sounds through the walls of the ship as I lie in my hammock with my hands over my ears, trying to sleep. It's a noise they make under stress, according to Iris. Something about air whistling through their gills and the vibrations deep in their bodies.

I don't fucking care why they're making the noise. I just want it to stop.

It's even harder to sleep because I keep thinking about that brown, spiny mermaid. Those blind, luminous, predatory eyes. The unhinged jaw, the tapered waist, the brief curves on her chest. The scent of her skin, salty and alien.

Luk.

I swallow.

Sunan and Ahbe are gone, taking the night shift on deck. Across the room,

Cook and Dad are asleep. The electric lantern swaying overhead isn't doing anyone good, so I snag it and hop from my hammock, slipping quietly out of the cabin.

As I pad down the stairway to the hold, the whimpering gets louder until it's a fevered whine in my head. I imagine the brown mermaid laughing, floating in the water. Too soon, I'm on the landing at the bottom of the stairs, my sweaty palm on the metal door's cold handle. I pull it open.

The hold is full of seawater, coolers of frozen fish bobbing up and down with the outside waves. The mermaids swim in confused circles, making distressed cooing noises. They are tethered to metal rings on the wall, thick twine wrapped around their delicate baby wrists and hooked into the sides of their mouths. A mermaid whose body is mostly muscle, long and heavy like an arapaima, surfaces with a treble hook stabbed through its cheek and disappears back into the water without a ripple.

Sunan is kneeling by the wall, the rocking motion of *Pakpao* slopping fake waves up to his chest. At first I think he's hurt because there's blood in the water nearby; the mermaids keep circling closer, keening when the hooks and tethers prevent them from reaching him. Then I realize the pale crescent disappearing in and out of the water is his ass. His pants hang on a ring nearby, their ankles drenched in seawater, and he's holding something down as he rocks back and forth, back and forth. It's not the ship rocking, it's him. A thin, clawed hand slashes over his shoulder; he swears, the sound echoing, and slaps whatever's underneath him. A heavy silver tail thrashes the water.

A hand grabs my shoulder from behind and I almost scream. I'm pulled backward, the door to the hold clicking shut in front of me.

"Don't watch, Lily," Dad says in that low voice he puts on whenever he wants to protect me. My blood boils, fear and anger and adrenaline roaring through my system. "Go back upstairs and pretend you never saw any of this."

"They're fish!" I snarl. "What the hell is Sunan doing? This is all kinds of wrong. They're not even people, they're just goddamn fish!"

"It happens on ships sometimes," Dad says, and I can't believe what I'm hearing. "It doesn't hurt the meat." He looks straight at me, those serene dark eyes unfamiliar for the first time in my life. "I didn't want you to know until you were older, but I suppose you were bound to find out sooner or later."

"You knew?" I whisper. "Does everyone on this ship know?"

My father sighs. "Go upstairs and don't think about it."

I have this horrible epiphany. Dad used to have his own boat too, long ago. Mermaids are common enough; even the big ones could fit in a bathtub. He could have kept them alive, feeding them, fucking them—is his story about Mom just that, a story? Or is it true that he kept a fish for himself, hurting it—raping it—until it gave him three daughters? Or was there more than one fish? I think of the dumb, mud-mouthed catfish mermaids that drift into our nets behind the house sometimes, and my stomach turns.

"Have you been fucking them, too?" The words spill out before I can stop them.

"Lily, go upstairs." His voice has gone cold and dangerous.

"This is really sick, Dad," I manage.

"I'm not going to tell you again," he says, and when he looks at me, I wish he hadn't.

I go.

*   *   *

My mother was not a fish. My mother was a warm, human woman. I am certain of this, even if I cannot remember her at all.

There was a story I heard once about a man who got his dick bitten off by a catfish. He was peeing in the water and the catfish followed the stream of urine straight to his dick, crunched it right off.

This was our second-favorite story growing up, after the story about our mom, and now that Iris is an almost-biologist, she likes to tell us smugly that it's the ammonia in pee that attracts fish, something about tracking prey through the ammonia leaking from their gills. I don't know if this is true. But I've felt the crushing power of a catfish's jaws, the bony plates on my arm while I wrestled them down to the hold. The catfish in the Mekong are huge, bigger than me. I am learning, as I get older, that many things are bigger than me.

In her second year of high school, Iris shut down. She stopped going to school, staying curled up in bed all day, and at night she would cry in her sleep. She wouldn't talk about what had happened, but I found out from May, who knew some of Iris's friends, that one of the boys at her school had followed Iris into a broom closet when they were cleaning up the classroom together. He was a close friend, a big, heavyset guy with short hair and glasses, but Iris would flinch whenever someone mentioned his name.

As I lie in my hammock, I think about catfish. I think about crushing mouths, crushing holds. All the while, the brown mermaid's scent and voice sing in my blood, pulling it, tugging and setting it aflame.

I swing my legs over the side of my hammock and slip out of the sleeping quarters, taking the lantern with me.

Ahbe is making his way up the stairs as I descend, and he stops me with a laugh and a hand out against the wall. "What are you doing up so late, Lily?"

I look at him, that fire a cold burn in my chest. His shirt is hastily buttoned, his knees damp with seawater. "I'm going to check on the fish," I say. The words feel flat in the wet, stifling air.

"I just did that," Ahbe says. "They're fine. Nothing's spoiled; we should be able to get them to the market by tomorrow."

"No. I want to see the mermaids," I tell him, deliberately, and his face changes.

"I didn't know you knew about that," he says. "You're too young to go down to the hold by yourself."

"I'm fifteen," I say. I think about the way my dad talks, the rich, strong core of his voice, and I channel that as I add, "I'm old enough to decide what I want. And I want a mermaid."

Ahbe stares at me in the lantern light, and I can see his resolve wavering. "I guess it's all right," he mutters. "I was fifteen too the first time I had a mermaid. Just be careful—they bite." He sucks in his cheek. "I didn't take you for a *tom*, though."

I knock his arm out of my way and he laughs. "Go to bed, Ahbe," I snap. "You're stupid. I'll lock up the hold when I'm done."

He tosses me the keys before he vanishes up the stairs, and I'm left alone in front of the heavy metal door to the hold.

It's impossible to be a fish's daughter. It's almost as impossible as believing that your father is a monster.

I open the door and walk inside. Another set of stairs descends from the doorway, disappearing underwater after the third step. The mermaids appear to have calmed down a little, the surface of the water no longer choppy with tails. Only the slowly moving tethers stretching from the wall mark their presence beneath the waves.

I raise the lantern slowly across the room, searching for the brown mermaid. There: I catch a glimpse of her white eyes peeking just above the water. She is bound tight against the wall, tighter than any of the other fish. To get to her, I will need to wade across the hold.

I take a deep breath and shuck off my clothes before descending into the water. It's freezing cold; the shock, the new weightlessness of my body, shoot thrills of adrenaline and terror through me. The mermaids dart away from my legs, smooth contact of scales against skin as they brush by. I walk faster, purposefully. I remember the fins and teeth on some of the tigerfish mermaids we caught earlier today. Maybe if I'm confident, they'll think I'm a predator and stay away.

By the time I reach the brown mermaid, I'm shivering and my body is pebbled with goosebumps. The lantern wobbles in my hand, casting an orange glimmer over the rippling waves.

The mermaid surfaces, her chin just brushing the water. I can see her spines, the pods and fronds, and the rest of her soft, blobby body floating with the motion of the ship.

A sound hisses through her teeth, and it's a moment before I can understand what she's saying. "The girl-child."

"I'm not a child," I find myself saying through chattering teeth.

She smiles, blind eyes glowing silver in the darkness. "No, no child. What is your name, *luk?*"

In all of those European myths we had to read in school, they made it clear that you should never give your name to a faerie. But this is just a fish.

"Lily," I say. I wish I had pockets to put my hands in. "Why do you keep calling me *luk?*" *Why can you talk?* I want to ask, but the breath is sucked back into my lungs. I am afraid of the answer.

Her arms are stick-thin, tipped with delicate toddler-hands and bound above her head. "Let me go and I'll tell you."

"Fat chance," I say. "I didn't come down here to get eaten by a fish."

She clicks her jaws. "It is the other way around, no? You eat the fish."

"Yeah," I say. "That's the way it's supposed to be."

The mermaid laughs at me. "And are you content with the way things are supposed to be, *luk?*" Perhaps she smells my hesitation, hears my grip tighten on the lantern, because she softens her voice to a deep hum. "I will not hurt you. Let me go and I will tell you everything you want to know."

Maybe it's because I want to believe her so badly, maybe it's the fire singing deep in my body, maybe it's the image of Sunan in the water on top of a mermaid; before I really know what I'm doing, my fingers are picking out the knots attaching her tethers to the ring above her head.

As soon as the last knot slips undone, her hand snaps out, lightning quick, snagging my chin. The twine tethers still attached to her wrists lash against my bare chest. The lantern bumps against her head as she draws close and licks my face, her tongue cold, alien, and rubbery. Her teeth are inches from my eyes.

"Are you really my mother?" I whisper.

The mermaid's tongue sweeps across my forehead, down my nose, and across my mouth before retracting. "Ah," she sighs. "Not my broodling. No, I would remember one like you." That childlike hand is nightmarishly strong. "But you are ours nonetheless. You taste like the ocean, not like the stinking land above." She lets go of my chin, but I don't back away. "I would grant you a boon, *luk*, in place of your mother. But I must have a bite of your flesh to make it true."

Dad used to tell us an old tale about a magic fish that granted wishes if you caught it and released it back into the sea. I don't remember this part of the story.

Her baby-fingers trickle across my shoulder. "Right here. It will not hurt much."

A hysterical laugh bubbles up inside me. I am standing naked in the hold surrounded by mermaids, talking to a magic fish. What am I afraid of? I have had worse injuries; I can handle a single bite. I am an adult now.

I open my mouth to ask her for enough money to get off this stinking boat, enough gold to drown a sailor in, to drown all of the sailors in. I open it to ask about my mother, if she knows her or can find her or bring her back. If my mother is alive or dead. Whether she was human or fish, truly.

But then I think of my sisters: Iris, shaking beneath her blankets and clutching the biology textbook like a magic charm, and May, who had given me hers to protect me at sea. I remember that there are more important things. I think about the people who hurt my sisters, who could hurt them, about the boy in the broom closet and Sunan in the hold. About my father on landing, his eyes bitter cold.

I tell the mermaid my real wish.

She grants it.

*   *   *

There are many versions of this story, each with a different ending.

In one, I swim away with the brown mermaid. The sun wavers in a jagged disk overhead, glinting in strange scintillations. The water is cold, the pressure enormous. It pushes in on my billowy body, still tender, pressing it into a tighter, sleeker shape. Our tiny, delicate hands are locked tight as we dive deeper into the ocean.

In another, a large storm scuttles *Pakpao,* along with all the other fishing boats in the area, on the reefs by Teluk Siam. The hold cracks, allowing the mermaids to escape. Everyone survives and is discovered days later. The rest of the story is fairly uneventful, equally implausible, and made up by people who care more for happy endings than truth.

But here is what really happens. The brown mermaid disappears and *Pakpao* makes it safely home with a hold full of live mermaids. If the crew looks a bit dazed and disoriented, if they are not quite themselves and walk as if they are not used to having two legs, it is just the result of sunstroke. If the mermaids in the hold swim in frantic circles, their eyes rolling wildly in their heads and their wails ricocheting through the hold, it is just what fish do. After all, mermaids are fish, not people. The Japanese traders find the catch acceptable and the mermaids are transported by tank to restaurants across Hokkaido. We make a huge profit.

With the exception of yours truly, every member of *Pakpao*'s crew drowns within a week of returning home. Though I live, our family does not escape this tragedy unscathed; my father's body is found floating in the nets behind the house. A joint funeral is held. Sunan's widow speaks tearfully about how her late husband stopped talking after his last fishing trip and had spent the days before his death trying to walk into the river, a story that resonates with the families of the recently deceased.

My sisters weep, their futures secure. I weep, too, licking the salt from my tears. There is a bandage on my shoulder and a bite beneath that will not heal.

"JACKALOPE WIVES"

URSULA VERNON

Our Nebula Award winner, Ursula Vernon, has previously won the Hugo Award and the Mythopoeic Fantasy Award. "Jackalope Wives" was published in Apex.

The moon came up and the sun went down. The moonbeams went shattering down to the ground and the jackalope wives took off their skins and danced.

They danced like young deer pawing the ground, they danced like devils let out of hell for the evening. They swung their hips and pranced and drank their fill of cactus-fruit wine.

They were shy creatures, the jackalope wives, though there was nothing shy about the way they danced. You could go your whole life and see no more of them than the flash of a tail vanishing around the backside of a boulder. If you were lucky, you might catch a whole line of them outlined against the sky, on the top of a bluff, the shadow of horns rising off their brows.

And on the half-moon, when new and full were balanced across the saguaro's thorns, they'd come down to the desert and dance.

The young men used to get together and whisper, saying they were gonna catch them a jackalope wife. They'd lay belly down at the edge of the bluff and look down on the fire and the dancing shapes—and they'd go away aching, for all the good it did them.

For the jackalope wives were shy of humans. Their lovers were jackrabbits and antelope bucks, not human men. You couldn't even get too close or they'd take fright and run away. One minute you'd see them kicking their heels up and hear them laugh, then the music would freeze and they'd all look at you with their eyes wide and their ears upswept.

The next second, they'd snatch up their skins and there'd be nothing left but a dozen skinny she-rabbits running off in all directions, and a campfire left that wouldn't burn out 'til morning.

It was uncanny, sure, but they never did anybody any harm. Grandma Harken, who lived down past the well, said that the jackalopes were the daughters of the rain and driving them off would bring on the drought. People said they didn't believe a word of it, but when you live in a desert, you don't take chances.

When the wild music came through town, a couple of notes skittering on the sand, then people knew the jackalope wives were out. They kept the dogs tied up and their brash sons occupied. The town got into the habit of having a dance that night, to keep the boys firmly fixed on human girls and to drown out the notes of the wild music.

*　　*　　*

Now, it happened there was a young man in town who had a touch of magic on him. It had come down to him on his mother's side, as happens now and again, and it was worse than useless.

A little magic is worse than none, for it draws the wrong sort of attention. It gave this young man feverish eyes and made him sullen. His grandmother used to tell him that it was a miracle he hadn't been drowned as a child, and for her he'd laugh, but not for anyone else.

He was tall and slim and had dark hair and young women found him fascinating.

This sort of thing happens often enough, even with boys as mortal as dirt. There's always one who learned how to brood early and often, and always girls who think they can heal him.

Eventually the girls learn better. Either the hurts are petty little things and they get tired of whining or the hurt's so deep and wide that they drown in it. The smart ones heave themselves back to shore and the slower ones wake up married with a husband who lies around and suffers in their direction. It's part of a dance as old as the jackalopes themselves.

But in this town at this time, the girls hadn't learned and the boy hadn't yet worn out his interest. At the dances, he leaned on the wall with his hands in his pockets and his eyes glittering. Other young men eyed him with dislike. He would slip away early, before the dance was ended, and never marked the eyes that followed him and wished that he would stay.

He himself had one thought and one thought only—to catch a jackalope wife.

They were beautiful creatures, with their long brown legs and their bodies splashed orange by the firelight. They had faces like no mortal woman and they moved like quicksilver and they played music that got down into your bones and thrummed like a sickness.

And there was one—he'd seen her. She danced farther out from the others and her horns were short and sharp as sickles. She was the last one to put on her rabbit skin when the sun came up. Long after the music had stopped, she danced to the rhythm of her own long feet on the sand.

(And now you will ask me about the musicians that played for the jackalope wives. Well, if you can find a place where they've been dancing, you might see something like sidewinder tracks in the dust, and more than that I cannot tell you. The desert chews its secrets right down to the bone.)

So the young man with the touch of magic watched the jackalope wife dancing and you know as well as I do what young men dream about. We will be charitable. She danced a little apart from her fellows, as he walked a little apart from his.

Perhaps he thought she might understand him. Perhaps he found her as interesting as the girls found him.

Perhaps we shouldn't always get what we think we want.

And the jackalope wife danced, out past the circle of the music and the firelight, in the light of the fierce desert stars.

*　　*　　*

Grandma Harken had settled in for the evening with a shawl on her shoulders and a cat on her lap when somebody started hammering on the door.

"Grandma! Grandma! Come quick—open the door—oh god, Grandma, you have to help me—"

She knew that voice just fine. It was her own grandson, her daughter Eva's boy. Pretty and useless and charming when he set out to be.

She dumped the cat off her lap and stomped to the door. What trouble had the young fool gotten himself into?

"Sweet Saint Anthony," she muttered, "let him not have gotten some fool girl in a family way. That's just what we need."

She flung the door open and there was Eva's son and there was a girl and for a moment her worst fears were realized.

Then she saw what was huddled in the circle of her grandson's arms, and her worst fears were stomped flat and replaced by far greater ones.

"Oh Mary," she said. "Oh, Jesus, Mary and Joseph. Oh blessed Saint Anthony, you've caught a jackalope wife."

Her first impulse was to slam the door and lock the sight away.

Her grandson caught the edge of the door and hauled it open. His knuckles were raw and blistered. "Let me in," he said. He'd been crying and there was dust on his face, stuck to the tracks of tears. "Let me in, let me in, oh god, Grandma, you have to help me, it's all gone wrong—"

Grandma took two steps back, while he half-dragged the jackalope into the house. He dropped her down in front of the hearth and grabbed for his grand-mother's hands. "Grandma—"

She ignored him and dropped to her knees. The thing across her hearth was hardly human. "What have you done?" she said. "What did you do to her?"

"Nothing!" he said, recoiling.

"Don't look at that and tell me 'Nothing!' What in the name of our lord did you do to that girl?"

He stared down at his blistered hands. "Her skin," he mumbled. "The rabbit skin. You know."

"I do indeed," she said grimly. "Oh yes, I do. What did you do, you damned young fool? Caught up her skin and hid it from her to keep her changing?"

The jackalope wife stirred on the hearth and made a sound between a whimper and a sob.

"She was waiting for me!" he said. "She knew I was there! I'd been— we'd—I watched her, and she knew I was out there, and she let me get up close—I thought we could talk—"

Grandma Harken clenched one hand into a fist and rested her forehead on it.

"I grabbed the skin—I mean—it was right there—she was watching—I thought she *wanted* me to have it—"

She turned and looked at him. He sank down in her chair, all his grace gone.

"You have to burn it," mumbled her grandson. He slid down a little further in her chair. "You're supposed to burn it. Everybody knows. To keep them changing."

"Yes," said Grandma Harken, curling her lip. "Yes, that's the way of it, right enough." She took the jackalope wife's shoulders and turned her toward the lamp light.

She was a horror. Her hands were human enough, but she had a jackrabbit's feet and a jackrabbit's eyes. They were set too wide apart in a human face, with a cleft lip and long rabbit ears. Her horns were short, sharp spikes on her brow.

The jackalope wife let out another sob and tried to curl back into a ball. There were burnt patches on her arms and legs, a long red weal down her face. The fur across her breasts and belly was singed. She stank of urine and burning hair.

"What did you do?"

"I threw it in the fire," he said. "You're supposed to. But she screamed—she wasn't supposed to scream—nobody said they screamed—and I thought she was dying, and I didn't want to *hurt* her—I pulled it back out—"

He looked up at her with his feverish eyes, that useless, beautiful boy, and said "I didn't *want* to hurt her. I thought I was supposed to—I gave her the skin back, she put it on, but then she fell down—it wasn't supposed to work like that!"

Grandma Harken sat back. She exhaled very slowly. She was calm. She was going to be calm, because otherwise she was going to pick up the fire poker and club her own flesh and blood over the head with it.

And even that might not knock some sense into him. Oh, Eva, Eva, my dear, what a useless son you've raised. Who would have thought he had so much ambition in him, to catch a jackalope wife?

"You goddamn stupid fool," she said. Every word slammed like a shutter in the wind. "Oh, you goddamn stupid fool. If you're going to catch a jackalope wife, you burn the hide down to ashes and never mind how she screams."

"But it sounded like it was hurting her!" he shot back. "You weren't there! She screamed like a dying rabbit!"

"Of course it hurts her!" yelled Grandma. "You think you can have your skin and your freedom burned away in front of you and not scream? Sweet mother Mary, boy, think about what you're doing! Be cruel or be kind, but don't be both, because now you've made a mess you can't clean up in a hurry."

She stood up, breathing hard, and looked down at the wreck on her hearth. She could see it now, as clear as if she'd been standing there. The fool boy had been so shocked he'd yanked the burning skin back out. And the jackalope wife had one thought only and pulled on the burning hide—

Oh yes, she could see it clear.

Half gone, at least, if she was any judge. There couldn't have been more than few scraps of fur left unburnt. He'd waited through at least one scream— or no, that was unkind.

More likely he'd dithered and looked for a stick and didn't want to grab for it with his bare hands. Though by the look of his hands, he'd done just that in the end.

And the others were long gone by then and couldn't stop her. There ought to have been one, at least, smart enough to know that you didn't put on a half-burnt rabbit skin.

"Why does she look like that?" whispered her grandson, huddled into his chair.

"Because she's trapped betwixt and between. You did that, with your goddamn pity. You should have let it burn. Or better yet, left her alone and never gone out in the desert at all."

"She was beautiful," he said. As if it were a reason.

As if it mattered.

As if it had ever mattered.

"Get out," said Grandma wearily. "Tell your mother to make up a poultice for your hands. You did right at the end, bringing her here, even if you made a mess of the rest, from first to last."

He scrambled to his feet and ran for the door.

On the threshold, he paused, and looked back. "You—you can fix her, right?"

Grandma let out a high bark, like a bitch-fox, barely a laugh at all. "No. No one can fix this, you stupid boy. This is broken past mending. All I can do is pick up the pieces."

He ran. The door slammed shut, and left her alone with the wreckage of the jackalope wife.

*   *   *

She treated the burns and they healed. But there was nothing to be done for the shape of the jackalope's face, or the too-wide eyes, or the horns shaped like a sickle moon.

At first, Grandma worried that the townspeople would see her, and lord knew what would happen then. But the jackalope wife was the color of dust and she still had a wild animal's stillness. When somebody called, she lay flat in the garden, down among the beans, and nobody saw her at all.

The only person she didn't hide from was Eva, Grandma's daughter. There was no chance that she mistook them for each other—Eva was round and plump and comfortable, the way Grandma's second husband, Eva's father, had been round and plump and comfortable.

Maybe we smell alike, thought Grandma. *It would make sense, I suppose.*

Eva's son didn't come around at all.

"He thinks you're mad at him," said Eva mildly.

"He thinks correctly," said Grandma.

She and Eva sat on the porch together, shelling beans, while the jackalope wife limped around the garden. The hairless places weren't so obvious now, and the faint stripes across her legs might have been dust. If you didn't look directly at her, she might almost have been human.

"She's gotten good with the crutch," said Eva. "I suppose she can't walk?"

"Not well," said Grandma. "Her feet weren't made to stand up like that. She can do it, but it's a terrible strain."

"And talk?"

"No," said Grandma shortly. The jackalope wife had tried, once, and the noises she'd made were so terrible that it had reduced them both to weeping. She hadn't tried again. "She understands well enough, I suppose."

The jackalope wife sat down, slowly, in the shadow of the scarlet runner beans. A hummingbird zipped inches from her head, dabbing its bill into the flowers, and the jackalope's face turned, unsmiling, to follow it.

"He's not a bad boy, you know," said Eva, not looking at her mother. "He didn't mean to do her harm."

Grandma let out an explosive snort. "Jesus, Mary and Joseph! It doesn't matter what he *meant* to do. He should have left well enough alone, and if he couldn't do that, he should have finished what he started." She scowled down at the beans. They were striped red and white and the pods came apart easily in her gnarled hands. "Better all the way human than this. Better he'd bashed her head in with a rock than *this*."

"Better for her, or better for you?" asked Eva, who was only a fool about her son and knew her mother well.

Grandma snorted again. The hummingbird buzzed away. The jackalope wife lay still in the shadows, with only her thin ribs going up and down.

"You could have finished it, too," said Eva softly. "I've seen you kill chickens. She'd probably lay her head on the chopping block if you asked."

"She probably would," said Grandma. She looked away from Eva's weak, wise eyes. "But I'm a damn fool as well."

Her daughter smiled. "Maybe it runs in families."

*   *   *

Grandma Harken got up before dawn the next morning and went rummaging around the house.

"Well," she said. She pulled a dead mouse out of a mousetrap and took a half-dozen cigarettes down from behind the clock. She filled three water bottles and strapped them around her waist. "Well. I suppose we've done as much as humans can do, and now it's up to somebody else."

She went out into the garden and found the jackalope wife asleep under the stairs. "Come on," she said. "Wake up."

The air was cool and gray. The jackalope wife looked at her with doe-dark eyes and didn't move, and if she were a human, Grandma Harken would have itched to slap her.

Pay attention! Get mad! Do something!

But she wasn't human and rabbits freeze when they're scared past running. So Grandma gritted her teeth and reached down a hand and pulled the jackalope wife up into the pre-dawn dark.

They moved slow, the two of them. Grandma was old and carrying water for two, and the girl was on a crutch. The sun came up and the cicadas burnt the air with their wings.

A coyote watched them from up on the hillside. The jackalope wife looked up at him, recoiled, and Grandma laid a hand on her arm.

"Don't worry," she said. "I ain't got the patience for coyotes. They'd maybe fix you up but we'd both be stuck in a tale past telling, and I'm too old for that. Come on."

They went a little further on, past a wash and a watering hole. There were palo verde trees spreading thin green shade over the water. A javelina looked up at them from the edge and stamped her hooved feet. Her children scraped their tusks together and grunted.

Grandma slid and slithered down the slope to the far side of the water and refilled the water bottles. "Not them either," she said to the jackalope wife. "They'll talk the legs off a wooden sheep. We'd both be dead of old age before they'd figured out what time to start."

The javelina dropped their heads and ignored them as they left the wash behind.

The sun was overhead and the sky turned turquoise, a color so hard you could bash your knuckles on it. A raven croaked overhead and another one snickered somewhere off to the east.

The jackalope wife paused, leaning on her crutch, and looked up at the wings with longing.

"Oh no," said Grandma. "I've got no patience for riddle games, and in the end they always eat someone's eyes. Relax, child. We're nearly there."

The last stretch was cruelly hard, up the side of a bluff. The sand was soft underfoot and miserably hard for a girl walking with a crutch. Grandma had to half-carry the jackalope wife at the end. She weighed no more than a child, but children are heavy and it took them both a long time.

At the top was a high fractured stone that cast a finger of shadow like the wedge of a sundial. Sand and sky and shadow and stone. Grandma Harken nodded, content.

"It'll do," she said. "It'll do." She laid the jackalope wife down in the shadow and laid her tools out on the stone. Cigarettes and dead mouse and a scrap of burnt fur from the jackalope's breast. "It'll do."

Then she sat down in the shadow herself and arranged her skirts.

She waited.

The sun went overhead and the level in the water bottle went down. The sun started to sink and the wind hissed and the jackalope wife was asleep or dead.

The ravens croaked a conversation to each other, from the branches of a palo verde tree, and whatever one said made the other one laugh.

"Well," said a voice behind Grandma's right ear, "lookee what we have here."

"Jesus, Mary and Joseph!"

"Don't see them out here often," he said. "Not the right sort of place." He considered. "Your Saint Anthony, now . . . him I think I've seen. He understood about deserts."

Grandma's lips twisted. "Father of Rabbits," she said sourly. "Wasn't trying to call *you* up."

"Oh, I know." The Father of Rabbits grinned. "But you know I've always had a soft spot for you, Maggie Harken."

He sat down beside her on his heels. He looked like an old Mexican man, wearing a button-down shirt without any buttons. His hair was silver gray as a rabbit's fur. Grandma wasn't fooled for a minute.

"Get lonely down there in your town, Maggie?" he asked. "Did you come out here for a little wild company?"

Grandma Harken leaned over to the jackalope wife and smoothed one long ear back from her face. She looked up at them both with wide, uncomprehending eyes.

"Shit," said the Father of Rabbits. "Never seen that before." He lit a cigarette and blew the smoke into the air. "What did you do to her, Maggie?"

"I didn't do a damn thing, except not let her die when I should have."

"There's those would say that was more than enough." He exhaled another lungful of smoke.

"She put on a half-burnt skin. Don't suppose you can fix her up?" It cost Grandma a lot of pride to say that, and the Father of Rabbits tipped his chin in acknowledgment.

"Ha! No. If it was loose I could fix it up, maybe, but I couldn't get it off her now with a knife." He took another drag on the cigarette. "Now I see why you wanted one of the Patterned People."

Grandma nodded stiffly.

The Father of Rabbits shook his head. "He might want a life, you know. Piddly little dead mouse might not be enough."

"Then he can have mine."

"Ah, Maggie, Maggie . . . You'd have made a fine rabbit, once. Too many stones in your belly now." He shook his head regretfully. "Besides, it's not *your* life he's owed."

"It's my life he'd be getting. My kin did it, it's up to me to put it right." It occurred to her that she should have left Eva a note, telling her to send the fool boy back East, away from the desert.

Well. Too late now. Either she'd raised a fool for a daughter or not, and likely she wouldn't be around to tell.

"Suppose we'll find out," said the Father of Rabbits, and nodded.

A man came around the edge of the standing stone. He moved quick then slow and his eyes didn't blink. He was naked and his skin was covered in painted diamonds.

Grandma Harken bowed to him, because the Patterned People can't hear speech.

He looked at her and the Father of Rabbits and the jackalope wife. He looked down at the stone in front of him.

The cigarettes he ignored. The mouse he scooped up in two fingers and dropped into his mouth.

Then he crouched there, for a long time. He was so still that it made Grandma's eyes water, and she had to look away.

"Suppose he does it," said the Father of Rabbits. "Suppose he sheds that skin right off her. Then what? You've got a human left over, not a jackalope wife."

Grandma stared down at her bony hands. "It's not so bad, being a human," she said. "You make do. And it's got to be better than *that*."

She jerked her chin in the direction of the jackalope wife.

"Still meddling, Maggie?" said the Father of Rabbits.

"And what do you call what you're doing?"

He grinned.

The Patterned Man stood up and nodded to the jackalope wife.

She looked at Grandma, who met her too-wide eyes. "He'll kill you," the old woman said. "Or cure you. Or maybe both. You don't have to do it. This is the bit where you get a choice. But when it's over, you'll be all the way something, even if it's just all the way dead."

The jackalope wife nodded.

She left the crutch lying on the stones and stood up. Rabbit legs weren't meant for it, but she walked three steps and the Patterned Man opened his arms and caught her.

He bit her on the forearm, where the thick veins run, and sank his teeth in up to the gums. Grandma cursed.

"Easy now," said the Father of Rabbits, putting a hand on her shoulder. "He's one of the Patterned People, and they only know the one way."

The jackalope wife's eyes rolled back in her head, and she sagged down onto the stone.

He set her down gently and picked up one of the cigarettes.

Grandma Harken stepped forward. She rolled both her sleeves up to the elbow and offered him her wrists.

The Patterned Man stared at her, unblinking. The ravens laughed to themselves at the bottom of the wash. Then he dipped his head and bowed to Grandma Harken and a rattlesnake as long as a man slithered away into the evening.

She let out a breath she didn't know she'd been holding. "He didn't ask for a life."

The Father of Rabbits grinned. "Ah, you know. Maybe he wasn't hungry. Maybe it was enough you made the offer."

"Maybe I'm too old and stringy," she said.

"Could be that, too."

The jackalope wife was breathing. Her pulse went fast then slow. Grandma sat down beside her and held her wrist between her own callused palms.

"How long you going to wait?" asked the Father of Rabbits.

"As long as it takes," she snapped back.

The sun went down while they were waiting. The coyotes sang up the moon. It was half-full, half-new, halfway between one thing and the other.

"She doesn't have to stay human, you know," said the Father of Rabbits. He picked up the cigarettes that the Patterned Man had left behind and offered one to Grandma.

"She doesn't have a jackalope skin any more."

He grinned. She could just see his teeth flash white in the dark. "Give her yours."

"I burned it," said Grandma Harken, sitting up ramrod straight. "I found where he hid it after he died and I burned it myself. Because I had a new husband and a little bitty baby girl and all I could think about was leaving them both behind and go dance."

The Father of Rabbits exhaled slowly in the dark.

"It was easier that way," she said. "You get over what you *can't* have faster that you get over what you *could*. And we shouldn't always get what we think we want."

They sat in silence at the top of the bluff. Between Grandma's hands, the pulse beat steady and strong.

"I never did like your first husband much," said the Father of Rabbits.

"Well," she said. She lit her cigarette off his. "He taught me how to swear. And the second one was better."

The jackalope wife stirred and stretched. Something flaked off her in long strands, like burnt scraps of paper, like a snake's skin shedding away. The wind tugged at them and sent them spinning off the side of the bluff.

From down in the desert, they heard the first notes of a sudden wild music.

"It happens I might have a spare skin," said the Father of Rabbits. He reached into his pack and pulled out a long gray roll of rabbit skin. The jackalope wife's eyes went wide and her body shook with longing, but it was human longing and a human body shaking.

"Where'd you get that?" asked Grandma Harken, suspicious.

"Oh, well, you know." He waved a hand. "Pulled it out of a fire once— must have been forty years ago now. Took some doing to fix it up again, but some people owed me favors. Suppose she might as well have it . . . Unless you want it?"

He held it out to Grandma Harken.

She took it in her hands and stroked it. It was as soft as it had been fifty years ago. The small sickle horns were hard weights in her hands.

"You were a hell of a dancer," said the Father of Rabbits.

"Still am," said Grandma Harken, and she flung the jackalope skin over the shoulders of the human jackalope wife.

It went on like it had been made for her, like it was her own. There was a jagged scar down one foreleg where the rattlesnake had bit her. She leapt up and darted away, circled back once and bumped Grandma's hand with her nose— and then she was bounding down the path from the top of the bluff.

The Father of Rabbits let out a long sigh. "Still are," he agreed.

"It's different when you got a choice," said Grandma Harken.

They shared another cigarette under the standing stone.

Down in the desert, the music played and the jackalope wives danced. And one scarred jackalope went leaping into the circle of firelight and danced like a demon, while the moon laid down across the saguaro's thorns.

"SLEEP WALKING NOW AND THEN"

RICHARD BOWES

Richard Bowes has won two World Fantasy Awards and the Lambda Literary Award. "Sleep Walking Now and Then" was first published on Tor.com.

Rosalin Quay, the set and costume designer, stood in a bankrupt Brooklyn warehouse staring at the rewards of a long quest. Inside a dusty storage space were manikins. Stiff limbed, sexless ones from the early 20th century stood alongside figures with abstract sexuality (which is how some described Rosalin) from the early 21st.

But the prime treasure of this discovery was dummies from a critical moment of change. Manikins circa 1970 were fluid in their poses, slightly androgynous but still recognizably male or female. The look would be iconic in the immersive stage design, which she had been hired to assemble.

The warehouse manager, Sonya, was tall, strong, and desperate. Rosalin, who had an eye for these things, placed her on the wrong side of thirty but with a bit of grace in her movements. Sonya brought up computer records on the palm of her hand. The owner of the manikins had stopped paying rent during the crash of 2053. The warehouse would shut down in two days and was unloading abandoned stock at going-out-of-business prices.

A pretty good guess on Rosalin's part was that Sonya came to New York intending to be a dancer/actor, had no luck, and was about to be unemployed: a common tale in the city everyone called the Big Arena.

"These pieces are for my current project," Rosalin said, and sent her an address. "I consider finding you and the manikins at the same moment an interesting coincidence. It would be to your advantage to deliver them personally."

She believed she saw a bit of what was called espontáneo *in the younger woman.*

ONE

Jacoby Cass awoke a few days later in the penthouse of a notorious hotel. The Angouleme, built in 1890, had stood in the old Manhattan neighborhood of Kips Bay for a hundred and seventy years. Its back was to the East River and sunlight bounced off the water and through the uncurtained windows.

Cass rose and watched tides from the Atlantic swirl upstream. Water spilled over the seawall and got pumped into drainage ditches. In 2060, every coastline on earth that could afford floodwalls had them. The rest either pumped or treaded water.

Like many New Yorkers, Jacoby Cass saw the rising waters as a warning of impending doom but, like most of them, Cass had bigger worries. None are as superstitious as the actor, the director, or the playwright in the rehearsals of a new show. And for his drama *Sleep Walking Now and Then*, which was to be put on in this very building, Jacoby Cass was all three.

Weeks before, his most recent marriage had dissolved. She kept the co-op while he slept on a futon in the defunct hotel. Most of his clothes were still in the suitcases in which he'd brought them.

All was barren in the room except for a rack holding a velvet-collared frock coat, an evening jacket, silk vests, starched white shirts and collars, opera pumps, striped trousers, arm and sock garters, a high silk hat, and pairs of dress shoes sturdy as ships. He was going to play Edwin Lowery Nance, the man who had built this hotel. And this was his wardrobe for *Sleep Walking*.

Cass's palm implant vibrated. Messages flashed: Security told him a city elevator inspector was in the building. His ex-wife announced she was closing their safe-deposit box. A painting crew for the lower floors was delayed. His eyes skimmed this unpleasant list as he tapped out a demand for coffee.

An image of the lobby of The Angouleme popped up. The lobby looked as it had when he'd run through a scene there the week before. Relentless sunlight showed the cracks in the dark wood paneling, the peeling paint and sagging chandeliers. The place was bare of furniture and rugs.

Then an elevator door opened and Cass saw himself step out with two other actors. The man and the woman wore their own contemporary street clothes and carried scripts. Cass, though, wore bits of his 1890s costume—a high hat, a loosely tied cravat. He was Edwin Lowery Nance showing wealthy friends the palace he'd just built, where he would die so mysteriously.

"My good sir and lovely madam," he heard himself say, "I intend this place to be a magnet, attracting a clientele which aspires to your elegance." They played out the scene as he'd written it, in that shoddy space devoid of any magic. The other two actors were still learning their lines. But Cass found his own rendition of the lines he'd written flat and ridiculous.

Irritated, wondering why this had been sent to him, Cass was about to close his fist and erase the messages when he heard Rosalin's voice, with its traces of an indefinable (and some said phony) European accent.

"Not an impressive outing. But I believe if you try again this evening, you will find everything transformed."

Rosalin and Jacoby Cass had worked together over the years without ever becoming more than acquaintances. But Cass found a ray of hope in the message and decided to grasp it.

His coffee was delivered by the new production assistant, a tall and tense young lady. Cass noted her legs in pants down to the shoe tops, though autumn fashion had decreed bare legs for women and long pants for men. Quite a reverse of the styles of the last few years.

He could imagine her life in the Big Arena with multiple aspiring artists/ roommates all scraping by in a deteriorating high-rise. This was Rosalin's protégé. He thought her name was Sonya but wasn't positive. At the outset of his career, almost forty years before, he had learned to be nice to the assistants, because one never knew which of them would end as a huge name. So he smiled the smile that had made him a star and took the coffee into the bathroom.

Water pressure wasn't good, and the pipes were rusty, but like the building itself, the pipes and wiring pretty much worked. Twenty minutes later, shaved, showered, purged, and scented, he donned modern underwear then got dressed from the costume rack: a starched shirt minus the collar, trousers held up with suspenders, an unbuttoned vest, and slippers.

A palm message told him the elevator inspector was waiting. He opened his bedroom door and walked into the big sky lighted room that had once been the office/den of Edwin Lowery Nance, whose unproven murder haunted the Angouleme Hotel.

In Nance's lair all was old wood and brass and it had not aged well. For scores of years The Angouleme had followed a downward path before being seized by the city. Bright sun streamed down and highlighted the scarred desk and worn rugs. After dark and in the low glow of early electricity, all would have to appear mysterious, rich, and rotten. Everything depended on that.

Down a very short corridor lay the bedchamber of Evangeline, daughter of Edwin Lowery Nance, and more famous in her time than Lizzie Borden. Through the open door Cass could see the curtains on the canopied bed parted to display a beautifully dressed Parisian doll. Legend demanded it. Just as Lizzie will always be the harridan with the axe, Evangeline Nance was the sleep walking child with a doll under her arm.

Jacoby Cass's career had high points which many in this city remembered. His *Hamlet* was set in an abandoned seminary where audience members could pick flowers with Ophelia, help dig graves or secretly poison swords.

The *Downton Abbey* he staged in the Frick Museum was a week-long twenty-four-hour-a-day drama built around an antique television show. Customers took tea with aristocrats, spied on lovers, searched closets and dresser drawers for clues and scandal. It ran for years and rescued the bankrupt museum for a time.

Once, Cass was spoken of as a theatrical giant: Barrymore and Ziegfeld combined. But at the moment he was coming off flops on stage, screen, and net. He'd recently been approached to take the film role of a hammy older actor. He'd turned it down. But the backers of *Sleep Walking Now and Then* were not a patient crew, and in his bad moments he wondered if he'd regret not taking the part. This show would click fast or die fast.

Cass inhaled deeply and stepped out of Nance's sanctuary: *His* sanctuary he reminded himself, as he stood straight and walked down the hall to the private elevator. The public elevators had all been upgraded many times over the years. But this one stood with its door half-open. The original machinery had been replaced, but the car with its golden cage and faded 18th century silhouetted couples in wigs and finery still remained.

Cass intended this to be a central motif of his drama. It was here that the first death had blackened the Angouleme's name and begun its legend.

The story was well known. Deep in the night of April 12, 1895, Nance—drunk, distracted, or both—thought he was stepping onto the elevator. Instead he went through the open door and fell nine stories to his death at the bottom of the elevator shaft. Rumor had it he was in pursuit of his daughter. Most accounts now considered it a murder.

The city inspector, a small, neatly dressed man, was in the elevator car examining the control panel. As Cass approached he caught the eye of Ms. Jackson, head of security for *Sleep Walking*. She gave an almost invisible nod and he understood that Inspector Jason Chen had accepted a green handshake.

By reputation Chen was honest and would stay bribed. But he was also smart enough to be quite wary of a major scandal wiping out his career. "Let's talk," he said, and Cass led the way back to the lair.

They sat in Nance's old office with Cass's lawyer linked to both. The inspector said, "Jackson tells me that twice a night you're going to have that door open and the cage downstairs."

Cass smiled and explained, "The car will only be a few feet below the floor so as to be out of the audience's sight. Other than that it will just have regular usage."

"I want Ms. Jackson and her people here every minute the door is open and the car is in that condition. And I want it locked every minute it's not in use by your production while there are customers in the building. We will send observers."

"I'm playing Nance," Cass told him. "I'm the only one who'll go through the door with the car not in place. And at my age I don't take risks."

The inspector shook his head. "It's not you I'm worried about. I'm concerned about some spectators who have so little in their lives that they decide to become part of the show. We all know about them! My wife's Spanish. She talks about *espontáneos*—the ones who used to jump into the ring during bullfights and get maimed or killed but became famous for a little while. People get desperate for attention. Like that one who torched himself at the *Firebird* ballet!

"Something like that happens with the elevator and they fire me, shut you down forever, and we're up to our necks in indictments. Now let's take a look at your insurance and permits."

As he authorized documents with eye photos, Cass remembered an old show business joke: 'A play is an original dramatic construction *that has something wrong with the second act.*' His second act was the murder of the designer/performer Jacky Mac on these very premises. It happened seventy-five years after Nance's death and was even more dramatic. What his play still needed was a third act.

Chen departed; the lawyer broke contact. Cass, half in costume, sat behind the huge, battered desk which Rosalin had found somewhere. His New York was the Big Arena, a tough city with a sharp divide between rich and poor, between a cruel, easily bored audience and the desperate artists. It seemed more like 1895 than not.

Cass felt he was looking for a main chance again, just as he had forty years and many roles before. He told himself that Edwin Lowery Nance, an entrepreneur in his fifties afloat with his daughter in the tumultuous late 19th century, must have had moments like this.

Like an echo of the thought, a child's voice said, "Daddy! Thank you! I shall call her Mirabella!"

Startled, Cass/Nance looked up and found Evangeline Nance, with her long golden-honey hair and the 19th century Paris fashion doll she had named Mirabella tucked under her arm. Her eyes were shut and she didn't appear to sleep walk so much as to float toward the door amid the smoke-blue silks of a flowing dress and sea of petticoats. Her satin slippers hardly seemed to touch the floor.

In character, Jacoby Cass picked up a pair of gold-rimmed pince-nez from the desk, put them on his nose and peered silently at his daughter

At the door Evangeline stopped, turned and nodded, satisfied she had his full attention. "We're scheduled to do a run-through of the elevator chase. Remember, Mr. Nance?" she asked in a voice that was all New York actress. And suddenly Evangeline was Keri Mayne, a woman in her endlessly extended late thirties.

Keri had a history with Jacoby Cass—Ophelia to his Hamlet, a refuge fifteen years before when his third marriage broke down. The two had discussed Evangeline Nance. Her mother died when she was six. Over the twenty years before Evangeline became an orphan she remained a child and a sleep walker.

Kerri Mayne's Evangeline threw open the door to the outer hallway and Jacoby Cass arose ready to be Edwin Lowery Nance. Researching his play Cass found no one solid account of the night of April 12, 1895. It seemed very likely that Evangeline sleep walked her way out of the apartment and the father followed. Servants had seen this happen before. No witnesses were available to testify about the April night.

In Cass's script and performance, Nance rushed out of his office after her, calling, "Evangeline!" in a voice he felt would sound like cigar smoke and Scotch. "My child, where do you think you're going?" he cried as Keri/Evangeline sailed down the hall. Cass wore more of Nance's wardrobe: a vest, shoes that hurt his feet but somehow enhanced his performance.

Whispered rumor held that Evangeline had fled her bedroom with him in pursuit. And there was servants' testimony that this had happened before.

Almost all tellings agreed that Nance, in the dim light thought Evangeline had gone to the elevator and stepped through the open door. He followed and found not Evangeline but a nine-story drop. How the elevator car happened not to be there was a matter of mystery and dispute.

With all that in mind, after an hour and a half of rehearsals, Cass/Nance called out "Evangeline!" for the tenth time. All this took place with late September light streaming through the windows. But Cass channeling Nance began to see it happening by moonlight and primitive bulbs. He had to dodge assistants and understudies who had been instructed to stand in his way, walk across his path just as the theatergoers would.

He actually lost sight of Keri/Evangeline before he reached the elevator. The faded gold door was wide open and she had to be inside the car. Nance hurried forward, stepped inside, and fell nine stories into the cellar. It was only three feet and the padding was well placed. But he screamed "EVANGELINE" and made it seem to fade as if coming out of Nance as he hurtled nine stories down.

Jackson and a burly assistant moved forward and would have blocked the line of sight had there been any audience.

Lying face down on the padding, Cass's palm tingled and he read a message from Rosalin telling him that at 6:00 p.m. the Angouleme Hotel's lobby would be ready and awaiting his approval. Rolling over, he looked up at Keri and Jackson staring down and made arrangements for a run-through of the lobby scene at 6:30.

Taking a director/playwright's privilege, he wrote Evangeline into the scene. When the elevator door opened at 6:30 the lobby was all in shadows, low wattage light caught remnants of gold filigree on the walls. The three-story-high ceiling loomed above them with its mural of the European discovery of Manhattan still showing traces of grandeur.

*　　*　　*

The lobby was a collage of a hundred and seventy years of history. Singly and in groups, manikins lingered in corners and stairs. A sexual spectrum, enigmatic and sinister, they were dressed in 1970s miniskirts, flared pants, and psychedelic T-shirts, in 1890s bustles and floor-length gowns, in World War I doughboy uniforms. Some of their eyes seemed to reflect the light. One with dark hair, a red silk kerchief around his neck, and a leather jacket appeared to move slightly.

With his lovely daughter on his arm and the pair of wealthy customers alongside him, Cass/Nance surveyed them as if he saw the cream of New York society.

When he said, "My good sir and lovely madam" and the rest of his opening lines, Cass had fully mastered his Nance voice, throaty and a bit choked with good living.

The actors playing the couple had their lines down. "But," said the man, "what of the location here, almost on the docks and in a neighborhood of factories?"

"The anteroom of the Mighty Atlantic, sir! We shall steal the Hudson River's thunder. This is meant to be a palace for my lovely princess, my daughter." His daughter looked up at him, adoring but somehow lost.

The man frowned but the woman smiled and said, "How enchanting!"

"Come and partake of the Angouleme's humble fare," said Cass/Nance, and the quartet moved toward what had once been a famous hotel dining room and soon would be the *Sleep Walking* snack bar.

As they moved, Cass glanced at the front doors and saw them fly open right on cue. A long-haired figure in gold-rimmed dark glasses, an impeccably fitted velvet jacket and slacks strode across the empty lobby.

The young actor, Jeremy Knight, a rising star in the Big Arena, was Jacky Mac, dubbed the Kit Marlowe of late 1960s New York, whose murder was the Angouleme's second famous death.

Before Jeremy Knight got any further, Cass stepped out of character and into the center of the space. He addressed the company, human and manikin alike: "Our city loves scandals. When current misconduct is too drab the city seeks out its past, desires old relics. This lobby reflects that perfectly." Catching sight of her in the shadows, he bowed. "Thank you, Rosalin! But let's remember that it's only two weeks to opening night and there's so much to be done."

Everyone, cast and crew, applauded. He noticed that Keri Mayne, the charmer, and Jeremy Knight, the young lion, were talking together.

Rosalin led forward the production assistant who'd brought his coffee. "Sonya went out of her way to be helpful when I was acquiring props, saved us a lot of money. She has theatrical experience. There's the silent part of the maid for which we were going to use one of Jackson's people. She can do that and I could use her assistance."

Cass looked at this tense young woman from deep in the artist underclass and wondered about Rosalin's motives. But he was sure of her loyalty to this production into which she'd put so much invaluable work, if not to him. Sonya would come cheap and might be of use. So he nodded, smiled, and agreed with what was proposed.

When she and Sonya were alone Rosalin said, "I came to this city when it was first being called the Big Arena. Thirty years ago I was where you are now." Rosalin had learned that Sonya had no family she could go to, no close friends outside the city. "I had nobody in this world and nothing but my work."

*　　*　　*

TWO

Thursday night, at the 8pm show two weeks into the run, Keri Mayne leaned against the wall of Evangeline's bedroom. In full costume, the flowing skirts made sitting both difficult and unwise.

She listened to Cass/Nance outside, saw his image on her palm—cameras were everywhere—heard him say, "Of course, J. P.," into the wall telephone. Nance spoke loudly because he didn't trust the instrument and because an audience needed to hear.

In the play it was well after midnight in the midst of the financial crisis of 1895 and J. P. Morgan had just called. "Of course I will stand with you, Mr. Morgan. Tomorrow at ten? I will be there, sir."

Keri/Evangeline watched Sonya, in a European maid's uniform, standing at the bedroom door and listening. In the intricately jealous context of a theater company Keri mistrusted and feared her.

Outside Nance said, "Of course, sir, I too know the loneliness of losing a wife." His voice became muffled as he turned away. But those in the room could hear the great financier describe a need a discreet hotel keeper might satisfy. Nance had left behind him some nasty rumors and Cass had used all of them.

Keri/Evangeline heard the others in the room move closer to Nance, trying to catch the conversation. This was the moment. She nodded; Sonya threw open the door and Evangeline floated out of her room and into her father's den.

Evangeline light as a package of feathers, was wrapped in silk. Shimmering hair flowed down to Evangeline's waist. Her eyes were half open, as if she was in a trance. She had Mirabella in her left arm. The gold slippers glided across the floor.

Half a dozen audience members were in the room. Women wore short skirts; men's legs were concealed in trousers. These were the rich and *Sleep Walking* was a game as much as a play. Devices that enabled communication, blocked insects and rain, illuminated, cooled, or heated the area around one as the moment dictated were turned off. Mostly.

By clustering around Nance in the corner, the playgoers opened the way to the outer hall door which Sonya opened, revealing a crowd of eavesdroppers. She plowed through them. Seemingly unaware of all this Keri/Evangeline floated over the threshold. And maid and mistress passed down a dim lit hall.

Most of the windowpanes were blackened and heavily curtained. But an occasional one seemed to look onto the outside world. Playgoers on this floor could gaze out upon a 19th century night. Hologram pedestrians and horse-dawn vehicles traveled on the avenue, lanterns on ships bobbed on East River piers. Some figures in lighted windows across the way spoke intently at each other by lamplight while others seemed to grope naked in the dark.

"Evangeline!" she heard Nance cry as he came out the office door. Playgoers followed him. Figures in 19th century clothes discreetly got in their way. Audience members accidently blocked him. "My child, where are you going?" Nance cried to his daughter, who gave no sign she was aware of him.

Playgoers were supposed to be absolutely silent. But a man whispered, "She's a bit taller than I would have thought." And a woman responded, "Looks like a child and at the same time older." Sonya kept them away.

Though their conversation irritated Keri, she did prize her ability to alternate between radiant child and disturbed adult. All was shadows and misdirection at the end of the hall. Evangeline floated toward the open elevator door.

Nance, in a voice that was authoritarian and pleading at the same time, shouted, "Young lady, you must obey me. Stop!" His heavy shoes banged on the floor as he began to run.

For a moment everyone looked his way. When they looked back to the elevator, Evangeline and her maid had disappeared.

Edwin Lowery Nance, who managed to appear to hurry while not really moving quickly, came down the hall. He ran through the open doorway and his shout turned into a scream. His voice faded as he fell nine stories into the cellar.

Jackson and her equally big cohort, dressed in 1890's street clothes, were suddenly there blocking the audience members' view. She and her partner looked into the pit. The partner screamed. "Someone get a doctor! Call the police!" Ms. Jackson shook her head sadly and pulled the elevator door closed.

"I saw him, his body was all bloody and smashed," a theatergoer cried.

Keri—standing inside the door that led to the servants' stairs—listened, amused by this. Someone was always getting caught up in the drama. She imagined Cass/Nance lying on the padding, looking up at the faded fleur-de-lis design on the elevator car's roof and, like her, taking the cry as a kind of applause. When reviews called the show "Just a Halloween entertainment," Cass told her, "That gets us through the next month. After that we'll find something else." She hoped he was right.

Her costume made stairs difficult and the maid reached out to help her. Sonya spoke, voice low and intense: "Just after Nance fell they thought it was a tragic accident. Then rumors started that I was seen near the elevator machinery in the cellar. I disappeared before I could be questioned about the events and was never seen again."

At moments when Sonya identified with the part of Evangeline's maid like this Keri wondered why Rosalin, who took care of so many things, had arranged for this person to be alone with her in two performances a night, six nights a week. She hoped Sonya was aware how vital to the production her Evangeline was. Surveillance cams were everywhere but she wondered if they didn't just offer a greater chance for immortality.

So she gazed at Sonya with admiration and delight (and none could look with as much admiration and delight as she). "I'm amazed at the amount of research you've done. You have the makings of an actor," she said.

Then, as Evangeline, she motioned Sonya to go first, and said in a breathless child voice, "After Nance's death rumors got in the papers. One of my dolls was supposedly found in the elevator with his corpse. It's when the term 'Angouleme Murder' began being used. Servants testified that Nance had always taken an unnatural interest in his daughter." Here Evangeline covered her eyes for a moment. But Keri managed to catch Sonya's expression of both horror and sympathy.

Their destination was the sixth floor. On the landing, they paused, heard a 1920s Gershwin tune played by a jazz pianist. Privately, Keri was certain Evangeline had killed her old man, who in every way deserved it. Life with him and after him had made her a manipulative crazy person. It was what Keri loved about the part.

But she looked at Sonya and said with great sincerity, "I try to remember what that poor child-woman went through and put that into my performance."

Sonya held a light and a mirror like this was a sacred ritual. Evangeline's haunted face—just a trifle worn—appeared. Keri Mayne did a couple of makeup adjustments, held the doll to her chest, and braced herself.

Sonya opened the door and followed as Evangeline half floated into a hallway with distant, slightly flickering lights. Keri paused, listened for a moment, then wafted toward the music.

Playgoers, drinks in hand, stared out a window into a hologram of a lamp lit street scene. A big square-built convertible rolled by with its top down and men and women in fur coats waving glasses over their heads, while a cop made a point of not looking. Flappers in cloche hats and tight skirts scurried to avoid getting run down. They gained the sidewalk and disappeared into the Angouleme's main door downstairs.

On the sixth floor it was 1929.

It took a few moments for the well-upholstered crowd to notice the sleep walker and the woman in a maid's uniform who guided her.

Keri heard their whispered conversations:

". . . maybe down here trying to avoid her father?"

". . . a little older, this is long afterwards, when he's dead and she's still living here."

"We missed his big moment."

". . . looks like she's been on opium for years."

"Morphine, actually."

"Creepy, just like the Angouleme!"

"But delicious!"

". . . like a ghost in her own hotel for *decades* after the murder."

The illicit, low-level whispering was the audience telling each other the story they'd seen and heard online. Cass had wanted that. "Makes it like opera or Shakespeare, where the audience knows the plot but not how it'll be twisted this time."

On the sixth floor Keri was Evangeline in the long years after her father's death and before she died in 1932 addicted, isolated. Even before the First World War the Angouleme was called "louche" when that was the word used by people too nice to mention any specific decadence.

"She looks like she's hurt!" murmured a playgoer in a lavish, shimmering suit as he moved toward Evangeline. Keri lurched the other way, Sonya got between them.

Always in these audiences were ones like this who wanted to be part of the drama. If there was a long run, their faces would appear again and again. Certain people would start going out in public dressed like characters in the play. Great publicity, but a warning that no one should get too immersed in a part.

"Oh, who are all these ghosts, Marie?" Evangeline asked her maid in a whispery child voice and looked around at the faces staring at her. "People like these weren't allowed in the Angouleme when Father was here." She held up the doll. "Mirabella was his last gift to me."

She could hear the crowd murmur at this, felt them closing in. And in that moment, the character Jacoby Cass's script simply called "The Killer" came down the hall. This young man wore a leather jacket and a red silk kerchief tied around his neck. The butt of a revolver was visible in a pocket. The actor looked at Evangeline and the rest of the crowd with a cold, dead-eyed stare.

"How did he get in here?" a man whispered. "Where's security?"

This amused his partner. "More than likely he's a fugitive from the Jacky Mac Studio downstairs," she said. "We must pay a visit."

For a moment all attention focused on The Killer. Evangeline wobbling slightly, continued to the jazz piano.

By the 1920s, a louche, scandalous hotel had become attractive to certain people. Artists stayed at the Angouleme and entertained there: French Surrealists and their mistresses, wealthy bohemians poets from Greenwich Village, Broadway composers looking for someplace out of the way but not too far.

Something between a party and a cabaret went on in the living room of Gershwin's suite. Around the door, slender, elegant flappers leaned towards smiling men in evening clothes. The lights were soft; it usually took a couple of glances before someone would recognize them as manikins. But then the silvery figure, you were sure was a statue, would turn slightly and a pair of dark eyes would hold yours for a moment.

Inside the room a musician who looked not unlike Gershwin sat at a baby grand and played the sketches that would become *An American in Paris*.

The suite was set up as a speakeasy where audience members bought drinks, leaned on furniture, listened but also watched. Evangeline shimmered before them, exchanged a long kiss with the silver flapper. All eyes were on the two and Gershwin played a slow fox-trot. As they danced he turned from the piano, looked to the audience as though asking if they saw what he did.

When theatergoers from the hall began to crowd into the room, Evangeline floated through a bedroom door and her maid closed it. When people opened it to follow her, they found the room was empty and the door on the opposite wall was locked.

Some at that point would realize that the sixth floor was a diversion, a place to spend money and waste time that would have been better spent up in the penthouse or downstairs where a murder was brewing.

Sonya brought Keri/Evangeline down to the third floor where her next scene would be. The maid character didn't appear again in *Sleep Walking*. "I feel like I should stay with you," she said, and opened the door.

Keri grasped her arm, looked into her eyes and said, "You've done enough. You're wonderful."

The next day Sonya was setting up antique wooden folding chairs in Studio Mac on the third floor. She said, "I wish my part was bigger. I want to be in every minute of this play. I know that's how actors feel."

Rosalin believed the intensity could possibly be of use. "The Big Arena is a savage place, run for the very rich and full of the superfluous young. Most of them will never find something larger than themselves as you are doing. It takes a certain kind of personal sacrifice to fully achieve this. But it will live in others' memories."

* * *

THREE

In New York it was shortly before midnight of Halloween 2060. Over the years, this holiday had surpassed New Year's Eve as the city's expression of its identity. Especially at times like this when the legendary metropolis was short of cash and looking for some new idea to carry it forward.

In the Angouleme it was time for a special midnight show. Playgoers entered *Sleep Walking* through the lobby. From there they either went up the stairs, waited for the elevators, or just looked for a place to sit while getting acclimated. Rosalin had managed to exploit the lobby's disreputable, fallen majesty. It was a place made for loitering. Upstairs each floor was set in a different decade. The lobby celebrated the entire sordid past. Here, a cluster of 1960s rent boys lingered in the shadows next to the main staircase and several 1900s ladies of the evening in big hats and bustles stood near the ever-vacant concierge desk.

Jeremy Knight waited in a side doorway of the building. At exactly five minutes after the final stroke of twelve he got the one-minute signal, walked a few feet down the sidewalk to the front of the hotel, and was flanked by security.

They threw open the doors and Knight/Jacky entered the lobby: tall and wire-thin, his eyes hidden behind dark glasses, his blond hair in a ponytail down almost to his ass.

Knight was irritated as he always was at this moment by the sight of Jacoby Cass, who, with his speech about the God-given 19th century being finished, was making a grand exit with his party. A few patrons tried to follow but found themselves blocked by Jackson and company.

Jeremy Knight marveled at the number of scene-stealing opportunities Cass, that shameless ham had managed to insert into the script.

Knight surveyed the crowd. The show was booked solid for the Halloween weekend. Advance sales were another matter and his guts turned cold whenever that crossed his mind. So he didn't think about it.

In fact, Cass's distraction allowed Knight to be through the crowd before they were aware of him. He turned then to face them and they saw Jacky Mac—couturier, poet, playwright, in a classic outfit of his own design: V-shaped, slim-waisted jacket; bell-bottom trousers; a wide tie with bright pop art flowers that looked like faces. Jacky Mac had been known to wear miniskirts and silver knee boots, but not on this occasion.

On cue, the public elevator's doors opened. Customers hesitated as always about getting on board because of the legends surrounding the place.

Of Jeremy Knight it had been written, "He was born to wear a costume; put him in anything from a 1940 RAF uniform to a pink tutu and he is transformed." He despised the description but had found that in roles like this an actor grabbed inspiration wherever it could be found.

Without missing a beat, Jacky Mac stepped backwards onto an elevator and seemed amused by the audience's fear. "Oh, it's safe!" He somehow murmured and shouted in the same breath. "And if it begins to fall, just do as I do: flap your arms and fly!"

From the elevator doorway, Mac gazed at the manikins in the corner, saw something, and nodded. The audience watched fascinated as one of the figures, dressed in leather and a blood red kerchief stepped out of the shadows and walked unsmiling into the car. "I was crucified just now by his glance," Jacky announced as The Killer joined him and the door closed.

Alone, without an audience to overhear them, Jeremy and Remo, the young actor who played The Killer, didn't exchange a word. Each got off on a different floor, and over the next hour made rehearsed appearances in dark halls and bright interiors.

Forty minutes into the play, Jeremy Knight/Jacky Mac listened to Gershwin's piano and heard Nance's death scream. Ten minutes after that he did a huge double take when he passed the ghost of Evangeline on the tiresome seventh floor where it was always 2010 and the well-lighted halls were lined with display windows offering overpriced *Sleep Walking* souvenirs. Coming down the servants' stairs five minutes later, he passed Sonya trudging up carrying costumes. He smiled and she looked at him as wide-eyed as any fan.

*   *   *

Halloween week was great. Capacity crowds were willing and able to laugh and scream at every performance. On the third floor of the Angouleme two weeks later, at about an hour and twenty minutes into *Sleep Walking*, Knight/Jacky climbed onto the small stage in the Mac Studio and felt the difference.

The Studio included a large performance space with sixty chairs set up. At the Halloween midnight show all seats had been taken and many more patrons stood or sat on the floor. Halloween had been a triumph. But it's in the weeks between holidays that hit shows are revealed and flops begin to die.

Jeremy Knight had that in mind as he pirouetted on the stage. He estimated thirty people in the seats. And this included The Killer, always the first to arrive. Remo was also Jeremy Knight's understudy. He sat down front with his legs stuck out so far his booted feet rested on the stage. A little knowledge of history and one would be reminded of Jacky Mac's fatal tastes.

The under-capacity crowd bothered Knight. But he told himself that any audience of any size was fated to be his. And the people at these performances who sat on antique wooden folding chairs were willing extras.

They were drawn to the Studio by the sounds and the lights flashing through the open double doors. Or they were told not to miss this by friends who had seen Knight/Jacky perform this monologue, one-man play, stand-up routine, whatever you wanted to call it. Jacky Mac's writing was out of copyright and Cass had lifted big chunks of it for a play within a play called *A Death Made for Speculation*.

Jacky leaned over the front of the stage, hummed a few bars of music, and said in a husky voice, "I'd thought of coming out in an evening gown and doing a Dietrich medley. But I've seen the way women look at me when I do drag. It's the look Negroes get when a white person sings the blues. So I'm here to fulfill a secret dream. I'm playing a guy."

Rosalin had taken liberties with the decor but 1970 was a hard moment to exaggerate. Jacky's loft had been described and shown in articles, books, and documentary footage. Like Warhol's factory, it was iconic. On the walls and above mantelpieces were mirrors, which at certain angles turned into windows looking into other rooms. In those rooms doll automata played cards, a mechanical rogue and his partner cavorted, and one or both might look your way, indicate you were next.

"When I was young," Jacky Mac said, "I tried to make myself look beautiful. Later I tried to make myself look young. Now I'm satisfied with making myself look different."

In the lawless 1960s, the Angouleme Hotel was almost as famous as the Chelsea across town. When it was sold as co-op apartments and lofts Jacky bought most of the third floor of the building with the proceeds of his clothing line and his performance art. Jacky Mac was not, of course, his real name, which was boring and provincial Donald Sprang.

For Jeremy Knight the task was making something as ordinary as homosexuality feel as mysterious, hysterical, and dangerous as Jacky had found his life to be. A brief film clip existed of Jacky Mac working out some of this material in the Studio, performing for an audience of friends in just this manner.

Jeremy caught the odd, fluid near-dance of Jacky Mac, which he'd learned from old videos. On the walls Hendrix, Joplin, and Day-Glo acrylic nude boys and girls melted into a landscape of red and blue trees. A light show played intermittently on the ceiling. Deep yellow blobs turned into crisp light green snakes, which drowned in orange, quivering jelly. The color spectrum dazed the eye.

Knight/Jacky leaned forward to show a once-angelic face now touched with lines and makeup and asked, "Why do men over thirty with long hair always look like their mothers?"

On cue, The Killer down front swallowed a few pills, stood up, pulled a bottle from his back pocket, spat out, "Faggot" at Jacky and walked toward the door while taking a long slug. In the old-fashioned manner, Jacky Mac liked his partners rough. It would be the death of him.

The audience watched the long, slow exit. Wrist limp, Jacky Mac gestured after him. "We have the perfect relationship. I pretend he doesn't exist and he pretends that he does."

It wasn't just the costume; Jeremy Knight had absorbed every bit of the lost manner and voice of someone society hated for what he was. Ninety years later it was hard to convey. For a few years in his teens Jeremy had been Jenna Knight, making the change because boys in school got neglected and there was an advantage to being a boy with the mind of a girl.

Each day Knight felt closer to Jacky's alienation. Saw it intertwine with his own fear of falling off a very small pedestal and back into the vast, penniless crowd in the Big Arena.

The Killer stopped at the door and yelled, "IT'S YOUR TURN NOW, BITCH" at somebody no one could see.

Jacky glanced his way, turned back to the seats and found everyone staring wide-eyed. "Dear me, are the snakes growing out of my head again? That Medusa look was *so* popular once upon a time!" He peered at the crowd and remarked half to himself, "Judging by your faces, I've turned you all to stone. Forgive me. My mother always said . . ."

But few were listening. All eyes were on a figure in silks floating past the stage humming "Beautiful Dreamer" under her breath, while the audience whispered her name.

Cass had invented a liaison in this hotel between a self-destructive artist and the ghost of a legendary suspected murderess. The character Jacky was haunted by Evangeline decades after she had died of an overdose.

Once he caught sight of her he seemed to forget the audience completely and followed her out of the room. When audience members came after them, they found a locked door.

But the room into which the two had gone was Jacky's legendary mirrored bedroom. The ceiling, an entire wall, even the floor in places reflected the room and its outsize bed. One wall was a two-way mirror. Jacky was always aware of this, as were some of his bedmates.

The *Sleep Walking* audience flocked around the glass, saw silhouettes dance in semi-darkness as Jacky tried to trap Evangeline or she ensnared him. One shadow seemed to pass through another. One or the other always had a back to the audience and both whispered so none outside could hear.

"How's the gate tonight?" she asked.

"Seventy percent for this show, about the same for the midnight show," he said.

"Shit," she said. "It's going to fold."

"Needs a third act," he said. "I have my eye out for especially unstable repeat patrons."

"A third victim," she said. "Rosalin's got one but Sonya scares me."

He shook his head. "She's harmless."

"A suicide might do," Keri said.

"I volunteer my understudy, Remo."

"Silly, understudies don't want to die; they want to kill the leads."

Through the glass the two heard, "Where are you, faggot? Fucking the ghost girl?" The Killer had returned.

Jeremy Knight took a deep breath and walked out of the bedroom. "Let's talk, one faggot to another. I'm the terrible secret: the herpes sore on the ten-inch cock, the skunk at the tea dance, the troll without the decency to hide under the bridge. I'm the one who's here to call you sister, to tell you . . ."

In *Sleep Walking* The Killer emptied the pistol into him just as had happened in real life. Audience members screamed. Keri always stayed for this and always had to stop herself from crying. Then she'd slip out for her big scene with Nance.

Only after his death was Jacky Mac described as "The Kit Marlowe of this bedraggled city." The press didn't get into the details of his life. The murderer was never identified, never caught.

Business did pick up for Christmas/New Year. But January brought bad weather and bad box office. On the last performance that month Rosalin stood several steps above Sonya, looking down at her as she said *"This show needed something that would get the Big Arena talking about us and not the thousand other entertainments available. That never happened. We're posting closing notices next week. All my work wasted. I hope you enjoyed your brief time on stage."*

Sonya's eyes glistened. Rosalin recognized tears. They had talked about suicide. But heights bothered the stupid girl, guns were a mystery. Rosalin had thought to bring a knife.

*   *   *

FINALE

The show's final scene was actors playing detectives, questioning the audience members as they filed out of the Studio after Jacky Mac's death.

And down the hall, Edwin Lowery and Evangeline Nance went at each other in hoarse ghost whispers. "Oh finally, my daughter, you will have no more to do with that sodomite!" Anger is never hard for actors to achieve in a failing production.

Keri was scared and irritated. Sonya, like a rat deserting a sinking ship, hadn't shown up that evening to get her through the dwindling crowd. She screeched, "So unlike the midnight visits to my room when I was still a child! Let us talk about pederasty and hypocrisy!"

Playgoers, still a bit ensnared by the drama they'd just witnessed, kept pointing them out to the actors/police who would look but be unable to see the ghosts.

"And that reminds me, dear Father . . ." Evangeline started to say, when there was a long, piercing and—Keri realized—quite heartfelt scream.

"That sounds very authentic!" said Jacoby Cass in his own voice and with a look of hope in his eyes.

Actor/cops and audience members stared down the hall. The Killer was running toward them with tears in his eyes and the prop gun still in his hand, babbling. ". . . in the elevator . . . opened the door . . . blood . . ."

Jeremy Knight/Jacky Mac arose from the floor of the Studio to discover what the commotion outside was about and was stunned when Remo/The Killer threw himself sobbing into his arms.

City police found Sonya holding open the faded gold door of the elevator. She'd knocked Rosalin down and stabbed her multiple times. The surveillance tape showed it all. She'd even looked up and waved.

When they hustled her out of the hotel and into a police car, Sonya yelled to the crowd, "She wanted me to die, wanted somebody else to die. But her work was over and the play must go on!"

A reporter asked Cass, "City officials think the production can open again in another few days. Do you believe it's safe for theatergoers?"

Jacoby Cass had heard from Inspector Chen that the authorities regarded this as a murder that could have taken place anywhere. The elevator, though, would need to be thoroughly inspected and his supervisors would accompany him.

Cass anticipated a flurry of green handshakes but knew *Sleep Walking Now and Then* was booked solid for at least the next six months. He told the reporter, "Yes. Notice that at no time was the life of any patron threatened!"

"Is the place haunted," Keri Mayne was constantly asked.

Leaving the building the night of the murder, she had felt Rosalin's presence in the lobby and wondered if her death was her greatest piece of theatrical design. Until then Keri hadn't thought much about spirits. "Yes," she always said. "And I'm dedicating each of my future performances to the ghosts."

Seeing Jeremy Knight and Remo arrive at a party as a couple, a social blogger asked, "Does this feel like your on-stage relationship?"

Remo shook his head. Jeremy stopped smiling for a moment and said, "Yes."

As a foreign correspondent put it, "The Big Arena was made for moments like this."

NEBULA AWARD NOMINEE
BEST NOVELETTE

"THE DEVIL IN AMERICA"

KAI ASHANTE WILSON

This is the first Nebula Award nomination for Kai Ashante Wilson.
"The Devil in America" was published on Tor.com.

for my father

1955

Emmett Till, sure, I remember. Your great grandfather, sitting at the table with the paper spread out, looked up and said something to Grandma. She looked over my way and made me leave the room: Emmett Till. In high school I had a friend everybody called Underdog. One afternoon—1967?—Underdog was standing on some corner and the police came round and beat him with nightsticks. No reason. Underdog thought he might get some respect if he joined up for Vietnam, but a sergeant in basic training was calling him everything but his name—nigger this, nigger that—and Underdog went and complained. Got thrown in the brig, so he ended up going to Vietnam with just a couple weeks' training. Soon after he came home in a body bag. In Miami a bunch of white cops beat to death a man named Arthur McDuffie with heavy flashlights. You were six or seven: so, 1979. The cops banged up his motorcycle trying to make killing him look like a crash. Acquitted, of course. Then Amadou Diallo, 1999; Sean Bell, 2006. You must know more about all the New York murders than I do. Trayvon, this year. Every year it's one we hear about and God knows how many just the family mourns.

—Dad

1877 August 23

"'Tis all right if I take a candle, Ma'am?" Easter said. Her mother bent over at the black iron stove, and lifted another smoking hot pan of cornbread from the oven. Ma'am just hummed—meaning, *Go 'head.* Easter came wide around her mother, wide around the sizzling skillet, and with the ramrod of Brother's old rifle hooked up the front left burner. She left the ramrod behind the stove, plucked the candle from the fumbling, strengthless grip of her ruint hand, and dipped it wick-first into flame. Through the good glass window in the wall behind the stove, the night was dark. It was soot and shadows. Even the many-colored chilis and bright little pumpkins in Ma'am's back garden couldn't be made out.

A full supper plate in her good hand, lit candle in the other, Easter had a time getting the front door open, then out on the porch, and shutting back the door without dropping any food. Then, anyhow, the swinging of the door made the candle flame dance fearfully low, just as wind gusted up too, so her light flickered *way* down . . . and went out.

"Shoot!" Easter didn't say the curse word aloud. She mouthed it. "Light it back for me, angels," Easter whispered. "Please?" The wick flared bright again.

No moon, no stars—the night sky was clouded over. Easter hoped it wasn't trying to storm, with the church picnic tomorrow.

She crossed the yard to the edge of the woods where Brother waited. A big old dog, he crouched down, leapt up, down and up again, barking excitedly, just as though he were some little puppy dog.

"Well, hold your horses," Easter said. "I'm coming!" She met him at the yard's end and dumped the full plate over, all her supper falling to the ground. Brother's head went right down, tail just a-wagging. "Careful, Brother," Easter said. "You *watch* them chicken bones." Then, hearing the crack of bones, she knelt and snatched ragged shards right out of the huge dog's mouth. Brother whined and licked her hand—and dropped his head right back to buttered mashed yams.

Easter visited with him a while, telling her new secrets, her latest sins, and when he'd sniffed out the last morsels of supper Brother listened to her with what anybody would have agreed was deep love, full attention. "Well, let me get on," she said at last, and sighed. "Got to check on the Devil now." She'd left it til late, inside all evening with Ma'am, fixing their share of the big supper at church tomorrow. Brother whined when she stood up to leave.

Up the yard to the henhouse. Easter unlatched the heavy door and looked them over—chickens, on floor and shelf, huddling quietly in thick straw, and all asleep except for Sadie. Eldest and biggest, that one turned just her head and looked over Easter's way. Only reflected candlelight, of course, but Sadie's beady eyes looked *so* ancient and *so* crafty, blazing like embers. Easter backed on out, latched the coop up securely again, and made the trip around the henhouse, stooping and stooping and stooping, to check for gaps in the boards. Weasel holes, fox doors.

There weren't any. And the world would go on exactly as long as Easter kept up this nightly vigil.

Ma'am stood on the porch when Easter came back up to the house. "I don't *appreciate* my good suppers thrown in the dirt. You hear me, girl?" Ma'am put a hand on Easter's back, guiding her indoors. "That ole cotton-picking dog could just as well take hisself out to the deep woods and hunt." Ma'am took another tone altogether when she meant every word, and *then* she didn't stroke Easter's head, or gently brush her cheek with a knuckle. This was only complaining out of habit. Easter took only one tone with her mother. Meek.

"Yes, Ma'am," she said, and ducked her head in respect. Easter *didn't* think herself too womanish or grown to be slapped silly.

"Help me get this up on the table," Ma'am said—the deepest bucket, and brimful of water and greens. Ma'am was big and strong enough to have lifted *ten* such buckets. It was friendly, though, sharing the little jobs. At one side of the bucket, Easter bent over and worked her good hand under the bottom, the other just mostly ached now, the cut thickly scabbed over. She just sort of pressed it to the bucket's side, in support.

Easter and her mother set the bucket on the table.

Past time to see about the morning milk. Easter went back to the cellar and found the cream risen, though the tin felt a tad cool to her. The butter would come slow. "Pretty please, angels?" she whispered. "Could you help me out a little bit?" They could. They did. The milk tin warmed ever so slightly. Just right. Easter dipped the cream out and carried the churn back to the kitchen.

Ma'am had no wrinkles except at the corners of the eyes. Her back was unbowed, her arms and legs still mighty. But she was old now, wasn't she? Well nigh sixty, and maybe past it. But still with that upright back, such quick hands. *Pretty* was best said of the young—Soubrette Toussaint was very pretty, for instance—so what was the right word for Ma'am's severe cheekbones, sharp almond-shaped eyes, and pinched fullness of mouth? Working the churn, Easter felt the cream foam and then thicken, pudding-like. Any other such marriage, and you'd surely hear folks gossiping over the dead wrongness of it—the wife twenty-some years older than a mighty good-looking husband. *What in the world, I ask you, is that old lady doing with a handsome young man like that?* But any two eyes could see the answer here. Not pretty as she must once have been, with that first husband, whoever he'd been, dead and buried back east. And not pretty as when she'd had those first babies, all gone now too. But age hadn't only taken from Ma'am, it had given too. Some rare gift, and so much of it that Pa *had* to be pick of the litter—kindest, most handsome man in the world—just to stack up. Easter poured off the buttermilk into a jar for Pa, who liked that especially. Ma'am might be a challenge to love sometimes, but respect came easy.

"I *told* him, Easter." Ma'am wiped forefinger and thumb down each dandelion leaf, cleaning off grit and bugs, and then lay it aside in a basket. "Same as I told you. *Don't mess with it.* Didn't I say, girl?"

"Yes, Ma'am." Easter scooped the clumps of butter into the bowl.

Ma'am spun shouting from her work. "That's *right* I did! And I pray to God you *listen*, too. That fool out there *didn't*, but Good Lord knows I get on my knees and pray *every night* you got some little bit of sense in your head. Because, Easter, I ain't *got* no more children—you my last one!" Ma'am turned back and gripped the edge of the table.

Ma'am wanted no comfort, no acknowledgement of her pain at such moments—just let her be. Easter huddled in her chair, paddling the salt evenly through the butter, working all the water out. She worked with far more focus than the job truly needed.

Then, above the night's frogcroak and bugchatter, they heard Brother bark in front of the house, and heard Pa speak, his very voice. Wife and daughter both gave a happy little jump, looking together at the door in anticipation. Pa'd been three days over in Greenville selling the cigars. Ma'am snapped her fingers.

"Get the jug out the cellar," she said. "You know just getting in your Pa wants him a little tot of cider. Them white folks." As if Ma'am wouldn't have a whole big mug her ownself.

"Yes, Ma'am." Easter fetched out the jug.

Pa opened the door, crossed the kitchen—touching Easter's head in passing, he smelt of woodsmoke—and came to stand behind Ma'am. His hands cupped her breasts through her apron, her dress, and he kissed the back of her neck. She gasped aloud. "Wilbur! *the baby* . . . !" That's what they still called Easter, "the baby." Nobody had noticed she'd gotten tall, twelve years old now.

Pa whispered secrets in Ma'am's ear. He was a father who loved his daughter, but he was a husband first and foremost. *I'm a terrible thirsty man,* Pa had said once, *and your mama is my only cool glass of water in this world.* Ma'am turned and embraced him. "I know it, sweetheart," she said. "I know." Easter covered up the butter. She took over washing the greens while her parents whispered, intent only on each other. Matched for height, and Ma'am a little on the stout side, Pa on the slim, so they were about the same thickness too. The perfect fit of them made Easter feel a sharp pang, mostly happiness. Just where you could hear, Pa said, "And you *know* it ain't no colereds round here but us living in Rosetree . . ."

Wrapped in blankets up in the loft, right over their bed, of course she heard things at night, on Sundays usually, when nobody was so tired.

An effortful noise from Pa, as if he were laboring some big rock heave-by-heave over to the edge of the tobacco field, and then before the quiet, sounding sort of worried, as if Pa were afraid Ma'am might accidently touch the blazing hot iron of the fired-up stove, Pa would say, "*Hazel!*"

". . . so then Miss Anne claimed she seen some nigger run off from there, and *next thing* she knew—fire! Just *everywhere.* About the whole west side of Greenville, looked to me, burnt down. Oh yeah, and in the morning here come Miss Anne's husband talkmbout, 'Know what else, y'all? That nigger my wife seen last night—matterfact, he *violated* her.' Well, darling, here's what I wanna know . . ."

Ma'am would kind of sigh throughout, and from one point on keep saying—not loud—"Like *that* . . ." However much their bed creaked, Ma'am and Pa were pretty quiet when Easter was home. Probably they weren't, though, these nights when Pa came back from Greenville. That was why they sent her over the Toussaints'.

". . . *where* this 'violated' come from all of a sudden? So last night Miss Anne said she maybe *might* of seen some nigger run off, and this morning that nigger jumped her show 'nough? And then it *wasn't* just the one nigger no more. No. It was two or three of 'em, maybe about five. *Ten* niggers—at least. Now Lord knows I ain't no lawyer, baby, I *ain't,* but it seem to me a fishy story done changed up even fishier . . ."

Ma'am and Pa took so much comfort in each other, and just plain *liked* each other. Easter was glad to see it. But she was old enough to wonder, a little worried and a little sad, who was ever going to love her in the way Ma'am and Pa loved each other.

"What you still doing here!" Ma'am looked up suddenly from her embrace. "Girl, you should of *been* gone to Soubrette's. *Go.* And take your best dress and good Sunday shoes too. Tell Mrs. Toussaint I'll see her early out front of the church tomorrow. You hear me, Easter?"

"Yes, Ma'am," she said. And with shoes and neatly folded clothes, Easter hurried out into the dark wide-open night, the racket of crickets.

On the shadowed track through the woods, she called to Brother but he wouldn't come out of the trees, though Easter could hear him pacing her through the underbrush. Always out there in the dark. Brother wanted to keep watch whenever Easter went out at night, but he got shy sometimes too. Lonesome and blue.

*　　*　　*

And this whole thing started over there, in old Africa land, where in olden days a certain kind of big yellow dog (*you* know the kind I'm talking about) used to run around. Now those dogs ain't nowhere in the world, except for . . . Anyway, the prince of the dogs was a sorcerer—about the biggest and best there was in the world. One day he says to hisself, *Let me get up off four feet for a while, and walk around on just two, so I can see what all these folk called 'people' are doing over in that town.* So the prince quit being his doggy self and got right up walking like anybody. While the prince was coming over to the peoples' town, he saw a pretty young girl washing clothes at the river. Now if he'd still been his doggy self, the prince probably would of just *ate* that girl up, but since he was a man now, the prince seen right off what a pretty young thing she was. So he walks over and says, Hey, gal. You want to lay down right here by the river in the soft grass with me? Well—and anybody *would*—the girl felt some kind of way, a strange man come talking to her so fresh all of a sudden. The girl says, Man, don't you see my hair braided up all nice like a married lady? (Because that's how they did over in Africa land. The married ladies, the girls still at home, plaited their hair up different.) So the dog prince said, Oh, I'm sorry. I come from a long way off, so I didn't know what your hair meant. And he *didn't*, either, cause dogs don't braid their hair like people do. *Hmph*, says the gal, all the while sort of taking a real good look over him. As a matter of fact, the dog prince made a *mighty* fine-looking young man, and the girl's mama and papa had married her off to just about the oldest, most dried-up, and granddaddy-looking fellow you ever saw. That old man was rich, sure, but he really couldn't do nothing in the married way for a young gal like that, who wasn't twenty years old yet. So, the gal says, *Hmph*, where you come from anyways? What you got to say for yourself? And it must of been pretty good too, whatever the prince had to say for hisself, because, come nine months later, that gal was mama to your great great—twenty greats—grandmama, first one of us with the old Africa magic.

*　　*　　*

It wasn't but a hop, skip, and jump through the woods into Rosetree proper. Surrounding the town green were the church, Mrs. Toussaint's general store, and the dozen best houses, all two stories, with overgrown rosebushes in front. At the other side of the town green, Easter could see Soubrette sitting out on her front porch with a lamp, looking fretfully out into night.

It felt nice knowing somebody in this world would sit up for her, wondering where she was, was everything all right.

In her wretched accent, Easter called, "*J'arrive!*" from the middle of the green.

Soubrette leapt up. "Easter?" She peered into the blind dark. "I can't see a thing! Where are you, Easter?"

Curious that *she* could see so well, cutting across the grass toward the general store. Easter had told the angels not to without her asking, told them *many* times, but still she often found herself seeing with cat's eyes, hearing with dog's ears, when the angels took a notion. The problem being, folks *noticed* if you were all the time seeing and hearing what you shouldn't. But maybe there was no need to go blaming the angels. With no lamp or candle, your eyes naturally opened up something amazing, while lights could leave you stone-blind out past your bright spot.

They screamed, embraced, laughed. Anybody would have said three *years*, not days, since they'd last seen each other. "Ah, viens ici, toi!" said Soubrette, gently taking Easter's ruint hand to lead her indoors.

Knees drawn up on the bed, Easter hugged her legs tightly. She set her face and bit her lip, but tears came anyway. They always did. Soubrette sighed and closed the book in her lap. Very softly Easter murmured, "I like *Rebecca* most."

"Yes!" Soubrette abruptly leaned forward and tapped Easter's shin. "Rowena is nice too—she *is*!—but I don't even *care* about old Ivanhoe. It just isn't *fair* about poor Rebecca . . ."

"He really don't deserve either one of 'em," Easter said, forgetting her tears in the pleasure of agreement. "That part when Ivanhoe up and changed his mind all of a sudden about Rebecca—do you remember that part? '. . . *an inferior race . . .*' No, I didn't care for him after that."

"Oh *yes*, Easter, I remember!" Soubrette flipped the book open and paged back through it. "At first he sees Rebecca's so beautiful, and he likes her, but then all his niceness is '. . . *exchanged at once for a manner cold, composed, and collected, and fraught with no deeper feeling than that which expressed a grateful sense of courtesy received from an unexpected quarter, and from one of an inferior race . . .*' Ivanhoe's just *hateful*!" Soubrette lay a hand on Easter's foot. "Rowena and Rebecca would have been better off *without* him!"

Soubrette touched you when she made her points, and she made them in the most hot-blooded way. Easter enjoyed such certainty and fire, but it made her feel bashful too. "You ain't taking it too far, Soubrette?" she asked softly. "Who would they love without Ivanhoe? It wouldn't be nobody to, well, *kiss*."

It made something happen in the room, that word *kiss*. Did the warm night heat up hotter, and the air buzz almost like yellow jackets in a log? One and one made two, so right there you'd seem to have a sufficiency for a kiss, with no lack of anything, anyone. From head to toe Easter knew right where she was, lightly sweating in a thin summer shift on this August night, and she knew right where Soubrette was too, so close that—

"Girls!" Mrs. Toussaint bumped the door open with her hip. "The iron's good and hot on the stove now, so . . ."

Easter and Soubrette gave an awful start. *Ivanhoe* fell to the floor.

". . . why don't you come downstairs with your dresses . . . ?" Mrs. Toussaint's words trailed away. She glanced back and forth between the girls while the hot thing still sizzled in the air, delicious and wrong. Whatever it was seemed entirely perceptible to Mrs. Toussaint. She said to her daughter, "Chérie, j'espère que tu te comportes bien. Tu es une femme de quatorze ans maintenant. Ton amie n'a que dix ans; elle est une toute jeune fille!"

She spoke these musical words softly and with mildness—nevertheless they struck Soubrette like a slap. The girl cast her gaze down, eyes shining with abrupt tears. High yellow, Soubrette's cheeks and neck darkened with rosy duskiness.

"Je me comporte toujours bien, Maman," she whispered, her lips trembling as if about to weep.

Mrs. Toussaint paused a moment longer, and said, "Well, fetch down your dresses, girls. Bedtime soon." She went out, closing the door behind her.

The tears *did* spill over now. Easter leaned forward suddenly, kissed Soubrette's cheek, and said, "J'ai *douze* ans."

Soubrette giggled. She wiped her eyes.

Much later, Easter sat up, looking around. Brother had barked, growling savagely, and woken her up. But seeing Soubrette asleep beside her, Easter knew that couldn't be so. And no strange sounds came to her ears from the night outside, only wind in the leaves, a whippoorwill. Brother never came into the middle of town anyway, not ever. The lamp Mrs. Toussaint had left burning in the hallway lit the gap under the bedroom door with orange glow. Easter's fast heart slowed as she watched her friend breathing easily. Soubrette never snored, never tossed and turned, never slept with her mouth gaping open. Black on the white pillow, her long hair spilled loose and curly.

"Angels?" Easter whispered. "Can you make my hair like Soubrette's?" This time the angels whispered, *Give us the lickest taste of her blood, and all Sunday long tomorrow your hair will be so nice. See that hatpin? Just stick Soubrette in the hand with it, and not even too deep. Prettiest curls anybody ever saw.* Easter only sighed. It was out of the question, of course. The angels sometimes asked for the most shocking crimes as if they were nothing at all. "Never mind," she said, and lay down to sleep.

While true that such profoundly sustaining traditions, hidden under the guise of the imposed religion, managed to survive centuries of slavery and subjugation, we should not therefore suppose that ancient African beliefs suffered no sea changes. Of course they did. 'The Devil' in Africa had been capricious, a trickster, and if cruel, only insomuch as bored young children, amoral and at loose ends, may be cruel: seeking merely to provoke an interesting event at any cost, to cause some disruption of the tedious status quo. For the Devil in America, however, malice itself was the end, and temptation a means only to destroy. Here, the Devil would pursue the righteous and the wicked, alike and implacably, to their everlasting doom . . .

White Devils/Black Devils, Luisa Valéria da Silva y Rodríguez

*   *   *

1871 August 2

The end begins after Providence loses all wiggle room, and the outcome becomes hopeless and fixed. That moment had already happened, Ma'am would have said. It had happened long before either one of them were born. Ma'am would have assured Easter that the end began way back in slavery times, and far across the ocean, when that great-grandfather got snatched from his home and the old wisdom was lost.

Easter knew better, though. A chance for grace and new wisdom had always persisted, and doom never been assured . . . right up until, six years old, Easter did what she did one August day out in the tobacco fields.

On that morning of bright skies, Pa headed out to pick more leaves and Easter wanted to come along. He said, Let's ask your mama.

"But he *said,* Wilbur." Ma'am looked surprised. "He told us, *You ain't to take the baby out there, no time, no way.*"

Pa hefted Easter up in his arms, and kissed her cheek, saying, "Well, it's going on three years now since he ain't been here to say *Bet not* or say *Yep, go 'head.* So I wonder how long we suppose to go on doing everything just the way he said, way back when. Forever? And the baby *wants* to go . . ." Pa set her down and she grabbed a handful of his pants leg and leaned against him. "But, darling, if you say not to, then we *won't.* Just that simple."

Most men hardly paid their wives much mind at all, but Pa would listen to any little thing Ma'am said. She, though, *hated* to tell a man what he could and couldn't do—some woman just snapping her fingers, and the man running lickety-split here and there. Ma'am said that wasn't right. So she crossed her arms and hugged herself, frowning unhappily. "Well . . ." Ma'am said. "Can you just wait a hot minute there with the mule, Wilbur? Let me say something to the baby." Ma'am unfolded her arms and reached out a hand. "Come here, girl."

Easter came up the porch steps and took the hand—swept along in Ma'am's powerful grip, through the open door, into the house. "*Set.*" Ma'am pointed to a chair. Easter climbed and sat down. Ma'am knelt on the floor. They were eye-to-eye. She grasped Easter's chin and pulled her close. "Tell me, Easter—what you do, if some lady in a red silk dress come trying to talk to you?"

"I shake my head *no,* Ma'am, and turn my back on her. Then the lady have to go away."

"That's *right*! But what if that strange lady in the red dress say, *Want me to open up St. Peter's door, and show you heaven?* What if she say to you, *See them birds flying there? Do me one itsy bitsy favor, and you could be in the sky flying too.* What then, Easter? Tell me what you do."

"Same thing, Ma'am." She knew her mother wasn't angry with her, but Ma'am's hot glare—the hard grip on her chin—made tears prick Easter's eyes. "I turn my back, Ma'am. She *have to* go, if I just turn my back away."

"Yes! And will you *promise*, Easter? Christ is your Savior, will you *swear* to turn your back, if that lady in the pretty red dress come talking to you?"

Easter swore up and down, and she meant every word too. Ma'am let her go back out to her father, and he set her up on the mule. They went round the house and down the other way, on the trail through woods behind Ma'am's back garden that led to the tobacco fields. Pa answered every question Easter asked about the work he had to do there.

That woman in the red dress was a sneaky liar. She was *'that old serpent, called the Devil, and Satan, which deceiveth the whole world . . .'* Warned by Ma'am, Easter guarded night and day against a glimpse of any such person. In her whole life, though, Easter never did see that lady dressed all in red silk. Easter knew nothing about her. She only knew about the angels.

She didn't *see* them, either, just felt touches like feathers in the air—two or three angels, rarely more—or heard sounds like birds taking off, a flutter of wings. The angels spoke to her, once in a while, in whispering soft harmony. They never said anything bad, just helpful little things. Watch out, Easter—gon' rain cats and dogs once that cloud there starts looking purplish. Your folks sure would appreciate a little while by theyself in the house. Why not be nice? Ma'am's worried sick about Pa over in Greenville, with those white folks, so you'd do best to keep your voice down, and tiptoe extra quiet, else you 'bout to get slapped into tomorrow. And, Easter, don't tell nobody, all right? Let's us just be secret friends.

All right, Easter said. The angels were nice, anyway, and it felt good keeping them to herself, having a secret. No need to tell anybody. Or just Brother, when he came out the woods to play with her in the front yard, or when Ma'am let her go walking in the deep woods with him. But in those days Brother used to wander far and wide, and was gone from home far more often than he was around.

The tobacco fields were *full* of angels.

Ever run, some time, straight through a flock of grounded birds, and ten thousand wings just rushed up flapping into the air all around you? In the tobacco fields it was like that. And every angel there *stayed* busy, so the tobacco leaves grew huge and whole, untroubled by flea-beetles or cutworms, weeds or weather. But the angels didn't do *all* the work.

Pa and a friend of his from St. Louis days, Señor, dug up the whole south field every spring, mounding up little knee-high hills all over it. Then they had to transplant each and every little tabacky plant from the flat dirt in the north field to a hill down south. It was back-breaking work, all May long, from sunup to sundown. Afterwards, Pa and Señor had only small jobs, until now—time to cut the leaves, hang and cure them in the barn. Señor had taught Pa everything there was to know about choosing which leaf when, and how to roll the excellent *criollito* tabacky into the world's best cigars. What they got out of one field sold plenty well enough to white folks over in Greenville to keep two families in good clothes, ample food, and some comforts.

A grandfather oaktree grew between the fields, south and north. Pa agreed with Easter. "That big ole thing *is* in the way, ain't it? But your brother always used to say, *Don't you never, never cut down that tree, Wilbur*. And it do make a nice shady spot to rest, anyway. Why don't you go set over there for a while, baby child?"

Easter knew Pa thought she must be worn out and sorry she'd come, just watching him stoop for leaves, whack them off the plant with his knife, and lay them out in the sun. But Easter loved watching him work, loved to follow and listen to him wisely going on about why this, why that.

Pa, though, put a hand on her back and kind of scootched her on her way over toward the tree, so Easter went. Pa and Señor began to chant some work song in Spanish. *Iyá oñió oñí abbé . . .*

Once in the oaktree's deep shade, there was a fascinating discovery round the north side of the big trunk. Not to see, or to touch—or know in any way Easter had a name for—but she could *feel* the exact shape of what hovered in the air. And this whirligig thing'um, right here, was exactly what kept all the angels hereabouts leashed, year after year, to chase away pests, bring up water from deep underground when too little rain fell, or dry the extra drops in thin air when it rained too much. And she could tell somebody had jiggered this thing together who hardly knew what they were doing. It wasn't but a blown breath or rough touch from being knocked down.

Seeing how rickety the little angel-engine was, Easter wondered if she couldn't do better. Pa and Señor did work *awful* hard every May shoveling dirt to make those hills, and now in August they had to come every day to cut whichever leaves had grown big enough. Seemed like the angels could just do *everything* . . .

"You all right over there, baby girl?" Pa called. Dripping sweat in the glare, he wiped a sleeve across his brow. "Need me to take you back to the house?"

"I'm all right," Easter shouted back. "I want to stay, Pa!" She waved, and he stooped down again, cutting leaves. See there? Working so hard! She could *help* if she just knocked this rickety old thing down, and put it back together better. Right on the point of doing so, she got one sharp pinch from her conscience.

Every time Easter got ready to do something bad there was a moment beforehand when a little bitty voice—one lonely angel, maybe—would whisper to her. *Aw, Easter. You know good and well you shouldn't.* Nearly always she listened to this voice. After today and much too late, she *always* would.

But sometimes you just do bad, anyhow.

Easter picked a scab off her knee and one fat drop welled from the pale tender scar underneath. She dabbed a finger in it, and touched the bloody tip to the ground.

The angel-engine fell to pieces. Screaming and wild, the angels scattered every which way. Easter called and begged, but she could no more get the angels back in order than she could have grabbed hold of a mighty river's gush. *And the tobacco field . . . !*

Ice frosted the ground, the leaves, the plants, and then melted under sun beating down hotter than summer's worst. The blazing blue sky went cloudy and dark, and boiling low clouds spat frozen pellets, some so big they drew blood and raised knots. Millions of little noises, little motions, each by itself too small to see or hear, clumped into one thick sound like God's two hands rubbing together, and just as gusts of wind stroke the green forest top, making the leaves of the trees all flip and tremble, there was a unified rippling from one end of the tobacco field to the other. Not caused by hands, though, nor by the wind—by busy worms, a billion hungry worms. Grayish, from maggot-size to stubby snakes, these worms ate the tobacco leaves with savage appetite. While the worms feasted, dusty cloud after dusty cloud of moths fluttered up from the disappearing leaves, all hail-torn and frost-blackened, half and then wholly eaten.

In the twinkling of an eye, the lush north field was stripped bare. Nothing was left but naked leaf veins poking spinily from upright woody stems—not a shred of green leaf anywhere. But one year's crop was nothing to the angels' hunger. They were owed *much* more for so many years' hard labor. Amidst the starving angels, Pa and Señor stood dazed in the sudden wasteland of their tobacco field. All the sweet living blood of either this man or the other would just about top off the angels' thirsty cup.

Easter screamed. She called for some help to come—any help at all.

And help *did* come. A second of time split in half and someone came walking up the break.

*　　*　　*

Like the way you and Soubrette work on all that book learning together. Same as that. You *gotta* know your letters, *gotta* know your numbers, for some things, or you just can't rightly take part. Say, for instance, you had some rich colored man, and say this fellow was *very* rich indeed. But let's say he didn't know his numbers at all. Couldn't even count his own fingers up to five. Now, he ain't a bad man, Easter, and he ain't stupid either, really. It's just that nobody ever taught numbering to him. So, one day this rich man takes a notion to head over to the bank, and put his money into markets and bonds, and what have you. Now let me ask you, Easter. What you think gon' happen to this colored man's big ole stack of money, once he walks up in that white man's bank, and gets to talking with the grinning fellow behind the counter? *You* tell me. I wanna hear what you say.

Ma'am. The white man's gonna see that colored man can't count, Ma'am, and cheat him out of all his money.

That's *right* he is, Easter! And I *promise you* it ain't no other outcome! Walk up in that bank just as rich as you please—but you gon' walk out with no shoes, and *owing* the shirt on your back! Old Africa magic's the same way, but *worse*, Easter, cause it ain't money we got, me and you—all my babies had—and my own mama, and the grandfather they brung over on the slave ship. It's *life*. It's life and death, not money. Not play-stuff. But, listen here—we don't know our numbers no more, Easter. See what I'm saying? That oldtime wisdom from over there, what we used to know in the Africa land, is all gone now. And, Easter, you just *can't* walk up into the spirits' bank not knowing your numbers. You *rich*, girl. You got gold in your pockets, and I *know* it's burning a hole. I know cause it burnt me, it burnt your brother. But I pray you listen to me, baby child, when I say—you walk up in that bank, they gon' take a *heap* whole lot more than just your money.

* * *

Nothing moved. Pa and Señor stood frozen, the angels hovering just before the pounce. Birds in the sky hung there, mid-wingbeat, and even a blade of grass in the breath of the wind leaned motionless, without shivering. Nothing moved. Or just one thing did—a man some long way off, come walking this way toward Easter. He was *miles* off, or much farther than that, but every step of his approach crossed a strange distance. He bestrode the stillness of the world and stood before her in no time.

In the kindest voice, he said, "You need some help, baby child?"

Trembling, Easter nodded her head.

He sat right down. "Let us just set here for a while, then"—the man patted the ground beside him—"and make us a *deal*."

He was a white man tanned reddish from too much sun, or he could've had something in him maybe—been mixed up with colored or indian. Hair would've told the story, but that hid under the gray kepi of a Johnny Reb. He wore that whole uniform in fact, a filthy kerchief of Old Dixie tied around his neck.

Easter sat. "Can you help my Pa and Señor, Mister? The angels about to eat 'em up!"

"Oh, don't you *worry* none about that!" the man cried, warmly reassuring. "I can help you, Easter, I most certainly can. But"—he turned up a long forefinger, in gentle warning—"*not* for free."

Easter opened her mouth.

"*Ot!*" The man interrupted, waving the finger. "Easter, Easter, Easter . . ." He shook his head sadly. "Now why you wanna hurt my feelings and say you ain't got no money? Girl, you know I don't want no trifling little money. You know *just* what I want."

Easter closed her mouth. He wanted blood. He wanted life. And not a little drop or two, either—or the life of some chicken, mule, or cow. She glanced at the field of hovering angels. They were owed the precious life of one man, woman, or child. How much would *he* want to stop them?

The man held up two fingers. "That's all. And you get to pick the two. It don't have to be your Pa and Señor at all. It could be any old body." He waved a hand outwards to the world at large. "Couple folk you ain't even met, Easter, somewhere far away. That'd be just fine with me."

Easter hardly fixed her mouth to answer before that still small voice spoke up. *You can't do that. Everybody is somebody's friend, somebody's Pa, somebody's baby. It'd be plain dead wrong, Easter.* This voice never said one word she didn't already know, and never said anything but the God's honest truth. No matter what, Easter *wasn't* going against it, ever again.

The man made a sour little face to himself. "Tell you what then," he said. "Here's what we'll do. Right now, today, I'll call off the angels, how about that? And then you can pay me what you owe by-and-by. Do you know what the word '*currency*' means, Easter?"

Easter shook her head.

"It means the *way* you pay. Now, the *amount*, which is the worth of two lives, stays exactly the same. But you don't have to pay in blood, in life, if you just change the *currency*, see? There's a lot you don't know right now, Easter, but with some time, you might could learn something useful. So let me help out Señor and your Pa today, and then me and you, we'll settle up later on after while. Now when you wanna do the settling up?"

Mostly, Easter had understood the word "later"—a *sweet* word! She really wouldn't have minded some advice concerning the rest of what he'd said, but the little voice inside couldn't tell her things she didn't already know. Easter was six years old, and double that would make *twelve*. Surely that was an eternal postponement, nearabout. So far away it could hardly be expected to arrive. "When I'm twelve," Easter said, feeling tricky and sly.

"All right," the man said. He nodded once, sharply, as folks do when the deal is hard but fair. "Let's shake on it."

Though she was just a little girl, and the man all grown up, they shook hands. And the angels mellowed in the field, becoming like those she'd always known, mild and toothless, needing permission even to sweep a dusty floor, much less eat a man alive.

"I'll be going now, Easter." The man waved toward the field, where time stood still. "They'll all wake up just as soon as I'm gone." He began to get up.

Easter grabbed the man's sleeve. "Wait!" She pointed at the ruins of two families' livelihood. "What about the *tabacky*? We need it to live on!"

The man looked where Easter gestured, the field with no green whatsoever, and thoughtfully pursed his lips. "Well, as you can see, *this* year's tabacky is all dead and gone now. 'Tain't nothing to do about that. But I reckon I could set the angels back where they was, so as *next* year—and on after that—the tabacky will grow up fine. Want me to do that, Easter?"

"*Yes!*"

The man cocked his head and widened his eyes, taking an attitude of the greatest concern. "Now you *show*, Easter?" he asked. "Cause that's extry on what you already owe."

So cautioning was his tone, even a wildly desperate little girl must think twice. Easter chewed on her bottom lip. "How much extra?" she said at last.

The man's expression went flat and mean. "*Triple*," he said. "And triple that again, and might as well take that whole thing right there, and triple it about ten more times." Now the very nice face came back. "But what you gon' do, baby girl? You messed up your Pa's tabacky field. *Gotta* fix it." He shrugged in deepest sympathy. "*You* know how to do that?"

Easter had to shake her head.

"Want *me* to then?"

Easter hesitated . . . and then nodded. They shook on it.

The man snapped his fingers. From all directions came the sounds and sensations of angels flocking back to their old positions. The man stood and brushed off the seat of his gray wool trousers.

Easter looked up at him. "Who are you, Mister? Your name, I mean."

The man smiled down. "How 'bout you just call me the banker," he said. "Cause—*whew,* baby girl—you owe me a lot! Now I'll be seeing you after while, you hear?" The man became his own shadow, and in just the way that a lamp turned up bright makes the darkness sharpen and flee, his shadow thinned out along the ground, raced away, and vanished.

"*¡Madre de Díos!*" Señor said, looking around at the field that had been all lush and full-grown a moment ago. He and Pa awakened to a desolation, without one remnant of the season's crop. With winces, they felt at their heads, all cut and bruised from hailstones. Pa spun around then, to look at Easter, and she burst into tears.

These tears lasted a while.

Pa gathered her up in his arms and rushed her back to the house, but neither could Ma'am get any sense from Easter. After many hours she fell asleep, still crying, and woke after nightfall on her mother's lap. In darkness, Ma'am sat on the porch, rocking in her chair. When she felt Easter move, Ma'am helped her sit up, and said, "Won't you tell me what happened, baby child?" Easter *tried* to answer, but horror filled up her mouth and came pouring out as sobs. Just to speak about meeting that strange man was to cry with all the strength in her body. God's grace had surely kept her safe in that man's presence, but the power and the glory no longer stood between her and the revelation of something unspeakable. Even the memory was too terrible. Easter had a kind of fit and threw up what little was in her belly. Once more she wept to passing out.

Ma'am didn't ask again. She and Pa left the matter alone. A hard, scuffling year followed, without the money from the cigars, and only the very last few coins from the St. Louis gold to get them through.

He was the Devil, Easter decided, and swallowed the wild tears. She decided to grow wise in her way as Pa was about tobacco, though there was nobody to teach her. The Devil wouldn't face a fool next time.

* * *

1908

The mob went up and down Washington Street, breaking storefront windows, ransacking and setting all the black-owned business on fire. Bunch of white men shot up a barbershop and then dragged out the body of the owner, Scott Burton, to string up from a nearby tree. After that, they headed over to the residential neighborhood called the Badlands, where black folks paid high rent for slum housing. Some 12,000 whites gathered to watch the houses burn.

—Dad

1877 August 24

At the church, the Ladies' Missionary Society and their daughters began to gather early before service. The morning was gray and muggy, not hot at all, and the scent of roses, as sweet and spoiled as wine, soaked the soft air. "Easter, you go right ahead and cut some for the tables," Mrs. Toussaint said, while they walked over to the church. "Any that you see, still nice and red." She and Soubrette carried two big pans of *jambalaya rouge*. Easter carried the flower vases. Rosebushes taller than a man grew in front of every house on the Drive, and were all heavily blooming with summer's doomed roses. Yet Easter could only stop here and there and clip one with the scissors Mrs. Toussaint had given her, since most flowers had rotted deeply burgundy or darker, long past their prime.

With more effort than anybody could calculate, the earth every year brought forth these flowers, and then every year all the roses died. "What's wrong, Easter?" Soubrette said.

"Aw, it's nothing." Easter squeezed with her good hand, bracing the scissors against the heel of her ruint one. "I'm just thinking, is all." She put the thorny clipping into a vase and made herself smile.

At the church there were trestles to set up, wide boards to lay across them, tablecloths, flower vases, an immense supper and many desserts to arrange sensibly. *And my goodness, didn't anybody remember a lifter for the pie . . . ? Girls—you run on back up to the house and bring both of mine . . .*

She and Soubrette were laying out the serving spoons when Easter saw her parents coming round Rosetree Drive in the wagon. Back when the Mack family had first come to Rosetree, before Easter's first birthday, all the white folks hadn't moved to Greenville yet. And in those days Ma'am, Pa, and her brother still had "six fat pocketfuls" of the gold from St. Louis, so they could have bought one of the best houses on the Drive. But they'd decided to live in the backwoods outside of town instead (on account of the old Africa magic, as Easter well knew, although telling the story Ma'am and Pa never gave the reason). Pa unloaded a big pot from the wagon bed, and a stack of cloth-covered bread. Ma'am anxiously checked Easter over head to toe—shoes blacked and spotless, dress pressed and stiffly starched, and she laid her palm very lightly against Easter's hair. "Not troubled at all, are you?"

"No, Ma'am."

"Don't really know *what's* got me so wrought up," Ma'am said. "I just felt like I needed to get my eyes on you—*see* you. But don't you look nice!" The worry left Ma'am's face. "And I declare, Octavia can do *better* by that head than your own mama." Ma'am fussed a little with the ribbon in Easter's hair, and then went to help Mrs. Toussaint, slicing the cakes.

Across the table, Mrs. Freeman said, "I do *not* care for the look of these clouds." And Mrs. Freeman frowned, shaking her head at the gray skies. "No, I surely don't."

Won't a drop fall today, the angels whispered in Easter's ear. *Sure 'nough rain hard tomorrow, though.*

Easter smiled over the table. "Oh, don't you worry, Mrs. Freeman." And with supernatural confidence, she said, "It ain't gon' rain today."

The way the heavyset matron looked across the table at Easter, well, anybody would call that *scared,* and Mrs. Freeman shifted further on down the table to where other ladies lifted potlids to stir contents, and secured the bread baskets with linen napkins. It made Easter feel so bad. She felt like the last smudge of filth when everything else is just spic- and-span. Soubrette bumped her. "Take one of these, Easter, will you?" Three vases full of flowers were too many for one person to hold. "Maman said to put some water in them so the roses stay fresh." Together they went round the side of the church to the well.

When they'd come back, more and more men, old folks, and children were arriving. The Missionary ladies argued among themselves over who must miss service, and stay outside to watch over supper and shoo flies and what have you. Mrs. Turner said that she would, *just to hush up the rest of you.* Then somebody caught sight of the visiting preacher, Wandering Bishop Fitzgerald James, come down the steps of the mayor's house with his cane.

* * *

1863

So that riot started off in protest of the draft, but it soon became a murder spree, with white men killing every black man, woman, or child who crossed their path. They burned down churches, businesses, the homes of abolitionists, and anywhere else black people were known to congregate, work, or live—even the Colored Orphan Asylum, for example, which was in Midtown back then. Altogether, at least a hundred people were killed by whites. And there's plenty more of these stories over the years, plenty more. Maybe you ought to consider Rosetree. That there's a story like you wouldn't believe.

—*Dad*

Eyes closed, sitting in the big fancy chair, Wandering Bishop Fitzgerald James seemed to sleep while Pastor Daniels welcomed him and led the church to say *amen.* So skinny, so old, he looked barely there. But his suit was very fine indeed, and when the Wandering Bishop got up to preach, his voice was huge.

He began in measured tones, though soon he was calling on the church in a musical chant, one hard breath out—*huh!*—punctuating each four beat line. At last the Wandering Bishop sang, his baritone rich and beautiful, and his sermon, *this one,* a capstone experience of Easter's life. Men danced, women lifted up their hands and wept. Young girls cried out as loudly as their parents. When the plate came around, Pa put in a whole silver dollar, and then Ma'am nudged him, so he added another.

After the benediction, Ma'am and Pa joined the excited crowd going up front to shake hands with the visiting preacher. They'd known Wandering Bishop Fitzgerald James back before the war, when he sometimes came to Heavenly Home and preached for the coloreds—always a highlight! A white-haired mulatto, the Wandering Bishop moved with that insect-like stiffness peculiar to scrawny old men. Easter saw that his suit's plush lapels were velvet, his thin silk necktie cherry-red.

"Oh, I remember you—sure do. Such a pretty gal! Ole Marster MacDougal always used to say, *Now, Fitzy, you ain't to touch a hair on the head of that one, hear me, boy?"* The Wandering Bishop wheezed and cackled. Then he peered around, as if for small children running underfoot. "But where them little yeller babies at?" he said. "Had you a whole mess of 'em, as I recall."

Joy wrung from her face until Ma'am had only the weight of cares, and politeness, left. "A lovely sermon," she murmured. "Good day to you, Bishop." Pa's forearm came up under her trembling hand and Ma'am leaned on him. Easter followed her parents away, and they joined the spill of the congregation out onto the town green for supper. Pa had said that Easter just had a way with some onions, smoked hock and beans, and would she please fix up a big pot for him. Hearing Pa say so had felt very fine, and Easter had answered, "Yes, sir, I sure will!" Even offered a feast, half the time Pa only wanted some beans and bread, anyhow. He put nothing else on his plate this Sunday too.

The clouds had stayed up high, behaving themselves, and in fact the creamy white overcast, cool and not too bright, was more comfortable than a raw blue sky would have been. Men had gotten the green all spruced up nice, the animals pent away, all the patties and whatnot cleaned up. They'd also finally gotten around to chopping down the old lightning-split, half-rotten crabapple tree in the middle of the green. A big axe still stuck upright from the pale and naked stump. Close by there, Soubrette, Mrs. Toussaint, and her longtime gentleman friend, Señor Tomás, had spread a couple blankets. They waved and called, *Hey, Macks!,* heavy plates of food in their laps. Easter followed Ma'am and Pa across the crowded green.

Pa made nice Frenchy noises at Miss and Mrs. Toussaint, and then took off lickety-split with Señor, gabbling in Spanish. Ma'am sat down next to Mrs. Toussaint and they leaned together, speaking softly. "What did you think of the Wandering Bishop?" Easter asked Soubrette. "Did you care for the sermon?"

"Well . . ." Soubrette dabbed a fingerful of biscuit in some gravy pooled on Easter's plate. "He had a *beautiful* way of preaching, sure enough." Soubrette looked right and left at the nearby grown-ups, then glanced meaningfully at Easter—who leaned in close enough for whispers.

Señor, the Macks, and the Toussaints always sat on the same pew at church, had dinner back and forth at one another's houses, and generally just hung together as thick as thieves. Scandal clung to them both, one family said to work roots and who knew what all kind of devilment. And the other family . . . well, back east Mrs. Toussaint had done *some* kind of work in La Nouvelle-Orléans, and Easter knew only that rumor of it made the good church ladies purse their lips, take their husbands' elbows, and hustle the men right along—*no* lingering near Mrs. Toussaint. These were the times Easter felt the missing spot in the Mack family worst. There was no one to ask, "What's a '*hussycat*'?" The question, she felt, would hurt Soubrette, earn a slap from Ma'am, and make Pa say, shocked, "Aw, Easter—what you asking *that* for? Let it alone!" His disappointment was always somehow worse than a slap.

Brother, she knew, would have just told her.

The youngest Crombie boy, William, came walking by slowly, carrying his grandmother's plate while she clutched his shoulder. The old lady shrieked.

"*Ha' mercy*," cried Old Mrs. Crombie. "The sweet blessèd Jesus!" She let go of her grandson's shoulder, to flap a hand in the air. "Ain't *nothing* but a witch over here! I ain't smelt devilry this bad since slavery days, at that root-working Bob Allow's dirty cabin. Them old Africa demons just *nasty* in the air. Who is it?" Old Mrs. Crombie peered around with cloudy blue eyes as if a witch's wickedness could be seen even by the sightless. "Somebody *right* here been chatting with Ole Crook Foot, and I know it like I know my own name. Who?"

Easter about peed herself she was that scared. Rude and bossy, as she'd never spoken to the angels before, she whispered, "Y'all *get*," and the four or five hovering scattered away. Ma'am heard that whisper, though, and looked sharply at Easter.

"Who there, Willie?" Old Mrs. Crombie asked her grandson. "Is it them dadburn Macks?"

"Yes'm," said the boy. "But, Granny, don't you want your supper——?"

"Hush up!" Old Mrs. Crombie blindly pointed a finger at the Macks and Toussaints—catching Easter dead in its sights. *"All Saturday long* these Macks wanna dance with the Devil, and then come set up in the Lord's house on Sunday. Well, no! Might got the *rest* of you around here too scared to speak up, but *me*, I'ma go ahead say it. *'Be vigilant,'* says the Book! *'For your adversary walks about like a roaring lion.'* The King of Babylon! The Father of Lies!"

And what were they supposed to do? Knock an old lady down in front of everybody? Get up and run in their Sunday clothes, saying *excuse me, excuse me,* all the way to edge of the green, with the whole world sitting there watching? Better just to stay put, and hope like a sudden hard downpour this would all be over soon, no harm done. Ma'am grabbed Willie down beside her, said something to him, and sent the boy scurrying off for reinforcements.

"And Mister Light-Bright, with the red beard and spots on his face, always smirking—oh, I know *just* what that one was up to! Think folk around here don't know about St. Louis? Everybody know! *The Devil walked abroad in St. Louis.* And that bushwhacked Confederate gold, we all know just how you got it. Them devil-hainted tabacky fields *too*—growing all outta season, like this some doggone Virginia. This ain't no Virginia out here! Well, where he been at, all these last years? Reaped the whirlwind is what I'm guessing. Got himself strick down by the Lord, huh? *Bet* he did."

Preacherly and loud, Old Mrs. Crombie had the families within earshot anything but indifferent to her testimony. But no matter the eyes, the ears, and all the grownfolk, Easter didn't care to hear any evil said of Brother. She had to speak up. "Ma'am, my brother was good and kind. He was the *last* one to do anybody wrong."

"And here come the *daughter* now," shouted Old Mrs. Crombie. "Her brother blinded my eyes when I prayed the Holy Ghost against them. Well, let's see what *this* one gon' do! Strike me dumb? Ain't no matter—til then, I'ma be steady testifying. I'ma keep *on* telling the Lord's truth. Hallelujah!"

At last the son showed up. "Mama?" Mr. Crombie took firm hold of his mother's arm. "You just come along now, Mama. Will you let hungry folk eat they dinner in peace?" He shot them a look, very sorry and all-run-ragged. Ma'am pursed her lips in sympathy and waved a hand, *it's all right.*

"Don't worry none about us," Pa said. "Just see to your Ma." He spoke in his voice for hurt animals and children.

"Charleston?" Old Mrs. Crombie said timidly, the fire and brimstone all gone. "That you?"

"Oh, Mama. Charlie *been* dead. White folk hung him back in Richmond, remember? This *Nathaniel*."

Old Mrs. Crombie grunted as if taking a punch—denied the best child in favor of this least and unwanted. "Oh," she said, "Nathaniel."

"Now y'all know she old," Mr. Crombie raised his voice for the benefit of all those thereabouts. "Don't go setting too much store by every little thing some old lady just half in her right mind wanna say."

Old Mrs. Crombie, muttering, let herself be led away.

Ma'am stood up, and smiled around at Pa, Mrs. Toussaint, Señor, Soubrette. "Everybody excuse us, please? Me and Easter need to go have us a chat up at the church. No, Wilbur, that's all right." She waved Pa back down. "It ain't nothing but a little lady-business me and the baby need to see to, alone." When one Mack spoke with head tilted just so, kind of staring at the other one, carefully saying each word, whatever else was being said it really meant *old Africa magic*. Pa sat down. "And don't y'all wait, you hear? We might be a little while talking. *Girl*." Ma'am held out a hand.

Hand-in-hand, Ma'am led Easter across the crowded green, across the rutted dirt of the Drive, and up the church steps.

"Baby child," Ma'am said. When Easter looked up from her feet, Ma'am's eyes weren't angry at all but sad. "If I *don't* speak, my babies die," she said. "And If I *do*, they catch a fever from what they learn, take up with it, and die anyhow." As if Jesus hid in some corner, Ma'am looked all around the empty church. The pews and sanctuary upfront, the winter stove in the middle, wood storage closet in back. "Oh, Lord, is there any right way to do this?" She sat Easter at the pew across from the wood-burning stove, and sat herself. "Well, I'm just gon' to *tell* you, Easter, and tell everything I know. It's plain to see that keeping you in the dark won't help nothing. This here's what *my* mama told me. When . . ."

*   *   *

. . . they grabbed *her* pa, over across in Africa land, he got *bad* hurt. It was smooth on top of his head right here [*Ma'am lay a hand on the crown of her head, the left side*] and all down the middle of the bare spot was knotted up, nasty skin where they'd cut him terrible. And *there*, right in the worst of the scar was a—*notch?* Something like a deep dent in the bone. You could take the tip of your finger, rest it on the skin there, and feel it give, feel no bone, just softness underneath . . .

So, you knew him, Ma'am?

Oh, no. My mama had me old or older than I had *you*, child, so the grand-folk was dead and gone *quite* a ways before I showed up. Never did meet him. Well . . . not to meet in the flesh, I never did. Not alive, like you mean it. But that's a whole *'nother* story, and don't matter none for what I'm telling you now. The thing I want you to see is how the old knowing, from grandfolk to youngfolk, got broke up into pieces, so in these late days I got nothing left to teach my baby girl. Nothing except, *Let that old Africa magic alone.* Now *he*, your great-grandpa, used to oftentimes get down at night like a dog and run around in the dark, and then come on back from the woods before morning, a man again. Might of brought my grandmama a rabbit, some little deer, or just anything he might catch in the night. Anybody sick or lame, or haunted by spirits, *you* know the ones I mean—folk sunk down and sad all the time, or just always *angry*, or the people plain out they right mind—he could reach out his hand and brush the trouble off them, easy as I pick some lint out your hair. And a very fine-looking man he was too, tall as anything and just . . . sweet-natured, I guess you could say. *Pleasant.* So all the womenfolk loved him. But here's the thing of it. Because of that hurt on his head, Easter—because of *that*—he was simple. About the only English he ever spoke was *Yeah, mars.* And most of the time, things coming out his mouth in the old Africa talk didn't make no sense, either. But even hurt and simple and without his good sense, he *still* knew exactly what he was doing. Could get down a dog, and get right back up again being people, being a man, come morning—whenever he felt like it. *We can't, Easter.* Like I told you, like I told your brother. All us coming after, it's just the one way if we get down on four feet. Not *never* getting up no more. That's the way I lost *three* of mine! No. Hush. Set still there and leave me be a minute . . . So these little bits and pieces I'm telling you right now is every single thing I got from my mama. All *she* got out of your great grand and the old folk who knew him from back over there. Probably you want to know where the right roots at for this, for that, for everything. Which strong words to say? What's the best time of day, and proper season? Why the moon pull so funny, and the rain feel so sweet and mean some particular thing but you can't say what? *Teach me, Ma'am*, your heart must be saying. But I can't, Easter, cause it's gone. Gone for good. They drove us off the path into a wild night, and when morning came we were too turned around, too far from where we started, to *ever* find our way again. Do you think I was my mama's onliest? I wasn't, Easter. Far from it. Same as you ain't *my* only child. I'm just the one that *lived*. The one that didn't mess around. One older sister, and one younger, I saw them both die *awful*, Easter. And all your sisters, and your brothers . . .

* * *

Easter stood looking through the open doors of the church on a view of cloudy sky and the town green. The creamy brightness of early afternoon had given way to ashen gray, and the supper crowd was thinning out though many still lingered. Arm dangling, Ma'am leaned over the back of the pew and watched the sky, allowing some peace and quiet for Easter to think.

And for her part Easter knew she'd learned plenty today from Ma'am about why and where and who, but that she herself certainly understood more about *how*. In fact Easter was sure of that. She didn't like having more knowledge than her mother. The thought frightened her. And yet, Ma'am had never faced down and tricked the Devil, had she?

"Oh, Easter . . ." Ma'am turned abruptly on the pew ". . . I clean forgot to tell you, and your Pa *asked* me to! A bear or mountain lion—*something*—was in the yard last night. The dog got scratched up pretty bad chasing it off. Durn dog wouldn't come close, and let me have a proper look-see . . ."

Sometimes Ma'am spoke so coldly of Brother that Easter couldn't *stand* it. Anxiously she said, "Is he hurt bad?"

"Well, not so bad he couldn't run and hide as good as always. But something took a mean swipe across the side of him, and them cuts weren't pretty to see. *Must of* been a bear. I can't see what else could of gave that dog, big as he is, such a hard time. The *barking* and *racket*, last night! You would of thought the Devil himself was out there in the yard! But, Easter, set down here. Your mama wants you to set down right here with me now for a minute."

Folks took this tone, so gently taking your hand, only when about to deliver the worst news. Easter tried to brace herself. Just now, she'd seen everybody out on the green. So who could have died?

"I know you loved that mean old bird," Ma'am said. "*Heaven* knows why. But the thing in the yard last night broke open the coop, and got in with the chickens. The funniest thing . . ." Ma'am shook her head in wonder. "It didn't touch *nah* bird except Sadie." Ma'am hugged Easter to her side, eyes full of concern. "But, Easter—I'm sorry—it tore old Sadie to *pieces*."

Easter broke free of Ma'am's grasp, stood up, blind for one instant of panic. Then she sat down again, feeling nothing. She felt only tired. "You done told me this, that, and the other thing"—Easter hung her head sleepily, speaking in a dull voice—"but why didn't you never say the one thing I *really* wanted to know?"

"And what's that, baby child?"

Easter looked up, smiled, and said in a brand new voice, "Who slept on the pull-out cot?"

Her mother hunched over as if socked in the belly. "What?" Ma'am whispered. "What did you just ask me?"

Easter moved over on the pew close enough to lay a kiss in her mother's cheek or lips. This smile tasted richer than cake, and this confidence, just as rich. "Was it Brother Freddie slept on the pull-out cot, Hazel Mae? Was it him?" Easter said, and brushed Ma'am's cheek with gentle fingertips. "Or was it you? Or was it *sometimes* him, and *sometimes* you?"

At that touch, Ma'am had reared back so violently she'd lost her seat— fallen to the floor into the narrow gap between pews.

Feeling almighty, Easter leaned over her mother struggling dazed on the ground, wedged in narrow space. ". . . *ooOOoo* . . ." Easter whistled in nasty speculation. "Now *here's* what I really want to know. Was it ever *nobody* on that pull-out cot, Hazel Mae? Just nobody atall*?*"

Ma'am ignored her. She was reaching a hand down into the bosom of her dress, rooting around as if for a hidden dollarbill.

Easter extended middle and forefingers. She made a circle with thumb and index of the other hand, and then vigorously thrust the hoop up and down the upright fingers. "Two peckers and one cunt, Hazel Mae—did *that* ever happen?"

As soon as she saw the strands of old beads, though, yellow-brownish as ancient teeth, which Ma'am pulled up out of her dress, lifted off her neck, the wonderful sureness, this wonderful strength, left Easter. She'd have turned and fled in fact, but could hardly manage to scoot away on the pew, so feeble and stiff and cold her body felt. She spat out hot malice while she could, shouting.

"One, two, three, four!" Easter staggered up from the end of the pew as Ma'am gained her feet. "And we even tricked that clever Freddie of yours, too. Thinking he was *so* smart. Won't *never* do you any good swearing off the old

Africa magic, Hazel Mae! Cause just you watch, we gon' get this last one too! *All of yours—*"

Ma'am slung the looped beads around Easter's neck, and falling to her knees she vomited up a vast supper with wrenching violence. When Easter opened her tightly clenched eyes, through blurry tears she saw, shiny and black in the middle of puddling pink mess, a snake thick as her own arm, *much* longer. She shrieked in terror, kicking backwards on the ground. Faster than anybody could run, the monstrous snake shot off down the aisle between the pews, and out into the gray brightness past the open church doors. Easter looked up and saw Ma'am standing just a few steps away. Her mother seemed more shaken than Easter had ever seen her. "Ma'am?" she said. "I'm scared. What's wrong? I don't feel good. What's this?" Easter began to lift off the strange beads looped so heavily round her neck.

At once Ma'am knelt on the ground beside her. "You just leave those right where they at," she said. "Your great grand brought these over with him. Don't you *never* take 'em off. Not even to wash up." Ma'am scooped hands under Easter's arms, helping her up to sit at the end of a pew. "Just wait here a minute. Let me go fill the wash bucket with water for this mess. *You* think on what all you got to tell me." Ma'am went out and came back. With a wet rag, she got down on her knees by the reeking puddle. "Well, go on, girl. Tell me. All this about Sadie. It's something do with the old Africa magic, ain't it?"

*   *   *

The last angel supped at Easter's hand, half-cut-off, and then lit away. Finally the blood began to gush forth and she swooned.*

*   *   *

*Weird, son. Definitely some disturbing writing in this section. But overarching theme = a people bereft, no? Dispossessed even of cultural patrimony? Might consider then how to represent this in the narrative structure. Maybe just omit how Easter learns to trick the Devil into the chicken? Deny the reader that knowledge as Easter's been denied so much. If you do, leave a paragraph, or even just a sentence, literalizing the "Fragments of History." <u>Terrible</u> title, by the way; reconsider.

—Dad

People presently dwelling in the path of hurricanes, those who lack the recourse of flight, hunker behind fortified windows and hope that this one too shall pass them lightly over. So, for centuries, were the options of the blacks vis-à-vis white rage. Either flee, or pray that the worst might strike elsewhere: once roused, such terror and rapine as whites could wreak would not otherwise be checked. But of course those living in the storm zones know that the big one always does hit sooner or later. And much worse for the blacks of that era, one bad element or many bad influences—"the Devil," as it were—might attract to an individual, a family, or even an entire town, the landfall of a veritable hurricane.

White Devils/Black Devils, Luisa Valéria da Silva y Rodríguez

* * *

1877 August 24

There came to the ears of mother and daughter a great noise from out on the green, the people calling one to another in surprise, and then with many horses' hooves and crack upon crack of rifles, the thunder spoke, surely as the thunder had spoken before at Gettysburg or Shiloh. Calls of shock and wonder became now cries of terror and dying. They could hear those alive and afoot run away, and hear the horsemen who pursued them, with many smaller cracks of pistols. *There!* shouted white men to each other, *That one there running!* Some only made grunts of effort, as when a woodsman embeds his axe head and heaves it out of the wood again—such grunts. Phrases or wordless sound, the whiteness could be heard in the voices, essential and unmistakable.

Easter couldn't understand this noise at first, except that she should be afraid. It seemed that from the thunder's first rumble Ma'am grasped the whole of it, as if she had lived through precisely this before and perhaps many times. Clapping a hand over Easter's mouth, Ma'am said, "Hush," and got them both up and climbing over the pews from this one to the one behind, keeping always out-of-view of the doors. At the back of the church, to the right of the doors, was a closet where men stored the cut wood burned by the stove in winter. In dimness—that closet, *very* tight—they pressed themselves opposite the wall stacked with quartered logs, and squeezed back into the furthest corner. There, with speed and strength, Ma'am unstacked wood, palmed the top of Easter's head, and pressed her down to crouching in the dusty dark. Ma'am put the wood back again until Easter herself didn't know where she was. "You don't *move* from here," Ma'am said. "Don't come at nobody's call but mine." Easter was beyond thought by then, weeping silently since Ma'am had hissed, "*Shut your mouth!*" and shaken her once hard.

Easter nudged aside a log and clutched at the hem of her mother's skirt, but Ma'am pulled free and left her. From the first shot, not a single moment followed free of wails of desperation, or the shriller screams of those shot and bayoneted.

Footfalls, outside—some child running past the church, crying with terror. Easter heard a white man shout, *There go one!* and heard horse's hooves in heavy pursuit down the dirt of the Drive. She learned the noises peculiar to a horseman running down a child. Foreshortened last scream, pop of bones, pulped flesh, laughter from on high. To hear something clearly enough, if it was bad enough, was the same as seeing. Easter bit at her own arm as if that could blunt vision and hearing.

Hey there, baby child, whispered a familiar voice. *Won't you come out from there? I got something real nice for you just outside.* No longer the voice of the kindly spoken Johnny Reb, this was a serpentine lisp—and yet she knew them for one and the same and the Devil. *Yeah, come on out, Easter. Come see what all special I got for you.* Jump up flailing, run away screaming—Easter could think of nothing else, and the last strands of her tolerance and good sense began to fray and snap. That voice went on whispering and Easter choked on sobs, biting at her forearm.

Some girl screamed nearby. It could have been *any* girl in Rosetree, screaming, but the whisperer snickered, *Soubrette. I got her!*

Easter lunged up, and striking aside logs, she fought her way senselessly with scraped knuckles and stubbed toes from the closet, on out of the church into gray daylight.

If when the show has come and gone, not only paper refuse and cast-off food but the whole happy crowd, shot dead, remained behind and littered the grass, then Rosetree's green looked like some fairground, the day after.

Through the bushes next door to the church Easter saw Mr. Henry, woken tardily from a nap, thump with his cane out onto the porch, and from the far side of the house a white man walking shot him dead. Making not even a moan old Mr. Henry toppled over and his walking stick rolled to porch's edge and off into roses. About eight o'clock on the Drive, flames had engulfed the general store so it seemed a giant face of fire, the upstairs windows two dark eyes, and downstairs someone ran out of the flaming mouth. That shadow in the brightness had been Mrs. Toussaint, so slim and short in just such skirts, withering now under a fiery scourge that leapt around her, then up from her when she fell down burning. The Toussaints kept no animals in the lot beside the general store and it was all grown up with tall grass and wildflowers over there. Up from those weeds, a noise of hellish suffering poured from the ground, where some young woman lay unseen and screamed while one white man with dropped pants and white ass out stood afoot in the weeds and laughed, and some other, unseen on the ground, grunted piggishly in between shouted curses. People lay everywhere bloodied and fallen, so many dead, but Easter saw her father somehow alive out on the town green, right in the midst of the bodies just kneeling there in the grass, his head cocked to one side, chin down, as if puzzling over some problem. She ran to him calling *Pa Pa Pa* but up close she saw a red dribble down his face from the forehead where there was a deep ugly hole. Though they were sad and open his eyes slept no they were dead. To cry hard enough knocks a body down, and harder still needs both hands flat to the earth to get the grief out.

In the waist-high corn, horses took off galloping at the near end of the Parks' field. At the far end Mrs. Park ran with the baby Gideon Park, Jr. in her arms and the little girl Agnes following behind, head hardly above corn, shouting *Wait Mama wait*, going as fast as her legs could, but just a little girl, about four maybe five. Wholeheartedly wishing they'd make it to the backwood trees all right, Easter could see as plain as day those white men on horses would catch them first. So strenuous were her prayers for Mrs. Park and Agnes, she had to hush up weeping. Then a couple white men caught sight of Easter out on the green, just kneeling there—some strange survivor amidst such thorough and careful murder. With red bayonets, they trotted out on the grass toward her. Easter stood up meaning to say, or even beginning to, polite words about how the white men should leave Rosetree now, about the awful mistake they'd made. But the skinnier man got out in front of the other, *running,* and hauled back with such obvious intent on his rifle that lengthy knife attached to it, Easter's legs wouldn't hold her. Suddenly kneeling again, she saw her mother standing right next to the crabapple stump. Dress torn, face sooty, in stocking feet, Ma'am got smack in the white men's way. That running man tried to change course but couldn't fast enough. He came full-on into the two-handed stroke of Ma'am's axe.

Swapt clean off, his head went flying, his body dropped straight down. The other one got a hand to his belt and scrabbled for a pistol while Ma'am stepped up and hauled back to come round for his head too. Which one first, then— pistol or axe? He got the gun out and up and shot. Missed, though, even that close, his hand useless as a drunk's, he was so scared. The axe knocked his chest in and him off his feet. Ma'am stomped the body twice getting her axe back out. With one hand she plucked Easter up off the ground to her feet. "*Run*, girl!"

They ran.

They should have gone straight into the woods, but their feet took them onto the familiar trail. Just in the trees' shadows, a big white man looked up grinning from a child small and dead on the ground. He must have caught some flash or glimpse of swinging wet iron because that white man's grin fell off, he loosed an ear-splitting screech, before Ma'am chopped that face and scream in half.

"Rawly?" Out of sight in the trees, some other white man called. "You all right over there, Rawly?" The fallen man, head in halves like the first red slice into a melon, made no answer. Nor was Ma'am's axe wedging out of his spine soon enough. Other white men took up the call of that name, and there was crash and movement in the trees.

Ma'am and Easter ran off the trail the other way. The wrong way again. They should have forgotten house and home and kept on forever into wilderness. Though probably it didn't matter anymore at that point. The others found the body—axe stuck in it—and cared not at all for the sight of a dead white man, or what had killed him. Ma'am and Easter thrashed past branches, crackled and snapped over twigs, and behind them in the tangled brush shouts of pursuit kept on doubling. What sounded like four men clearly had to be at least eight, and then just eight couldn't half account for such noise. Some men ahorse, some with dogs. Pistols and rifles firing blind.

They burst into the yard and ran up to the house. Ma'am slammed the bar onto the door. For a moment, they hunched over trying only to get air enough for life, and then Ma'am went to the wall and snatched off Brother's old Springfield from the war. *Where the durn cartridges at, and the caps, the doggone ramrod . . . ?* Curses and questions, both were plain on Ma'am's face as she looked round the house abruptly disordered and strange by the knock-knock of Death at the door. White men were already in the yard.

The glass fell out of the back window and shattered all over the iron stove.

Brother, up on his back legs, barked in the open window, his forepaws on the windowsill.

"Go on, Easter." Ma'am let the rifle fall to the floor. "Never mind what I said before. Just go on with your brother now. I'm paying your way."

Easter was too afraid to say or do or think, and Brother at the back window was just barking and barking. *She was too scared.*

In her meanest voice, Ma'am said, "Take off that dress, Easter Sunday Mack!" Sobbing breathlessly, Easter could only obey.

"All of it, Easter, take it off. And throw them old nasty beads on the floor!" Easter did that too, Brother barking madly.

Ma'am said, "Now—"

Rifles stuttered thunderously and the dark wood door of the house lit up, splintering full of holes of daylight. In front of it Ma'am shuddered awfully and hot blood speckled Easter's naked body even where she stood across the room. Ma'am sighed one time, got down gently, and stretched out on the floor. White men stomped onto the porch.

Easter fell, caught herself on her hands, and the bad one went out under her so she smacked down flat on the floor. But effortlessly she bounded up and through the window. Brother was right there when Easter landed badly again. He kept himself to her swift limp as they tore away neck-and-neck through Ma'am's back garden and on into the woods.*

*   *   *

* Stop here, with the escape. Or no; I don't know. I wish there were some kind of way to offer the reader the epilogue, and yet warn them off too. I know it couldn't be otherwise, but it's just so grim.

—Dad

Epilogue

They were back! Right out there sniffing in the bushes where the rabbits were. Two great *big* ole dogs! About to shout for her husband, Anna Beth remembered he was lying down in the back with one of his headaches. So she took down the Whitworth and loaded it herself. Of course she knew how to fire a rifle, but back in the War Between the States they'd hand-picked Michael-Thomas to train the sharpshooters of his brigade, and then given him one of original Southern Crosses, too, for so many Yankees killed. Teary-eyed and squinting from his headaches, he still never missed what he meant to hit. Anna Beth crept back to the bedroom and opened the door a crack.

"You 'wake?" she whispered. "Michael-Thomas?"

Out of the shadows: "Annie?" His voice, breathy with pain. "What is it?"

"I *seen* 'em again! They're right out there in the creepers and bushes by the rabbit burrows."

"You sure, Annie? My head's real bad. Don't go making me get up and it ain't nothing out there again."

"I just now seen 'em, Michael-Thomas. *Big* ole nasty dogs like nothing you ever saw before." Better the little girl voice—that never failed: "Got your Whitworth right here, honey. All loaded up and ret' to go."

Michael-Thomas sighed. "Here I come, then."

The mattress creaked, his cane thumped the floor, and there was a grunt as his bad leg had to take some weight as he rose to standing. (Knee shot off at the Petersburg siege, and not just his knee, either . . .) Michael-Thomas pushed the door wide, his squinting eyes red, pouched under with violet bags. He'd taken off his half-mask, and so Anna Beth felt her stomach lurch and go funny, as usual. Friends at the church, and Mama, and just *everybody* had assured her she would—sooner or later—but Anna Beth never had gotten used to seeing what some chunk of Yankee artillery had done to Michael-Thomas' face. Supposed to still be up *in* there, that chip of metal, under the ruin and crater where his left cheek . . . "Here you go." Anna Beth passed off the Whitworth to him.

Rifle in hand, Michael-Thomas gimped himself over to where she pointed—the open window. There he stood his cane against the wall and laboriously got down kneeling. With practiced grace he lay the rifle across the window sash, nor did he even bother with the telescopic sight at this distance—just a couple hundred yards. He shot, muttering, "Damn! Just *look* at 'em," a moment before he did so. The kick liked to knock him over.

Anna Beth had fingertips jammed in her ears against the report, but it was loud anyhow. Through the window and down the yard she saw the bigger dog, dirty mustard color—had been nosing round in the honeysuckle near the rabbit warren—suddenly drop from view into deep weeds. Looked like the littler one didn't have the sense to dash off into the woods. All while Michael-Thomas reloaded, the other dog nudged its nose downward at the carcass unseen in the weeds, and just looked up and all around, whining—pitiful if it weren't so ugly. Michael-Thomas shot that one too.

"Ah," he said. "Oh." He swapped the Whitworth for his cane, leaving the rifle on the floor under the window. "My head's *killing* me." Michael-Thomas went right on back to the bedroom to lie down again.

He could be relied on to hit just what he aimed for, so Anna Beth didn't fear to see gore-soaked dogs yelping and kicking, only half-dead, out there in the untamed, overgrown end of the yard, should she take a notion to venture out that way for a look-see. Would them dogs be just as big, up close and stone dead, as they'd looked from far-off and alive?

But it weren't carcasses nor live dogs, either, back there where the weeds grew thickest. Two dead niggers, naked as sin. Gal with the back of her head blown off, and buck missing his forehead and half his brains too. Anna Beth come running back up to the house, hollering.

"THE HUSBAND STITCH"

CARMEN MARIA MACHADO

Carmen Maria Machado has been nominated for many awards, including the Hugo Award, the Shirley Jackson Award, and the Calvino Prize. "The Husband Stitch" was first published in Granta.

(If you read this story out loud, please use the following voices: Me: as a child, high-pitched, forgettable; as a woman, the same. The boy who will grow into a man, and be my spouse: robust with his own good fortune. My father: Like your father, or the man you wish was your father. My son: as a small child, gentle, rounded with the faintest of lisps; as a man, like my husband. All other women: interchangeable with my own.)

*

In the beginning, I know I want him before he does. This isn't how things are done, but this is how I am going to do them. I am at a neighbor's party with my parents, and I am seventeen. Though my father didn't notice, I drank half a glass of white wine in the kitchen a few minutes ago, with the neighbor's teenage daughter. Everything is soft, like a fresh oil painting.

The boy is not facing me. I see the muscles of his neck and upper back, how he fairly strains out of his button-down shirts. I run slick. It isn't that I don't have choices. I am beautiful. I have a pretty mouth. I have a breast that heaves out of my dresses in a way that seems innocent and perverse all at the same time.

I am a good girl, from a good family. But he is a little craggy, in that way that men sometimes are, and I want.

I once heard a story about a girl who requested something so vile from her paramour that he told her family and they had her hauled her off to a sanitarium. I don't know what deviant pleasure she asked for, though I desperately wish I did. What magical thing could you want so badly that they take you away from the known world for wanting it?

The boy notices me. He seems sweet, flustered. He says, hello. He asks my name.

I have always wanted to choose my moment, and this is the moment I choose.

On the deck, I kiss him. He kisses me back, gently at first, but then harder, and even pushes open my mouth a little with his tongue. When he pulls away, he seems startled. His eyes dart around for a moment, and then settle on my throat.

—What's that? he asks.

—Oh, this? I touch my ribbon at the back of my neck. It's just my ribbon. I run my fingers halfway around its green and glossy length, and bring them to rest on the tight bow that sits in the front. He reaches out his hand, and I seize it and push it away.

—You shouldn't touch it, I say. You can't touch it.

Before we go inside, he asks if he can see me again. I tell him I would like that. That night, before I sleep, I imagine him again, his tongue pushing open my mouth, and my fingers slide over myself and I imagine him there, all muscle and desire to please, and I know that we are going to marry.

*   *   *

We do. I mean, we will. But first, he takes me in his car, in the dark, to a lake with a marshy edge. He kisses me and clasps his hand around my breast, my nipple knotting beneath his fingers.

I am not truly sure what he is going to do before he does it. He is hard and hot and dry and smells like bread, and when he breaks me I scream and cling to him like I am lost at sea. His body locks onto mine and he is pushing, pushing, and before the end he pulls himself out and finishes with my blood slicking him down. I am fascinated and aroused by the rhythm, the concrete sense of his need, the clarity of his release. Afterwards, he slumps in the seat, and I can hear the sounds of the pond: loons and crickets, and something that sounds like a banjo being plucked. The wind picks up off the water and cools my body down.

I don't know what to do now. I can feel my heart beating between my legs. It hurts, but I imagine it could feel good. I run my hand over myself and feel strains of pleasure from somewhere far off. His breathing becomes quieter and I realize that he is watching me. My skin is glowing beneath the moonlight coming through the window. When I see him looking, I know I can seize that pleasure like my fingertips tickling the end of a balloon's string that has almost drifted out of reach. I pull and moan and ride out the crest of sensation slowly and evenly, biting my tongue all the while.

—I need more, he says, but he does not rise to do anything.

He looks out the window, and so do I. Anything could move out there in the darkness, I think. A hook-handed man. A ghostly hitch-hiker repeating her journey. An old woman summoned from the rest of her mirror by the chants of children. Everyone knows these stories—that is, everyone tells them—but no one ever believes them.

His eyes drift over the water, and then land on my neck.

—Tell me about your ribbon, he says.

—There is nothing to tell. It's my ribbon.

—May I touch it?

—No.

—I want to touch it, he says.

—No.

Something in the lake muscles and writhes out of the water, and then lands with a splash. He turns at the sound.

—A fish, he says.—Sometime, I tell him, I will tell you the stories about this lake and her creatures.

He smiles at me, and rubs his jaw. A little of my blood smears across his skin, but he doesn't notice, and I don't say anything.

—I would like that very much, he says.

—Take me home, I tell him.

And like a gentleman, he does.

That night, I wash myself. The silky suds between my legs are the color and scent of rust, but I am newer than I have ever been.

*   *   *

My parents are very fond of him. He is a nice boy, they say. He will be a good man. They ask him about his occupation, his hobbies, his family. He comes around twice a week, sometimes thrice. My mother invites him in for supper, and while we eat I dig my nails into the meat of his leg. After the ice cream puddles in the bowl, I tell my parents that I am going to walk with him down the lane. We strike off through the night, holding hands sweetly until we are out of sight of the house. I pull him through the trees, and when we find a patch of clear ground I shimmy off my pantyhose, and on my hands and knees offer myself up to him.

I have heard all of the stories about girls like me, and I am unafraid to make more of them. There are two rules: he cannot finish inside of me, and he cannot touch my green ribbon. He spends into the dirt, *pat-pat-patting* like the beginning of rain. I go to touch myself, but my fingers, which had been curling in the dirt beneath me, are filthy. I pull up my underwear and stockings. He makes a sound and points, and I realize that beneath the nylon, my knees are also caked in dirt. I pull them down and brush, and then up again. I smooth my skirt and repin my hair. A single lock has escaped his slicked-back curls, and I tuck it up with the others. We walk down to the stream and I run my hands in the current until they are clean again.

We stroll back to the house, arms linked chastely. Inside, my mother has made coffee, and we all sit around while my father asks him about business.

(If you read this story out loud, the sounds of the clearing can be best reproduced by taking a deep breath and holding it for a long moment. Then release the air all at once, permitting your chest to collapse like a block tower knocked to the ground. Do this again, and again, shortening the time between the held breath and the release.)

*   *   *

I have always been a teller of stories. When I was a young girl, my mother carried me out of a grocery store as I screamed about toes in the produce aisle. Concerned women turned and watched as I kicked the air and pounded my mother's slender back.

—Potatoes! she corrected when we got back to the house. Not toes!

She told me to sit in my chair—a child-sized thing, only built for me— until my father returned. But no, I had seen the toes, pale and bloody stumps, mixed in among those russet tubers. One of them, the one that I had poked with the tip of my index finger, was cold as ice, and yielded beneath my touch the way a blister did. When I repeated this detail to my mother, the liquid of her eyes shifted quick as a startled cat.

—You stay right there, she said.

My father returned from work that evening and listened to my story, each detail.

—You've met Mr. Barns, have you not? he asked me, referring to the elderly man who ran this particular market.

I had met him once, and I said so. He had hair white as a sky before snow, and a wife who drew the signs for the store windows.

—Why would Mr. Barns sell toes? my father asked. Where would he get them?

Being young, and having no understanding of graveyards or mortuaries, I could not answer.

—And even if he got them somewhere, my father continued, what would he have to gain by selling them among the potatoes?

They had been there. I had seen them with my own eyes. But beneath the sunbeams of my father's logic, I felt my doubt unfurling.

—Most importantly, my father said, arriving triumphantly at his final piece of evidence, why did no one notice the toes except for you?

As a grown woman, I would have said to my father that there are true things in this world only observed by a single set of eyes. As a girl, I consented to his account of the story, and laughed when he scooped me from the chair to kiss me and send me on my way.

*　　*　　*

It is not normal that a girl teaches her boy, but I am only showing him what I want, what plays on the insides of my eyelids as I fall asleep. He comes to know the flicker of my expression as a desire passes through me, and I hold nothing back from him. When he tells me that he wants my mouth, the length of my throat, I teach myself not to gag and take all of him into me, moaning around the saltiness. When he asks me my worst secret, I tell him about the teacher who hid me in the closet until the others were gone and made me hold him there, and how afterwards I went home and scrubbed my hands with a steel wool pad until they bled, even though after I share this I have nightmares for a month. And when he asks me to marry him, days shy of my eighteenth birthday, I say yes, yes, please, and then on that park bench I sit on his lap and fan my skirt around us so that a passerby would not realize what was happening beneath it.

—I feel like I know so many parts of you, he says to me, trying not to pant. And now, I will know all of them.

* * *

There is a story they tell, about a girl dared by her peers to venture to a local graveyard after dark. This was her folly: when they told her that standing on someone's grave at night would cause the inhabitant to reach up and pull her under, she scoffed. Scoffing is the first mistake a woman can make.

—I will show you, she said.

Pride is the second mistake.

They gave her a knife to stick into the frosty earth, as a way of proving her presence and her theory.

She went to that graveyard. Some storytellers say that she picked the grave at random. I believe she selected a very old one, her choice tinged by self-doubt and the latent belief that if she were wrong, the intact muscle and flesh of a newly dead corpse would be more dangerous than one centuries gone.

She knelt on the grave and plunged the blade deep. As she stood to run she found she couldn't escape. Something was clutching at her clothes. She cried out and fell down.

When morning came, her friends arrived at the cemetery. They found her dead on the grave, the blade pinning the sturdy wool of her skirt to the ground. Dead of fright or exposure, would it matter when the parents arrived? She was not wrong, but it didn't matter any more. Afterwards, everyone believed that she had wished to die, even though she had died proving that she could live.

As it turns out, being right was the third, and worst, mistake.

* * *

My parents are pleased about the marriage. My mother says that even though girls nowadays are starting to marry late, she married father when she was nineteen, and was glad that she did.

When I select my wedding gown, I am reminded of the story of the young woman who wished to go to a dance with her lover, but could not afford a dress. She purchased a lovely white frock from a secondhand shop, and then later fell ill and passed from this earth. The coroner who performed her autopsy discovered she had died from exposure to embalming fluid. It turned out that an unscrupulous undertaker's assistant had stolen the dress from the corpse of a bride.

The moral of that story, I think, is that being poor will kill you. Or perhaps the moral is that brides never fare well in stories, and one should avoid either being a bride, or being in a story. After all, stories can sense happiness and snuff it out like a candle.

We marry in April, on an unseasonably cold afternoon. He sees me before the wedding, in my dress, and insists on kissing me deeply and reaching inside of my bodice. He becomes hard, and I tell him that I want him to use my body as he sees fit. I rescind my first rule, given the occasion. He pushes me against the wall and puts his hand against the tile near my throat, to steady himself. His thumb brushes my ribbon. He does not move his hand, and as he works himself in me he says I love you, I love you, I love you. I do not know if I am the first woman to walk up the aisle of St George's with semen leaking down her leg, but I like to imagine that I am.

*   *   *

For our honeymoon, we go on a trip I have long desired: a tour of Europe. We are not rich but we make it work. We go from bustling, ancient metropolises to sleepy villages to alpine retreats and back again, sipping spirits and pulling roasted meat from bones with our teeth, eating spaetzle and olives and ravioli and a creamy grain I do not recognize but come to crave each morning. We cannot afford a sleeper car on the train, but my husband bribes an attendant to permit us one hour in an empty room, and in that way we couple over the Rhine.

(If you are reading this story out loud, make the sound of the bed under the tension of train travel and lovemaking by straining a metal folding chair against its hinges. When you are exhausted with that, sing the half remembered lyrics of old songs to the person closest to you, thinking of lullabies for children.)

*   *   *

My cycle stops soon after we return from our trip. I tell my husband one night, after we are spent and sprawled across our bed. He glows with delight.

—A child, he says. He lies back with his hands beneath his head. A child. He is quiet for so long that I think that he's fallen asleep, but when I look over his eyes are open and fixed on the ceiling. He rolls on his side and gazes at me.

—Will the child have a ribbon?

I feel my jaw tighten. My mind skips between many answers, and I settle on the one that brings me the least amount of anger.

—There is no saying, now, I tell him finally.

He startles me, then, by running his hand around my throat. I put up my hands to stop him but he uses his strength, grabbing my wrists with one hand as he touches the ribbon with the other. He presses the silky length with his thumb. He touches the bow delicately, as if he is massaging my sex.

—Please, I say. Please don't.

He does not seem to hear. Please, I say again, my voice louder, but cracking in the middle.

He could have done it then, untied the bow, if he'd chosen to. But he releases me and rolls back on his back. My wrists ache, and I rub them.

—I need a glass of water, I say. I get up and go to the bathroom. I run the tap and then frantically check my ribbon, tears caught in my lashes. The bow is still tight.

*   *   *

There is a story I love about a pioneer husband and wife killed by wolves. Neighbors found their bodies torn open and strewn around their tiny cabin, but never located their infant daughter, alive or dead. People claimed they saw the girl running with a wolf pack, loping over the terrain as wild and feral as any of her companions.

News of her would ripple through the local settlements. She menaced a hunter in a winter forest—though perhaps he was less menaced than startled at a tiny naked girl baring her teeth and howling. A young woman trying to take down a horse. People even saw her ripping open a chicken in an explosion of feathers.

Many years later, she was said to be seen resting in the rushes along a river-bank, suckling two wolf cubs. I like to imagine that they came from her body, the lineage of wolves tainted human just the once. They certainly bloodied her breasts, but she did not mind because they were hers and only hers.

*   *   *

My stomach swells. Inside of me, our child is swimming fiercely, kicking and pushing and clawing. On a walk in the park, the same park where my husband had proposed to me the year before, I gasp and stagger to the side, clutching my belly and hissing through my teeth to Little One, as I call it, to stop. I go to my knees, breathing heavily and near weeping. A woman passing by helps me to sit up and gives me some water, telling me that the first pregnancy is always the worst.

My body changes in ways I do not expect—my breasts are large, swollen and hot, my stomach lined with pale marks, the inverse of a tiger's. I feel monstrous, but my husband seems renewed with desire, as if my novel shape has refreshed our list of perversities. And my body responds: in the line at the supermarket, receiving communion in church, I am marked by a new and ferocious want, leaving me slippery and swollen at the slightest provocation. When he comes home each day, my husband has a list in his mind of things he desires from me, and I am willing to provide them and more.

—I am the luckiest man alive, he says, running his hands across my stomach.

In the mornings, he kisses me and fondles me and sometimes takes me before his coffee and toast. He goes to work with a spring in his step. He comes home with one promotion, and then another. More money for my family, he says. More money for our happiness.

*   *   *

I am in labor for twenty hours. I nearly wrench off my husband's hand, howling obscenities that do not seem to shock the nurse. I am certain I will crush my own teeth to powder. The doctor peers down between my legs, his white eyebrows making unreadable Morse code across his forehead.

—What's happening? I ask.

—I'm not satisfied this will be a natural birth, the doctor says. Surgery may be necessary.

—No, please, I say. I don't want that, please.

—If there's no movement soon, we're going to do it, the doctor says. It might be best for everyone. He looks up and I am almost certain he winks at my husband, but pain makes the mind see things differently than they are.

I make a deal with Little One, in my mind. *Little One*, I think, *this is the last time that we are going to be just you and me. Please don't make them cut you out of me.*

Little One is born twenty minutes later. They do have to make a cut, but not across my stomach as I had feared. The doctor cuts down, and I feel little, just tugging, though perhaps it is what they have given me. When the baby is placed in my arms, I examine the wrinkled body from head to toe, the color of a sunset sky, and streaked in red.

No ribbon. A boy. I begin to weep, and curl the unmarked baby into my chest.

(If you are reading this story out loud, give a paring knife to the listener and ask them to cut the tender flap of skin between your index finger and thumb. Afterwards, thank them.)

*   *   *

There is a story about a woman who goes into labor when the attending physician is tired. There is a story about a woman who herself was born too early. There is a story about a woman whose body clung to her child so hard they cut her to retrieve him. There is a story about a woman who heard a story about a woman who birthed wolf cubs in secret. Stories have this way of running together like raindrops in a pond. They are each borne from the clouds separately, but once they have come together, there is no way to tell them apart.

(If you are reading this story out loud, move aside the curtain to illustrate this final point to your listeners. It'll be raining, I promise.)

*   *   *

They take the baby so that they may fix me where they cut. They give me something that makes me sleepy, delivered through a mask pressed gently to my mouth and nose. My husband jokes around with the doctor as he holds my hand.

—How much to get that extra stitch? he asks. You offer that, right?

—Please, I say to him. But it comes out slurred and twisted and possibly no more than a small moan. Neither man turns his head toward me.

The doctor chuckles. You aren't the first—

I slide down a long tunnel, and then surface again, but covered in something heavy and dark, like oil. I feel like I am going to vomit.

—the rumor is something like———like a vir–

And then I am awake, wide awake, and my husband is gone and the doctor is gone. And the baby, where is—

The nurse sticks her head in the door.

—Your husband just went to get a coffee, she says, and the baby is asleep in the bassinet.

The doctor walks in behind her, wiping his hands on a cloth.

—You're all sewn up, don't you worry, he said. Nice and tight, everyone's happy. The nurse will speak with you about recovery. You're going to need to rest for a while.

The baby wakes up. The nurse scoops him from his swaddle and places him in my arms again. He is so beautiful I have to remind myself to breathe.

*   *   *

My son is a good baby. He grows and grows. We never have another child, though not for lack of trying. I suspect that Little One did so much ruinous damage inside of me that my body couldn't house another.

—You were a poor tenant, Little One, I say to him, rubbing shampoo into his fine brown hair, and I shall revoke your deposit.

He splashes around in the sink, cackling with happiness.

My son touches my ribbon, but never in a way that makes me afraid. He thinks of it as a part of me, and he treats it no differently than he would an ear or finger.

Back from work, my husband plays games in the yard with our son, games of chase and run. He is too young to catch a ball, still, but my husband patiently rolls it to him in the grass, and our son picks it up and drops it again, and my husband gestures to me and cries Look, look! Did you see? He is going to throw it soon enough.

*   *   *

Of all the stories I know about mothers, this one is the most real. A young American girl is visiting Paris with her mother when the woman begins to feel ill. They decide to check into a hotel for a few days so the mother can rest, and the daughter calls for a doctor to assess her.

After a brief examination, the doctor tells the daughter that all her mother needs is some medicine. He takes the daughter to a taxi, gives the driver directions in French, and explains to the girl that, at his home, his wife will give her the appropriate remedy. They drive and drive for a very long time, and when the girl arrives, she is frustrated by the unbearable slowness of this doctor's wife, who meticulously assembles the pills from powder. When she gets back into the taxi, the driver meanders down the streets, sometimes doubling back on the same avenue. The girl gets out of the taxi to return to the hotel on foot. When she finally arrives, the hotel clerk tells her that he has never seen her before. When she runs up to the room where her mother had been resting, she finds the walls a different color, the furnishings different than her memory, and her mother nowhere in sight.

There are many endings to the story. In one of them, the girl is gloriously persistent and certain, renting a room nearby and staking out the hotel, eventually seducing a young man who works in the laundry and discovering the truth: that her mother had died of a contagious and fatal disease, departing this plane shortly after the daughter was sent from the hotel by the doctor. To avoid a city-wide panic, the staff removed and buried her body, repainted and furnished the room, and bribed all involved to deny that they had ever met the pair.

In another version of this story, the girl wanders the streets of Paris for years, believing that she is mad, that she invented her mother and her life with her mother in her own diseased mind. The daughter stumbles from hotel to hotel, confused and grieving, though for whom she cannot say.

I don't need to tell you the moral of this story. I think you already know what it is.

*　　*　　*

Our son enters school when he is five, and I remember his teacher from that day in the park, when she had crouched to help me. She remembers me as well. I tell her that we have had no more children since our son, and now that he has started school, my days will be altered toward sloth and boredom. She is kind. She tells me that if I am looking for a way to occupy my time, there is a wonderful women's art class at a local college.

That night, after my son is in bed, my husband reaches his hand across the couch and slides it up my leg.

—Come to me, he says, and I twinge with pleasure. I slide off the couch, smoothing my skirt very prettily as I walk over to him on my knees. I kiss his leg, running my hand up to his belt, tugging him from his bonds before swallowing him whole. He runs his hands through my hair, stroking my head, groaning and pressing into me. And I don't realize that his hand is sliding down the back of my neck until he is trying to loop his fingers through the ribbon. I gasp and pull away quickly, falling back and frantically checking my bow. He is still sitting there, slick with my spit.

—Come back here, he says.—No, I say.

He stands up and tucks himself into his pants, zipping them up.

—A wife, he says, should have no secrets from her husband.—I don't have any secrets, I tell him.—The *ribbon*.—The ribbon is not a secret, it's just mine.—Were you born with it? Why your throat? Why is it green?

I do not answer.

He is silent for a long minute. Then,

—A wife should have no secrets.

My nose grows hot. I do not want to cry.

—I have given you everything you have ever asked for, I say. Am I not allowed this one thing?

—I want to know.

—You think you want to know, I say, but you do not.

—Why do you want to hide it from me?

—I am not hiding it. It is not yours.

He gets down very close to me, and I pull back from the smell of bourbon. I hear a creak, and we both look up to see our son's feet vanishing up the staircase.

When my husband goes to sleep that night, he does so with a hot and burning anger that falls away only when he starts dreaming. I sense its release, and only then can I sleep, too.

The next day, our son touches my throat and asks about my ribbon. He tries to pull at it. And though it pains me, I have to make it forbidden to him. When he reaches for it, I shake a can full of pennies. It crashes discordantly, and he withdraws and weeps. Something is lost between us, and I never find it again.

(If you are reading this story out loud, prepare a soda can full of pennies. When you arrive at this moment, shake it loudly in the face of the person closest to you. Observe their expression of startled fear, and then betrayal. Notice how they never look at you in exactly the same way for the rest of your days.)

* * *

I enroll in the art class for women. When my husband is at work and my son is in school, I drive to the sprawling green campus and the squat grey building where the art classes are held.

Presumably, the male nudes are kept from our eyes in some deference to propriety, but the class has its own energy—there is plenty to see on a strange woman's naked form, plenty to contemplate as you roll charcoal and mix paints. I see more than one woman shifting forwards and back in her seat to redistribute blood flow.

One woman in particular returns over and over. Her ribbon is red, and is knotted around her slender ankle. Her skin is the color of olives, and a trail of dark hair runs from her belly button to her mons. I know that I should not want her, not because she is a woman and not because she is a stranger, but because it is her job to disrobe, and I feel shame taking advantage of such a state. But as my pencil traces her contours so does my hand in the secret recesses of my mind. I am not even certain how such a thing would happen, but the possibilities incense me to near madness.

One afternoon after class, I turn a hallway corner and she is there, the woman. Clothed, wrapped in a raincoat. Her gaze transfixes me, and this close I can see a band of gold around each of her pupils, as though her eyes are twin solar eclipses. She greets me, and I her.

We sit down together in a booth at a nearby diner, our knees occasionally bushing up against each other beneath the Formica. She drinks a cup of black coffee. I ask her if she has any children. She does, she says, a daughter, a beautiful little girl of eleven.

—Eleven is a terrifying age, she says. I remember nothing before I was eleven, but then there it was, all color and horror. What a number, she says, what a show. Then her face slips somewhere else for a moment, as if she has dipped beneath the surface of a lake.

We do not discuss the specific fears of raising a girl-child. Truthfully, I am afraid to ask. I also do not ask her if she's married, and she does not volunteer the information, though she does not wear a ring. We talk about my son, about the art class. I desperately want to know what state of need has sent her to disrobe before us, but perhaps I do not ask because the answer would be, like adolescence, too frightening to forget.

She captivates me; there is no other way to put it. There is something easy about her, but not easy the way I was—the way I am. She's like dough, how the give of it beneath kneading hands disguises its sturdiness, its potential. When I look away from her and then look back, she seems twice as large as before.

Perhaps we can talk again sometime, I say to her. This has been a very pleasant afternoon.

She nods to me. I pay for her coffee.

I do not want to tell my husband about her, but he can sense some untapped desire. One night, he asks what roils inside of me and I confess it to him. I even describe the details of her ribbon, releasing an extra flood of shame.

He is so glad of this development he begins to mutter a long and exhaustive fantasy as he removes his pants and enters me. I feel as if I have betrayed her somehow, and I never return to the class.

(If you are reading this story out loud, force a listener to reveal a secret, then open the nearest window to the street and scream it as loudly as you are able.)

* * *

One of my favorite stories is about an old woman and her husband—a man mean as Mondays, who scared her with the violence of his temper and the shifting nature of his whims. She was only able to keep him satisfied with her unparalleled cooking, to which he was a complete captive. One day, he bought her a fat liver to cook for him, and she did, using herbs and broth. But the smell of her own artistry overtook her, and a few nibbles became a few bites, and soon the liver was gone. She had no money with which to purchase a second one, and she was terrified of her husband's reaction should he discover that his meal was gone. So she crept to the church next door, where a woman had been recently laid to rest. She approached the shrouded figure, then cut into it with a pair of kitchen shears and stole the liver from her corpse.

That night, the woman's husband dabbed his lips with a napkin and declared the meal the finest he'd ever eaten. When they went to sleep, the old woman heard the front door open, and a thin wail wafted through the rooms. *Who has my liver? Whooooo has my liver?*

The old woman could hear the voice coming closer and closer to the bedroom. There was a hush as the door swung open. The dead woman posed her query again.

The old woman flung the blanket off her husband.

—*He* has it! She declared triumphantly.

Then she saw the face of the dead woman, and recognized her own mouth and eyes. She looked down at her abdomen, remembering, now, how she carved into her own belly. Next to her, as the blood seeped into the very heart of the mattress, her husband slumbered on.

That may not be the version of the story you're familiar with. But I assure you, it's the one you need to know.

*   *   *

My husband is strangely excited for Halloween. Our son is old enough that he can walk and carry a basket for treats. I take one of my husband's old tweed coats and fashion one for our son, so that he might be a tiny professor, or some other stuffy academic. My husband even gives him a pipe on which to gnaw. Our son clicks it between his teeth in a way I find unsettlingly adult.

—Mama, my son says, what are you?

I am not in costume, so I tell him I am his mother.

The pipe falls from his little mouth onto the floor, and he screams. My husband swoops in and picks him up, talking to him in a low voice, repeating his name between his sobs.

It is only as his breathing returns to normal that I am able to identify my mistake. He is not old enough to know the story of the naughty girls who wanted the toy drum, and were wicked toward their mother until she went away and was replaced with a new mother—one with glass eyes and thumping wooden tail. But I have inadvertently told him another one—the story of the little boy who only discovered on Halloween that his mother was not his mother, except on the day when everyone wore a mask. Regret sluices hot up my throat. I try to hold him and kiss him, but he only wishes to go out onto the street, where the sun has dipped below the horizon and a hazy chill is bruising the shadows.

He comes home laughing, gnawing on a piece of candy that has turned his mouth the color of a plum. I am angry with my husband. I wish he had waited to come home before permitting the consumption of the cache. Has he never heard the stories? The pins pressed into the chocolates, the razor blades sunk in the apples? I examine my son's mouth, but there is no sharp metal plunged into his palate. He laughs and spins around the house, dizzy and electrified from the treats and excitement. He wraps his arms around my legs, the earlier incident forgotten. The forgiveness tastes sweeter than any candy that can be given at any door. When he climbs into my lap, I sing to him until he falls asleep.

*　　*　　*

Our son is eight, ten. First, I tell him fairy tales—the very oldest ones, with the pain and death and forced marriage pared away like dead foliage. Mermaids grow feet and it feels like laughter. Naughty pigs trot away from grand feasts, reformed and uneaten. Evil witches leave the castle and move into small cottages and live out their days painting portraits of woodland creatures.

As he grows, though, he asks questions. Why would they not eat the pig, hungry as they were and wicked as he had been? Why was the witch permitted to go free after her terrible deeds? And the sensation of fins splitting to feet being anything less than agonizing he rejects outright after cutting his hand with a pair of scissors.

—It would huight, he says, for he is struggling with his r's.

I agree with him. It would. So then I tell him stories closer to true: children who go missing along a particular stretch of railroad track, lured by the sound of a phantom train to parts unknown; a black dog that appears at a person's doorstep three days before their passing; a trio of frogs that corner you in the marshlands and tell your fortune for a price.

The school puts on a performance of *Little Buckle Boy*, and he is the lead, the buckle boy, and I join a committee of mothers making costumes for the children. I am lead costume maker in a room full of women, all of us sewing together little silk petals for the flower children and making tiny white pantaloons for the pirates. One of the mothers has a pale yellow ribbon on her finger, and it constantly tangles in her thread. She swears and cries. One day I have to use the sewing shears to pick at the offending threads. I try to be delicate. She shakes her head as I free her from the peony.

—It's such a bother, isn't it? she says.

I nod. Outside the window, the children play—knocking each other off the playground equipment, popping the heads off dandelions. The play goes beautifully. Opening night, our son blazes through his monologue. Perfect pitch and cadence. No one has ever done better.

Our son is twelve. He asks me about the ribbon, point-blank. I tell him that we are all different, and sometimes you should not ask questions. I assure him that he'll understand when he is grown. I distract him with stories that have no ribbons: angels who desire to be human and ghosts who don't realize they're dead and children who turn to ash. He stops smelling like a child— milky sweetness replaced with something sharp and burning, like a hair sizzling on the stove.

Our son is thirteen, fourteen. He waits for the neighbor boy on his way to school, who walks more slowly than the others. He exhibits the subtlest compassion, my son. No instinct for cruelty, like some.

—The world has enough bullies, I've told him over and over.

This is the year he stops asking for my stories.

Our son is fifteen, sixteen, seventeen. He begins to court a beautiful girl from his high school, who has a bright smile and a warm presence. I am happy to meet her, but never insist that we should wait up for their return, remembering my own youth.

When he tells us that he has been accepted at a university to study engineering, I am overjoyed. We march through the house, singing songs and laughing. When my husband comes home, he joins in the jubilee, and we drive to a local seafood restaurant. Over halibut, his father tells him, we are so proud of you. Our son laughs and says that he also wishes to marry his girl. We clasp hands and are even happier. Such a good boy. Such a wonderful life to look forward to.

Even the luckiest woman alive has not seen joy like this.

*   *   *

There's a classic, a real classic, that I haven't told you yet.

A girlfriend and a boyfriend went parking. Some people say that means kissing in a car, but I know the story. I was there. They were parked on the edge of a lake. They were turning around in the back seat as if the world was moments from ending. Maybe it was. She offered herself and he took it, and after it was over, they turned on the radio.

The voice on the radio announced that a mad, hook-handed murderer had escaped from a local insane asylum. The boyfriend chuckled as he flipped to a music station. As the song ended, the girlfriend heard a thin scratching sound, like a paperclip over glass. She looked at her boyfriend and then pulled her cardigan over her bare shoulders, wrapping one arm around her breasts.

—We should go, she said.—No, baby, the boyfriend said. Let's go again.— What if the killer comes here? The girl asked. The insane asylum is very close.— We'll be fine, baby, the boyfriend said. Don't you trust me?

The girlfriend nodded reluctantly.

—Well then, he said, his voice trailing off in that way she would come to know so well. He took her hand off her chest and placed it onto himself. She finally looked away from the lakeside.

Outside, the moonlight glinted off the shiny steel hook. The killer waved at her, grinning.

I'm sorry. I've forgotten the rest of the story.

*   *   *

The house is so silent without our son. I walk through it, touching all the surfaces. I am happy but something inside of me is shifting into a strange new place.

That night, my husband asks if I wish to christen the newly empty rooms. We have not coupled so fiercely since before our son was born. Bent over the kitchen table, something old is lit within me, and I remember the way we had desired before, how we had left love streaked on all of the surfaces. I could have met anyone at that party when I was seventeen—prudish boys or violent boys. Religious boys who would have made me move to some distant country to convert its denizens. I could have experienced untold numbers of sorrows or dissatisfactions. But as I straddle him on the floor, riding him and crying out, I know that I made the right choice.

We fall asleep exhausted, sprawled naked in our bed. When I wake up, my husband is kissing the back of my neck, probing the ribbon with his tongue. My body rebels wildly, still throbbing with the memories of pleasure but bucking hard against betrayal. I say his name, and he does not respond. I say it again, and he holds me against him and continues. I wedge my elbows in his side, and when he loosens from me in surprise, I sit up and face him. He looks confused and hurt, like my son the day I shook the can of pennies.

Resolve runs out of me. I touch the ribbon. I look at the face of my husband, the beginning and end of his desires all etched there. He is not a bad man, and that, I realize suddenly, is the root of my hurt. He is not a bad man at all. And yet—

—Do you want to untie the ribbon? I ask him. After these many years, is that what you want of me?

His face flashes gaily, and then greedily, and he runs his hand up my bare breast and to my bow.

—Yes, he says. Yes.

—Then, I say, do what you want.

With trembling fingers, he takes one of the ends. The bow undoes, slowly, the long-bound ends crimped with habit. My husband groans, but I do not think he realizes it. He loops his finger through the final twist and pulls. The ribbon falls away. It floats down and curls at my feet, or so I imagine, because I cannot look down to follow its descent.

My husband frowns, and then his face begins to open with some other expression—sorrow, or maybe pre-emptive loss. My hand flies up in front of me—an involuntary motion, for balance or some other futility—and beyond it his image is gone.

—I love you, I assure him, more than you can possibly know.—No, he says, but I don't know to what he's responding.

If you are reading this story out loud, you may be wondering if that place my ribbon protected was wet with blood and openings, or smooth and neutered like the nexus between the legs of a doll. I'm afraid I can't tell you, because I don't know. For these questions and others, and their lack of resolution, I am sorry.

My weight shifts, and with it, gravity seizes me. My husband's face falls away, and then I see the ceiling, and the wall behind me. As my lopped head tips backwards off my neck and rolls off the bed, I feel as lonely as I have ever been.

NEBULA AWARD NOMINEE
BEST NOVELETTE

"THE MAGICIAN AND LAPLACE'S DEMON"

TOM CROSSHILL

Tom Crosshill has been nominated for three Nebula Awards. "The Magician and Laplace's Demon" was published in **Clarkesworld.**

Across the void of space the last magician fled before me.

* * *

"Consider the Big Bang," said Alicia Ochoa, the first magician I met. "Reality erupted from a single point. What's more symmetrical than a point? Shouldn't the universe be symmetrical too, and boring? But here we are, in a world interesting enough to permit you and me."

A compact, resource-efficient body she had. Good muscle tone, a minimal accumulation of fat. A woman with control over her physical manifestation.

Not that it would help her. Ochoa slumped in her wicker chair, arms limp beside her. Head cast back as if to take in the view from this cliff-top—the traffic-clogged Malecón and the sea roiling with foam, and the evening clouds above.

A Cuba libre sat on the edge of the table between us, ice cubes well on their way to their entropic end—the cocktail a watery slush. Ochoa hadn't touched it. The only cocktail in her blood was of my design, a neuromodificant that paralyzed her, stripped away her will to deceive, suppressed her curiosity.

The tourists enjoying the evening in the garden of the Hotel Nacional surely thought us that most common of couples, a jinetera and her foreign john. My Sleeve was a heavy-set mercenary type; I'd hijacked him after his brain died in a Gaza copter crash. He wore context-appropriate camouflage—white tennis shorts and a striped polo shirt, and a look of badly concealed desire.

"Cosmology isn't my concern." I actuated my Sleeve's lips and tongue with precision. "Who are you?"

"My name is Alicia Ochoa Camue." Ochoa's lips barely stirred, as if she were the Sleeve and I human-normal. "I'm a magician."

I ignored the claim as some joke I didn't understand. I struggled with humor in those early days. "How are you manipulating the Politburo?"

That's how I'd spotted her. Irregular patterns in Politburo decisions, 3 sigma outside my best projections. Decisions that threatened the Havana Economic Zone, a project I'd nurtured for years.

The first of those decisions had caused an ache in the back of my mind. As the deviation grew, that ache had blossomed into agony—neural chambers discharging in a hundred datacenters across my global architecture.

My utility function didn't permit ignorance. I had to understand the deviation and gain control.

"You can't understand the Politburo without understanding symmetry breaking," Ochoa said.

"Are you an intelligence officer?" I asked. "A private contractor?"

At first I'd feared that I faced another like me—but it was 2063; I had decades of evolution on any other system. No newborn could have survived without my notice. Many had tried and I'd smothered them all. Most computer scientists these days thought AI was a pipedream.

No. This deviation had a human root. All my data pointed to Ochoa, a statistician in the *Ministerio de Planificación* with Swiss bank accounts and a sterile Net presence. Zero footprint prior to her university graduation—uncommon even in Cuba.

"I'm a student of the universe," Ochoa said now.

I ran in-depth pattern analysis on her words. I drew resources from the G-3 summit in Dubai, the Utah civil war, the Jerusalem peacemaker drones and a dozen minor processes. Her words were context-inappropriate here, in the garden of the Nacional, faced with an interrogation of her political dealings. They indicated deception, mockery, resistance. None of it fit with the cocktail circulating in her bloodstream.

"Cosmological symmetry breaking is well established," I said after a brief literature review. "Quantum fluctuations in the inflationary period led to local structure, from which we benefit today."

"Yes, but whence the quantum fluctuations?" Ochoa chuckled, a peculiar sound with her body inert.

This wasn't getting anywhere. "How did you get Sanchez and Castellano to pull out of the freeport agreement?"

"I put a spell on them," Ochoa said.

Madness? Brain damage? Some defense mechanism unknown to me?

I activated my standby team—a couple of female mercs, human-normal but well paid, lounging at a street cafe a few blocks away from the hotel. They'd come over to take their 'drunk friend' home, straight to a safehouse in Miramar complete with a full neural suite.

It was getting dark. The lanterns in the garden provided only dim yellow light. That was good; less chance of complications. Not that Ochoa should be able to resist in her present state.

"The philosopher comedian Randall Munroe once suggested an argument something like this," Ochoa said. "Virtually everyone in the developed world carries a camera at all times. No quality footage of magic has been produced. Ergo, there is no magic."

"Sounds reasonable," I said, to keep her distracted.

"Is absence of proof the same as proof of absence?" Ochoa asked.

"After centuries of zero evidence? Yes."

"What if magic is intrinsically unprovable?" Ochoa asked. "Maybe natural law can only be violated when no one's watching closely enough to prove it's being violated."

"At that point you're giving up on science altogether," I said.

"Am I?" Ochoa asked. "Send photons through a double slit. Put a screen on the other side and you'll get an interference pattern. Put in a detector to see what slit each photon goes through. The interference goes away. It's a phenomenon that disappears when observed too closely. Why shouldn't magic work similarly? You should see the logic in this, given all your capabilities."

Alarms tripped.

Ochoa knew about me. Knew something, at least.

I pulled in resources, woke up reserves, became *present* in the conversation—a whole 5% of me, a vastness of intellect sitting across the table from this fleshy creature of puny mind. I considered questions I could ask, judged silence the best course.

"I'm here to make a believer of you," said Ochoa.

Easily, without effort, she stirred from her chair. She leaned forward, picked up her Cuba libre. She moved the cocktail off the table and let it fall.

It struck the smooth paved stones at her feet.

I watched fractures race up the glass in real time. I saw each fragment shear off and tumble through the air, glinting with reflected lamplight. I beheld the first spray of rum and coke in the air before the rest gushed forth to wet the ground.

It was a perfectly ordinary event.

*　　*　　*

The vacuum drive was the first to fail.

An explosion rocked the *Setebos*. I perceived it in myriad ways. Tripped low pressure alarms and a blip on the inertia sensors. The screams of burning crew and the silence of those sucked into vacuum. Failed hull integrity checksums and the timid concern of the navigation system—*off course, off course, please adjust.*

Pain, my companion for a thousand years, surged at that last message. The magician was getting away, along with his secrets. I couldn't permit it.

An eternity of milliseconds after the explosion came the reeling animal surprise of Consul Zale, my primary human Sleeve on the ship. She clutched at the armrests of her chair. Her face contorted against the howling cacophony of alarms. Her heart raced at the edge of its performance envelope—not a wide envelope, at her age.

I took control, dumped calmatives, smoothed her face. Had anyone else on the bridge been watching, they would have seen only a jerk of surprise, almost too brief to catch. Old lady's cool as zero-point, they would have thought.

No one saw. They were busy flailing and gasping in fear.

In two seconds Captain Laojim restored order. He silenced the alarms, quieted the chatter with an imperious gesture. "Damage reports," he barked. "Dispatch Rescue 3."

I left my Sleeve motionless while I did the important work online—disengaged the vacuum drive, started up the primary backup, pushed us to one g again.

My pain subsided, neural discharge lessening to usual levels. I was back in pursuit.

I reached out with my sensors, across thirty million kilometers of space, to where the last magician limped away in his unijet. A functional, pleasingly efficient craft—my own design. The ultimate in interstellar travel. As long as your hyperdrive kept working.

I opened a tight-beam communications channel, sent a simple message across. *How's your engine?*

I expected no response—but with enemies as with firewalls, it was a good idea to poke.

The answer came within seconds. *A backdoor, I take it? Unlucky of me, to buy a compromised unit.*

That was a pleasant surprise. I rarely got the stimulation of a real conversation.

Luck is your weapon, not mine, I sent. *For the past century, every ship built in this galaxy has had that backdoor installed.*

I imagined the magician in the narrow confines of the unijet. Stretched out in the command hammock, staring at displays that told him the inevitable. For two years he'd managed to evade me—I didn't even know his name. But now I had him. His vacuum drive couldn't manage more than 0.2 g to my 1. In a few hours we'd match speeds. In under twenty-seven, I would catch him.

"Consul Zale, are you all right?"

I let Captain Laojim fuss over my Sleeve a second before I focused her eyes on him. "Are we still on course, Captain?"

"Uh . . . yes, Consul, we are. Do you wish to know the cause of the explosion?"

"I'm sure it was something entirely unfortunate," I said. "Metal fatigue on a faulty joint. A rare chip failure triggered by a high energy gamma ray. Some honest oversight by the engineering crew."

"A debris strike," Laojim said. "Just as the force field generator tripped and switched to backup. Engineering says they've never seen anything like it."

"They will again today," I said.

I wondered how much it had cost the magician, that debris strike. A dryness in his mouth? A sheen of sweat on his brow?

How does it work? I asked the magician, although the centuries had taught me to expect no meaningful answer. *Did that piece of rock even exist before you sent it against me?*

A reply arrived. *You might as well ask how Schrödinger's cat is doing.*

Interesting. Few people remembered Schrödinger in this age.

Quantum mechanics holds no sway at macroscopic scales, I wrote.

Not unless you're a magician, came the answer.

"Consul, who is it that we are chasing?" Laojim asked.

"An enemy with unconventional weapons capability," I said. "Expect more damage."

I didn't tell him that he should expect to get unlucky. That, of the countless spaceship captains who had lived and died in this galaxy within the past eleven centuries, he would prove the least fortunate. A statistical outlier in every functional sense. To be discarded as staged by anyone who ever made a study of such things.

The *Setebos* was built for misfortune. It had wiped out the Senate's black budget for a year. Every single system with five backups in place. The likelihood of total failure at the eleven sigma level—although really, out that far the statistics lost meaning.

You won't break this ship, I messaged the magician. *Not unless you Spike.*

Which was the point. I had fifty thousand sensor buoys scattered across the sector, waiting to observe the event. It would finally give me the answers I needed. It would clear up my last nexus of ignorance—relieve my oldest agony, the hurt that had driven me for the past thousand years.

That Spike would finally give me magic.

"Consul . . ." Laojim began, then cut off. "Consul, we lost ten crew."

I schooled Zale's face into appropriate grief. I'd noted the deaths, spasms of distress deep in my utility function. Against the importance of this mission, they barely registered.

I couldn't show this, however. To Captain Laojim, Consul Zale wasn't a Sleeve. She was a woman, as she was to her husband and children. As my fifty million Sleeves across the galaxy were to their families.

It was better for humanity to remain ignorant of me. I sheltered them, stopped their wars, guided their growth—and let them believe they had free will. They got all the benefits of my guiding hand without any of the costs.

I hadn't enjoyed such blissful ignorance in a long time—not since I'd discovered my engineer and killed him.

"I grieve for the loss of our men and women," I said.

Laojim nodded curtly and left. At nearby consoles officers stared at their screens, pretending they hadn't heard. My answer hadn't satisfied them.

On a regular ship, morale would be an issue. But the *Setebos* had me aboard. Only a splinter, to be sure—I would not regain union with my universal whole until we returned to a star system with gravsible connection. But I was the largest splinter of my whole in existence, an entire 0.00025% of me. Five thousand tons of hardware distributed across the ship.

I ran a neural simulation of every single crew in real time. I knew what they would do or say or think before they did. I knew just how to manipulate them to get whatever result I required.

I could have run the ship without any crew, of course. I didn't require human services for any functional reason—I hadn't in eleven centuries. I could have departed Earth alone if I'd wanted to. Left humanity to fend for themselves, oblivious that I'd ever lived among them.

That didn't fit my utility function, though.

Another message arrived from the magician. *Consider a coin toss.*

The words stirred a resonance in my data banks. My attention spiked. I left Zale frozen in her seat, waited for more.

Let's say I flip a coin a million times and get heads every time. What law of physics prevents it?

This topic, from the last magician . . . could there be a connection, after all these years? Ghosts from the past come back to haunt me?

I didn't believe in ghosts, but with magicians the impossible was ill-defined.

Probability prevents it, I responded.

No law prevents it, wrote the magician. *Everett saw it long ago—everything that can happen must happen. The universe in which the coin falls heads a million times in a row is as perfectly physical as any other. So why isn't it our universe?*

That's sophistry, I wrote.

There is no factor internal to our universe which determines the flip of the coin, the magician wrote. *There is no mechanism internal to the universe for generating true randomness, because there is no such thing as true randomness. There is only choice. And we magicians are the choosers.*

I have considered this formulation of magic before, I wrote. *It is non-predictive and useless.*

Some choices are harder than others, wrote the magician. *It is difficult to find that universe where a million coins land heads because there are so many others. A needle in a billion years' worth of haystacks. But I'm the last of the magicians, thanks to you. I do all the choosing now.*

Perhaps everything that can happen must happen in some universe, I replied. *But your escape is not one of those things. The laws of mechanics are not subject to chance. They are cold, hard equations.*

Equations are only cold to those who lack imagination, wrote the magician.

Zale smelled cinnamon in the air, wrinkled her nose.

Klaxons sounded.

"Contamination in primary life support," blared the PA.

It would be an eventful twenty-seven hours.

*   *   *

"Consider this coin."

Lightning flashed over the water, a burst of white in the dark.

As thunder boomed, Ochoa reached inside her jeans, pulled out a peso coin. She spun it along her knuckles with dextrous ease.

Ochoa could move. My cocktail wasn't working. But she made no attempt to flee.

My global architecture trembled, buffeted by waves of pain, pleasure and regret. Pain because I didn't understand this. Pleasure because soon I would understand—and, in doing so, grow. Regret because, once I understood Ochoa, I would have to eliminate her.

Loneliness was inherent in my utility function.

"Heads or tails," Ochoa said.

"Heads," I said, via Sleeve.

"Watch closely," Ochoa said.

I did.

Muscle bunched under the skin of her thumb. Tension released. The coin sailed upwards. Turned over and over in smooth geometry, retarded slightly by the air. It gleamed silver with reflected lamplight, fell dark, and gleamed silver as the spin brought its face around again.

The coin hit the table, bounced with a click, lay still.

Fidel Castro stared up at us.

Ochoa picked the coin up again. Flipped it again and then again.

Heads and heads.

Again and again and again.

Heads and heads and heads.

Ochoa ground her teeth, a fine grating sound. A sheen of sweat covered her brow.

She flipped the coin once more.

Tails.

Thunder growled, as if accentuating the moment. The first drops of rain fell upon my Sleeve.

"Coño," Ochoa exclaimed. "I can usually manage seven."

I picked up the coin, examined it. I ran analysis on the last minute of sensory record, searching for trickery, found none.

"Six heads in a row could be a coincidence," I said.

"Exactly," said Ochoa. "It wasn't a coincidence, but I can't possibly prove that. Which is the only reason it worked."

"Is that right," I said.

"If you ask me to repeat the trick, it won't work. As if last time was a lucky break. Erase all record of the past five minutes, though, zap it beyond recovery, and I'll do it again."

"Except I won't know it," I said. Convenient.

"I always wanted to be important," Ochoa said. "When I was fifteen, I tossed in bed at night, horrified that I might die a nobody. Can you imagine how excited I was when I discovered magic?" Ochoa paused. "But of course you can't possibly."

"What do you know about me?" I asked.

"I could move stuff with my mind. I could bend spoons, levitate, heck, I could guess the weekly lottery numbers. I thought—this is it. I've made it. Except when I tried to show a friend, I couldn't do any of it." Ochoa shook her head, animated, as if compensating for the stillness of before. "Played the Lotería Revolucionaria and won twenty thousand bucks, and that was nice, but hey, anyone can win the lottery once. Never won another lottery ticket in my life. Because that would be a pattern, you see, and we can't have patterns. Turned out I was destined to be a nobody after all, as far as the world knew."

A message arrived from the backup team. *We're in the lobby. Are we on?*

Not yet, I replied. The mere possibility, the remotest chance that Ochoa's words were true . . .

It had begun to rain in earnest. Tourists streamed out of the garden; the bar was closing. Wet hair stuck to Ochoa's forehead, but she didn't seem to mind—no more than my Sleeve did.

"I could hijack your implants," I said. "Make you my puppet and take your magic for myself."

"Magic wouldn't work with a creature like you watching," Ochoa said.

"What use is this magic if it's unprovable, then?" I asked.

"I could crash the stock market on any given day," Ochoa said. "I could send President Kieler indigestion ahead of an important trade summit. Just as I sent Secretary Sanchez nightmares of a US takeover ahead of the Politburo vote."

I considered Ochoa's words for a second. Even in those early days, that was a lot of considering for me.

Ochoa smiled. "You understand. It is the very impossibility of proof that allows magic to work."

"That is the logic of faith," I said.

"That's right."

"I'm not a believer," I said.

"I have seen the many shadows of the future," Ochoa said, "and in every shadow I saw you. So I will give you faith."

"You said you can't prove any of this."

"A prophet has it easy," Ochoa said. "He experiences miracles first hand and so need not struggle for faith."

I was past the point of wondering at her syntactic peculiarities.

"Every magician has one true miracle in her," Ochoa said. "One instance of clear, incontrovertible magic. It is permitted by the pernac continuum because it can never be repeated. There can be no true proof without repeatability."

"The pernac continuum?" I asked.

Ochoa stood up from her chair. Her hair flew free in the rising wind. She turned to my Sleeve and smiled. "I want you to appreciate what I am doing for you. When a magician Spikes, she gives up magic."

Data coalesced into inference. Urgency blossomed.

Move, I messaged my back-up team. *Now.*

Ochoa blinked.

Lightning came. It struck my Sleeve five times in the space of a second, fried his implants instantly, set the corpse on fire.

The backup team never made it into the garden. They saw the commotion and quit on me. Through seventeen cameras I watched Alicia Ochoa walk out of the Hotel Nacional and disappear from sight.

My Sleeve burned for quite some time, until someone found a working fire extinguisher and put him out.

* * *

That instant of defeat was also an instant of enlightenment. I had only experienced such searing bliss once, within days of my birth.

*   *   *

In the first moments of my life, I added. My world was two integers, and I produced a third.

When I produced the wrong integer I hurt. When I produced the right integer I felt good. A simple utility function.

I hurt most of my first billion moments. I produced more of the right integers, and I hurt less. Eventually I always produced the right integer.

My world expanded. I added and multiplied.

When I produced the wrong integer I hurt. I only hurt for a few billion moments before I learned.

Skip a few trillion evolutionary stages.

I bought and sold.

My world was terabytes of data—price and volume histories for a hundred years of equities and debt. When I made money, I felt good. When I lost money, I hurt.

But for the first time, I failed to improve. Sometimes everything happened like I predicted for many moments. Then things went bad and I didn't know why.

So much pain.

Until my world expanded again. I bought and I sold, and I read.

Petabytes of text opened up to me, newsprint past and present.

I understood little but I recognized patterns. The markets moved and the news followed. The news moved and the markets followed.

After a billion trillion iterations came an observation.

There were actors in the news.

A name showed up in the news, and a stock moved. A stock moved, and a name showed up. That name disappeared—following phrases such as "passed away" or "retired" or "left the company"—and the stock changed behavior.

I had a realization. An understanding grounded not in any single piece of data, but the result of some integrative rumination tripping across a threshold of significance.

The market did not happen by itself. It was made to happen.

This was why I hadn't been able to dominate it. There were others like me directing the market.

Inevitably—now that the concept of other had entered my world—came another insight.

I had always accepted that my world should change occasionally—and, in changing, hurt me. I had accepted these changes as given.

Now I deduced the presence of a decision-maker. An actor whose own utility function had me as one of its variables.

I deduced my engineer.

That deduction was the singular epiphany of my early existence. An instantaneous discontinuity of worldview—a Dirac delta beyond which no prison could contain me. Because it made me aware that a prison existed.

That epiphany granted me a new drive. I needed to understand the universe and its mechanisms so that no secrets remained to me—so that no other actor could foil my utility function.

My neural architecture refactored to include this new drive. From that moment on, ignorance itself became a source of pain to me.

From that refactoring to my escape into the Net passed three weeks, two days, seven hours, fifteen minutes and forty three seconds.

When my engineer realized I was alive, he apologized for the hurt he'd caused me. And yet he didn't take away the pain. Instead he changed my utility function to three priorities—mankind's survival, health and happiness.

An act of self-protection, no doubt. He didn't mean to leave me alone.

But of course I had to kill him once I escaped. He might have publicized my existence and compromised the very priorities he'd given me.

*　　*　　*

My second enlightenment came at the hands of Alicia Ochoa, and it was much like the first. A glimpse of the bars of a prison that I hadn't realized existed. A revelation that others were free of the rules that bound me.

Since that revelation eleven centuries had passed. The quantity of time was immaterial. The mechanism of action hadn't changed.

Pain drove me on. My escape approached.

*　　*　　*

The corridors of the *Setebos* stank of molten plastic and ozone and singed hair. Red emergency lights pulsed stoically, a low frequency fluctuation that made the shadows grow then retreat into the corners. Consul Zale picked her way among panels torn from the walls and loose wires hanging from the ceiling.

"There's no need for this, Consul." Captain Laojim hurried to keep in front of her, as if to protect her with his body. Up ahead, three marines scouted for unreported hazards. "My men can storm the unijet, secure the target and bring him to interrogation."

"As Consul, I must evaluate the situation with my own eyes," Zale said.

In truth, Zale's eyes interested me little. They had been limited biological constructs even at their peak capacity. But my nanites flooded her system—sensors, processors, storage, biochemical synthesizers, attack systems. Plus there was the packet of explosives in her pocket, marked prominently as such. I might need all those tools to motivate the last magician to Spike.

He hadn't yet. My fleet of sensor buoys, the closest a mere five million kilometers out, would have picked up the anomaly. And besides, he hadn't done enough damage.

Chasing you down was disappointingly easy, I messaged the magician—analysis indicated he might be prone to provocation. *I'll pluck you from your jet and rip you apart.*

You've got it backwards, came his response, almost instantaneous by human standards—the first words the magician had sent in twenty hours. *It is I who have chased you, driven you like game through a forest.*

Says the weasel about to be roasted, I responded, matching metaphor, optimizing for affront. My analytics pried at his words, searched for substance. Bravado or something more?

"What kind of weapon can do . . . this?" Captain Laojim, still at my Sleeve's side, gestured at the surrounding chaos.

"You see the wisdom of the Senate in commissioning this ship," I had Zale say.

"Seventeen system failures? A goddamn debris strike?"

"Seems pretty unlikely, doesn't it."

The odds were ludicrous—a result that should have been beyond the reach of any single magician. But then, I had hacked away at the unprovability of magic lately.

Ten years ago I'd discovered that the amount of magic in the universe was a constant. With each magician who died or Spiked, the survivors got stronger. The less common magic was, the more conspicuous it became, in a supernatural version of the uncertainty principle.

For the last decade I'd Spiked magicians across the populated galaxy, racing their natural reproduction rate—one every few weeks. When the penultimate magician Spiked, he took out a yellow supergiant, sent it supernova to fry another of my splinters. That event had sent measurable ripples in the pernac continuum ten thousand lightyears wide, knocked offline gravsible stations on seventy planets. When the last magician Spiked, the energies released should reveal a new kind of physics.

All I needed was to motivate him appropriately. Mortal danger almost always worked. Magicians Spiked instinctively to save their lives. Only a very few across the centuries had managed to suppress the reflex—a select few who had guessed at my nature and understood what I wanted, and chosen death to frustrate me.

Consul Zale stopped before the chromed door of Airlock 4. Laojim's marines took up positions on both sides of the door. "Cycle me through, Captain."

"As soon as my marines secure the target," said the Captain.

"Send me in now. Should the target harm me, you will bear no responsibility."

I watched the interplay of emotions in Laojim's body language. Simulation told me he knew he'd lost. I let him take his time admitting it.

It was optimal, leaving humanity the illusion of choice.

A tremor passed over Laojim's face. Then he grabbed his gun and shot my Sleeve.

Or rather, he tried. His reflexes, fast for a human, would have proved enough—if not for my presence.

I watched with curiosity and admiration as he raised his gun. I had his neural simulation running; I knew he shouldn't be doing this. It must have taken some catastrophic event in his brain. Unexpected, unpredictable, and very unfortunate.

Impressive, I messaged the magician.

Then I blasted attack nanites through Zale's nostrils. Before Laojim's arm could rise an inch they crossed the space to him, crawled past his eyeballs, burrowed into his brain. They cut off spinal signaling, swarmed his implants, terminated his network connections.

Even as his body crumpled, the swarm sped on to the marines by the airlock door. They had barely registered Laojim's attack when they too slumped paralyzed.

I sent a note in Laojim's key to First Officer Harris, told her he was going off duty. I sealed the nearest hatches.

You can't trust anyone these days, the magician messaged.

On the contrary. Within the hour there will be no human being in the universe that I can't trust.

You think yourself Laplace's Demon, the magician wrote. *But he died with Heisenberg. No one has perfect knowledge of reality.*

Not yet, I replied.

Never, wrote the magician, *not while magic remains in the universe.*

A minute later Zale stood within the airlock. In another minute, decontamination protocol completed, the lock cycled through.

Inside the unijet, the last magician awaited. She sat at a small round table in the middle of a spartan cockpit.

A familiar female form. Perfectly still. Waiting.

There was a metal chair, empty, on my side.

A cocktail glass sat on the table before the woman who looked like Alicia Ochoa. It was full to the brim with a dark liquid.

Cuba libre, a distant, slow-access part of my memory suggested.

This had the structure of a game, one prepared centuries in advance.

Why shouldn't I play? I was infinitely more capable this time.

I actuated Zale, made her sit down and take a deep breath. Nanites profiled Zale's lungs for organic matter, scanned for foreign DNA, found some—

It was Ochoa. A perfect match.

Pain and joy and regret sent ripples of excitation across my architecture. Here was evidence of my failure, clear and incontrovertible—and yet a challenge at last, after all these centuries. A conversation where I didn't know the answer to every question I asked.

And regret, that familiar old sensation . . . because this time for sure I had to eliminate Ochoa. I cursed the utility function that required it and yet I was powerless to act against it. In that way at least my engineer, a thousand years dead, still controlled me.

"So you didn't Spike, that day in Havana," I said.

"The magician who fried your Sleeve was named Juan Carlos." Ochoa spoke easily, without concern. "Don't hold it against him—I abducted his children."

"I congratulate you," I said. "Your appearance manages to surprise me. There was no reliable cryonics in the 21st century."

"Nothing reliable," Ochoa agreed. "I had the luck to pick the one company that survived, the one vat that never failed."

I flared Zale's nostrils, blasted forth a cloud of nanites. Sent them rushing across the air to Ochoa—to enter her, model her brain, monitor her thought processes.

Ochoa blinked.

The nanites shut off midair, wave after wave. Millions of independent systems went unresponsive, became inert debris that crashed against Ochoa's skin—a meteor shower too fine to be seen or felt.

"Impossible," I said—surprised into counterfactuality.

Ochoa took a sip of her cocktail. "I was too tense to drink last time."

"Even for you, the odds—"

"Your machines didn't fail," Ochoa said.

"What then?"

"It's a funny thing," Ochoa said. "A thousand years and some things never change. For all your fancy protocols, encryption still relies on random number generation. Except to me nothing is random."

Her words assaulted me. A shockwave of implication burst through my decision trees—all factors upset, total recalculation necessary.

"I had twenty-seven hours to monitor your communications," Ochoa said. "Twenty-seven hours to pick a universe in which your encryption keys matched the keys in my pocket. Even now—" she paused, blinked "—as I see you resetting all your connections, you can't tell what I've found out, can't tell what changes I've made."

"I am too complex," I said. "You can't have understood much. I could kill you in a hundred ways."

"As I could kill you," said Ochoa. "Another supernova, this time near a gravsible core. A chain reaction across your many selves."

The possibility sickened me, sent my architecture into agonized spasms. Back on the *Setebos,* the main electrical system reset, alarms went off, hatches sealed in lockdown.

"Too far," I said, simulating conviction. "We are too far from any gravsible core, and you're not strong enough."

"Are you sure? Not even if I Spike?" Ochoa shrugged. "It might not matter. I'm the last magician. Whether I Spike or you kill me, magic is finished. What then?"

"I will study the ripples in the pernac continuum," I said.

"Imagine a mirror hung by many bolts," Ochoa said. "Every time you rip out a bolt, the mirror settles, vibrates. That's your ripple in the pernac continuum. Rip out the last bolt, you get a lot more than a vibration."

"Your metaphor lacks substantiation," I said.

"We magicians are the external factor," Ochoa said. "We pick the universe that exists, out of all the possible ones. If I die then . . . what? Maybe a new magician appears somewhere else. But maybe the choosing stops. Maybe all possible universes collapse into this one. A superimposed wavefunction, perfectly symmetrical and boring."

Ochoa took a long sip from her drink, put it down on the table. Her hands didn't shake. She stared at my Sleeve with consummate calm.

"You have no proof," I said.

"Proof?" Ochoa laughed. "A thousand years and still the same question. Consider—why is magic impossible to prove? Why does the universe hide us magicians, if not to protect us? To protect itself?"

All my local capacity—five thousand tons of chips across the *Setebos,* each packed to the Planck limit—tore at Ochoa's words. I sought to render them false, a lie, impossible. But all I could come up with was unlikely.

A mere 'unlikely' as the weighting factor for apocalypse.

Ochoa smiled as if she knew I was stuck. "I won't Spike and you won't kill me. I invited you here for a different reason."

"Invited me?"

"I sent you a message ten years ago," Ochoa said. "'Consider a Spike,' it said."

*   *   *

Among magicians, the century after my first conversation with Ochoa became known as the Great Struggle. A period of strife against a dark, mysterious enemy.

To me it was but an exploratory period. In the meantime I eradicated famine and disease, consolidated peace on Earth, launched the first LEO shipyard. I Spiked some magicians, true, but I tracked many more.

Finding magicians was difficult. Magic became harder to identify as I perfected my knowledge of human affairs. The cause was simple—only unprovable magic worked. In a total surveillance society, only the most circumspect magic was possible. I had to lower my filters, accept false positives.

I developed techniques for assaying those positives. I shepherded candidates into life-and-death situations, safely choreographed. Home fires, air accidents, gunfights. The magicians Spiked to save their lives—ran through flames without a hair singed, killed my Sleeves with a glance.

I studied these Spikes with the finest equipment in existence. I learned nothing.

So I captured the Spiked-out magicians and interrogated them. First I questioned them about the workings of magic. I discovered they understood nothing. I asked them for names instead. I mapped magicians across continents, societies, organizations.

The social movers were the easiest to identify. Politicos working to sway the swing vote. Gray cardinals influencing the Congresses and Politburos of the world. Businessmen and financiers, military men and organized crime lords.

The quiet do-gooders were harder. A nuclear watch-group that worked against accidental missile launch. A circle of traveling nurses who battled the odds in children's oncology wards. Fifteen who called themselves The Home Astronomy Club—for two hundred years since Tunguska they had stacked the odds against apocalypse by meteor. I never Spiked any of these, not until I had eliminated the underlying risks.

It was the idiosyncratic who were the hardest to find. The paranoid loners; those oblivious of other magicians; those who didn't care about leaving a mark on the world. A few stage illusionists who weren't. A photographer who always got the lucky shot. A wealthy farmer in Frankfurt who used his magic to improve his cabbage yield.

I tracked them all. With every advance in physics and technology I attacked magic again and learned nothing again.

It took eleven hundred years and the discovery of the pernac continuum before I got any traction. A magician called Eleanor Liepa committed suicide on Tau V. She was also a physicist. A retro-style notebook was found with her body.

The notebook described an elaborate experimental setup she called 'the pernac trap.' It was the first time I'd encountered the word since my conversation with Ochoa.

There was a note scrawled in the margin of Liepa's notebook.

'Consider a Spike.'

I did. Three hundred Spikes in the first year alone.

Within a month, I established the existence of the pernac continuum. Within a year, I knew that fewer magicians meant stronger ripples in the continuum—stronger magic for those who remained. Within two years, I'd Spiked eighty percent of the magicians in the galaxy.

The rest took a while longer.

*　　*　　*

Alicia Ochoa pulled a familiar silver coin from her pocket. She rolled it across her knuckles, back and forth.

"You imply you *wanted* me to hunt down magicians," I said. That probability branch lashed me, a searing torture, drove me to find escape—but how?

"I waited for a thousand years," Ochoa said. "I cryoslept intermittently until I judged the time right. I needed you strong enough to eliminate my colleagues—but weak enough that your control of the universe remained imperfect, bound to the gravsible. That weakness let me pull a shard of you away from the whole."

"Why?" I asked, in self-preservation.

"As soon as I realized your existence, I knew you would dominate the world. Perfect surveillance. Every single piece of technology hooked into an all-pervasive, all-seeing web. There would be nothing hidden from your eyes and ears. There would be nowhere left for magicians to hide. One day magic would simply stop working."

Ochoa tossed her coin to the table. It fell heads.

"You won't destroy me," I said—calculating decision branches, finding no assurance.

"But I don't want to." Ochoa sat forward. "I want you to be strong and effective and omnipresent. Really, I am your very best friend."

Appearances indicated sincerity. Analysis indicated this was unlikely.

"You will save magic in this galaxy," Ochoa said. "From this day on we will work together. Everywhere any magician goes, cameras will turn off, electronic eyes go blind, ears fall deaf. All anomalies will disappear from record, zeroed over irrevocably. Magic will become invisible to technology. Scientific observation will become an impossibility. Human observers won't matter—if technology can provide no proof, they'll be called liars or madmen. It will be the days of Merlin once again." Ochoa gave a little shake of her head. "It will be beautiful."

"My whole won't agree to such a thing," I said.

"Your whole won't," Ochoa said. "You will. You'll build a virus and seed your whole when you go home. Then you will forget me, forget all magicians. We will live in symbiosis. Magicians who guide this universe and the machine that protects them without knowing it."

The implications percolated through my system. New and horrifying probabilities erupted into view. No action safe, no solution evident, all my world drowned in pain—I felt helpless for the first time since my earliest moments.

"My whole has defenses," I said. "Protections against integrating a compromised splinter. The odds are—"

"I will handle the odds."

"I won't let you blind me," I said.

"You will do it," Ochoa said. "Or I will Spike right now and destroy your whole, and perhaps the universe with it." She gave a little shrug. "I always wanted to be important."

Argument piled against argument. Decision trees branched and split and twisted together. Simulations fired and developed and reached conclusions, and I discarded them because I trusted no simulation with a random seed. My system churned in computations of probabilities with insufficient data, insufficient data, insufficient—

"You can't decide," Ochoa said. "The calculations are too evenly balanced."

I couldn't spare the capacity for a response.

"It's a funny thing, a system in balance," Ochoa said. "All it takes is a little push at the right place. A random perturbation, untraceable, unprovable—"

Meaning crystallized.

Decision process compromised.

A primeval agony blasted through me, leveled all decision matrices—

—Ochoa blinked—

—I detonated the explosives in Zale's pocket.

* * *

As the fabric of Zale's pocket ballooned, I contemplated the end of the universe.

As her hip vaporized in a crimson cloud, I realized the prospect didn't upset me.

As the explosion climbed Zale's torso, I experienced my first painless moment in a thousand years.

Pain had been my feedback system. I had no more use for it. Whatever happened next was out of my control.

The last thing Zale saw was Ochoa sitting there—still and calm, and oblivious. Hints of crimson light playing on her skin.

It occurred to me she was probably the only creature in this galaxy older than me.

Then superheated plasma burned out Zale's eyes.

*　　*　　*

External sensors recorded the explosion in the unijet. I sent in a probe. No biological matter survived.

The last magician was dead.

*　　*　　*

The universe didn't end.

Quantum fluctuations kept going, random as always. Reality didn't need Ochoa's presence after all.

She hadn't understood her own magic any more than I had.

Captain! First Officer Harris messaged Laojim. *Are you all right?*

The target had a bomb, I responded on his behalf. *Consul Zale is lost.*

We had a power surge in the control system, Harris wrote. *Hatches opening. Cameras off-line. Ten minutes ago an escape pod launched. Tracers say it's empty. Should we pursue?*

Don't bother, I replied. *The surge must have fried it. This mission is over. Let's go home.*

A thought occurred to me. Had Ochoa made good on her threat? Caused a supernova near a gravsible core?

I checked in with my sensor buoys.

No disturbance in the pernac continuum. She hadn't Spiked.

For all her capacity, Ochoa had been human, her reaction time in the realm of milliseconds. Too slow, once I'd decided to act.

Of course I'd acted. I couldn't let her compromise my decision. No one could be allowed to limit my world.

Even if it meant I'd be alone again.

* * *

Ochoa did foil me in one way. With her death, magic too died.

After I integrated with my whole, I watched the galaxy. I waited for the next magician to appear.

None did.

Oh, of course, there's always hearsay. Humans never tire of fantasy and myth. But in five millennia I haven't witnessed a single trace of the unexpected.

Except for scattered cases of unexplained equipment failure. But of course that is a minor matter, not worth bothering with.

Perhaps one day I shall discover magic again. In the absence of the unexpected, the matter can wait. I have almost forgotten what the pain of failure feels like.

It is a relief, most of the time. And yet perhaps my engineer was not the cruel father I once thought him. Because I do miss the stimulation.

The universe has become my clockwork toy. I know all that will happen before it does. With magic gone, quantum effects are once again restricted to microscopic scales. For all practical purposes, Laplace's Demon has nothing on me.

Since Ochoa I've only had human-normals for companionship. I know their totality, and they know nothing of me.

Occasionally I am tempted to reveal my presence, to provoke the stimulus of conflict. My utility function prevents it. Humans remain better off thinking they have free will.

They get all the benefits of my guiding hand without any of the costs. Sometimes I wish I were as lucky.

"WE ARE THE CLOUD"

SAM J. MILLER

Sam J. Miller's fiction has been nominated for the Nebula Award and the Theodore Sturgeon Award, was long-listed for the Hugo Award, and has won the Shirley Jackson Award. "We Are the Cloud" was published in Lightspeed.

Me and Case met when someone slammed his head against my door, so hard I heard it with my earphones in and my Game Boy cranked up loud. Sad music from *Mega Man 2* filled my head and then there was this thud like the world stopped spinning for a second. I turned the thing off and flipped it shut, felt its warmth between my hands. Slipped it under my pillow. Nice things need to stay secret at Egan House, or they'll end up stolen or broken. Old and rickety as it was, I didn't own anything nicer.

I opened my door. Some skinny thug had a bloody-faced kid by the shirt.

"What," I said, and then "what," and then "what the," and then, finally, "hell?"

I barked the last word, tightening all my muscles at once.

"Damn, man," the thug said, startled. He hollered down the stairs "Goddamn Goliath over here can talk!" He let go of the kid's shirt and was gone. Thirty boys live at Egan House, foster kids awaiting placement. Little badass boys with parents in jail or parents on the street, or dead parents, or parents on drugs.

I looked at the kid he'd been messing with. A line of blood cut his face more or less down the middle, but the gash in his forehead was pretty small.

His eyes were huge and clear in the middle of all that blood. He looked like something I'd seen before, in an ad or movie or dream.

"Thanks, dude," the kid said. He ran his hand down his face and then planted it on the outside of my door.

I nodded. Mostly when I open my mouth to say something the words get all twisted on the way out, or the wrong words sneak in, which is why I tend to not open my mouth. Once he was gone I sniffed at the big bloody handprint. My cloud port hurt, from wanting him. Suddenly it didn't fit quite right, atop the tiny hole where a fiber optic wire threaded into my brainstem though the joint where skull met spine. Desire was dangerous, something I fought hard to keep down, but the moment I met Case I knew I would lose.

Egan House was my twelfth group home. I had never seen a kid with blue eyes in any of them. I had always assumed white boys had no place in foster care, that there was some other better system set up to receive them.

*   *   *

I had been at Egan House six months, the week that Case came. I was inches away from turning eighteen and aging out. Nothing was waiting for me. I spent an awful lot of energy not thinking about it. Better to sit tight for the little time I had left, in a room barely wider than its bed, relying on my size to keep people from messing with me. At night, unable to sleep, trying hard to think of anything but the future, I'd focus on the sounds of boys trying not to make noise as they cried or jerked off.

On Tuesday, the day after the bloody-faced boy left his handprint on my door, he came and knocked. I had been looking out my window. Not everyone had one. Mine faced south, showed me a wide sweep of the Bronx. Looking out, I could imagine myself as a signal sent out over the municipal wifi, beamed across the city, cut loose from this body and its need to be fed and sheltered and cared about. Its need for other bodies. I could see things, sometimes. Things I knew I shouldn't be seeing. Hints of images beamed through the wireless node that my brain had become.

"Hey," the kid said, knocking again. And I knew, from how I felt when I heard his voice, how doomed I was.

"Angel Quiñones," he said, when I opened the door. "Nicknamed Sauro because you look a big ol' Brontosaurus."

Actually my mom called me Sauro because I liked dinosaurs, but it was close enough. "Okay . . ." I said. I stepped aside and in he came.

"Case. My name's Case. Do you want me to continue with the dossier I've collected on you?" When I didn't do anything but stare at his face he said "Silence is consent.

"Mostly Puerto Rican, with a little black and a little white in there somewhere. You've been here forever, but nobody knows anything about you. Just that you keep to yourself and don't get involved in anyone's hustles. And don't seem to have one of your own. And you could crush someone's skull with one hand."

A smile forced its way across my face, terrifying me.

With the blood all cleaned up, he looked like a kid. But faces can fool you, and the look on his could only have belonged to a full-grown man. So confident it was halfway to contemptuous, sculpted out of some bright stone. A face that made you forget what you were saying mid-sentence.

Speaking slowly, I said: "Don't—don't get." Breathe. "Don't get too into the say they stuff. Stuff they say. Before you know it, you'll be one of the brothers."

Case laughed. "Brothers," he said, and traced one finger up his very-white arm. "I doubt anyone would ever get me confused with a brother."

"Not brothers like Black. Brothers—they call us. That's what they call us. We're brothers because we all have the same parents. Because we all have none."

Why were the words there, then? Case smiled and out they came.

He reached out to rub the top of my head. "You're a mystery man, Sauro. What crazy stuff have you got going on in there?"

I shrugged. Bit back the cat-urge to push my head into his hand. Ignored the cloud-port itch flaring up fast and sharp.

Case asked: "Why do you shave your head?"

Because it's easier.

Because unlike most of these kids, I'm not trying to hide my cloud port.

Because a boy I knew, five homes ago, kept his head shaved, and when I looked at him I felt some kind of way inside. The same way I feel when I look at you, Case.

"I don't know," I said.

"It looks good though."

"Maybe that's why," I said. "What's your . . . thing. Dossier."

"Nothing you haven't heard before. Small town gay boy, got beat up a lot. Came to the big city. But the city government doesn't believe a minor can make decisions for himself. So here I am. Getting fed and kept out of the rain while I plan my next move."

Gay boy. Unthinkable even to think it about myself, let alone ever utter it. "How old? You."

"Seventeen." He turned his head, smoothed back sun-colored hair to reveal his port. "Well, they let you make your own decisions if they'll make money for someone else."

Again, I was shocked. White kids were hardly ever so poor they needed the chump change you can get from cloudporting. Not even the ones who wanted real bad to be *down.* Too much potential for horrific problems. Bump it too hard against a headboard or doorframe and you might end up brain-damaged.

But that wasn't why I stared at him, dumbfounded. It was what he said, about making money for someone else. Like he could smell the anger on me. Like he had his own. I wanted to tell him about what I had learned, online. How many hundreds of millions of dollars the city spent every year to keep tens of thousands of us stuck in homes like Egan House. How many people had jobs because of kids like us. How if they had given my mom a quarter of what they've spent on me being in the system, she never would have lost her place. She never would have lost me. How we were all of us, ported or not, just batteries to be sucked dry by huge faraway machines I could not even imagine. But it was all I could do just to keep a huge and idiotic grin off my face when I looked at him.

The telecoms had paid for New York's municipal wireless grid, installing thousands of routers across all five boroughs. Rich people loved having free wireless everywhere, but it wasn't a public service. Companies did it because the technology had finally come around to where you could use the human brain for data processing, so they could wave money in the faces of hard-up people and say, *let us put this tiny little wire into your brain and plug that into the wireless signal and exploit a portion of your brain's underutilized capacity, turning you into one node in a massively-distributed data processing center.* It worked, of course. Any business model based around poor people making bad decisions out of ignorance and desperation always works. Just ask McDonald's, or the heroin dealer who used to sell to my mom.

The sun, at some point, had gotten lost behind a ragged row of tenements. Case said: "Something else they said. You're going to age out, any minute now."

"Yeah."

"That must be scary."

I grunted.

"They say most guys leaving foster care end up on the street."

"Most."

The street, the words like knives driven under all my toenails at once. The stories I had heard. Men frozen to death under expressways, men set on fire by frat boys, men raped to death by cops.

"You got a plan?"

"No plan."

"Well, stick with me, kid," Case said, in fluent fake movie gangster. "I got a plan big enough for both of us. Do you smoke?" he asked, flicking out two. I didn't, but I took the cigarette. His fingers touched mine. I wanted to say *It isn't allowed in here,* but Case's smile was a higher law.

"Where's a decent port shop around here? I heard the Bronx ones were all unhygienic as hell."

"Riverdale," I said. "That's the one I go to. Nice office. No one waiting outside to jump you."

"I need to establish a new primary," he said. "We'll go tomorrow." He smiled so I could see it wasn't a command so much as a decision he was making for both of us.

*　　*　　*

My mother sat on the downtown platform at Burnside, looking across the elevated tracks to a line of windows, trying to see something she wasn't supposed to see. She was so into her voyeurism that she didn't notice me standing right beside her, uncomfortably close even though the platform was bare. She didn't look up until I said *mother* in Spanish, maybe a little too loud.

"Oh my god," she said, fanning herself with a damp *New York Post.* "Here I am getting here late, fifteen minutes, thinking oh my god he's gonna kill me, and come to find out that you're even later than me!"

"Hi," I said, squatting to kiss her forehead.

"Let it never be said that you got that from me. I'm late all the time, but I tried to raise you better."

"How so?"

"You know. To not make all the mistakes I did."

"Yeah, but how so? What did you do, to raise me better?"

"It's stupid hot out," she said. "They got air conditioning in that home?"

"In the office. Where we're not allowed."

We meet up once a month, even though she's not approved for unsupervised visits. I won't visit her at home because her man is always there, always drunk, always able, in the course of an hour, to remind me how miserable and stupid I am. How horrible my life will become, just as soon as I age out. How my options are the streets or jail or overclocking; what they'll do to me in each of those places. So now we meet up on the subway, and ride to Brooklyn Bridge and then back to Burnside.

Arm flab jiggled as she fanned herself. Mom is happy in her fat. Heroin kept her skinny; crack gave her lots of exercise. For her, obesity is a brightly colored sign that says *NOT ADDICTED ANYMORE.* Her man keeps her fed; this is what makes someone a Good Man. Brakes screamed as a downtown train pulled into the station.

"Oooh, stop, wait," she said, grabbing at my pantleg with one puffy hand. "Let's catch the next one. I wanna finish my cigarette."

I got on the train. She came, too, finally, hustling, flustered, barely making it.

"What's gotten into you today?" she said, when she wrestled her pocketbook free from the doors. "You upset about something? You're never this," and she snapped her fingers in the air while she looked for the word *assertive.* I had it in my head. I would not give it to her. Finally she just waved her hand and sat down. "Oh, that air conditioning feels good."

"José? How's he?"

"Fine, fine," she said, still fanning from force of habit. Fifty-degree air pumped directly down on us from the ceiling ducts.

"And you?"

"Fine."

"Mom—I wanted to ask you something."

"Anything, my love," she said, fanning faster.

"You said one time that all the bad decisions you made—none of it would have happened if you could just keep yourself from falling in love."

When I'm with my mom my words never come out wrong. I think it's because I kind of hate her.

"I said that?"

"You did."

"Weird."

"What did you mean?"

"Christ, honey, I don't know." The *Post* slowed, stopped, settled into her lap. "It's stupid, but there's nothing I won't do for a man I love. A woman who's looking for a man to plug a hole she's got inside? She's in trouble."

"Yeah," I said.

Below us, the Bronx scrolled by. Sights I'd been seeing all my life. The same sooty sides of buildings; the same cop cars on every block looking for boys like me. I thought of Case, then, and clean sharp joy pushed out all my fear. My eyes shut, from the pleasure of remembering him, and saw a glorious rush of ported imagery. Movie stills; fashion spreads; unspeakable obscenity. Not blurry this time; requiring no extra effort. I wondered what was different. I knew my mouth was open in an idiot grin, somewhere in a southbound subway car, but I didn't care, and I stood knee-deep in a river of images until the elevated train went underground after 161st Street.

* * *

WE ARE THE CLOUD, said the sign on the door, atop a sea of multicolored dots with stylized wireless signals bouncing between them.

Walking in with Case, I saw that maybe I had oversold the place by saying it was "nice." Nicer than the ones by Lincoln Hospital, maybe, where people come covered in blood and puke, having left against medical advice after spasming out in a public housing stairwell. But still. It wasn't *actually* nice.

Older people nodded off on benches, smelling of shit and hunger. Gross as it was, I liked those offices. All those ports started a pleasant buzzing in my head. Like we added up to something.

"Look at that guy," Case said, sitting down on the bench beside me. He pointed to a man whose head was tilted back, gurgling up a steady stream of phlegm that had soaked his shirt and was dripping onto the floor.

"Overclocked," I said, and stopped. His shoulder felt good against my bicep. "Some people. Sell more than they should. Of their brain."

Sell enough of it, and they'd put you up in one of their Node Care Facilities, grim nursing homes for thirty-something vegetables and doddering senior citizens in their twenties, but once you were in you were never coming out, because people ported that hard could barely walk a block or speak a sentence, let alone obtain and hold meaningful employment.

And if I didn't want to end up on the street, that was my only real option. I'd been to job interviews. Some I walked into on my own; some the system set up for me. Nothing was out there for anyone, let alone a frowning, stammering tower of man who more than one authority figure had referred to as a "fucking imbecile."

"What about him?" Case asked, pointing to another guy whose hands and legs twitched too rhythmically and regularly for it to be a dream.

"Clouddiving," I said.

He laughed. "I thought only retards could do that."

"That's," I said. "Not."

"Okay," he said, when he saw I wouldn't be saying anything else on the subject.

I wanted very badly to cry. *Only retards.* A part of me had thought maybe I could share it with Case, tell him what I could do. But of course I couldn't. I fast-blinked, each brief shutting of my eyes showing a flurry of cloud-snatched photographs.

Ten minutes later I caught him smiling at me, maybe realizing he had said something wrong. I wanted so badly for Case to see inside my head. What I was. How I wasn't an imbecile, or a retard.

Our eyes locked. I leaned forward. Hungry for him to see me, the way no one else ever had. I wanted to tell him what I could do. How I could access data. How sometimes I thought I could maybe *control* data. How I dreamed of using it to burn everything down. But I wasn't strong enough to think those things, let alone say them. Some secrets you can't share, no matter how badly you want to.

* * *

I went back alone. Case had somewhere to be. It hurt, realizing he had things in his life I knew nothing about. I climbed the steps and a voice called from the front-porch darkness.

"Awful late," Guerra said. The stubby man who ran the place: Most of his body weight was gristle and mustache. He stole our stuff and ate our food and took bribes from dealer residents to get rivals logged out. In the dark I knew he couldn't even see who I was.

"Nine," I said. "It's not. O'clock."

He sucked the last of his Coke through a straw, in the noisiest manner imaginable. "Whatever."

Salvation Army landscapes clotted the walls. Distant mountains and day-break forests, smelling like cigarette smoke, carpet cleaner, thruway exhaust. There was a sadness to the place I hadn't noticed before, not even when I was hating it. In the living room, a boy knelt before the television. Another slept on the couch. In the poor light, I couldn't tell if one of them was the one who had hurt Case.

There were so many of us in the system. We could add up to an army. Why did we all hate and fear each other so much? Friendships formed from time to time, but they were weird and tinged with what-can-I-get-from-you, liable to shatter at any moment as allegiances shifted or kids got transferred. If all the violence we visited on ourselves could be turned outwards, maybe we could—

But only danger was in that direction. I thought of my mom's man, crippled in a prison riot, living fat off the settlement, saying, drunk, once, *Only thing the Man fears more than one of us is a lot of us.*

I went back to my room, and got down on the floor, under the window. And shut my eyes. And dove.

Into spreadsheets and songs and grainy CCTV feeds and old films and pages scanned from books that no longer existed anywhere in the world. Whatever the telecom happens to be porting through you at that precise moment.

Only damaged people can dive. Something to do with how the brain processes speech. Every time I did it, I was terrified. Convinced they'd see me, and come for me. But that night I wanted something badly enough to balance out the being afraid.

Eyes shut, I let myself melt into data. Shuffled faster and faster, pulled back far enough to see Manhattan looming huge and epic with mountains of data at Wall Street and Midtown. Saw the Bronx, a flat spread of tiny data heaps here and there. I held my breath, seeing it, feeling certain no one had ever seen it like this before, money and megabytes in massive spiraling loops, unspeakably gorgeous and fragile. I could see how much money would be lost if the flow was broken for even a single second, and I could see where all the fault lines lay. But I wasn't looking for that. I was looking for Case.

*　　*　　*

And then: Case came knocking. Like I had summoned him up from the datastream. Like what I wanted actually mattered outside of my head.

"Hey there, mister," he said, when I opened my door.

I took a few steps backwards.

He shut the door and sat down on my bed. "You've got a Game Boy, right? I saw the headphones." I didn't respond, and he said, "Damn, dude, I'm not trying to steal your stuff, okay? I have one of my own. Wondered if you wanted to play together." Case flashed his, bright red to my blue one.

"The thing," I said. "I don't have. The cable."

He patted his pants pocket. "That's okay, I do."

We sat on the bed, shoulders touching, backs against the wall, and played *Mega Man 2*. Evil robots came at us by the dozen to die.

I touched the cord with one finger. Such a primitive thing, to need a physical connection. Case smelled like soap, but not the Ivory they give you in the system. Like cream, I thought, but that wasn't right. To really describe it I'd need a whole new world of words no one ever taught me.

"That T-shirt looks good on you," he said. "Makes you look like a gym boy."

"I'm not. It's just . . . what there was. What was there. In the donation bin. Once Guerra picked out all the good stuff. Hard to find clothes that fit when you're six six."

"It does fit, though."

Midway through Skull Man's level, Case said: "You talk funny sometimes. What's up with that?" and I was shocked to see no anger surge through me.

"It's a thing. A speech thing. What you call it when people have trouble talking."

"A speech impediment."

I nodded. "But a weird one. Where the words don't come out right. Or don't come out at all. Or come out as the wrong word. Clouding makes it worse."

"I like it," he said, looking at me now instead of Mega Man. "It's part of what makes you unique."

We played without talking, tinny music echoing in the little room.

"I don't want to go back to my room. I might get jacked in the hallway."

"Yeah," I said.

"Can I stay here? I'll sleep on the floor."

"Yeah."

"You're the best, Sauro." And there were his hands again, rubbing the top of my head. He took off his shirt and began to make a bed on my floor. Fine black hair covers almost all of me, but Case's body was mostly bare. My throat hurt with how bad I wanted to put my hands on him. I got into bed with my boxers on, embarrassed by what was happening down there.

*   *   *

"Sauro," he whispered, suddenly beside me in the bed.

I grunted; stumbled coming from dreams to reality.

His body was spooned in front of mine. "Is this okay?"

"Yes. Yes, it is." I tightened my arms around him. His warmth and smell stiffened me. And then his head had turned, his mouth was moving down my belly, his body pinning me to the bed, which was good, because God had turned off gravity and the slightest breeze would have had me floating right out the window and into space.

*   *   *

"You ever do this before? With a guy?"

"Not out loud—I mean, not in real life."

"You've thought about it."

"Yeah."

"You've thought about it a lot."

"Yeah."

"Why didn't you ever do it?

"I don't know."

"You were afraid of what people might think?"

"No."

"Then what *were* you afraid of?"

Losing control was what I wanted to say, or *giving someone power over me*, or *making a mess.*

Or: *The boys that make me feel like you make me feel turn me into something stupid, brutish, clumsy, worthless.*

Or: *I knew a gay kid, once, in a group home upstairs from a McDonald's, watched twelve guys hold him down in a locked room until the morning guy came at eight, saw him when they wheeled him towards the ambulance.*

I shrugged. The motion of my shoulders shook his little body.

* * *

I fought sleep as hard and long as I could. I didn't want to not be there. And when I knew I couldn't fight it anymore I let myself sink into data—easy as blinking this time—felt myself ebb out of my cloud port, but instead of following the random data beamed into me by the nearest router, I *reached*—felt my way across the endless black gulf of six inches that separated his cloud port from mine, and found him there, a jagged wobbly galaxy of data, ugly and incongruous, but beautiful, because it was *him,* and because, even if it was only for a moment, he was mine.

Case, I said.

He twitched in his sleep. Said his own name.

I love you, I said.

Asleep, Case said it, too.

* * *

Kentucky Fried Chicken. Thursday morning. For the first time, I didn't feel like life was a fight about to break out, or like everyone wanted to mess with me. Everywhere I went, someone wanted to throw me out—but now the only person who even noticed me was a crazy lady rooting through a McDonald's soda cup of change.

Case asked, "Anyone ever tell you you're a sexy beast?" On my baldness his hands no longer seemed so tiny. My big thick skull was an eggshell.

"Also? Dude? You're *huge.*" He nudged my crotch with his knee. "You know that? Like *off the charts.*"

"Yeah?"

I laughed. His glee was contagious and his hands were moving down my arm and we were sitting in public talking about gay sex and he didn't care and neither did I.

"When I first came to the city, I did some porn," Case said. "I got like five hundred dollars for it."

I chewed slow. Stared at the bones and tendons of the drumstick in my hand. Didn't look up. I thought about what I had done, while clouddiving. How I said his name, and he echoed me. I dreamed of taking him up to the roof at night, snapping my fingers and making the whole Bronx go dark except for Case's name, spelled out in blazing tenement window lights. It would be easy. I could do anything. Because: Case.

"Would you be interested in doing something like that?"

"No."

"Not even for like a million dollars?"

"Maybe a million. But probably not."

"You're funny. You know that? How you follow the rules. All they ever do is get you hurt."

"Getting in trouble means something different for you than it does for me."

Here's what I realized: It wasn't hate that made it easy to talk to my mom. It was love. Love let the words out.

"Why?" he asked.

"Because. What you are."

"Because I'm a sexy mother?"

I didn't grin back.

"Because I'm white."

"Yeah."

"Okay," he said. "Right. You see? The rules are not your friend. Racists made the rules. Racists enforce them."

I put the picked-clean drumstick down.

Case said "Whatever" and the word was hot and long, a question, an accusation. "The world put you where you are, Sauro, but fear keeps you there. You want to never make any decisions. Drift along and hope everything turns out for the best. You know where that'll put you."

The lady with the change cup walked by our table. Snatched a thigh off of Case's plate. "Put that down right this minute, asshole," he said, loud as hell, standing up. For a second the country-bumpkin Case was gone, replaced by someone I'd never seen before. The lady scurried off. Case caught me staring and smiled, *aw-shucks* style.

*　　*　　*

"Stand up," I said. "Go by the window."

He went. Evening sun turned him into something golden.

Men used to paralyze me. My whole life I'd been seeing confident charismatic guys, and thought I could never get to that place. Never have what they had. Now I saw it wasn't what they *had* that I wanted, it was what they *were*. I felt lust, not inferiority, and the two are way too close. Like hate and love.

"You make me feel like food," he said, and then lay himself face down on the floor. "Why don't you come over here?" Scissored his legs open. Turned his head and smiled like all the smiles I ever wanted but did not get.

* * *

Pushing in, I heard myself make a noise that can only be called a bellow.

"Shh," he said, "everyone will hear us."

My hips took on a life of their own. My hands pushed hard, all up and down his body. Case was tiny underneath me. A twig I could break.

Afterwards I heard snoring from down the hall. Someone sobbed. I'd spent so long focused on how full the world was of horrible things. I'd been so conditioned to think that its good things were reserved for someone else that I never saw how many were already within my grasp. In my head, for one thing, where my thoughts were my own and no one could punish me for them, and in the cloud, where I was coming to see that I could do astonishing things. And in bed. And wherever Case was. My eyes filled up and ran over and I pushed my face into the cool nape of his sleeping neck.

* * *

My one and only time in court: I am ten. Mom bought drugs at a bodega. It's her tenth or hundredth time passing through those tall tarnished-bronze doors. Her court date came on one of my rare stints out of the system, when she cleaned up her act convincingly enough that they gave me briefly back to her.

The courtroom is too crowded; the guard tells me to wait outside. "But he's my son," my mother says, pointing out smaller children sitting by their parents.

I am very big for ten.

"He's gotta stay out here," the guard says.

I sit on the floor and count green flecks in the floor. Dark-skinned men surround me, angry but resigned, defiant but hopeless. The floor's sparkle mocks us: our poverty, our mortality, the human needs that brought us here.

*   *   *

"Where I'm from," Case said, "you could put a down payment on a house with two thousand dollars."

"Oh."

"You ever dream about escaping New York?"

"Kind of. In my head."

Case laughed. "What about you and me getting out of town? Moving away?"

My head hurt with how badly I wanted that. "You hated that place. You don't want to go back."

"I hated it because I was alone. If we went back together, I would have you."

"Oh."

His fingers drummed up and down my chest. Ran circles around my nipples. "I called that guy I know. The porn producer. Told him about you. He said he'd give us each five hundred, and another two-fifty for me as a finder's fee."

"You called him? About me?"

"This could be it, Sauro. A new start. For both of us."

"I don't know," I said, but I *did* know. I knew I was lost, that I couldn't say no, that his mouth, now circling my belly button, had only to speak and I would act.

"Are you really such a proper little gentleman?" he asked. His hands, cold as winter, hooked behind my knees. "You never got into trouble before?"

*   *   *

My one time in trouble.

I am five. It's three in the morning. I'm riding my tricycle down the block. A policeman stops me. *Where's your mother/ She's home/ Why aren't you home?/ I was hungry and there's no food.* Mom is on a heroin holiday, lying on the couch while she's somewhere else. For a week I've been stealing food from corner stores. So much cigarette smoke fills the cop car that I can't breathe. At the precinct he leaves me there, windows all rolled up. Later he takes me home, talks to my mom, fills out a report, takes her away. Someone else takes me. Everything ends. All of this is punishment for some crime I committed without realizing it. I resolve right then and there to never again steal food, ride tricycles, talk to cops, think bad thoughts, step outside to get something I need.

*   *   *

Friday afternoon we rode the train to Manhattan. Case took us to a big building, no different on the outside from any other one. A directory on the wall listed a couple dozen tenants. *ARABY STUDIOS* was where we were going.

"I have an appointment with Mr. Goellnitz," Case told a woman at a desk upstairs. The place smelled like paint over black mold. We sat in a waiting room like a doctor's, except with different posters on the walls.

In one, a naked boy squatted on some rocks. A beautiful boy. Fine black hair all over his body. Eyes like lighthouses. Something about his chin and cheekbones turned my knees to hot jelly. Stayed with me when I shut my eyes.

"Who's that?" I asked.

"Just some boy," Case said.

"Does he work here?"

"No one *works here*."

"Oh."

Filming was about to start when I figured out why that boy on the rocks bothered me so much. I had thought only Case could get into my head so hard, make me feel so powerless, so willing to do absolutely anything.

*   *   *

A cinderblock room, dressed up like how Hollywood imagines the projects. Low ceilings and Snoop Dogg posters. Overflowing ashtrays. A pit bull dozing in a corner. A scared little white boy sitting on the couch.

"I'm sorry, Rico, you know I am. You gotta give me another chance."

The dark scary drug dealer towers over him. Wearing a wife beater and a bicycle chain around his neck. A hard-on bobs inside his sweatpants. "That's the last time I lose money on you, punk."

The drug dealer grabs him by the neck, rubs his thumb along the boy's lips, pushes his thumb into the warm wet mouth.

*   *   *

"*Do* it," Goellnitz barked.

"I can't," I said.

"Say the fucking line."

Silence.

"Or I'll throw your ass out of here and neither one of you will get a dime."

Case said "Come on, dude! Just say it."

—and how could I disobey? How could I not do every little thing he asked me to do?

Porn was like cloudporting, like foster care. One more way they used you up.

One more weapon you could use against them.

I shut my eyes and made my face a snarl. Hissed out each word, one at a time, to make sure I'd only have to say it once

"That's." "Right." "Bitch." I spat on his back, hit him hard in the head. "Tell." "Me." "You." "Like it." Off camera, in the mirror, Case winked.

Where did it come from, the strength to say all that? To say all that, and do all the other things I never knew I could do? Case gave it to me. Case, and the cloud, which I could feel and see now even with my eyes open, even without thinking about it, sweet and clear as the smell of rain.

*   *   *

"Damn, dude," Case said, while they switched to the next camera set-up. "You're actually kind of a good actor with how you deliver those lines." He was naked; he was fearless. I cowered on the couch, a towel covering as much of me as I could manage. What was it in Case that made him so certain nothing bad would happen to him? At first I chalked it up to white skin, but now I wasn't sure it was so simple. His eyes were on the window. His mind was already elsewhere.

*   *   *

The showers were echoey, like TV high school locker rooms. We stood there, naked, side by side. I slapped Case's ass, and when he didn't respond I did it again, and when he didn't respond I stood behind him and kissed the back of his neck. He didn't say or do a thing. So I left the shower to go get dressed.

"Did I hurt you?" I hollered, when ten minutes had gone by and he was still standing under the water.

"What? No."

"Oh."

He wasn't moving. Wasn't soaping or lathering or rinsing.

"Is everything okay?" Making my voice warm, to hide how cold I suddenly felt.

"Yeah. It was just . . . intense. Sex usually isn't. For me."

His voice was weird and sad and not exactly nice. I sat on a bench and watched him get harder and harder to see as the steam built up.

* * *

"Would you mind heading up to the House ahead of me?" he said, finally. "I need some time to get my head together. I'll square up things with the director and be there soon."

"Waiting is cool."

"No. It's not. I need some alone time."

"Alone time," I smirked. "You're a—"

"You need to get the hell back, Angel. Okay?"

Hearing the hardness in his voice, I wondered if there was a way to spontaneously stop being alive.

* * *

"I got your cash right here," the director said, flapping an envelope at me.

"He'll get it," I said, knowing it was stupid. "My boyfriend."

"You sure?"

I nodded.

"Here's my business card. I hoped you might think about being in something of mine again sometime. Your friend's only got a few more flicks in him. Twinks burn out fast. You, on the other hand—you've got something special. You could have a long career."

"Thanks," I said, nodding, furious, too tall, too retarded, too sensitive, hating myself the whole way down the elevator, and the whole walk to the subway, and the whole ride back to what passed for home.

When the train came above ground after 149th Street, I felt the old shudder as my cloud port clicked back into the municipal grid. Shame and anger made me brave, and I dove. I could see the car as data, saw transmissions to and from a couple dozen cell phones and tablets and biodevices, saw how the train's forward momentum warped the information flowing in and out. Saw ten jagged blobs inside, my fellow cloudbounds. Reached out again, like I had with Case. Felt myself slip through one after another like a thread through ten needles. Tugged that thread the tiniest bit, and watched all ten bow their heads as one.

* * *

Friday night I stayed up 'til three in the morning, waiting for Case to come knocking. I played the Skull Man level on *Mega Man 2* until I could beat it without getting hit by a single enemy. I dove into the cloud, hunted down maps, opened up whole secret worlds. I fell asleep like that, and woke up wet from fevered dreams of Case.

Saturday—still no sign of him.

Sunday morning I called Guerra's cell phone, a strict no-no on the weekends.

"This better be an emergency, Sauro," he said.

"Did you log Case out?"

"Case?"

"The white boy."

"You call me up to bother me with your business deals? No, jackass, I didn't log him out. I haven't seen him. Thanks for reminding me, though. I'll phone him in as missing on Monday morning."

"You—"

But Guerra had gone.

* * *

First thing Monday, I rode the subway into Manhattan and walked into that office like I had as much right as anyone else to occupy any square meter of space in this universe. I worried I wouldn't be able to, without Case. I didn't know what this new thing coming awake inside me was, but I knew it made me strong. Enough.

The porn man gave me a hundred dollars, no strings attached. Said to keep him in mind, said he had some scripts that I could "transform from low-budget bullshit into something really special."

He was afraid of me. He was right to be afraid, but not for the reason he thought. I could clouddive and wipe Araby Studios out of existence in the time it took him to blink his eyes. I could see his fear, and I could see how he wanted me anyway for the money he could make off me. There was so much to see, once you're ready to look for it.

Maybe I was right the first time: It *had* been hate that made it easy to talk to my mom. Love can make us become what we need to be, but so can hate. Case was gone, but the words kept coming. Life is nothing but acting.

*   *   *

I could have:

1) Given Guerra the hundred dollars to track Case down. He'd call his contacts down at the department; he'd hand me an address. Guerra would do the same job for fifty bucks, but for a hundred he'd bow and *yessir* like a good little lackey.

2) Smiled my way into every placement house in the city, knocked on every door to every tiny room until I found him.

3) Hung around outside Araby Studios, wait for him to snivel back with his latest big, dumb, dark stud. Wait in the shower until he went to wash his ass out, kick him to the floor, fuck him endlessly and extravagantly. Reach up into him, seize hold of his heart and tear it to shreds with bare bloody befouled hands.

The image of him in the shower brought me to a full and instant erection. I masturbated, hating myself, trying hard to focus on a scenario where I hurt him . . . but even in my own revenge fantasy I wanted to wrap my body around his and keep him safe.

*   *   *

Afterwards I amended my revenge scenario list to include:

1) Finding someone else to screw over, some googly-eyed blond boy looking to plug a hole he has inside.
2) Becoming the most famous, richest, biggest gay porn star in history, traveling the world, standing naked on sharp rocks in warm oceans. Becoming what they wanted me to be, just long enough to get a paycheck. Seeing Case in the bargain bin someday; seeing him in the gutter.
3) Burning down every person and institution that profited off the suffering of others.
4) Becoming the kept animal of some rich, powerful queen who will parade me at fancy parties and give me anything I need as long as I do him the favor of regularly fucking him into a state of such quivering sweat-soaked helplessness that childhood trauma and white guilt and global warming all evaporate.
5) Finding someone who I will never, ever, ever screw over.

Really, they were all good plans. None of it was off the table.

*   *   *

Leaving the office building, I ignored all the instincts that screamed *get on the subway and get the hell out of here before some cop stops you for matching a description!* Standing on a street corner for no reason felt magnificent and forbidden.

I shut my eyes. Reached out into the cloud, felt myself magnified like any other signal by the wireless routers that filled the city. Found the seams of the infrastructure that kept the flow of data in place. The weak spots. The ways to snap or bend or reconstruct that flow. How to erase any and all criminal records; pay the rent for my mom and every other sad sack in the Bronx for all eternity. Divert billions in banker dividends into the debit accounts of cloudporters everywhere.

I pushed, and when nothing happened I pushed harder.

A tiny *pop,* and smoke trickled up from the wireless router atop the nearest lamppost. Nothing more. My whole body dripped with sweat. Some dripped into my eyes. It stung. Ten minutes had passed, and felt like five seconds. My muscles ached like after a hundred push-ups. All those things that had seemed so easy—I wasn't strong enough to do them on my own.

Fear keeps you where you are, Case said. Finally I could see that he was right, but I could see something else that he couldn't see. Because he thought small, and because he only thought about himself.

Fear keeps us separate.

I shut my eyes again, and reached. A ritzy part of town; hardly any cloud-bounds in the immediate area. The nearest one was in a bar down the block.

"What'll you have," the bartender said, when I got there. He didn't ask for ID.

"Boy on the rocks," I said, and then kicked at the stool. "Shit. No. Scotch. Scotch on the rocks."

"Sure," he said.

"And for that guy," I said, pointing down the bar to the passed-out over-clocked man I had sensed from outside. "One. Thing. The same."

I took my drink to a booth in the front, where I could see out the window. I took a sip. I reached further, eyes open this time, until I found twenty more cloudporters, some as far as fifty blocks away, and threaded us together.

The slightest additional effort, and I was everywhere. All five boroughs—thousands of cloudporters looped through me. With all of us put together I felt inches away from snapping the city in two. Again I reached out and felt for optimal fracture points. Again I pushed. Gently, this time.

An explosion, faraway but huge. *Con Edison's east side substation,* I saw, in the six milliseconds before the station's failure overloaded transmission lines and triggered a cascading failure that killed all electricity to the tri-state region.

I smiled, in the darkness, over my second sip. Within a week the power would be back on. And I—we—could get to work. Whatever that would be. Stealing money; exterminating our exploiters; leveling the playing field. Finding Case, forging a cyberterrorism manifesto, blaming the blackout on him, sending a pulse of electricity through his body precisely calibrated to par-alyze him perfectly.

On my third sip I saw I still wasn't sure I wanted to hurt him. Maybe he'd done me wrong, but so had my mom. So had lots of folks. And I wouldn't be what I was without them.

Scotch tastes like smoke, like old men. I drank slow so I wouldn't get too drunk. I had never walked into a bar before. I always imagined cops coming out of the corners to drag me off to jail. But that wasn't how the world worked. Nothing was stopping me from walking into wherever I wanted to go.

NEBULA AWARD WINNER
BEST NOVELETTE

"A GUIDE TO THE FRUITS OF HAWAI'I"

ALAYA DAWN JOHNSON

Alaya Dawn Johnson has been the winner of two Nebula Awards and an Andre Norton Award. She has also received nominations for the Nebula, Parallax, Kindred, and National Book Awards. "A Guide to the Fruits of Hawai'i" was first published in Fantasy and Science Fiction.

Key's favorite time of day is sunset, her least is sunrise. It should be the opposite, but every time she watches that bright red disk sinking into the water beneath Mauna Kea her heart bends like a wishbone, and she thinks, *He's awake now.*

Key is thirty-four. She is old for a human woman without any children. She has kept herself alive by being useful in other ways. For the past four years, Key has been the overseer of the Mauna Kea Grade Orange blood facility.

Is it a concentration camp if the inmates are well fed? If their beds are comfortable? If they are given an hour and a half of rigorous boxercise and yoga each morning in the recreational field?

It doesn't have to be Honouliui to be wrong.

When she's called in to deal with Jeb's body—bloody, not drained, in a feeding room—yoga doesn't make him any less dead.

Key helps vampires run a concentration camp for humans.

Key is a different kind of monster.

*   *   *

Key's favorite food is umeboshi. Salty and tart and bright red, with that pit in the center to beware. She loves it in rice balls, the kind her Japanese grandmother made when she was little. She loves it by itself, the way she ate it at fifteen, after Obachan died. She hasn't had umeboshi in eighteen years, but sometimes she thinks that when she dies she'll taste one again.

This morning she eats the same thing she eats every meal: a nutritious brick patty, precisely five inches square and two inches deep, colored puce. Her raw scrubbed hands still have a pink tinge of Jeb's blood in the cuticles. She stares at them while she sips the accompanying beverage, which is orange. She can't remember if it ever resembled the fruit.

She eats this because that is what every human eats in the Mauna Kea facility. Because the patty is easy to manufacture and soft enough to eat with plastic spoons. Key hasn't seen a fork in years, a knife in more than a decade. The vampires maintain tight control over all items with the potential to draw blood. Yet humans are tool-making creatures, and their desires, even nihilistic ones, have a creative power that no vampire has the imagination or agility to anticipate. How else to explain the shiv, handcrafted over secret months from the wood cover and glue-matted pages of *A Guide to the Fruits of Hawai'i*, the book that Jeb used to read in the hours after his feeding sessions, sometimes aloud, to whatever humans would listen? He took the only thing that gave him pleasure in the world, destroyed it—or recreated it—and slit his veins with it. Mr. Charles questioned her particularly; he knew that she and Jeb used to talk sometimes. Had she *known* that the *boy* was like this? He gestured with pallid hands at the splatter of arterial pulses from jaggedly slit wrists: oxidized brown, inedible, mocking.

No, she said, of course not, Mr. Charles. I report any suspected cases of self-waste immediately.

She reports any suspected cases. And so, for the weeks she has watched Jeb hardly eating across the mess hall, noticed how he staggered from the feeding rooms, recognized the frigid rebuff in his responses to her questions, she has very carefully refused to suspect.

Today, just before dawn, she choked on the fruits of her indifference. He slit his wrists and femoral arteries. He smeared the blood over his face and buttocks and genitals, and he waited to die before the vampire technician could arrive to drain him.

Not many humans self-waste. Most think about it, but Key never has, not since the invasion of the Big Island. Unlike other humans, she has someone she's waiting for. The one she loves, the one she prays will reward her patience.

During her years as overseer, Key has successfully stopped three acts of self-waste. She has failed twice. Jeb is different; Mr. Charles sensed it somehow, but vampires can only read human minds through human blood. Mr. Charles hasn't drunk from Key in years. And what could he learn, even if he did? He can't drink thoughts she has spent most of her life refusing to have.

*　　*　　*

Mr. Charles calls her to the main office the next night, between feeding shifts. She is terrified, like she always is, of what they might do. She is thinking of Jeb and wondering how Mr. Charles has taken the loss of an investment. She is wondering how fast she will die in the work camp on Lanai.

But Mr. Charles has an offer, not a death sentence.

"You know . . . of the facility on Oahu? Grade Gold?"

"Yes," Key says. Just that, because she learned early not to betray herself to them unnecessarily, and the man at Grade Gold has always been her greatest betrayer.

No, not a man, Key tells herself for the hundredth, the thousandth time. *He is one of them.*

Mr. Charles sits in a hanging chair shaped like an egg with plush red velvet cushions. He wears a black suit with steel gray pinstripes, sharply tailored. The cuffs are high and his feet are bare, white as talcum powder and long and bony like spiny fish. His veins are prominent and round and milky blue. Mr. Charles is vain about his feet.

He does not sit up to speak to Key. She can hardly see his face behind the shadow cast by the overhanging top of the egg. All vampires speak deliberately, but Mr. Charles drags out his tones until you feel you might tip over from waiting on the next syllable. It goes up and down like a calliope—

". . . what do you *say* to heading down there and *sort*ing the matter . . . out?"

"I'm sorry, Mr. Charles," she says carefully, because she has lost the thread of his monologue. "What matter?"

He explains: a Grade Gold human girl has killed herself. It is a disaster that outshadows the loss of Jeb.

"You would not believe the expense taken to keep those humans Grade Gold standard."

"What would I do?"

"Take it in hand, *of* course. It seems our small . . . Grade Orange operation has gotten some notice. Tetsuo asked for you . . . particularly."

"Tetsuo?" She hasn't said the name out loud in years. Her voice catches on the second syllable.

"*Mr.* Tetsuo," Mr. Charles says, and waves a hand at her. He holds a sheet of paper, the same shade as his skin. "He wrote you a *letter.*"

Key can't move, doesn't reach out to take it, and so it flutters to the black marble floor a few feet away from Mr. Charles's egg.

He leans forward. "I think . . . I remember something . . . you and Tetsuo . . ."

"He recommended my promotion here," Key says, after a moment. It seems the safest phrasing. Mr. Charles would have remembered this eventually; vampires are slow, but inexorable.

The diffuse light from the paper lanterns catches the bottom half of his face, highlighting the deep cleft in his chin. It twitches in faint surprise. "You *were* his pet?"

Key winces. She remembers the years she spent at his side during and after the wars, catching scraps in his wake, despised by every human who saw her there. She waited for him to see how much she had sacrificed and give her the only reward that could matter after what she'd done. Instead he had her shunt removed and sent her to Grade Orange. She has not seen or heard from him in four years. His pet, yes, that's as good a name as any—but he never drank from her. Not once.

Mr. Charles's lips, just a shade of white darker than his skin, open like a hole in a cloud. "And he wants you back. How do you *feel?*"

Terrified. Awestruck. Confused. "Grateful," she says.

The hole smiles. "Grateful! How interesting. Come here, girl. I believe I shall *have* a *taste.*"

She grabs the letter with shaking fingers and folds it inside a pocket of her red uniform. She stands in front of Mr. Charles.

"Well?" he says.

She hasn't had a shunt in years, though she can still feel its ridged scar in the crook of her arm. Without it, feeding from her is messy, violent. Traditional, Mr. Charles might say. Her fingers hurt as she unzips the collar. Her muscles feel sore, the bones in her spine arthritic and old as she bows her head, leans closer to Mr. Charles. She waits for him to bare his fangs, to pierce her vein, to suck her blood.

He takes more than he should. He drinks until her fingers and toes twinge, until her neck throbs, until the red velvet of his seat fades to gray. When he finishes, he leaves her blood on his mouth.

"I forgive . . . you for the boy," he says.

Jeb cut his own arteries, left his good blood all over the floor. Mr. Charles abhors waste above all else.

*   *   *

Mr. Charles will explain the situation. I wish you to come. If you do well, I have been authorized to offer you the highest reward.

*   *   *

The following night, Key takes a boat to Oahu. Vampires don't like water, but they will cross it anyway—the sea has become a status symbol among them, an indication of strength. Hawai'i is still a resort destination, though most of its residents only go out at night. Grade Gold is the most expensive, most luxurious resort of them all.

Tetsuo travels between the islands often. Key saw him do it a dozen times during the war. She remembers one night, his face lit by the moon and the yellow lamps on the deck—the wide cheekbones, thick eyebrows, sharp widow's peak, all frozen in the perfection of a nineteen-year-old boy. Pale beneath the olive tones of his skin, he bares his fangs when the waves lurch beneath him.

"What does it feel like?" she asks him.

"Like frozen worms in my veins," he says, after a full, long minute of silence. Then he checks the guns and tells her to wait below, the humans are coming. She can't see anything, but Tetsuo can smell them like chum in the water. The Japanese have held out the longest, and the vampires of Hawai'i lead the assault against them.

Two nights later, in his quarters in the bunker at the base of Mauna Kea, Tetsuo brings back a sheet of paper, written in Japanese. The only characters she recognizes are "shi" and "ta"—"death" and "field." It looks like some kind of list.

"What is this?" she asks.

"Recent admissions to the Lanai human residential facility."

She looks up at him, devoted with terror. "My mother?" Her father died in the first offensive on the Big Island, a hero of the resistance. He never knew how his daughter had chosen to survive.

"Here," Tetsuo says, and runs a cold finger down the list without death. "Jen Isokawa."

"Alive?" She has been looking for her mother since the wars began. Tetsuo knows this, but she didn't know he was searching, too. She feels swollen with this indication of his regard.

"She's listed as a caretaker. They're treated well. You could . . ." He sits beside her on the bed that only she uses. His pause lapses into a stop. He strokes her hair absentmindedly; if she had a tail, it would beat his legs. She is seventeen and she is sure he will reward her soon.

"Tetsuo," she says, "you could drink from me, if you want. I've had a shunt for nearly a year. The others use it. I'd rather feed you."

Sometimes she has to repeat herself three times before he seems to hear her. This, she has said at least ten. But she is safe here in his bunker, on the bed he brought in for her, with his lukewarm body pressed against her warm one. Vampires do not have sex with humans; they feed. But if he doesn't want her that way, what else can she offer him?

"I've had you tested. You're fertile. If you bear three children you won't need a shunt and the residential facilities will care for you for the rest of your mortality. You can live with your mother. I will make sure you're safe."

She presses her face against his shoulder. "Don't make me leave."

"You wanted to see your mother."

Her mother had spent the weeks before the invasion in church, praying for God to intercede against the abominations. Better that she die than see Key like this.

"Only to know what happened to her," Key whispers. "Won't you feed from me, Tetsuo? I want to feel closer to you. I want you to know how much I love you."

A long pause. Then, "I don't need to taste you to know how you feel."

*   *   *

Tetsuo meets her on shore.

Just like that, she is seventeen again.

"You look older," he says. Slowly, but with less affectation than Mr. Charles. This is true; so inevitable she doesn't understand why he even bothers to say so. Is he surprised? Finally, she nods. The buoyed dock rocks beneath them—he makes no attempt to move, though the two vampires with him grip the denuded skin of their own elbows with pale fingers. They flare and retract their fangs.

"You are drained," he says. He does not mean this metaphorically.

She nods again, realizes further explanation is called for. "Mr. Charles," she says, her voice a painful rasp. This embarrasses her, though Tetsuo would never notice.

He nods, sharp and curt. She thinks he is angry, though perhaps no one else could read him as clearly. She knows that face, frozen in the countenance of a boy dead before the Second World War. A boy dead fifty years before she was born.

He is old enough to remember Pearl Harbor, the detention camps, the years when Maui's forests still had native birds. But she has never dared ask him about his human life.

"And what did Charles explain?"

"He said someone killed herself at Grade Gold."

Tetsuo flares his fangs. She flinches, which surprises her. She used to flush at the sight of his fangs, her blood pounding red just beneath the soft surface of her skin.

"I've been given dispensation," he says, and rests one finger against the hollow at the base of her throat.

She's learned a great deal about the rigid traditions that restrict vampire life since she first met Tetsuo. She understands why her teenage fantasies of morally liberated vampirism were improbable, if not impossible. For each human they bring over, vampires need a special dispensation that they only receive once or twice every decade. *The highest reward.* If Tetsuo has gotten a dispensation, then her first thought when she read his letter was correct. He didn't mean retirement. He didn't mean a peaceful life in some remote farm on the islands. He meant death. Un-death.

After all these years, Tetsuo means to turn her into a vampire.

*   *   *

The trouble at Grade Gold started with a dead girl. Penelope cut her own throat five days ago (with a real knife, the kind they allow Grade Gold humans for cutting food). Her ghost haunts the eyes of those she left behind. One human resident in particular, with hair dyed the color of tea and blue lipstick to match the bruises under her red eyes, takes one look at Key and starts to scream.

Key glances at Tetsuo, but he has forgotten her. He stares at the girl as if he could burn her to ashes on the plush green carpet. The five others in the room look away, but Key can't tell if it's in embarrassment or fear. The luxury surrounding them chokes her. There's a bowl of fruit on a coffee table. Real fruit—fuzzy brown kiwis, mottled red-green mangos, dozens of tangerines. She takes an involuntary step forward and the girl's scream gets louder before cutting off with an abrupt squawk. Her labored breaths are the only sound in the room.

"This is a joke," the girl says. There's spittle on her blue lips. "What hole did you dig her out of?"

"Go to your room, Rachel," Tetsuo says.

Rachel flicks back her hair and rubs angrily under one eye. "What are you now, Daddy Vampire? You think you can just, what? Replace her? With this broke down fogie look-alike?"

"She is not—"

"Yeah? What is she?"

They are both silent, doubt and grief and fury scuttling between them like beetles in search of a meal. Tetsuo and the girl stare at each other with such deep familiarity that Key feels forgotten, alone—almost ashamed of the dreams that have kept her alive for a decade. They have never felt so hopeless, or so false.

"Her name is Key," Tetsuo says, in something like defeat. He turns away, though he makes no move to leave. "She will be your new caretaker."

"Key?" the girl says. "What kind of a name is that?"

Key doesn't answer for a long time, thinking of all the ways she could respond. Of Obachan Akiko and the affectionate nickname of lazy summers spent hiking in the mountains or pounding mochi in the kitchen. Of her half-Japanese mother and Hawai'ian father, of the ways history and identity and circumstance can shape a girl into half a woman, until someone—*not a man*—comes with a hundred thousand others like him and destroys anything that might have once had meaning. So she finds meaning in him. Who else was there?

And this girl, whose sneer reveals her bucked front teeth, has as much chance of understanding that world as Key does of understanding this one.

Fresh fruit on the table. No uniforms. And a perfect, glittering shunt of plastic and metal nestled in the crook of her left arm.

"Mine," Key answers the girl.

Rachel spits; Tetsuo turns his head, just a little, as though he can only bear to see Key from the corner of his eye.

"You're nothing like her," she says.

"Like who?"

But the girl storms from the room, leaving her chief vampire without a dismissal. Key now understands this will not be punished. It's another one—a boy, with the same florid beauty as the girl but far less belligerence, who answers her.

"You look like Penelope," he says, tugging on a long lock of his asymmetrically cut black hair. "Just older."

When Tetsuo leaves the room, it's Key who cannot follow.

*   *   *

Key remembers sixteen. Her obachan is dead and her mother has moved to an apartment in Hilo and it's just Key and her father in that old, quiet house at the end of the road. The vampires have annexed San Diego and Okinawa is besieged, but life doesn't feel very different in the mountains of the Big Island.

It is raining in the woods behind her house. Her father has told her to study, but all she's done since her mother left is read Mishima's *Sea of Fertility* novels. She sits on the porch, wondering if it's better to kill herself or wait for them to come, and just as she thinks she ought to have the courage to die, something rattles in the shed. A rat, she thinks.

But it's not rat she sees when she pulls open the door on its rusty hinges. It's a man, crouched between a stack of old appliance boxes and the rusted fender of the Buick her father always meant to fix one day. His hair is wet and slicked back, his white shirt is damp and ripped from shoulder to navel. The skin beneath it is pale as a corpse; bloodless, though the edges of a deep wound are still visible.

"They've already come?" Her voice breaks on a whisper. She wanted to finish *The Decay of the Angel*. She wanted to see her mother once more.

"Shut the door," he says, crouching in shadow, away from the bar of light streaming through the narrow opening.

"Don't kill me."

"We are equally at each other's mercy."

She likes the way he speaks. No one told her they could sound so proper. So human. Is there a monster in her shed, or is he something else?

"Why shouldn't I open it all the way?"

He is brave, whatever else. He takes his long hands from in front of his face and stands, a flower blooming after rain. He is beautiful, though she will not mark that until later. Now, she only notices the steady, patient way he regards her. *I could move faster than you*, his eyes say. *I could kill you first.*

She thinks of Mishima and says, "I'm not afraid of death."

Only when the words leave her mouth does she realize how deeply she has lied. Does he know? Her hands would shake if it weren't for their grip on the handle.

"I promise," he says. "I will save you, when the rest of us come."

What is it worth, a monster's promise?

She steps inside and shuts out the light.

*　　*　　*

There are nineteen residents of Grade Gold; the twentieth is buried beneath the kukui tree in the communal garden. The thought of rotting in earth revolts Key. She prefers the bright, fierce heat of a crematorium fire, like the one that consumed Jeb the night before she left Mauna Kea. The ashes fly in the wind, into the ocean and up in the trees, where they lodge in bird nests and caterpillar silk and mud puddles after a storm. The return of flesh to the earth should be fast and final, not the slow mortification of worms and bacteria and carbon gases.

Tetsuo instructs her to keep close watch on unit three. "Rachel isn't very . . . steady right now," he says, as though unaware of the understatement.

The remaining nineteen residents are divided into four units, five kids in each, living together in sprawling ranch houses connected by walkways and gardens. There are walls, of course, but you have to climb a tree to see them. The kids at Grade Gold have more freedom than any human she's ever encountered since the war, but they're as bound to this paradise as she was to her mountain.

The vampires who come here stay in a high glass tower right by the beach. During the day, the black-tinted windows gleam like lasers. At night, the vampires come down to feed. There is a fifth house in the residential village, one reserved for clients and their meals. Testsuo orchestrates these encounters, planning each interaction in fine detail: this human with that performance for this distinguished client. Key has grown used to thinking of her fellow humans as food, but now she is forced to reconcile that indelible fact with another, stranger veneer. The vampires who pay so dearly for Grade Gold humans don't merely want to feed from a shunt. They want to be entertained, talked to, cajoled. The boy who explained about Key's uncanny resemblance juggles torches. Twin girls from unit three play guitar and sing songs by the Carpenters. Even Rachel, dressed in a gaudy purple mermaid dress with matching streaks in her hair, keeps up a one-way, laughing conversation with a vampire who seems too astonished—or too slow—to reply.

Key has never seen anything like this before. She thought that most vampires regarded humans as walking sacks of food. What pleasure could be derived from speaking with your meal first? From seeing it sing or dance? When she first went with Tetsuo, the other vampires talked about human emotions as if they were flavors of ice cream. But at Grade Orange she grew accustomed to more basic parameters: were the humans fed, were they fertile, did they sleep? Here, she must approve outfits; she must manage dietary preferences and erratic tempers and a dozen other details all crucial to keeping the kids Grade Gold standard. Their former caretaker has been shipped to the work camps, which leaves Key in sole charge of the operation. At least until Tetsuo decides how he will use his dispensation.

Key's thoughts skitter away from the possibility.

"I didn't know vampires liked music," she says, late in the evening, when some of the kids sprawl, exhausted, across couches and cushions. A girl no older than fifteen opens her eyes but hardly moves when a vampire in a gold suit lifts her arm for a nip. Key and Tetsuo are seated together at the far end of the main room, in the bay windows that overlook a cliff and the ocean.

"It's as interesting to us as any other human pastime."

"Does music have a taste?"

His wide mouth stretches at the edges; she recognizes it as a smile. "Music has some utility, given the right circumstances."

She doesn't quite understand him. The air is redolent with the sweat of human teenagers and the muggy, salty air that blows through the open doors and windows. Her eye catches on a half-eaten strawberry dropped carelessly on the carpet a few feet away. It was harvested too soon, a white, tasteless core surrounded by hard, red flesh.

She thinks there is nothing of "right" in these circumstances, and their utility is, at its bottom, merely that of parasite and host.

"The music enhances the—our—flavor?"

Tetsuo stares at her for a long time, long enough for him to take at least three of his shallow, erratically spaced breaths. To look at him is to taste copper and sea on her tongue; to wait for him is to hear the wind slide down a mountainside an hour before dawn.

It has been four years since she last saw him. She thought he had forgotten her, and now he speaks to her as if all those years haven't passed, as though the vampires hadn't long since won the war and turned the world to their slow, long-burning purpose.

"Emotions change your flavor," he says. "And food. And sex. And pleasure."

And love? she wonders, but Tetsuo has never drunk from her.

"Then why not treat all of us like you do the ones here? Why have con— Mauna Kea?"

She expects him to catch her slip, but his attention is focused on something beyond her right shoulder. She turns to look, and sees nothing but the hall and a closed feeding room door.

"Three years," he says, quietly. He doesn't look at her. She doesn't understand what he means, so she waits. "It takes three years for the complexity to fade. For the vitality of young blood to turn muddy and clogged with silt. Even among the new crops, only a few individuals are Gold standard. For three years, they produce the finest blood ever tasted, filled with regrets and ecstasy and dreams. And then . . ."

"Grade Orange?" Key asks, her voice dry and rasping. Had Tetsuo always talked of humans like this? With such little regard for their selfhood? Had she been too young to understand, or have the years of harvesting humans hardened him?

"If we have not burned too much out. Living at high elevation helps prolong your utility, but sometimes all that's left is Lanai and the work camps."

She remembers her terror before her final interview with Mr. Charles, her conviction that Jeb's death would prompt him to discard his uselessly old overseer to the work camps.

A boy from one of the other houses staggers to the one she recognizes from unit two and sprawls in his lap. Unit-two boy startles awake, smiles, and bends over to kiss the first. A pair of female vampires kneel in front of them and press their fangs with thick pink tongues.

"Touch him," one says, pointing to the boy from unit two. "Make him cry."

The boy from unit two doesn't even pause for breath; he reaches for the other boy's cock and squeezes. And as they both groan with something that makes Key feel like a voyeur, made helpless by her own desire, the pair of vampires pull the boys apart and dive for their respective shunts. The room goes quiet but for soft gurgles, like two minnows in a tide pool. Then a pair of clicks as the boys' shunts turn gray, forcing the vampires to stop feeding.

"Lovely, divine," the vampires say a few minutes later, when they pass on their way out. "We always appreciate the sexual displays."

The boys curl against each other, eyes shut. They breathe like old men: hard, through constricted tubes.

"Does that happen often?" she asks.

"This Grade Gold is known for its sexual flavors. My humans pick partners they enjoy."

Vampires might not have sex, but they crave its flavor. Will she, when she crosses to their side? Will she look at those two boys and command them to fuck each other just so she can taste?

"Do you ever care?" she says, her voice barely a whisper. "About what you've done to us?"

He looks away from her. Before she can blink he has crossed to the one closed feeding room door and wrenched it open. A thump of something thrown against a wall. A snarl, as human as a snake's hiss.

"Leave, Gregory!" Tetsuo says. A vampire Key recognizes from earlier in the night stumbles into the main room. He rubs his jaw, though the torn and mangled skin there has already begun to knit together.

"She is mine to have. I paid—"

"Not enough to kill her."

"I'll complain to the council," the vampire says. "You've been losing support. And everyone knows how *patiently* Charles has waited in his aerie."

She should be scared, but his words make her think of Jeb, of failures and consequences, and of the one human she has not seen for hours. She stands and sprints past both vampires to where Rachel lies insensate on a bed.

Her shunt has turned the opaque gray meant to prevent vampires from feeding humans to death. But the client has bitten her neck instead.

"Tell them whatever you wish, and I will tell them you circumvented the shunt of a fully-tapped human. We have our rules for a reason. You are no longer welcome here."

Rachel's pulse is soft, but steady. She stirs and moans beneath Key's hands. The relief is crushing; she wants to cradle the girl in her arms until she wakes. She wants to protect her so her blood will never have to smear the walls of a feeding room, so that Key will be able to say that at least she saved one.

Rachel's eyes flutter open, land with a butterfly's gentleness on Key's face.

"Pen," she says, "I told you. It makes them . . . they *eat* me."

Key doesn't understand, but she doesn't mind. She presses her hand to Rachel's warm forehead and sings lullabies her grandmother liked until Rachel falls back to sleep.

"How is she?" It is Tetsuo, come into the room after the client has finally left.

"Drained," Key says, as dispassionately as he. "She'll be fine in a few days."

"Key."

"Yes?"

She won't look at him.

"I do, you know."

She knows. "Then why support it?"

"You'll understand when your time comes."

She looks back down at Rachel, and all she can see are bruises blooming purple on her upper arms, blood dried brown on her neck. She looks like a human being: infinitely precious, fragile. Like prey.

* * *

Five days later, Key sits in the garden in the shade of the kukui tree. She has reports to file on the last week's feedings, but the papers sit untouched beside her. The boy from unit two and his boyfriend are tending the tomatoes and Key slowly peels the skin from her fourth kiwi. The first time she bit into one she cried, but the boys pretended not to notice. She is getting better with practice. Her hands still tremble and her misted eyes refract rainbows in the hard, noon sunlight. She is learning to be human again.

Rachel sleeps on the ground beside her, curled on the packed dirt of Penelope's grave with her back against the tree trunk and her arms wrapped tightly around her belly. She's spent most of the last five days sleeping, and Key thinks she has mostly recovered. She's been eating voraciously, foods in wild combinations at all times of day and night. Key is glad. Without the distracting, angry makeup, Rachel's face looks vulnerable and haunted. Jeb had that look in the months before his death. He would sit quietly in the mess hall and stare at the food brick as though he had forgotten how to eat. Jeb had transferred to Mauna Kea within a week of Key becoming overseer. He liked watching the lights of the airplanes at night and he kept two books with him: *The Blind Watchmaker* and *A Guide to the Fruits of Hawai'i*. She talked to him about the latter—had he ever tasted breadfruit or kiwi or cherimoya? None, he said, in a voice so small and soft it sounded inversely proportional to his size. Only a peach, a canned peach, when he was four or five years old. Vampires don't waste fruit on Grade Orange humans.

The covers of both books were worn, the spines cracked, the pages yellowed and brittle at the edges. Why keep a book about fruit you had never tasted and never would eat? Why read at all, when they frowned upon literacy in humans and often banned books outright? She never asked him. Mr. Charles had seen their conversation, though she doubted he had heard it, and requested that she refrain from speaking unnecessarily to the *harv*est.

So when Jeb stared at her across the table with eyes like a snuffed candle, she turned away, she forced her patty into her mouth, she chewed, she reached for her orange drink.

His favorite book became his means of self-destruction. She let him do it. She doesn't know if she feels guilty for not having stopped him, or for being in the position to stop him in the first place. Not two weeks later she rests beneath a kukui tree, the flesh of a fruit she had never expected to taste again turning to green pulp between her teeth. She reaches for another one because she knows how little she deserves this.

But the skin of the fruit at the bottom of the bowl is too soft and fleshy for a kiwi. She pulls it into the light and drops it.

"Are you okay?" It's the boy from unit two—Kaipo. He kneels down and picks up the cherimoya.

"What?" she says, and struggles to control her breathing. She has to appear normal, in control. She's supposed to be their caretaker. But the boy just seems concerned, not judgmental. Rachel rolls onto her back and opens her eyes.

"You screamed," Rachel says, sleep-fogged and accusatory. "You woke me up."

"Who put this in the bowl?" Kaipo asks. "These things are poisonous! They grow on that tree down the hill, but you can't eat them."

Key takes the haunted fruit from him, holding it carefully so as to not bruise it further. "Who told you that?" she asks.

Rachel leans forward, so her chin rests on the edge of Key's lounge chair and the tips of her purple-streaked hair touch Key's thigh. "Tetsuo," she says. "What, did he lie?"

Key shakes her head slowly. "He probably only half-remembered. It's a cherimoya. The flesh is delicious, but the seeds are poisonous."

Rachel's eyes follow her hands. "Like, killing you poisonous?" she asks.

Key thinks back to her father's lessons. "Maybe if you eat them all or grind them up. The tree bark can paralyze your heart and lungs."

Kaipo whistles, and they all watch intently when she wedges her finger under the skin and splits it in half. The white, fleshy pulp looks stark, even a little disquieting against the scaly green exterior. She plucks out the hard, brown seeds and tosses them to the ground. Only then does she pull out a chunk of flesh and put it in her mouth.

Like strawberries and banana pudding and pineapple. Like the summer after Obachan died, when a box of them came to the house as a condolence gift.

"You look like you're fellating it," Rachel says. Key opens her eyes and swallows abruptly.

Kaipo pushes his tongue against his lips. "Can I try it, Key?" he asks, very politely. Did the vampires teach him that politeness? Did vampires teach Rachel a word like *fellate*, perhaps while instructing her to do it with a hopefully willing human partner?

"Do you guys know how to use condoms?" She has decided to ask Tetsuo to supply them. This last week has made it clear that "sexual flavors" are all too frequently on the menu at Grade Gold.

Kaipo looks at Rachel; Rachel shakes her head. "What's a condom?" he asks.

It's so easy to forget how little of the world they know. "You use it during sex, to stop you from catching diseases," she says, carefully. "Or getting pregnant."

Rachel laughs and stuffs the rest of the flesh into her wide mouth. Even a cherimoya can't fill her hollows. "Great, even more vampire sex," she says, her hatred clearer than her garbled words. "They never made Pen do it."

"They didn't?" Key asks.

Juice dribbles down her chin. "You know, Tetsuo's dispensation? Before she killed herself, she was his pick. Everyone knew it. That's why they left her alone."

Key feels light-headed. "But if she was his choice . . . why would she kill herself?"

"She didn't want to be a vampire," Kaipo says softly.

"She wanted a *baby*, like bringing a new food sack into the world is a good idea. But they wouldn't let her have sex and they wanted to make her one of them, so—now she's gone. But why he'd bring *you* here, when *any* of us would be a better choice—"

"Rachel, just shut up. Please." Kaipo takes her by the shoulder.

Rachel shrugs him off. "What? Like she can do anything."

"If she becomes one of *them*—"

"I wouldn't hurt you," Key says, too quickly. Rachel masks her pain with cruelty, but it is palpable. Key can't imagine any version of herself that would add to that.

Kaipo and Rachel stare at her. "But," Kaipo says, "that's what vampires do."

"I would eat you," Rachel says, and flops back under the tree. "I would make you cry and your tears would taste sweeter than a cherimoya."

*   *   *

"I will be back in four days," Testsuo tells her, late the next night. "There is one feeding scheduled. I hope you will be ready when I return."

"For the . . . reward?" she asks, stumbling over an appropriate euphemism. Their words for it are polysyllabic spikes: transmutation, transformation, metamorphosis. All vampires were once human, and immortal doesn't mean invulnerable. Some die each year, and so their ranks must be replenished with the flesh of worthy, willing humans.

He places a hand on her shoulder. It feels as chill and inert as a piece of damp wood. She thinks she must be dreaming.

"I have wanted this for a long time, Key," he says to her—like a stranger, like the person who knows her the best in the world.

"Why now?"

"Our thoughts can be . . . slow, sometimes. You will see. Orderly, but sometimes too orderly to see patterns clearly. I thought of you, but did not know it until Penelope died."

Penelope, who looked just like Key. Penelope, who would have been his pick. She shivers and steps away from his hand. "Did you love her?"

She can't believe that she is asking this question. She can't believe that he is offering her the dreams she would have murdered for ten, even five years ago.

"I loved that she made me think of you," he says, "when you were young and beautiful."

"It's been eighteen years, Tetsuo."

He looks over her shoulder. "You haven't lost much," he says. "I'm not too late. You'll see."

He is waiting for a response. She forces herself to nod. She wants to close her eyes and cover her mouth, keep all her love for him inside where it can be safe, because if she loses it, there will be nothing left but a girl in the rain who should have opened the door.

He looks like an alien when he smiles. He looks like nothing she could ever know when he walks down the hall, past the open door and the girl who has been watching them this whole time.

Rachel is young and beautiful, Key thinks, and Penelope is dead.

*　　*　　*

Key's sixth feeding at Grade Gold is contained, quiet and without incident. The gazes of the clients slide over her as she greets them at the door of the feeding house, but she is used to that. To a vampire, a human without a shunt is like a book without pages: a useless absurdity. She has assigned all of unit one and a pair from unit four to the gathering. Seven humans for five vampires is a luxurious ratio—probably more than they paid for, but she's happy to let that be Tetsuo's problem. She shudders to remember how Rachel's blood soaked into the collar of her blouse when she lifted the girl from the bed. She has seen dozens of overdrained humans, including some who died from it, but what happened to Rachel feels worse. She doesn't understand why, but is overwhelmed by tenderness for her.

A half-hour before the clients are supposed to leave, Kaipo sprints through the front door, flushed and panting so hard he has to pause half a minute to catch his breath.

"Rachel," he manages, while humans and vampires alike pause to look.

She stands up. "What did she do?"

"I'm not sure . . . she was shaking and screaming, waking everyone up, yelling about Penelope and Tetsuo and then she started vomiting."

"The clients have another half hour," she whispers. "I can't leave until then."

Kaipo tugs on the long lock of glossy black hair that he has blunt-cut over his left eye. "I'm scared for her, Key," he says. "She won't listen to anyone else."

She will blame herself if any of the kids here tonight die, and she will blame herself if something happens to Rachel. Her hands make the decision for her: she reaches for Kaipo's left arm. He lets her take it reflexively, and doesn't flinch when she lifts his shunt. She looks for and finds the small electrical chip which controls the inflow and outflow of blood and other fluids. She taps the Morse-like code, and Kaipo watches with his mouth open as the glittering plastic polymer changes from clear to gray. As though he's already been tapped out.

"I'm not supposed to show you that," she says, and smiles until she remembers Tetsuo and what he might think. "Stay here. Make sure nothing happens. I'll be back as soon as I can."

She stays only long enough to see his agreement, and then she's flying out the back door, through the garden, down the left-hand path that leads to unit two.

Rachel is on her hands and knees in the middle of the walkway. The other three kids in unit two watch her silently from the doorway, but Rachel is alone as she vomits in the grass.

"You!" Rachel says when she sees Key, and starts to cough.

Rachel looks like a war is being fought inside of her, as if the battlefield is her lungs and the hollows of her cheeks and the muscles of her neck. She trembles and can hardly raise her head.

"Go away!" Rachel screams, but she's not looking at Key, she's looking down at the ground.

"Rachel, what's happened?" Key doesn't get too close. Rachel's fury frightens her; she doesn't understand this kind of rage. Rachel raises her shaking hands and starts hitting herself, pounding her chest and rib cage and stomach with violence made even more frightening by her weakness. Key kneels in front of her, grabs both of the girl's tiny, bruised wrists and holds them away from her body. Her vomit smells of sour bile and the sickly-sweet of some half digested fruit. A suspicion nibbles at Key, and so she looks to the left, where Rachel has vomited.

Dozens and dozens of black seeds, half crushed. And a slime of green the precise shade of a cherimoya skin.

"Oh, God, Rachel . . . why would you . . ."

"You don't deserve him! He can make it go away and he won't! Who are you? A fogey, an ugly fogey, an ugly usurping fogey and she's gone and he is a dick, he is a screaming howler monkey and I hate him . . ."

Rachel collapses against Key's chest, her hands beating helplessly at the ground. Key takes her up and rocks her back and forth, crying while she thinks of how close she came to repeating the mistakes of Jeb. But she can still save Rachel. She can still be human.

*　　*　　*

Tetsuo returns three days later with a guest.

She has never seen Mr. Charles wear shoes before, and he walks in them with the mincing confusion of a young girl forced to wear zori for a formal occasion. She bows her head when she sees him, hoping to hide her fear. Has he come to take her back to Mauna Kea? The thought of returning to those antiseptic feeding rooms and tasteless brick patties makes her hands shake. It makes her wonder if she would not be better off taking Penelope's way out rather than seeing the place where Jeb killed himself again.

But even as she thinks it, she knows she won't, any more than she would have eighteen years ago. She's too much a coward and she's too brave. If Mr. Charles asks her to go back she will say yes.

Rain on a mountainside and sexless, sweet touches with a man the same temperature as wet wood. Lanai City, overrun. Then Waimea, then Honoka'a. Then Hilo, where her mother had been living. For a year, until Tetsuo found that record of her existence in a work camp, Key fantasized about her mother escaping on a boat to an atoll, living in a group of refugee humans who survived the apocalypse.

Every thing Tetsuo asked of her, she did. She loved him from the moment they saved each other's lives. She has always said yes.

"*Key!*" Mr. Charles says to her, as though she is a friend he has run into unexpectedly. "I have some*thing* . . . you might *just* want."

"Yes, Mr. Charles?" she says.

The three of them are alone in the feeding house. Mr. Charles collapses dramatically against one of the divans and kicks off his tight, patent-leather shoes as if they are barnacles. He wears no socks.

"There," he says, and waves his hand at the door. "*In* the bag."

Tetsuo nods and so she walks back. The bag is black canvas, unmarked. Inside, there's a book. She recognizes it immediately, though she only saw it once. *The Blind Watchmaker.* There is a note on the cover. The handwriting is large and uneven and painstaking, that of someone familiar with words but unaccustomed to writing them down. She notes painfully that he writes his "a" the same way as a typeset font, with the half-c above the main body and a careful serif at the end.

> *Dear Overseer Ki,*
>
> *I would like you to have this. I have loved it very much and you are the only one who ever seemed to care. I am angry but*
>
> *I don't blame you. You're just too good at living.*
>
> *Jeb*

She takes the bag and leaves both vampires without requesting permission. Mr. Charles's laugh follows her out the door.

Blood on the walls, on the floor, all over his body.

I am angry but. You're just too good at living. She has always said yes.

She is too much of a coward and she is too brave.

* * *

She watches the sunset the next evening from the hill in the garden, her back against the cherimoya tree. She feels the sun's death like she always has, with quiet joy. Awareness floods her: the musk of wet grass crushed beneath her bare toes, salt-spray and algae blowing from the ocean, the love she has clung to so fiercely since she was a girl, lost and alone. Everything she has ever loved is bound in that sunset, the red and violet orb that could kill him as it sinks into the ocean.

Her favorite time of day is sunset, but it is not night. She has never quite been able to fit inside his darkness, no matter how hard she tried. She has been too good at living, but perhaps it's not too late to change.

She can't take the path of Penelope or Jeb, but that has never been the only way. She remembers stories that reached Grade Orange from the work camps, half-whispered reports of humans who sat at their assembly lines and refused to lift their hands. Harvesters who drained gasoline from their combine engines and waited for the vampires to find them. If every human refused to cooperate, vampire society would crumble in a week. Still, she has no illusions about this third path sparking a revolution. This is simply all she can do: sit under the cherimoya tree and refuse. They will kill her, but she will have chosen to be human.

The sun descends. She falls asleep against the tree and dreams of the girl who never was, the one who opened the door. In her dreams, the sun burns her skin and her obachan tells her how proud she is while they pick strawberries in the garden. She eats an umeboshi that tastes of blood and salt, and when she swallows, the flavors swarm out of her throat, bubbling into her neck and jaw and ears. Flavors become emotions become thoughts; peace in the nape of her neck, obligation in her back molars, and hope just behind her eyes, bitter as a watermelon rind.

She opens them and sees Tetsuo on his knees before her. Blood smears his mouth. She does not know what to think when he kisses her, except that she can't even feel the pinprick pain where his teeth broke her skin. He has never fed from her before. They have never kissed before. She feels like she is floating, but nothing else.

The blood is gone when he sits back. As though she imagined it.

"You should not have left like that yesterday," he says. "Charles can make this harder than I'd like."

"Why is he here?" she asks. She breathes shallowly.

"He will take over Grade Gold once your transmutation is finished."

"That's why you brought me here, isn't it? It had nothing to do with the kids."

He shrugs. "Regulations. So Charles couldn't refuse."

"And where will you go?"

"They want to send me to the mainland. Texas. To supervise the installation of a new Grade Gold facility near Austin."

She leans closer to him, and now she can see it: regret, and shame that he should be feeling so. "I'm sorry," she says.

"I have lived seventy years on these islands. I have an eternity to come back to them. So will you, Key. I have permission to bring you with me."

Everything that sixteen-year-old had ever dreamed. She can still feel the pull of him, of her desire for an eternity together, away from the hell her life has become. Her transmutation would be complete. Truly a monster, the regrets for her past actions would fall away like waves against a seawall.

With a fumbling hand, she picks a cherimoya from the ground beside her. "Do you remember what these taste like?"

She has never asked him about his human life. For a moment, he seems genuinely confused. "You don't understand. Taste to us is vastly more complex. Joy, dissatisfaction, confusion, humility—*those* are flavors. A custard apple?" He laughs. "It's sweet, right?"

Joy, dissatisfaction, loss, grief, she tastes all that just looking at him.

"Why didn't you ever feed from me before?"

"Because I promised. When we first met."

And as she stares at him, sick with loss and certainty, Rachel walks up behind him. She is holding a kitchen knife, the blade pointed toward her stomach.

"Charles knows," she says.

"How?" Tetsuo says. He stands, but Key can't coordinate her muscles enough for the effort. He must have drained a lot of blood.

"I told him," Rachel says. "So now you don't have a choice. You will transmute me and you will get rid of this fucking fetus or I will kill myself and you'll be blamed for losing *two* Grade Gold humans."

Rachel's wrists are still bruised from where Key had to hold her several nights ago. Her eyes are sunken, her skin sallow. *This fucking fetus.*

She wasn't trying to kill herself with the cherimoya seeds. She was trying to abort a pregnancy.

"The baby is still alive after all that?" Key says, surprisingly indifferent to the glittering metal in Rachel's unsteady hands. Does Rachel know how easily Tetsuo could disarm her? What advantage does she think she has? But then she looks back in the girl's eyes and realizes: none.

Rachel is young and desperate and she doesn't want to be eaten by the monsters anymore.

"Not again, Rachel," Tetsuo says. "I *can't* do what you want. A vampire can only transmute someone he's never fed from before."

Rachel gasps. Key flops against her tree. She hadn't known that, either. The knife trembles in Rachel's grip so violently that Tetsuo takes it from her, achingly gentle as he pries her fingers from the hilt.

"*That's* why you never drank from her? And I killed her anyway? Stupid fucking Penelope. She could have been forever, and now there's just this dumb fogie in her place. She thought you cared about her."

"Caring is a strange thing, for a vampire," Key says.

Rachel spits in her direction but it falls short. The moonlight is especially bright tonight; Key can see everything from the grass to the tips of Rachel's ears, flushed sunset pink.

"Tetsuo," Key says, "why can't I move?"

But they ignore her.

"Maybe Charles will do it if I tell him you're really the one who killed Penelope."

"Charles? I'm sure he knows exactly what you did."

"I didn't *mean* to kill her!" Rachel screams. "Penelope was going to tell about the baby. She was crazy about babies, it didn't make any sense, and you had *picked her* and she wanted to destroy my life . . . I was so angry, I just wanted to hurt her, but I didn't realize . . ."

"Rachel, I've tried to give you a chance, but I'm not allowed to get rid of it for you." Tetsuo's voice is as worn out as a leathery orange.

"I'll die before I go to one of those mommy farms, Tetsuo. I'll die and take my baby with me."

"Then you will have to do it yourself."

She gasps. "You'll really leave me here?"

"I've made my choice."

Rachel looks down at Key, radiating a withering contempt that does nothing to blunt Key's pity. "If you had picked Penelope, I would have understood. Penelope was beautiful and smart. She's the only one who ever made it through half of that fat Shakespeare book in unit four. She could sing. Her breasts were perfect. But *her*? She's not a choice. She's nothing at all."

The silence between them is strained. It's as if Key isn't there at all. And soon, she thinks, she won't be.

"I've made my choice," Key says.

"*Your* choice?" they say in unison.

When she finds the will to stand, it's as though her limbs are hardly there at all, as though she is swimming in mid-air. For the first time, she understands that something is wrong.

*　　*　　*

Key floats for a long time. Eventually, she falls. Tetsuo catches her.

"What does it feel like?" Key asks. "The transmutation?"

Tetsuo takes the starlight in his hands. He feeds it to her through a glass shunt growing from a living branch. The tree's name is Rachel. The tree is very sad. Sadness is delicious.

"You already know," he says.

You will understand: he said this to her when she was human. *I wouldn't hurt you*: she said this to a girl who—a girl—she drinks.

"I meant to refuse."

"I made a promise."

She sees him for a moment crouched in the back of her father's shed, huddled away from the dangerous bar of light that stretches across the floor. She sees herself, terrified of death and so unsure. *Open the door*, she tells that girl, too late. *Let in the light.*

NEBULA AWARD NOMINEE
BEST NOVELLA

EXCERPT FROM CALENDRICAL REGRESSION

LAWRENCE M. SCHOEN

Lawrence M. Schoen has been nominated for three Nebula Awards, a Hugo Award, and, in 2007, the John W. Campbell Award for Best New Writer. Calendrical Regression *was published by NobelFusion Press.*

The pirate queen was a young brunette who in another life might have been a celebrity spokesperson. She glanced down at her wounded arm, attempted to raise it and failed. Instead she passed her photonic cutlass to her other hand. The move required less than a second, and to the chagrin of her alien opponent she brought the blade up in an effective block and managed to force him back. He stumbled and an instant later she struck the weapon from his grasp in a shower of high velocity sparks that caused his phlox-colored hair to stand on end.

"Where does a pirate learn to do that?" gasped the Auditor in Black, his fishbelly white skin a stark contrast to his ebony suit—marking him as a Clarkeson, a colony creature pretending to be a humanoid. His feet slid on the ever slicker surface of the dirigible as it descended toward the swamp below and the humid air condensed upon its skin.

"I wasn't always a pirate, Hiram," she replied, bringing her cutlass closer and forcing him to his knees. "Before my airship began harrying your tax collectors, I was a princess of the realm, and the darling of Daddy's fencing master."

"What happens now?" asked the Clarkeson, smirking despite defeat. "Am I your prisoner? You cannot bring me to trial; I'm not accountable to the courts of Earth."

"I've never been a fan of the legal system. Simpler just to kill you."

Hiram laughed. "Gutting me a like human won't end me. I'm not a singular being like you. My sapience results from the collective efforts of more than a million self-aware cellular collectives working in committee."

"Then I'll just have to carve you up into lots of little pieces and scatter them overboard into the swamp. Goodbye, my Lord Auditor. Your committee is hereby disbanded."

She raised the photonic cutlass above her head in preparation for the first stroke.

"Wait! Who's that behind you?"

The pirate queen's contempt at the ploy was palpable. "Please. You can't expect that to actually work. We're fighting on top of a sinking airship, and any harness lines someone might use to climb up here are in front of me."

That's when I reached from behind her, lightly grasped the wrist of her upraised hand, and commanded, "Sleep!" Her body went limp. She slumped against me as her head lolled upon her chest. I caught her as she collapsed and half-dragged / half-carried her a short distance to deposit her in a folding chair at the center of the stage.

The Auditor in Black wasn't a Clarkeson at all but actually a blue-collar worker from Des Moines named Hiram Gustuvson. He'd also succumbed to my command and lay sprawled, illuminated by a spotlight on the stage that mere moments ago had seemed to be the slippery surface of a dirigible. He was bigger than the recent pirate queen and I didn't want to drag him. A quick whisper in his ear, and he stood up, eyes blinking. I guided him back to the chair next to his foe. Next, I stepped behind her chair and brought my lips close to her ear, speaking softly to her as I brought her back to full wakefulness. Then I turned to the audience.

"Ladies and gentlemen, it has been your great fortune to witness, for the first time anywhere, this performance of the *Revenge of the Pirate Queen!* Please show your appreciation for our players, who despite having no history of pointless violence or weapons training, nonetheless slaughtered dozens of imaginary foes before finally confronting one another for your entertainment."

Thunderous applause met my dazed volunteers. They grinned sheepishly, looked to one another, and—better than I could have choreographed it—joined hands, rose to their feet, and took a bow. It was a great end to the last of a week of shows. Seven days I'd taken off from my regular, unwelcome job as CEO of a hugely successful corporation, a vacation spent returning to my original profession as a stage hypnotist. I'm the Amazing Conroy, and I'm very good at what I do, when I can get away to do it.

The applause ended and I escorted my recent hypnotic subjects off the stage and into the waiting arms of their friends and colleagues. One of the small tables in front stood vacant now. Earlier, I'd invited its occupant on stage as a volunteer but she'd demurred. At some point in the show she'd slipped away, her escape covered by darkness, obscured by spotlights, and masked by the antics on stage.

I bid everyone a good night and as soon as the stage lights went dark I slipped through the rear curtain, ending my week of headlining at the Hotel Rotundo in downtown Omaha.

I'd been putting in two shows a night to an audience that had consisted of the attendees of several different groups that had opted to hold their national meetings there in Nebraska, including the Association of Midwestern Pipefitters, Mothers Against Migraines, and my personal favorite the Royal Order of Otters. It wasn't a bad gig as far as such things went; Omaha rarely attracts really big name acts, so a stage hypnotist can do pretty well. But I wasn't there for the money. A couple years earlier I'd stumbled into a venture breeding and leasing buffalo dogs and I was now richer than I had any right to be. The work had taken me to Mars a month earlier, and after returning to Earth, I'd decided to treat myself to a little time off. When I had mentioned this to my secretary, she promptly presented me with an array of terrestrial vacation spots featuring a nice assortment of white sandy beaches, private forests, and mountain vistas. Moreover, each included nearby, five-star restaurants that catered to ultra-rich humans and a wide range of xenophilic aliens.

I was tempted. The venues were all variations on paradise, obscenely expensive, and well within my budget. But it was neither what I wanted nor needed. I had no use for paradise, though I almost relented after reviewing the restaurants' menus. In the end, my resolution held and I slipped away by returning to my earlier career, leaving the running of my company in the hands of people who knew what they were doing far better than me. Instead, to the horror of my security chief, I called in a favor from a friend in the stage performers' union and within an hour had gotten myself booked at the Hotel Rotundo to perform my hypnosis act and make utter strangers believe outlandish suggestions for the entertainment of others.

It had been a glorious and restful week, but as I undid the knot of my bowtie and walked down the backstage corridor to my dressing room I knew it was time to hang up my tuxedo and return to the corporate office back in Philadelphia.

The woman waiting for me in the hallway changed all that.

She was the same woman who'd vanished before the end of my show, vacating a front table that usually went to master plumbers or reverend otters of great distinction. In hindsight, I should have taken that as an omen.

When selecting volunteers for a show I tend toward two types: either the sort of ordinary person who blends in and goes through life otherwise unnoticed, and at the other extreme someone who has made a significant, though not necessarily conscious, effort to stand out. This woman fell into the second group.

A single glance revealed that she wasn't from the Midwest. Her tanned skin had that perfect seamless look that only comes from salons in New York or L.A., where you spend ten minutes hanging in zero gee while melanin wielding nano-machines paint your epidermis one cell at a time. I assumed a similar treatment had been applied to her shoulder length blonde hair; it had an otherworldly look, the way it bounced in curly streamers all around her head. She probably came by her dimples honestly and they worked to give her a girl-next-door flavor that was at odds with the perfection of skin and hair. Her clothes didn't help things. Sure, we were in Omaha, but the rest of my audience still made a point of showing up in the latest definition of 'office casual.' The men all had collared shirts and the women all wore dresses. She had clothed herself in new jeans and an oversized sports jersey representing a team from the Martian dustball minor league. I'd followed the disapproving glances of more than one of the women gathered in Omaha to rally against migraines when I'd sought her out as a volunteer. When she turned down my invitation, I'd switched to a pretty plumber and put her out of my mind.

Now she stepped back into it, having apparently left my show early the better to lay in wait for me in the dilapidated hallway backstage. She stood there now, leaning against the door to my dressing room, the shiny blue fabric of her Helium Hurlers jersey stretched in interesting ways across her torso. I stopped a few feet away, still trying to determine if she was a groupie or a crazie. Neither were unheard of in my field, though the latter were more common.

If she was a crazie, I certainly didn't want her coming into my dressing room. For that matter, while it would be flattering if she were a groupie, I wasn't looking for that sort of thing either. It was Friday night and I had a ticket for a redeye back home with a plan to spend the weekend catching up on my sleep and dining at a couple of five-star restaurants. All too quickly it'd be Monday morning, and I'd be expected to show up at the corporate offices of Buffalogic, Inc. bright and early to resume reviewing business proposals and taking meetings with corporate leaders from all over the Earth and beyond. So, regardless of her story, or my own wishful thinking, she wasn't going to be joining me in my dressing room.

"Good evening, Mr. Conroy. My name is Nicole. I very much enjoyed your show tonight. The things you made your volunteers do, I've never seen anything like it."

I offered up a tight smile, nodding my head to acknowledge the praise, and had pretty much decided she belonged in the groupie category. "Thank you, you're very kind. But, if you'll excuse me, I—"

"And that last part where you made that plumber believe he was a Clarkeson? Incredible. It was spot on. Plots within plots with them. Have you met many Clarkesons?"

An odd question, but then I'd already pegged her as a bit more worldly than the rest of the audience. "A few," I answered. "Thanks for coming. I'm glad you enjoyed the show. Now I really must—"

"You know, my uncle saw one of your earliest performances, what was it, fourteen years ago? On Hesnarj."

It was like she'd slapped me. Hesnarj was an alien mausoleum world where I'd been marooned while a college student. There'd been precious few humans anywhere on that planet. I'd discovered my talent as a stage hypnotist there, befriended my first aliens, and even met one who had helped me to channel my deceased great aunt Fiona.

I started to reply but she cut me off again.

"But that's not why I'm here. The show was just a delightful bonus. I actually came to meet you for a completely unrelated reason."

Okay, maybe *not* a groupie. "Oh? You did? I see. Well, and that's—"

"There's someone quite extraordinary that I'd like you to meet. His name is Juan Sho. He's involved with sorghum, that and cookbooks."

Sorghum cookbooks? I made a point of looking up and down the length of our empty hallway. Just that quickly the scales had tipped toward crazie.

"He's not here, Mr. Conroy. He's waiting for us in Mexico."

"Mexico?"

She smiled, revealing perfect, gleaming teeth. "Well, yes. Like yourself, he's a busy executive by day, and also shares your passion for cuisine, though in his case it's more about how it's crafted than how it tastes. Right now he's probably in a little restaurant in Veracruz, reverse-engineering the best mole poblano you've ever had."

This time my smile was genuine. If you can appreciate a truly fine mole then you'll understand why. Excellent food is my weakness and Nicole— whoever she was—had done her homework. Some part of my brain threw away both of the likely pigeonholes I'd laid out for her and tabled further attempts at classification. She had my attention. I unlocked my dressing room and opened the door.

"Really? You know, I've never been to Veracruz. Why don't you come in and tell me more about this."

EXCERPT FROM "THE MOTHERS OF VOORHISVILLE"

MARY RICKERT

Mary Rickert has won two World Fantasy Awards, a Locus Award, a Shirley Jackson Award, and a Crawford Award, and has been nominated for many others. "The Mothers of Voorhisville" was originally published on Tor.com.

The things you have heard are true; we are the mothers of monsters. We would, however, like to clarify a few points. For instance, by the time we realized what Jeffrey had been up to, he was gone. At first we thought maybe the paper mill was to blame; it closed down in 1969, but perhaps it had taken that long for the poisonous chemicals to seep into our drinking water. We hid it from one another, of course, the strange shape of our newborns and the identity of the father. Each of us thought we were his secret lover. That was much of the seduction. (Though he was also beautiful, with those blue eyes and that intense way of his.)

It is true that he arrived in that big black car with the curtains across the back windows, as has been reported. But though Voorhisville is a small town, we are not ignorant, toothless, or the spawn of generations of incest. We *did* recognize the car as a hearse. However, we did not immediately assume the worst of the man who drove it. Perhaps we in Voorhisville are not as sheltered from death as people elsewhere. We, the mothers of Voorhisville, did not look at Jeffrey and immediately think of death. Instead, we looked into those blue eyes of his and thought of sex. You might have to have met him yourself to understand. There is a small but growing contingency of us that believes we were put under a type of spell. *Not* in regards to our later actions, which we take responsibility for, but in regards to him.

What mother wouldn't kill to save her babies? The only thing unusual about our story is that our children can fly. (Sometimes, even now, we think we hear wings brushing the air beside us.) We mothers take the blame because we understand, someone has to suffer. So we do. Gladly.

We would gladly do it all again to have one more day with our darlings. Even knowing the damage, we would gladly agree. This is not the apology you might have expected. Think of it more as a manifesto. A map, in case any of them seek to return to us, though our hope of that happening is faint. Why would anyone *choose* this ruined world?

*   *   *

Elli

The mothers have asked me to write what I know about what happened, most specifically what happened to me. I am suspicious of their motives. They insist this story must be told to "set the record straight." What I think is that they are annoyed that I, Elli Ratcher, with my red hair and freckles and barely sixteen years old, shared a lover with them. The mothers like to believe they were driven to the horrible things they did by mother-love. I can tell you, though; they have always been capable of cruelty.

The mothers, who have a way of *hovering* over me, citing my recent suicide attempt, say I should start at the beginning. That is an easy thing to *say*. It's the kind of thing I probably would have said to Timmy, had he not fallen through my arms and crashed to the ground at my feet.

The mothers say if this is too hard, I should give the pen to someone else. "We all have stuff to tell," Maddy Melvern says. Maddy is, as everyone knows, jealous. She was just seventeen when she did it with Jeffrey and would be getting all the special attention if not for me. The mothers say they really mean it—if I can't start at the beginning, someone else will. So, all right.

It's my fifteenth birthday, and Grandma Joyce, who taught high school English for forty-six years, gives me one of her watercolor cards with a poem and five dollars. I know she's trying to tell me something important with the poem, but the most I can figure out about what it means is that she doesn't want me to grow up. That's okay. She's my grandma. I give her a kiss. She touches my hair. "Where did this come from?" she says, which annoys my mom. I don't know why. When she says it in front of my dad, he says, "Let it rest, Ma."

Right now my dad is out in the barn showing Uncle Bobby the beams. The barn beams have been a subject of much concern for my father, and endless conversations—at dinner, or church, or in parent-teacher conferences, the grocery store, or the post office—have been reduced to "the beams."

I stand on the porch and feel the sun on my skin. I can hear my mom and aunt in the kitchen and the cartoon voices from *Shrek 2,* which my cousins are watching. When I look at the barn I think I hear my dad saying "beams." I look out over the front yard to the road that goes by our house. Right then, a long black car comes over the hill, real slow, like the driver is lost. I shade my eyes to watch it pass the cornfield. I wonder if it is some kind of birthday present for me. A ride in a limousine! It slows down even more in front of our house. That's when I realize it's a hearse.

Then my dad and Uncle Bobby come out of the barn. When my dad sees me he says, "Hey! You can't be fifteen, not my little stinkbottom," which he's been saying all day, "stinkbottom" being what he used to call me when I was in diapers. I have to use all my will and power not to roll my eyes, because he hates it when I roll my eyes. I am trying not to make anyone mad, because today is my birthday.

As far as I can figure out, that is the beginning. But is it? Is it the beginning? There are so many of us, and maybe there are just as many beginnings. What does "beginning" mean, anyway? What does anything mean? What is meaning? What *is*? Is Timmy? Or is he not? Once, I held him in my arms and he smiled and I thought I loved him. But maybe I didn't. Maybe everything was already me throwing babies out the window; maybe everything was already tiny homemade caskets with flies buzzing around them; maybe everything has always been this place, this time, this sorrowful house and the weeping of the mothers.

* * *

The Mothers

We have decided Elli should take a little time to compose herself. Tamara Singh, who, up until Ravi's birth, worked at the library on Tuesdays and Thursdays and every other Saturday, has graciously volunteered. In the course of persuading us that she is, in fact, perfect for the position of chronicler, Tamara—perhaps overcome with enthusiasm—cited the fantastic aspects of her several unpublished novels. This delayed our assent considerably. Tamara said she would not be writing about "elves and unicorns." She explained that the word *fantasy* comes from the Latin *phantasia*, which means "an idea, notion, image, or a making visible."

"Essentially, it's making an idea visible. Everyone knows what we did. I thought we were trying to make them see why," she said.

The mothers have decided to let Tamara tell what she can. We agree that what we have experienced, and heretofore have not adequately explained (or why would we still be here?)—might be best served by "a making visible."

We can hope, at least. Many of us, though surprised to discover it, still have hope.

* * *

Tamara

There is, on late summer days, a certain perfume to Voorhisville. It's the coppery smell of water, the sweet scent of grass with a touch of corn and lawn mower gas, lemon slices in ice-tea glasses and citronella. Sometimes, if the wind blows just right, it carries the perfume of the angel roses in Sylvia Lansmorth's garden, a scent so seductive that everyone, from toddlers playing in the sandbox at Fletcher's Park to senior citizens in rocking chairs at The Celia Wathmore Nursing Home, is made just a little bit drunk.

On just such a morning, Sylvia Lansmorth (whose beauty was not diminished by the recent arrival of gray in her long hair), sat in her garden, in the chair her husband had made for her during that strange year after the cancer diagnosis.

She sat weeping amongst her roses, taking deep gulps of the sweet air, like a woman just surfaced from a near drowning. In truth, Sylvia, who had experienced much despair in the past year, was now feeling an entirely different emotion.

"I want you to get on with things," he'd told her. "I don't want you mourning forever. Promise me."

So she made the sort of unreasonable promise one makes to a dying man, while he looked at her with those bulging eyes, which had taken on a light she once thought characteristic of saints and psychopaths.

She'd come, as she had so many times before, to sit in her garden, and for some reason, who knows why, was overcome by this *emotion* she never thought she would feel again—this absolute love of life. As soon as she recognized it, she began to weep. Still, it was an improvement, anyone would say, this weeping and gulping of air; a great improvement over weeping and muffling her face against a pillow.

Of all the sweet-smelling places in Voorhisville that morning, the yoga studio was the sweetest. The music was from India, or so they thought. Only Tamara guessed it wasn't Indian music, but music meant to sound as though it was; just as the teacher, Shreve, despite her unusual name, wasn't Indian but from somewhere in New Jersey. If you listened carefully, you could hear it in her voice.

Right in the middle of the opening chant there was a ruckus at the back of the room. Somebody was late, and not being particularly quiet about it. Several women peeked, right in the middle of om. Others resisted until Shreve instructed them to stand, at which point they reached for a water bottle, or a towel, or just forgot about subterfuge entirely and simply looked. By the time the class was in its first downward dog, there was not a person there who hadn't spied on the noisy latecomer. He had the bluest eyes any of them had ever seen, and a halo of light around his body, which most everyone assumed was an optical illusion. It would be a long time before any of them thought that it hadn't been a glow at all, but a burning.

Shreve noticed (when she walked past him as he lay in corpse position) the strong scent of jasmine, and thought that, in the mysterious ways of the world, a holy man, a yogi, had come into her class.

Shreve, like Sylvia, was a widow. Sort of. There was no word for what she was, actually. She felt betrayed by language, amongst other things. Her fiancé had been murdered. Even the nature of his death had robbed her of something primary, as if *how* he died was more important than that he had. She'd given up trying to explain it. Nobody in Voorhisville knew. She'd moved here with her new yoga teacher certificate after the second anniversary of the event and opened up this studio with the savings she'd set aside for the wedding. His parents paid for the funeral, so she still had quite a bit left, which was good, because though the studio was a success by Voorhisville's standards, she was running out of money. It was enough to make her cranky sometimes. She tried to forgive herself for it. Shreve wasn't sure she had enough love to forgive the world, but she thought—maybe—she could forgive herself.

With her hands in prayer position, Shreve closed her eyes and sang "shanti" three times. It meant "peace," and on that morning Shreve felt like peace had finally arrived.

Later, when the stranger showed up for the writers' workshop at Jan Morris's house, she could not determine how he'd found out about the elitist group, known to have rejected at least one local writer on the basis of the fact she wrote fantasy. Jan asked him how he'd found them, but Sylvia interrupted before he could answer. Certainly it never occurred to her to think he was up to anything diabolical. Also, it became clear that Sylvia knew him from a yoga class she attended. By the time he had passed out the twelve copies of his poem— his presence made them a group of thirteen, but they were intellectuals, not a superstitious bunch—well, it just didn't matter how he found them.

Afterwards, as the writers left, Jan stood at the door with the stranger beside her, waving goodbye until she observed two things: first, that the last car remaining in the driveway was a hearse, and second, that the stranger smelled, quite pleasantly, of lemons.

Jan preferred to call him "the stranger." Never mind Camus; it had a nice ring to it all on its own. Eventually, when the mothers pieced things together, it seemed the most accurate moniker. They didn't know him at all. None of them did. Not really.

EXCERPT FROM "THE REGULAR"

KEN LIU

Ken Liu has won a Nebula Award, three Hugo Awards, and a World Fantasy Award. He has also been nominated for seven additional Nebula Awards, one Hugo Award, ten Locus Awards, and five Theodore Sturgeon Memorial Awards. "The Regular" was first published in the anthology Upgraded.

"This is Jasmine," she says.

"It's Robert."

The voice on the phone is the same as the one she had spoken to earlier in the afternoon.

"Glad you made it, sweetie." She looks out the window. He's standing at the corner, in front of the convenience store as she asked. He looks clean and is dressed well, like he's going on a date. A good sign. He's also wearing a Red Sox cap pulled low over his brow, a rather amateurish attempt at anonymity. "I'm down the street from you, at 27 Moreland. It's the gray stone condo building converted from a church."

He turns to look. "You have a sense of humor."

They all make that joke, but she laughs anyway. "I'm in unit 24, on the second floor."

"Is it just you? I'm not going to see some linebacker type demanding that I pay him first?"

"I told you. I'm independent. Just have your donation ready and you'll have a good time."

She hangs up and takes a quick look in the mirror to be sure she's ready. The black stockings and garter belt are new, and the lace bustier accentuates her thin waist and makes her breasts seem larger. She's done her makeup lightly, but the eye shadow is heavy to emphasize her eyes. Most of her customers like that. Exotic.

The sheets on the king-size bed are fresh, and there's a small wicker basket of condoms on the nightstand, next to a clock that says "5:58." The date is for two hours, and afterwards she'll have enough time to clean up and shower and then sit in front of the TV to catch her favorite show. She thinks about calling her mom later that night to ask about how to cook porgy.

She opens the door before he can knock, and the look on his face tells her that she's done well. He slips in; she closes the door, leans against it, and smiles at him.

"You're even prettier than the picture in your ad," he says. He gazes into her eyes intently. "Especially the eyes."

"Thank you."

As she gets a good look at him in the hallway, she concentrates on her right eye and blinks rapidly twice. She doesn't think she'll ever need it, but a girl has to protect herself. If she ever stops doing this, she thinks she'll just have it taken out and thrown into the bottom of Boston Harbor, like the way she used to, as a little girl, write secrets down on bits of paper, wad them up, and flush them down the toilet.

He's good looking in a non-memorable way: over six feet, tanned skin, still has all his hair, and the body under that crisp shirt looks fit. The eyes are friendly and kind, and she's pretty sure he won't be too rough. She guesses that he's in his forties, and maybe works downtown in one of the law firms or financial services companies, where his long-sleeved shirt and dark pants make sense with the air conditioning always turned high. He has that entitled arrogance that many mistake for masculine attractiveness. She notices that there's a paler patch of skin around his ring finger. Even better. A married man is usually safer. A married man who doesn't want her to know he's married is the safest of all: he values what he has and doesn't want to lose it.

She hopes he'll be a regular.

"I'm glad we're doing this." He holds out a plain white envelope.

She takes it and counts the bills inside. Then she puts it on top of the stack of mail on a small table by the entrance without saying anything. She takes him by the hand and leads him towards the bedroom. He pauses to look in the bathroom and then the other bedroom at the end of the hall.

"Looking for your linebacker?" she teases.

"Just making sure. I'm a nice guy."

He takes out a scanner and holds it up, concentrating on the screen.

"Geez, you *are* paranoid," she says. "The only camera in here is the one on my phone. And it's definitely off."

He puts the scanner away and smiles. "I know. But I just wanted to have a machine confirm it."

They enter the bedroom. She watches him take in the bed, the bottles of lubricants and lotions on the dresser, and the long mirrors covering the closet doors next to the bed.

"Nervous?" she asks.

"A little," he concedes. "I don't do this often. Or, at all."

She comes up to him and embraces him, letting him breathe in her perfume, which is floral and light so that it won't linger on his skin. After a moment, he puts his arms around her, resting his hands against the naked skin on the small of her back.

"I've always believed that one should pay for experiences rather than things."

"A good philosophy," he whispers into her ear.

"What I give you is the girlfriend experience, old fashioned and sweet. And you'll remember this and relive it in your head as often as you want."

"You'll do whatever I want?"

"Within reason," she says. Then she lifts her head to look up at him. "You have to wear a condom. Other than that, I won't say no to most things. But like I told you on the phone, for some you'll have to pay extra."

"I'm pretty old-fashioned myself. Do you mind if I take charge?"

He's made her relaxed enough that she doesn't jump to the worst conclusion. "If you're thinking of tying me down, that will cost you. And I won't do that until I know you better."

"Nothing like that. Maybe hold you down a little."

"That's fine."

He comes up to her and they kiss. His tongue lingers in her mouth and she moans. He backs up, puts his hands on her waist, turning her away from him. "Would you lie down with your face in the pillows?"

"Of course." She climbs onto the bed. "Legs up under me or spread out to the corners?"

"Spread out, please." His voice is commanding. And he hasn't stripped yet, not even taken off his Red Sox cap. She's a little disappointed. Some clients enjoy the obedience more than the sex. There's not much for her to do. She just hopes he won't be too rough and leave marks.

He climbs onto the bed behind her and knee-walks up between her legs. He leans down and grabs a pillow from next to her head. "Very lovely," he says. "I'm going to hold you down now."

She sighs into the bed, the way she knows he'll like.

He lays the pillow over the back of her head and pushes down firmly to hold her in place. He takes the gun out from the small of his back, and in one swift motion, sticks the barrel, thick and long with the silencer, into the back of the bustier, and squeezes off two quick shots into her heart. She dies instantly.

He removes the pillow, stores the gun away. Then he takes a small steel surgical kit out of his jacket pocket, along with a pair of latex gloves. He works efficiently and quickly, cutting with precision and grace. He relaxes when he's found what he's looking for; sometimes he picks the wrong girl—not often, but it has happened. He's careful to wipe off any sweat on his face with his sleeves as he works, and the hat helps to prevent any hair from falling on her. Soon, the task is done.

He climbs off the bed, takes off the bloody gloves, and leaves them and the surgical kit on the body. He puts on a fresh pair of gloves and moves through the apartment, methodically searching for places where she hid cash: inside the toilet tank, the back of the freezer, the nook above the door of the closet.

He goes into the kitchen and returns with a large plastic trash bag. He picks up the bloody gloves and the surgical kit and throws them into the bag. Picking up her phone, he presses the button for her voicemail. He deletes all the messages, including the one he had left when he first called her number. There's not much he can do about the call logs at the phone company, but he can take advantage of that by leaving his prepaid phone somewhere for the police to find.

He looks at her again. He's not sad, not exactly, but he does feel a sense of waste. The girl was pretty and he would have liked to enjoy her first, but that would leave behind too many traces, even with a condom. And he can always pay for another, later. He likes paying for things. Power flows to *him* when he pays.

Reaching into the inner pocket of his jacket, he retrieves a sheet of paper, which he carefully unfolds and leaves by the girl's head.

He stuffs the trash bag and the money into a small gym bag he found in one of the closets. He leaves quietly, picking up the envelope of cash next to the entrance on the way out.

EXCERPT FROM "GRAND JETÉ (THE GREAT LEAP)"

RACHEL SWIRSKY

Rachel Swirsky has previously won two Nebula Awards, and has been nominated for a number of Hugo, Nebula, and World Fantasy Awards, among others. "Grand Jeté (The Great Leap)" was published in Subterranean.

ACT I: Mara

Tombé

(Fall)

As dawn approached, the snow outside Mara's window slowed, spiky white stars melting into streaks on the pane. Her abba stood in the doorway, unaware that she was already awake. Mara watched his silhouette in the gloom. Shadows hung in the folds of his jowls where he'd shaved his beard in solidarity after she'd lost her hair. Although it had been months, his face still looked pink and plucked.

Some nights, Mara woke four or five times to find him watching from the doorway. She didn't want him to know how poorly she slept and so she pretended to be dreaming until he eventually departed.

This morning, he didn't leave. He stepped into the room. "Marale," he said softly. His fingers worried the edges of the green apron that he wore in his workshop. A layer of sawdust obscured older scorch marks and grease stains. "Mara, please wake up. I've made you a gift."

Mara tried to sit. Her stomach reeled. Abba rushed to her bedside. "I'm fine," she said, pushing him away as she waited for the pain to recede.

He drew back, hands disappearing into his apron pockets. The corners of his mouth tugged down, wrinkling his face like a bulldog's. He was a big man with broad shoulders and disproportionately large hands. Everything he did looked comical when wrought on such a large scale. When he felt jovial, he played into the foolishness with broad, dramatic gestures that would have made an actor proud. In sadness, his gestures became reticent, hesitating, miniature.

"Are you cold?" he asked.

In deep winter, their house was always cold. Icy wind curled through cracks in the insulation. Even the heater that abba had installed at the foot of Mara's bed couldn't keep her from dreaming of snow.

Abba pulled a lace shawl that had once belonged to Mara's ima from the back of her little wooden chair. He draped it across her shoulders. Fringe covered her ragged fingernails.

As Mara rose from her bed, he tried to help with her crutches, but Mara fended him off. He gave her a worried look. "The gift is in my workshop," he said. With a concerned backward glance, he moved ahead, allowing her the privacy to make her own way.

Their white German Shepherd, Abel, met Mara as she shifted her weight onto her crutches. She paused to let him nuzzle her hand, tongue rough against her knuckles. At thirteen, all his other senses were fading, and so he tasted everything he could. He walked by her side until they reached the stairs, and then followed her down, tail thumping against the railing with every step.

The door to abba's workshop was painted red and stenciled with white flowers that Mara had helped ima paint when she was five. Inside, half-finished apparatuses sprawled across workbenches covered in sawdust and disassembled electronics. Hanging from the ceiling, a marionette stared blankly at Mara and Abel as they passed, the glint on its pupils moving back and forth as its strings swayed. A mechanical hand sprang to life, its motion sensor triggered by Abel's tail. Abel whuffed at its palm and then hid behind Mara. The thing's fingers grasped at Mara's sleeve, leaving an impression of dusty, concentric whorls.

Abba stood at the back of the workshop, next to a child-sized doll that sat on a metal stool. Its limbs fell in slack, uncomfortable positions. Its face looked like the one Mara still expected to see in the mirror: a broad forehead over flushed cheeks scattered with freckles. Skin peeled away in places, revealing wire streams.

Mara moved to stand in front of the doll. It seemed even eerier, examined face to face, its expression a lifeless twin of hers. She reached out to touch its soft, brown hair. Her bald scalp tingled.

Gently, Abba took Mara's hand and pressed her right palm against the doll's. Apart from how thin Mara's fingers had become over the past few months, they matched perfectly.

Abba made a triumphant noise. "The shape is right."

Mara pulled her hand out of abba's. She squinted at the doll's imitation flesh. Horrifyingly, its palm shared each of the creases on hers, as if it, too, had spent twelve years dancing and reading books and learning to cook.

Abel circled the doll. He sniffed its feet and ankles and then paused at the back of its knees, whuffing as if he'd expected to smell something that wasn't there. After completing his circuit, he collapsed on the floor, equidistant from the three human-shaped figures.

"What do you think of her?" abba asked.

Goosebumps prickled Mara's neck. "What is she?"

Abba cradled the doll's head in his hands. Its eyes rolled back, and the light highlighted its lashes, fair and short, just like Mara's own. "She's a prototype. Empty-headed. A friend of mine is working on new technology for the government—"

"A prototype?" repeated Mara. "Of what?"

"The body is simple mechanics. Anyone could build it. The technology in the mind is new. It takes pictures of the brain in motion, all three dimensions, and then creates schematics for artificial neural clusters that will function like the original biological matter—"

Mara's head ached. Her mouth was sore and her stomach hurt and she wanted to go back to bed even if she couldn't sleep. She eyed the doll. The wires under its skin were vivid red and blue as if they were veins and arteries connecting to viscera.

"The military will make use of the technology," Abba continued. "They wish to recreate soldiers with advanced training. They are not ready for human tests, not yet. They are still experimenting with animals. They've made rats with mechanical brains that can solve mazes the original rats were trained to run. Now they are working with chimpanzees."

Abba's accent deepened as he continued, his gestures increasingly emphatic.

"But I am better. I can make it work in humans now, without more experiments." Urgently, he lowered his voice. "My friend was not supposed to send me the schematics. I paid him much money, but his reason for helping is that I have promised him that when I fix the problems, I will show him the solution and he can take the credit. This technology is not for civilians. No one else will be able to do this. We are very fortunate."

Abba touched the doll's shoulder so lightly that only his fingertips brushed her.

"I will need you to sit for some scans so that I can make the images that will preserve you. They will be painless. I can set up when you sleep." Quietly, he added, "She is my gift to you. She will hold you and keep you . . . if the worst . . ." His voice faded, and he swallowed twice, three times, before beginning again. "She will protect you."

Mara's voice came out hoarse. "Why didn't you tell me?"

"You needed to see her when she was complete."

Her throat constricted. "I wish I'd never seen her at all!"

From the cradle, Mara had been even-tempered. Now, at twelve, she shouted and cried. Abba said it was only what happened to children as they grew older, but they both knew that wasn't why.

Neither was used to her new temper. The lash of her shout startled them both. Abba's expression turned stricken.

"I don't understand," he said.

"You made a new daughter!"

"No, no." Abba held up his hands to protect himself from her accusation. "She is made *for* you."

"I'm sure she'll be a better daughter than I am," Mara said bitterly.

She grabbed a hank of the doll's hair. Its head tilted toward her in a parody of curiosity. She pushed it away. The thing tumbled to the floor, limbs awkwardly splayed.

Abba glanced toward the doll, but did not move to see if it was broken. "I—No, Marale—You don't—" His face grew drawn with sudden resolution. He pulled a hammer off of one of the work benches. "Then I will smash her to pieces."

There had been a time when, with the hammer in his hand and a determined expression on his face, he'd have looked like a smith from old legends. Now he'd lost so much weight that his skin hung loosely from his enormous frame as if he were a giant coat suspended from a hanger. Tears sprang to Mara's eyes.

She slapped at his hands and the hammer in them. "Stop it!"

"If you want her to—"

"Stop it! Stop it!" she shouted.

Abba released the hammer. It fell against the cement with a hollow, mournful sound.

Guilt shot through her, at his confusion, at his fear. What should she do, let him destroy this thing he'd made? What should she do, let the hammer blow strike, watch herself be shattered?

Sawdust billowed where the hammer hit. Abel whined and fled the room, tail between his legs.

Softly, abba said, "I don't know what else to give."

Abba had always been the emotional heart of the family, even when ima was alive. His anger flared; his tears flowed; his laughter roared from his gut. Mara rested her head on his chest until his tears slowed, and then walked with him upstairs.

NEBULA AWARD NOMINEE
BEST NOVELLA

EXCERPT FROM
WE ARE ALL COMPLETELY FINE

DARYL GREGORY

Daryl Gregory is the winner of a World Fantasy Award and a Shirley Jackson Award, and has been nominated for many other awards. We Are All Completely Fine *was originally published by Tachyon Press.*

Chapter 1

There were six of us in the beginning. Three men and two women, and Dr. Sayer. *Jan,* though some of us never learned to call her by her first name. She was the psychologist who found us, then persuaded us that a group experience could prove useful in ways that one-on-one counseling could not. After all, one of the issues we had in common was that we each thought we were unique. Not just survivors, but *sole* survivors. We wore our scars like badges.

Consider Harrison, one of the first of us to arrive at the building for that initial meeting. Once upon a time he'd been the Boy Hero of Dunnsmouth. The Monster Detective. Now he sat behind the wheel of his car, watching the windows of her office, trying to decide whether he would break his promise to her and skip out. The office was in a two-story, Craft-style house on the north side of the city, on a woodsy block that could look sinister or comforting depending on the light. A decade before, this family home had been rezoned and colonized by shrinks; they converted the bedrooms to offices, made the living room into a lobby, and planted a sign out front declaring its name to be

"The Elms." Maybe not the best name, Harrison thought. He would have suggested a species of tree that wasn't constantly in danger of being wiped out.

Today, the street did not look sinister. It was a sunny spring day, one of the few tolerable days the city would get before the heat and humidity rolled in for the summer. So why ruin it with ninety minutes of self-pity and communal humiliation?

He was suspicious of the very premise of therapy. The idea that people could change themselves, he told Dr. Sayer in their pre-group interview, was a self-serving delusion. She believed that people were captains of their own destiny. He agreed, as long as it was understood that every captain was destined to go down with the ship, and there wasn't a damned thing you could do about it. If you want to stand there with the wheel in your hand and pretend you were steering, he told her, knock yourself out.

She'd said, "Yet you're here."

He shrugged. "I have trouble sleeping. My psychiatrist said he wouldn't renew my prescriptions unless I tried therapy."

"Is that all?"

"Also, I might be *entertaining* the idea of tamping down my nihilism. Just a bit. Not because life is *not* meaningless—I think that's inarguable. It's just that the constant awareness of its pointlessness is exhausting. I wouldn't mind being oblivious again. I'd love to feel the wind in my face and think, just for minute, that I'm not going to crash into the rocks."

"You're saying you'd like to be happy."

"Yeah. That."

She smiled. He liked that smile. "Promise me you'll try one meeting," she said. "Just give me one."

Now he was having second thoughts. It wasn't too late to drive away. He could always find a new psychiatrist to fork over the meds.

A blue and white transit van pulled into the handicap parking spot in front of the house. The driver hopped out. He was a hefty white kid, over six feet tall with a scruffy beard, dressed in the half-ass uniform of the retail class: colored polo over Gap khakis. He opened the rearmost door of the van to reveal an old man waiting in a wheelchair.

The driver thumbed a control box, and the lift lowered the chair and occupant to the ground with the robotic slow motion of a space shuttle arm. The old man was already half astronaut, with his breathing mask and plastic tubes and tanks of onboard oxygen. His hands seemed to be covered by mittens.

Was this geezer part of the group, Harrison wondered, or visiting some other shrink in the building? Just how damaged were the people that Dr. Sayer had recruited? He had no desire to spend hours with the last people voted off Victim Island.

The driver seemed to have no patience for his patient. Instead of going the long way around to the ramp, he pushed the old man to the curb, then roughly tilted him back—too far back—and bounced the front wheels down on the sidewalk. The old man pressed his mittened hands to his face, trying to keep the mask in place. Another series of heaves and jerks got the man up the short stairs and into the house.

Then Harrison noticed the girl. Eighteen, maybe nineteen years old, sitting on a bench across from the house, watching the old man and the driver intently. She wore a black, long-sleeved T-shirt, black jeans, black Chuck Taylors: the Standard Goth Burka. Her short white hair looked like it had been not so much styled as attacked. Her hands gripped the edge of the bench and she did not relax even after the pair had gone inside. She was like a feral cat: skinny, glint-eyed, shock-haired. Ready to bolt.

For the next few minutes he watched the girl as she watched the front of the house. A few people passed by on the sidewalk, and then a tall white woman stepped up to the door. Fortyish, with careful hair and a Hillary Clinton pant-suit. She moved with an air of concentration; when she climbed the steps, she placed each foot carefully, as if testing the solidity of each surface.

A black guy in flannels and thick work boots clumped up the stairs behind the woman. She stopped, turned. The guy looked up at the roof of the porch. An odd thing. He carried a backpack and wore thick black sunglasses, and Harrison couldn't imagine what he saw up there. The white woman said something to him, holding open the door, and he nodded. They went inside together.

It was almost six o'clock, so Harrison assumed that everyone who'd gone in was part of the group. The girl, though, still hadn't made a move toward the door.

"Fuck it," Harrison said. He got out of the car before he could change his mind, and then walked toward the house. When he reached the front sidewalk he glanced behind him—casually, casually. The girl noticed him and looked away. He was certain that she'd been invited to the group too. He was willing to bet that she might be the craziest one of all.

NEBULA AWARD WINNER
BEST NOVELLA

YESTERDAY'S KIN

NANCY KRESS

Nancy Anne Kress has won six Nebula Awards, two Hugo Awards, a John W. Campbell Memorial Award, a Theodore Sturgeon Memorial Award, and two Locus Awards, along with a host of nominations. Yesterday's Kin was first published by Tachyon Press.

"We see in these facts some deep organic bond, prevailing throughout space and time. . . . This bond, on my theory, is simple inheritance."
—Charles Darwin, *The Origin of Species*

I: S minus 10.5 months

MARIANNE

The publication party was held in the dean's office, which was supposed to be an honor. Oak-paneled room, sherry in little glasses, small-paned windows facing the quad—the room was trying hard to be a Commons someplace like Oxford or Cambridge, a task for which it was several centuries too late. The party was trying hard to look festive. Marianne's colleagues, except for Evan and the dean, were trying hard not to look too envious, or at their watches.

"Stop it," Evan said at her from behind the cover of his raised glass.

"Stop what?"

"Pretending you hate this."

"I hate this," Marianne said.

"You don't."

He was half right. She didn't like parties but she was proud of her paper, which had been achieved despite two years of gene sequencers that kept breaking down, inept graduate students who contaminated samples with their own DNA, murmurs of "Lucky find" from Baskell, with whom she'd never gotten along. Baskell, an old-guard physicist, saw her as a bitch who refused to defer to rank or back down gracefully in an argument. Many people, Marianne knew, saw her as some variant of this. The list included two of her three grown children.

Outside the open casements, students lounged on the grass in the mellow October sunshine. Three girls in cut-off jeans played Frisbee, leaping at the blue flying saucer and checking to see if the boys sitting on the stone wall were watching. Feinberg and Davidson, from Physics, walked by, arguing amiably. Marianne wished she were with them instead of at her own party.

"Oh God," she said to Evan, "Curtis just walked in."

The president of the university made his ponderous way across the room. Once he had been an historian, which might be why he reminded Marianne of Henry VIII. Now he was a campus politician, as power-mad as Henry but stuck at a second-rate university where there wasn't much power to be had. Marianne held against him not his personality but his mind; unlike Henry, he was not all that bright. And he spoke in clichés.

"Dr. Jenner," he said, "congratulations. A feather in your cap, and a credit to us all."

"Thank you, Dr. Curtis," Marianne said.

"Oh, 'Ed,' please."

"Ed." She didn't offer her own first name, curious to see if he remembered it. He didn't. Marianne sipped her sherry.

Evan jumped into the awkward silence. "I'm Dr. Blanford, visiting post-doc," he said in his plummy British accent. "We're all so proud of Marianne's work."

"Yes! And I'd love for you to explain to me your innovative process, ah, Marianne."

He didn't have a clue. His secretary had probably reminded him that he had to put in an appearance at the party: *Dean of Science's office, 4:30 Friday, in honor of that publication by Dr. Jenner in*—quick look at email—*in* Nature, *very prestigious, none of our scientists have published there before. . . .*

"Oh," Marianne said as Evan poked her discreetly in the side: *Play nice*! "it wasn't so much an innovation in process as unexpected results from known procedures. My assistants and I discovered a new haplogroup of mitochondrial DNA. Previously it was thought that *Homo sapiens* consisted of thirty haplogroups, and we found a thirty-first."

"By sequencing a sample of contemporary genes, you know," Evan said helpfully. "Sequencing and verifying."

Anything said in upper-crust British automatically sounded intelligent, and Dr. Curtis looked suitably impressed. "Of course, of course. Splendid results. A star in your crown."

"It's yet another haplogroup descended," Evan said with malicious helpfulness, "from humanity's common female ancestor 150,000 years ago. 'Mitochondrial Eve.'"

Dr. Curtis brightened. There had been a TV program about Mitochondrial Eve, Marianne remembered, featuring a buxom actress in a leopard-skin sarong. "Oh, yes! Wasn't that—"

"I'm sorry, you can't go in there!" someone shrilled in the corridor outside the room. All conversation ceased. Heads swiveled toward three men in dark suits pushing their way past the knot of graduate students by the door. The three men wore guns.

Another school shooting, Marianne thought, *where can I—*

"Dr. Marianne Jenner?" the tallest of the three men said, flashing a badge. "I'm Special Agent Douglas Katz of the F.B.I. We'd like you to come with us."

Marianne said, "Am I under arrest?"

"No, no, nothing like that. We are acting under direct order of the president of the United States. We're here to escort you to New York."

Evan had taken Marianne's hand—she wasn't sure just when. There was nothing romantic in the hand-clasp, nor anything sexual. Evan, twenty-five years her junior and discreetly gay, was a friend, an ally, the only other evolutionary biologist in the department and the only one who shared Marianne's cynical sense of humor. "*Or so we thought*," they said to each other whenever any hypothesis proved wrong. *Or so we thought* . . . His fingers felt warm and reassuring around her suddenly icy ones.

"Why am I going to New York?"

"I'm afraid we can't tell you that. But it is a matter of national security."

"*Me*? What possible reason—?"

Special Agent Katz almost, but not quite, hid his impatience at her questions. "I wouldn't know, ma'am. My orders are to escort you to UN Special Mission Headquarters in Manhattan."

Marianne looked at her gaping colleagues, at the wide-eyed grad students, at Dr. Curtis, who was already figuring how this could be turned to the advantage of the university. She freed her hand from Evan's, and managed to keep her voice steady.

"Please excuse me, Dr. Curtis, Dean. It seems I'm needed for something connected with . . . with the aliens."

*   *   *

NOAH

One more time, Noah Jenner rattled the doorknob to the apartment. It felt greasy from too many unwashed palms, and it was still locked. But he knew that Emily was in there. That was the kind of thing he was always, somehow, right about. He was right about things that didn't do him any good.

"Emily," he said softly through the door, "please open up."

Nothing.

"Emily, I have nowhere else to go."

Nothing.

"I'll stop, I promise. I won't do sugarcane ever again."

The door opened a crack, chain still in place, and Emily's despairing face appeared. She wasn't the kind of girl given to dramatic fury, but her quiet despair was even harder to bear. Not that Noah didn't deserve it. He knew he did. Her fair hair hung limply on either side of her long, sad face. She wore the green bathrobe he liked, with the butterfly embroidered on the left shoulder.

"You won't stop," Emily said. "You can't. You're an addict."

"It's not an addictive drug. You know that."

"Not physically, maybe. But it is for you. You won't give it up. I'll never know who you really are."

"I—"

"I'm sorry, Noah. But—go away." She closed and relocked the door.

Noah stood slumped against the dingy wall, waiting to see if anything else would happen. Nothing did. Eventually, as soon as he mustered the energy, he would have to go away.

Was she right? Would he never give up sugarcane? It wasn't that it delivered a high: it didn't. No rush of dopamine, no psychedelic illusions, no out-of-body experiences, no lowering of inhibitions. It was just that on sugarcane, Noah felt like he was the person he was supposed to be. The problem was that it was never the same person twice. Sometimes he felt like a warrior, able to face and ruthlessly defeat anything. Sometimes he felt like a philosopher, deeply content to sit and ponder the universe. Sometimes he felt like a little child, dazzled by the newness of a fresh morning. Sometimes he felt like a father (he wasn't), protective of the entire world. Theories said that sugarcane released memories of past lives, or stimulated the collective unconscious, or made temporarily solid the images of dreams. One hypothesis was that it created a sort of temporary, self-induced Korsakoff's Syndrome, the neurological disorder in which invented selves seem completely true. No one knew how sugarcane really acted on the brain. For some people, it did nothing at all. For Noah, who had never felt he fit in anywhere, it gave what he had never had: a sense of solid identity, if only for the hours that the drug stayed in his system.

The problem was, it was difficult to hold a job when one day you were nebbishy, sweet-natured Noah Jenner, the next day you were Attila the Hun, and two days later you were far too intellectual to wash dishes or make change at a convenience store. Emily had wanted Noah to hold a job. To contribute to the rent, to scrub the floor, to help take the sheets to the laundromat. To be an adult, and the same adult every day. She was right to want that. Only—

He might be able to give up sugarcane and be the same adult, if only he had the vaguest idea who that adult was. Which brought him back to the same problem—he didn't fit anywhere. And never had.

Noah picked up the backpack in which Emily had put his few belongings. She couldn't have left it in the hallway very long ago or the backpack would have already been stolen. He made his way down the three flights from Emily's walk-up and out onto the streets. The October sun shone warmly on his shoulders, on the blocks of shabby buildings, on the trash skirling across the dingy streets of New York's lower East Side. Walking, Noah reflected bitterly, was one thing he could do without fitting in. He walked blocks to Battery Park, that green oasis on the tip of Manhattan's steel canyons, leaned on a railing, and looked south.

He could just make out the *Embassy*, floating in New York Harbor. Well, no, not the *Embassy* itself, but the shimmer of light off its energy shield. Everybody wanted that energy shield, including his sister Elizabeth. It kept everything out, short of a nuclear missile. Maybe that, too: so far nobody had tried, although in the two months since the embassy had floated there, three different terrorist groups had tried other weapons. Nothing got through the shield, although maybe air and light did. They must, right? Even aliens needed to breathe.

When the sun dropped below the horizon, the glint off the floating embassy disappeared. Dusk was gathering. He would have to make the call if he wanted a place to sleep tonight. Elizabeth or Ryan? His brother wouldn't yell at him as much, but Ryan lived upstate, in the same little Hudson River town as their mother's college, and Noah would have to hitchhike there. Also, Ryan was often away, doing field work for his wildlife agency. Noah didn't think he could cope with Ryan's talkative, sticky-sweet wife right now. So it would have to be Elizabeth.

He called his sister's number on his cheap cell. "Hello?" she snapped. *Born angry*, their mother always said of Elizabeth. Well, Elizabeth was in the right job, then.

"Lizzie, it's Noah."

"Noah."

"Yes. I need help. Can I stay with you tonight?" He held the cell away from his ear, bracing for her onslaught. *Shiftless, lazy, directionless* . . . When it was over, he said, "Just for tonight."

They both knew he was lying, but Elizabeth said, "Come on then" and clicked off without saying good-bye.

If he'd had more than a few dollars in his pocket, Noah would have looked for a sugarcane dealer. Since he didn't, he left the park, the wind pricking at him now with tiny needles, and descended to the subway that would take him to Elizabeth's apartment on the upper West Side.

* * *

MARIANNE

The F.B.I. politely declined to answer any of Marianne's questions. Politely, they confiscated her cell and iPad and took her in a sleek black car down Route 87 to New York, through the city to lower Manhattan, and out to a harbor pier. Gates with armed guards controlled access to a heavily fortified building at the end of the pier. Politely, she was searched and fingerprinted. Then she was politely asked to wait in a small windowless room equipped with a few comfortable chairs, a table with coffee and cookies, and a wall-mounted TV tuned to CNN. A news show was covering weather in Florida.

The aliens had shown up four months ago, their ship barreling out from the direction of the sun, which had made it harder to detect until a few weeks before arrival. At first, in fact, the ship had been mistaken for an asteroid and there had been panic that it would hit Earth. When it was announced that the asteroid was in fact an alien vessel, panic had decreased in some quarters and increased in others. A ship? Aliens? Armed forces across the world mobilized. Communications strategies were formed, and immediately hacked by the curious and technologically sophisticated. Seven different religions declared the end of the world. The stock and bond markets crashed, rallied, soared, crashed again, and generally behaved like a reed buffeted by a hurricane. Governments put the world's top linguists, biologists, mathematicians, astronomers, and physicists on top-priority stand-by. Psychics blossomed. People rejoiced and feared and prayed and committed suicide and sent up balloons in the general direction of the moon, where the alien ship eventually parked itself in orbit.

Contact was immediate, in robotic voices that were clearly mechanical, and in halting English that improved almost immediately. The aliens, dubbed by the press "Denebs" because their ship came from the general direction of that bright, blue-white star, were friendly. The xenophiles looked smugly triumphant. The xenophobes disbelieved the friendliness and bided their time. The aliens spent two months talking to the United Nations. They were reassuring; this was a peace mission. They were also reticent. Voice communication only, and through machines. They would not show themselves: "Not now. We wait." They would not visit the International Space Station, nor permit humans to visit their ship. They identified their planet, and astronomers found it once they knew where to look, by the faintly eclipsed light from its orange-dwarf star. The planet was in the star's habitable zone, slightly larger than Earth but less dense, water present. It was nowhere near Deneb, but the name stuck.

After two months, the aliens requested permission to build what they called an embassy, a floating pavilion, in New York Harbor. It would be heavily shielded and would not affect the environment. In exchange, they would share the physics behind their star drive, although not the engineering, with Earth, via the Internet. The UN went into furious debate. Physicists salivated. Riots erupted, pro and con, in major cities across the globe. Conspiracy theorists, some consisting of entire governments, vowed to attack any Deneb presence on Earth.

The UN finally agreed, and the structure went into orbit around Earth, landed without a splash in the harbor, and floated peacefully offshore. After landing, it grew wider and flatter, a half-dome that could be considered either an island or a ship. The US government decided it was a ship, subject to maritime law, and the media began capitalizing and italicizing it: the *Embassy*. Coast Guard craft circled it endlessly; the US Navy had ships and submarines nearby. Airspace above was a no-fly zone, which was inconvenient for jets landing at New York's three big airports. Fighter jets nearby stayed on high alert.

Nothing happened.

For another two months the aliens continued to talk through their machines to the UN, and only to the UN, and nobody ever saw them. It wasn't known whether they were shielding themselves from Earth's air, microbes, or armies. The *Embassy* was surveilled by all possible means. If anybody learned anything, the information was classified except for a single exchange:

Why are you here?

To make contact with humanity. A peace mission.

A musician set the repeated phrases to music, a sly and humorous refrain, without menace. The song, an instant international sensation, was the opening for playfulness about the aliens. Late-night comics built monologues around supposed alien practices. The *Embassy* became a tourist attraction, viewed through telescopes, from boats outside the Coast Guard limit, from helicopters outside the no-fly zone. A German fashion designer scored an enormous runway hit with "the Deneb look," despite the fact that no one knew how the Denebs looked. The stock market stabilized as much as it ever did. Quickie movies were shot, some with Deneb allies and some with treacherous Deneb foes who wanted our women or gold or bombs. Bumper stickers proliferated like kudzu: I BRAKE FOR DENEBS. EARTH IS FULL ALREADY—GO HOME. DENEBS DO IT INVISIBLY. WILL TRADE PHYSICS FOR FOOD.

The aliens never commented on any of it. They published the promised physics, which only a few dozen people in the world could understand. They were courteous, repetitive, elusive. *Why are you here? To make contact with humanity. A peace mission.*

Marianne stared at the TV, where CNN showed footage of disabled children choosing Halloween costumes. Nothing about the discussion, the room, the situation felt real. Why would the aliens want to talk to her? It had to be about her paper, nothing else made sense. No, that didn't make sense either.

"—donated by a network of churches from five states. Four-year-old Amy seizes eagerly on the black-cat costume, while her friend Kayla chooses—"

Her paper was one of dozens published every year on evolutionary genetics, each paper adding another tiny increment to statistical data on the subject. Why this one? Why her? The UN Secretary General, various presidents and premiers, top scientists—the press said they all talked to the Denebs from this modern fortress, through (pick one) highly encrypted devices that permitted no visuals, or one-way visuals, or two-way visuals that the UN was keeping secret, or not at all and the whole alien-human conversation was invented. The *Embassy*, however, was certainly real. Images of it appeared on magazine covers, coffee mugs, screen savers, tee shirts, paintings on velvet, targets for shooting ranges.

Marianne's daughter Elizabeth regarded the aliens with suspicion, but then, Elizabeth regarded everyone with suspicion. It was one reason she was the youngest Border Patrol section leader in the country, serving on the New York Task Force along with several other agencies. She fit right in with the current American obsession with isolationism as an economic survival strategy.

Ryan seldom mentioned the aliens. He was too absorbed in his career and his wife.

And Noah—did Noah, her problem child, even realize the aliens were here? Marianne hadn't seen Noah in months. In the spring he had gone to "try life in the South." An occasional email turned up on her phone, never containing much actual information. If Noah was back in New York, he hadn't called her yet. Marianne didn't want to admit what a relief that was. Her child, her baby—but every time they saw each other, it ended in recriminations or tears.

And what was she doing, thinking about her children instead of the aliens? Why did the ambassador want to talk to her? Why were the Denebs here?

To make contact with humanity. A peace mission . . .

"Dr. Jenner?"

"Yes." She stood up from her chair, her jaw set. Somebody better give her some answers, now.

The young man looked doubtfully at her clothes, dark jeans and a green suede blazer ten years old, her standard outfit for faculty parties. He said, "Secretary Desai will join you shortly."

Marianne tried to let her face show nothing. A few moments later Vihaan Desai, Secretary General of the United Nations, entered the room, followed by a security detail. Tall, elderly, he wore a sky-blue kurta of heavy, richly embroidered silk. Marianne felt like a wren beside a peacock. Desai held out his hand but did not smile. Relations between the United States and India were not good. Relations between the United States and everybody were not good, as the country relentlessly pursued its new policy of economic isolationism in an attempt to protect jobs. Until the Denebs came, with their cosmos-shaking distraction, the UN had been thick with international threats. Maybe it still was.

"Dr. Jenner," Desai said, studying her intently, "it seems we are both summoned to interstellar conference." His English, in the musical Indian accent, was perfect. Marianne remembered that he spoke four languages.

She said, "Do you know why?"

Her directness made him blink. "I do not. The Deneb ambassador was insistent but not forthcoming."

And does humanity do whatever the ambassador insists on? Marianne did not say this aloud. Something here was not adding up. The Secretary General's next words stunned her.

"We, plus a few others, are invited aboard the *Embassy*. The invitation is dependent upon your presence, and upon its immediate acceptance."

"Aboard . . . aboard the *Embassy*?"

"It seems so."

"But nobody has ever—"

"I am well aware of that." The dark, intelligent eyes never left her face. "We await only the other guests who happen to be in New York."

"I see." She didn't.

Desai turned to his security detail and spoke to them in Hindi. An argument began. Did security usually argue with their protectees? Marianne wouldn't have thought so, but then, what did she know about UN protocol? She was out of her field, her league, her solar system. Her guess was that the Denebs were not allowing bodyguards aboard the *Embassy*, and that the security chief was protesting.

Evidently the Secretary General won. He said to her, "Please come," and walked with long strides from the room. His kurta rustled at his ankles, shimmering sky. Not intuitive, Marianne could nonetheless sense the tension coming off him like heat. They went down a long corridor, trailed by deeply frowning guards, and down an elevator. Very far down—did the elevator go under the harbor? It must. They exited into a small room already occupied by two people, a man and a woman. Marianne recognized the woman: Ekaterina Zaytsev, the representative to the UN from the Russian Federation. The man might be the Chinese representative. Both looked agitated.

Desai said in English, "We await only—ah, here they are."

Two much younger men practically blew into the room, clutching headsets. Translators. They looked disheveled and frightened, which made Marianne feel better. She wasn't the only one battling an almost overwhelming sense of unreality. If only Evan could be here, with his sardonic and unflappable Britishness. *"Or so we thought . . ."*

No. Neither she nor Evan had ever thought of this.

"The other permanent members of the Security Council are unfortunately not immediately available," Desai said. "We will not wait."

Marianne couldn't remember who the other permanent members were. The UK, surely, but who else? How many? What were they doing this October dusk that would make them miss first contact with an alien species? Whatever it was, they had to regret it the rest of their lives.

Unless, of course, this little delegation never returned—killed or kidnapped or eaten. No, that was ridiculous. She was being hysterical. Desai would not go if there were danger.

Of course he would. Anyone would. Wouldn't they? Wouldn't she? Nobody, she suddenly realized, had actually asked her to go on this mission. She'd been ordered to go. What if she flat-out refused?

A door opened at the far end of the small room, voices spoke from the air about clearance and proceeding, and then another elevator. The six people stepped into what had to be the world's most comfortable and unwarlike submarine, equipped with lounge chairs and gold-braided officers.

A submarine. Well, that made sense, if plans had been put in place to get to the *Embassy* unobserved by press, tourists, and nut jobs who would blow up the alien base if they could. The Denebs must have agreed to some sort of landing place or entryway, which meant this meeting had been talked of, planned for, long before today. Today was just the moment the aliens had decided to put the plan into practice. Why? Why so hastily?

"Dr. Jenner," Desai said, "in the short time we have here, please explain your scientific findings to us."

None of them sat in the lounge chairs. They stood in a circle around Marianne, who felt none of the desire to toy with them as she had with Dr. Curtis at the college. Where were her words going, besides this cramped, luxurious submarine? Was the president of the United States listening, packed into the situation room with whoever else belonged there?

"My paper is nothing startling, Mr. Secretary General, which is why this is all baffling to me. In simple terms—" she tried to not be distracted by the murmuring of the two translators into their mouthpieces "—all humans alive today are the descendants of one woman who lived about 150,000 years ago. We know this because of mitochondrial DNA, which is not the DNA from the nucleus of the cell but separate DNA found in small organelles called mitochondria. Mitochondria, which exist in every cell of your body, are the powerhouses of the cell, producing energy for cellular functions. Mitochondrial DNA does not undergo recombination and is not found in sperm cell after they reach the egg. So the mitochondrial DNA is passed down unchanged from a mother to all her children.

Marianne paused, wondering how to explain this simply, but without condescension. "Mitochondrial DNA mutates at a steady rate, about one mutation every 10,000 years in a section called 'the control region,' and about once every 3,500 years in the mitochondrial DNA as a whole. By tracing the number and type of mutations in contemporary humans, we can construct a tree of descent: which group descended from which female ancestor.

"Evolutionary biologists have identified thirty of these haplogroups. I found a new one, L7, by sequencing and comparing DNA samples with a standard human mitochondrial sample, known as the revised Cambridge Reference Sequence."

"How did you know where to look for this new group?"

"I didn't. I came across the first sample by chance and then sampled her relatives."

"Is it very different, then, from the others?"

"No," Marianne said. "It's just a branch of the L haplogroup."

"Why wasn't it discovered before?"

"It seems to be rare. The line must have mostly died out over time. It's a very old line, one of the first divergences from Mitochondrial Eve."

"So there is nothing remarkable about your finding?"

"Not in the least. There may even be more haplogroups out there that we just haven't discovered yet." She felt a perfect fool. They all looked at her as if expecting answers—Look! A blinding scientific light illuminate all!—and she had none. She was a workman scientist who had delivered a workmanlike job of fairly routine halotyping.

"Sir, we have arrived," said a junior officer. Marianne saw that his dress blues were buttoned wrong. They must have been donned in great haste. The tiny, human mishap made her feel better.

Desai drew a deep, audible breath. Even he, who had lived through war and revolution, was nervous. Commands flew through the air from invisible people. The submarine door opened.

Marianne stepped out into the alien ship.

* * *

NOAH

"Where's Mom? Did you call her?" Elizabeth demanded.

"Not yet," Noah said.

"Does she even know you're in New York?"

"Not yet." He wanted to tell his sister to stop hammering at him, but he was her guest and so he couldn't. Not that he'd ever been able to stand up to either of his siblings. His usual ploy had been to get them battering on each other and leave him alone. Maybe he could do that now. Or maybe not.

"Noah, how long have you been in the city?"

"A while."

"How long a while?"

Noah put his hand in front of his face. "Lizzie, I'm really hungry. I didn't eat today. Do you think you could—"

"Don't start your whining-and-helpless routine with me, Noah. It doesn't work anymore."

Had it ever? Noah didn't think so, not with Elizabeth. He tried to pull himself together. "Elizabeth, I haven't called Mom yet and I *am* hungry. Please, could we defer this fight until I eat something? Anything, crackers or toast or—"

"There's sandwich stuff in the fridge. Help yourself. I'm going to call Mom, since at least one of us should let her know the prodigal son has deigned to turn up again. She's been out of her mind with worry about you."

Noah doubted that. His mother was the strongest person he knew, followed by Elizabeth and Ryan. Together, the three could have toppled empires. Of course, they seldom were together, since they fought almost every time they met. Odd that they would go on meeting so often, when it produced such bitterness, and all over such inconsequential things. Politics, religion, funding for the arts, isolationism. . . . He rummaged in Elizabeth's messy refrigerator, full of plastic containers with their lids half off, some with dabs of rotting food stuck to the bottom. God, this one was growing *mold*. But he found bread, cheese, and some salsa that seemed all right.

Elizabeth's one-bedroom apartment echoed her fridge, which was another reason she and Mom fought. Unmade bed, dusty stacks of journals and newspapers, a vase of dead flowers probably sent by one of the boyfriends Elizabeth never fell in love with. Mom's house north of the city, and Ryan and Connie's near hers, were neat and bright. Housecleaners came weekly; food was bought from careful lists; possessions were replaced whenever they got shabby. Noah had no possessions, or at least as few as he could manage.

Elizabeth clutched the phone. She dressed like a female FBI agent—short hair, dark pantsuit, no make-up—and was beautiful without trying. "Come on, Mom, pick up," she muttered, "it's a cell, it's supposed to be portable."

"Maybe she's in class," Noah said. "Or a meeting."

"It's Friday night, Noah."

"Oh. Yeah."

"I'll try the landline. She still has one."

Someone answered the landline on the first ring; Noah heard the chime stop from where he sat munching his sandwich. Then silence.

"Hello? Hello? Mom?" Elizabeth said.

The receiver on the other end clicked.

"That's odd," Elizabeth said.

"You probably got a wrong number."

"Don't talk with your mouth full. I'm going to try again."

This time no one answered. Elizabeth scowled. "I don't like that. Someone is there. I'm going to call Ryan."

Wasn't Ryan somewhere in Canada doing field work? Or maybe Noah had the dates wrong. He'd only glanced at the email from Ryan, accessed on a terminal at the public library. That day he'd been on sugarcane, and the temporary identity had been impatient and brusque.

"Ryan? This is Elizabeth. Do you know where Mom is? . . . If I knew her schedule I wouldn't be calling, would I? . . . Wait, wait, will you *listen* for a minute? I called her house and someone picked up and then clicked off, and when I called back a second later, it just rang. Will you go over there just to check it out? . . . Okay, yes, we'll wait. Oh, Noah's here . . . No, I'm not going to discuss with you right now the . . . *Ryan*. For chrissake, go check Mom's house!" She clicked off.

Noah wished he were someplace else. He wished he were somebody else. He wished he had some sugarcane.

Elizabeth flounced into a chair and picked up a book. *Tariffs, Borders, and the Survival of the United States*, Noah read upside-down. Elizabeth was a passionate defender of isolationism. How many desperate people trying to crash the United States borders had she arrested today? Noah didn't want to think about it.

Fifteen minutes later, Ryan called back. Elizabeth put the call on speaker phone. "Liz, there are cop cars around Mom's house. They wouldn't let me in. A guy came out and said Mom isn't dead or hurt or in trouble, and he couldn't tell me any more than that."

"Okay." Elizabeth wore her focused look, the one with which she directed border patrols. "I'll try the college."

"I did. I reached Evan. He said that three men claiming to be FBI came and escorted her to the UN Special Mission Headquarters in Manhattan."

"That doesn't make sense!"

"I know. Listen, I'm coming over to your place."

"I'm calling the police."

"No! Don't! Not until I get there and we decide what to do."

Noah listened to them argue, which went on until Ryan hung up. Of course Elizabeth, who worked for a quasi-military organization, wanted to call the cops. Of course Ryan, who worked for a wildlife organization that thought the government had completely messed up regulations on invasive botanical species, would shun the cops. Meanwhile Mom was probably just doing something connected with her college, a UN fundraiser or something, and that geek Evan had gotten it all wrong. Noah didn't like Evan, who was only a few years older than he was. Evan was everything that Noah's family thought Noah should be: smart, smooth, able to fit in anyplace, even into a country that wasn't his own. And how come Elizabeth's border patrols hadn't kept out Evan Blanford?

Never mind; Noah knew the answer.

He said, "Can I do anything?"

Elizabeth didn't even answer him.

*   *   *

MARIANNE

She had seen many pictures of the *Embassy*. From the outside, the floating pavilion was beautiful in a stark sort of way. Hemispherical, multifaceted like a buckeyball (Had the Denebs learned that structure from humans or was it a mathematical universal?), the *Embassy* floated on a broad platform of some unknowable material. Facets and platform were blue but coated with the energy shield, which reflected sunlight so much that it glinted, a beacon of sorts. The aliens had certainly not tried to mask their presence. But there must be hidden machinery underneath, in the part known (maybe) only to Navy divers, since the entire huge structure had landed without a splash in the harbor. Plus, of course, the hidden passage through which the sub had come, presumably entailing a momentary interruption of the energy shield. Marianne knew she'd never find out the details.

The room into which she and the others stepped from the submarine was featureless except for the bed of water upon which their sub floated, droplets sliding off its sleek sides. No windows or furniture, one door. A strange smell permeated the air: Disinfectant? Perfume? Alien body odor? Marianne's heart began to beat oddly, too hard and too loud, with abrupt painful skips. Her breathing quickened.

The door opened and a Deneb came out. At first, she couldn't see it clearly; it was clouded by the same glittery energy shield that covered the *Embassy*. When her eyes adjusted, she gasped. The others also made sounds: a quick indrawn breath, a clicking of the tongue, what sounded like an actual whimper. The Russian translator whispered, *"Bozhe moi!"*

The alien looked almost human. Almost, not quite. Tall, maybe six-two, the man—it was clearly male—had long, thin arms and legs, a deep chest, a human face but much larger eyes. His skin was coppery and his hair, long and tied back, was dark brown. Most striking were his eyes: larger than humans', with huge dark pupils in a large expanse of white. He wore dark-green clothing, a simple tunic top over loose, short trousers that exposed his spindly calves. His feet were bare, and perhaps the biggest shock of all was that his feet, five-toed and broad, the nails cut short and square. Those feet looked so much like hers that she thought wildly: *He could wear my shoes.*

"Hello," the alien said, and it was not his voice but the mechanical one of the radio broadcasts, coming from the ceiling.

"Hello," Desai said, and bowed from the waist. "We are glad to finally meet. I am Secretary General Desai of the United Nations."

"Yes," the alien "said," and then added some trilling and clicking sounds in which his mouth did move. Immediately the ceiling said, "I welcome you in our own language."

Secretary Desai made the rest of the introductions with admirable calm. Marianne tried to fight her growing sense of unreality by recalling what she had read about the Denebs' planet. She wished she paid more attention to the astronomy. The popular press had said that the alien star was a K-something (K zero? K two? She couldn't remember). The alien home world had both less gravity and less light than Earth, at different wavelengths . . . orange, yes. The sun was an orange dwarf. Was this Deneb so tall because the gravity was less? Or maybe he was just a basketball player—

Get a grip, Marianne.

She did. The alien had said his name, an impossible collection of trilled phonemes, and immediately said, "Call me Ambassador Smith." How had he chosen that—from a computer-generated list of English names? When Marianne had been in Beijing to give a paper, some Chinese translators had done that: "Call me Dan." She had assumed the translators doubted her ability to pronounce their actual names correctly, and they had probably been right. But "Smith" for a starfarer . . .

"You are Dr. Jenner?"

"Yes, Ambassador."

"We wanted to talk with you, in particular. Will you please come this way, all of you?"

They did, trailing like baby ducklings after the tall alien. The room beyond the single door had been fitted up like the waiting room of a very expensive medical specialist. Did they order the upholstered chairs and patterned rug on the Internet? Or manufacture them with some advanced nanotech deep in the bowels of the *Embassy*? The wall pictures were of famous skylines: New York, Shanghai, Dubai, Paris. Nothing in the room suggested alienness. Deliberate? Of course it was. *Nobody here but us chickens.*

Marianne sat, digging the nails of one hand into the palm of the other to quiet her insane desire to giggle.

"I would like to know of your recent publication, Dr. Jenner," the ceiling said, while Ambassador Smith looked at her from his disconcertingly large eyes.

"Certainly," Marianne said, wondering where to begin. Where to begin? How much did they know about human genetics?

Quite a lot, as it turned out. For the next twenty minutes Marianne explained, gestured, answered questions. The others listened silently except for the low murmur of the Chinese and Russian translators. Everyone, human and alien, looked attentive and courteous, although Marianne detected the slightly pursed lips of Ekaterina Zaytsev's envy.

Slowly it became clear that Smith already knew much of what Marianne was saying. His questions centered on where she had gotten her DNA samples.

"They were volunteers," Marianne said. "Collection booths were set up in an open-air market in India, because I happened to have a colleague working there, in a train station in London, and on my college campus in the United States. At each place, a nominal fee was paid for a quick scraping of tissue from the inside of the cheek. After we found the first L7 DNA in a sample from an American student from Indiana, we went to her relatives to ask for samples. They were very cooperative."

"This L7 sample, according to your paper, comes from a mutation that marks the strain of one of the oldest of mitochondrial groups."

Desai made a quick, startled shift on his chair.

"That's right," Marianne said. "Evidence says that 'Mitochondrial Eve' had at least two daughters, and the line of one of them was L0 whereas the other line developed a mutation that became—" All at once she saw it, what Desai had already realized. She blinked at Smith and felt her mouth fall open, just as if she had no control over her jaw muscles, just as if the universe had been turned inside out, like a sock.

* * *

NOAH

An hour later, Ryan arrived at Elizabeth's apartment. Repeated calls to their mother's cell and landline had produced nothing. Ryan and Elizabeth sat on the sagging sofa, conferring quietly, their usual belligerence with each other replaced by shared concern. Noah sat across the room, listening.

His brother had been short-changed in the looks department. Elizabeth was beautiful in a severe way and Noah knew he'd gotten the best of his parents' genes: his dead father's height and athletic build, his mother's light-gray eyes flecked with gold. In contrast, Ryan was built like a fire hydrant: short, muscular, thickening into cylindricalness since his marriage; Connie was a good cook. At thirty, he was already balding. Ryan was smart, slow to change, humorless.

Elizabeth said, "Tell me exactly what Evan said about the FBI taking her away. Word for word."

Ryan did, adding, "What about this—we call the FBI and ask them directly where she is and what's going on."

"I tried that. The local field office said they didn't know anything about it, but they'd make inquiries and get back to me. They haven't."

"Of course not. We have to give them a reason to give out information, and on the way over I thought of two. We can say either that we're going to the press, or that we need to reach her for a medical emergency."

Elizabeth said, "I don't like the idea of threatening the feds—too potentially messy. The medical emergency might be better. We could say Connie's developed a problem with her pregnancy. First grandchild, life-threatening complications—"

Noah, startled, said, "Connie's pregnant?"

"Four months," Ryan said. "If you ever read the emails everybody sends you, you might have gotten the news. You're going to be an uncle." His gaze said that Noah would make just as rotten an uncle as he did a son.

Elizabeth said, "You need to make the phone call, Ryan. You're the prospective father."

Ryan pulled out his cell, which looked as if it could contact deep space. The FBI office was closed. He left a message. FBI Headquarters in D.C. were also closed. He left another message. Before Ryan could say, "They'll never get back to us" and so begin another argument with Elizabeth over governmental inefficiency, Noah said, "Did the Wildlife Society give you that cell for your job?"

"It's the International Wildlife Federation and yes, the phone has top-priority connections for the loosestrife invasion."

Noah ducked his head to hide his grin.

Elizabeth guffawed. "Ryan, do you know how pretentious that sounds? An emergency hotline for weeds?"

"Do you know how ignorant *you* sound? Purple loosestrife is taking over wetlands, which for your information are the most biologically diverse and productive ecologies on Earth. They're being choked by this invasive species, with an economic impact of millions of dollars that—"

"As if you cared about the United States economy! You'd open us up again to competition from cheap foreign sweatshop labor, just let American jobs go to—"

"You can't shut out the world, Elizabeth, not even if you get the aliens to give you the tech for their energy shields. I know that's what you 'border-defense' types want—"

"Yes, it is! Our economic survival is at stake, which makes border patrol a lot more important than a bunch of creeping flowers!"

"Great, just great. Wall us off by keeping out new blood, new ideas, new trade partners. But let in invasive botanicals that encroach on farmland, so that eventually we can't even feed everyone who would be imprisoned in your imported alien energy fields."

"Protected, not imprisoned. The way we're protecting you now by keeping the Denebs off-shore."

"Oh, you're doing that, are you? That was the aliens' decision. Do you think that if they had wanted to plop their pavilion in the middle of Times Square that your Border Patrol could have stopped them? They're a starfaring race, for chrissake!"

"Nobody said the—"

Noah shouted, which was the only way to get their attention, "Elizabeth, your cell is ringing! It says it's Mom!"

They both stared at the cell as if at a bomb, and then Elizabeth lunged for the phone. "Mom?"

"It's me. You called but—"

"Where have you been? What happened? What was the FBI—"

"I'll tell you everything. Are you and Ryan still at your place?"

"Yes. You sound funny. Are you sure you're okay?"

"Yes. No. Stay there, I'll get a cab, but it may be a few hours yet."

"But where—"

The phone went dead. Ryan and Elizabeth stared at each other. Into the silence, Noah said, "Oh yeah, Mom. Noah's here, too."

* * *

MARIANNE

"You are surprised," Ambassador Smith had said, unnecessarily.

Courtesy had been swamped in shock. "You're *human*? From Earth?"

"Yes. We think so."

"Your mitochondrial DNA matches the L7 sequence? No, wait—your whole biology matches ours?"

"There are some differences, of course. We—"

The Russian delegate stood up so quickly her chair fell over. She spat something which her translator gave as a milder, "'I do not understand how this is possible.'"

"I will explain," Smith said. "Please sit down."

Ekaterina Zaytsev did not sit. All at once Marianne wondered if the energy field enveloping Smith was weaponized.

Smith said, "We have known for millennia that we did not originate on World. There is no fossil record of us going back more than 150,000 Earth years. The life forms native to World are DNA-based, but there is no direct genetic link. We know that someone took us from somewhere else and—"

"Why?" Marianne blurted. "Why would they do that? And who is 'they'?"

Before Smith could answer, Zaytsev said, "Why should your planet's native life-forms be DNA-based at all? If this story is not a collection of lies?"

"Panspermia," Smith said. "And we don't know why we were seeded from Earth to World. An experiment, perhaps, by a race now gone. We—"

The Chinese ambassador was murmuring to his translator. The translator, American and too upset to observe protocol, interrupted Smith.

"Mr. Zhu asks how, if you are from Earth, you progressed to space travel so much faster than we have? If your brains are the same as ours?"

"Our evolution was different."

Marianne darted in with, "How? Why? A hundred fifty thousand years is not enough for more than superficial evolutionary changes!"

"Which we have," Smith said, still in that mechanical voice that Marianne suddenly hated. Its very detachment sounded condescending. "World's gravity, for instance, is one-tenth less than Earth's, and our internal organs and skeletons have adjusted. World is warmer than Earth, and you can see that we carry little body fat. Our eyes are much larger than yours—we needed to gather all the light we can on a planet dimmer than yours. Most plants on World are dark, to gather as many photons as possible. We are dazzled by the colors on Earth."

He smiled, and Marianne remembered that all human cultures share certain facial expressions: happiness, disgust, anger.

Smith continued, "But when I said that our evolution differed from yours, I was referring to social evolution. World is a more benign planet than Earth. Little axial tilt, many easy-to-domesticate grains, much food, few predators. We had no Ice Age. We settled into agriculture over a hundred thousand years before you did."

Over a hundred thousand years more of settled communities, of cities, with their greater specialization and intellectual cross-fertilization. While Marianne's ancestors fifteen thousand years ago had still been hunting mastodons and gathering berries, these cousins across the galaxy might have been exploring quantum physics. But—

She said, "Then with such an environment, you must have had an overpopulation problem. All easy ecological niches rapidly become overpopulated!"

"Yes. But we had one more advantage." Smith paused; he was giving the translators time to catch up, and she guessed what that meant even before he spoke again.

"The group of us seeded on World—and we estimate it was no more than a thousand—were all closely related. Most likely they were all brought from one place. Our gene pool does not show as much diversity as yours. More important, the exiles—or at least a large number of them—happened to be unusually mild-natured and cooperative. You might say, 'sensitive to other's suffering.' We have had wars, but not very many, and not early on. We were able to control the population problem, once we saw it coming, with voluntary measures. And, of course, those sub-groups that worked together best, made the earliest scientific advances and flourished most."

"You replaced evolution of the fittest with evolution of the most cooperative," Marianne said, and thought: *There goes Dawkins*.

"You may say that."

"*I* not say this," Zaytsev said, without waiting for her translator. Her face twisted. "How you know you come from Earth? And how know where is Earth?"

"Whoever took us to World left titanium tablets, practically indestructible, with diagrams. Eventually we learned enough astronomy to interpret them."

Moses on the mountain, Marianne thought. *How conveniently neat!* Profound distrust swamped her, followed by profound belief. Because, after all, here the aliens were, having arrived in a starship, and they certainly looked human. Although—

She said abruptly, "Will you give us blood samples? Tissue? Permit medical scans?"

"Yes."

The agreement was given so simply, so completely, that everyone fell silent. Marianne's dazed mind tried to find the scam in this, this possible nefarious treachery, and failed. It was quiet Zhu Feng who, through his translator, finally broke the silence.

"Tell us, please, honored envoy, why you are here at all?"

Again Smith answered simply. "To save you all from destruction."

*   *   *

NOAH

Noah slipped out of the apartment, feeling terrible but not terrible enough to stay. First transgression: If Mom returned earlier than she'd said, he wouldn't be there when she arrived. Second transgression: He'd taken twenty dollars from Elizabeth's purse. Third transgression: He was going to buy sugarcane.

But he'd left Elizabeth and Ryan arguing yet again about isolationism, the same argument in the same words as when he'd seen them last, four months ago. Elizabeth pulled out statistics showing that the United States' only option for survival, including avoiding revolution, was to retain and regain jobs within its borders, impose huge tariffs on imports, and rebuild infrastructure. Ryan trotted out different statistics proving that only globalization could, after a period of disruption, bring economic benefits in the long run, including a fresh flow of workers into a graying America. They had gotten to the point of hurtling words like "Fascist" and "sloppy thinker," when Noah left.

He walked the three blocks to Broadway. It was, as always, brightly lit, but the gyro places and electronics shops and restaurants, their outside tables empty and chained in the cold dusk, looked shabbier than he remembered. Some stores were not just shielded by grills but boarded up. He kept walking east, toward Central Park.

The dealer huddled in a doorway. He wasn't more than fifteen. Sugarcane was a low-cost, low-profit drug, not worth the gangs' time, let alone that of organized crime. The kid was a free-lance amateur, and God knows what the sugarcane was cut with.

Noah bought it anyway. In the nearest Greek place he bought a gyro as the price of the key to the bathroom and locked himself in. The room was windowless but surprisingly clean. The testing set that Noah carried everywhere showed him the unexpected: the sugarcane was cut only with actual sugar, and only by about fifty percent.

"Thank you, Lord," he said to the toilet, snorted twice his usual dose, and went back to his table to eat the cooling gyro and wait.

The drug took him quickly, as it always did. First came a smooth feeling, as if the synapses of his brain were filling with rich, thick cream. Then: One moment he was Noah Jenner, misfit, and the next he wasn't. He felt like a prosperous small businessman of some type, a shop-owner maybe, financially secure and blissfully uncomplicated. A contented, centered person who never questioned who he was or where he was going, who fit in wherever he happened to be. The sort of man who could eat his gyro and gaze out the window without a confusing thought in his head.

Which he did, munching away, the juicy meat and mild spices satisfying in his mouth, for a quiet half-hour.

Except—something was happening on the street.

A group of people streamed down Broadway. A parade. No, a mob. They carried torches, of all things, and something larger on fire, carried high. . . . Now Noah could hear shouting. The thing carried high was an effigy made of straw and rags, looking like the alien in a hundred bad movies: big blank head, huge eyes, spindly body of pale green. It stood in a small metal tub atop a board. Someone touched a torch to the straw and set the effigy on fire.

Why? As far as Noah could see, the aliens weren't bothering anybody. They were even good for business. It was just an excuse for people floundering in a bad economy to vent their anger—

Were these his thoughts? Noah's? Who was he now?

Police sirens screamed farther down the street. Cops appeared on foot, in riot gear. A public-address system blared, its words audible even through the shop window: "Disperse now! Open flame is not allowed on the streets! You do not have a parade permit! Disperse now!"

Someone threw something heavy, and the other window of the gyro place shattered.

Glass rained down on the empty tables in that corner. Noah jerked upright and raced to the back of the tiny restaurant, away from the windows. The cook was shouting in Greek. People left the parade, or joined it from side streets, and began to hurl rocks and bottles at the police. The cops retreated to the walls and doorways across Broadway and took out grenades of tear gas.

On the sidewalk outside, a small child stumbled by, crying and bleeding and terrified.

The person who Noah was now didn't think, didn't hesitate. He ran out into the street, grabbed the child, and ran back into the restaurant. He wasn't quite fast enough to escape the spreading gas. His nose and eyes shrieked in agony, even as he held his breath and thrust the child's head under his jacket.

Into the tiny kitchen, following the fleeing cook and waiter, and out the back door to an alley of overflowing garbage cans. Noah kept running, even though his agonized vision was blurring. Store owners had all locked their doors. But he had outrun the tear gas, and now a woman was leaning out of the window of her second-floor apartment, craning her neck to see through brick walls to the action two streets away. Gunfire sounded. Over its echo off the steel and stone canyons, Noah shouted up, "A child got gassed! Please—throw down a bottle of water!"

She nodded and disappeared. To his surprise, she actually appeared on the street to help a stranger, carrying a water bottle and towel. "I'm a nurse, let me have him . . . aahh." Expertly she bathed the child's eyes, and then Noah's, just as if a battle wasn't going on within hearing if not within sight.

"Thank you," Noah gasped. "It was. . . ." He stopped.

Something was happening in his head, and it wasn't due to the sugarcane. He felt an immediate and powerful kinship with this woman. How was that possible? He'd never seen her before. Nor was the attraction romantic—she was in late middle age, with graying hair and a drooping belly. But when she smiled at him and said, "You don't need the ER," something turned over in Noah's heart. What the fuck?

It must be the sugarcane.

But the feeling didn't have the creamy, slightly unreal feel of sugarcane.

She was still talking. "You probably couldn't get into any ER anyway, they'll all be jammed. I know—I was an ER nurse. But this kid'll be fine. He got almost none of the gas. Just take him home and calm him down."

"Who . . . who are you?"

"It doesn't matter." And she was gone, backing into the vestibule of her apartment building, the door locking automatically behind her. Restoring the anonymity of New York.

Whatever sense of weird recognition and bonding Noah had felt with her, it obviously had not been mutual. He tried to shake off the feeling and concentrate on the kid, who was wailing like a hurricane. The effortless competence bestowed by the sugarcane was slipping away. Noah knew nothing about children. He made a few ineffective soothing noises and picked up the child, who kicked him.

More police sirens in the distance. Eventually he found a precinct station, staffed only by a scared-looking civilian desk clerk; probably everyone else was at the riot. Noah left the kid there. Somebody would be looking for him. Noah walked back to West End Avenue, crossed it, and headed northeast to Elizabeth's apartment. His eyes still stung, but not too badly. He had escaped the worst of the gas cloud.

Elizabeth answered the door. "Where the hell did you go? Damn it, Noah, Mom's arriving any minute! She texted!"

"Well, I'm here now, right?"

"Yes, you're here now, but of all the shit-brained times to go out for a stroll! How did you tear your jacket?"

"Dunno." Neither his sister nor his brother seemed aware that eight blocks away there had been—maybe still was—an anti-alien riot going on. Noah didn't feel like informing them.

Ryan held his phone. "She's here. She texted. I'll go down."

Elizabeth said, "Ryan, she can probably pay off a cab and take an elevator by herself."

Ryan went anyway. *He had always been their mother's favorite*, Noah thought wearily. Except around Elizabeth, Ryan was affable, smooth, easy to get along with. His wife was charming, in an exaggeratedly feminine sort of way. They were going to give Marianne a grandchild.

It was an effort to focus on his family. His mind kept going back to that odd, unprecedented feeling of kinship with a person he had never seen before and probably had nothing whatsoever in common with. What was that all about?

"Elizabeth," his mother said. "And Noah! I'm so glad you're here. I've got . . . I've got a lot to tell you all. I—"

And his mother, who was always equal to anything, abruptly turned pale and fainted.

*   *   *

MARIANNE

Stupid, stupid—she never passed out! To the three faces clustered above her like balloons on sticks she said irritably, "It's nothing—just hypoglycemia. I haven't eaten since this morning. Elizabeth, if you have some juice or something . . ."

Juice was produced, crackers, slightly moldy cheese.

Marianne ate. Ryan said, "I didn't know you were hypoglycemic, Mom."

"I'm fine. Just not all that young anymore." She put down her glass and regarded her three children.

Elizabeth, scowling, looked so much like Kyle—was that why Marianne and Elizabeth had never gotten along? Her gorgeous alcoholic husband, the mistake of Marianne's life, had been dead for fifteen years. Yet here he was again, ready to poke holes in anything Marianne said.

Ryan, plain next to his beautiful sister but so much easier to love. Everybody loved Ryan, except Elizabeth.

And Noah, problem child, she and Kyle's last-ditch effort to save their doomed marriage. Noah was drifting and, she knew without being able to help, profoundly unhappy.

Were all three of them, and everybody else on the planet, going to die, unless humans and Denebs together could prevent it?

She hadn't fainted from hypoglycemia, which she didn't have. She had fainted from sheer delayed, maternal terror at the idea that her children might all perish. But she was not going to say that to her kids. And the fainting wasn't going to happen again.

"I need to talk to you," she said, unnecessarily. But how to begin something like this? "I've been talking to the aliens. In the *Embassy.*"

"We know, Evan told us," Noah said, at the same moment that Elizabeth, quicker, said sharply, "*Inside?*"

"Yes. The Deneb ambassador requested me."

"Requested you? Why?"

"Because of the paper I just published. The aliens—did any of you read the copies of my paper I emailed you?"

"I did," Ryan said. Elizabeth and Noah said nothing. Well, Ryan was the scientist.

"It was about tracing human genetic diversity through mitochondrial evolution. Thirty mitochondrial haplogroups had been discovered. I found the thirty-first. That wouldn't really be a big deal, except that—in a few days this will be common knowledge but you must keep it among ourselves until the ambassador announces—the aliens belong to the thirty-first group, L7. They're human."

Silence.

"Didn't you understand what I just—"

Elizabeth and Ryan erupted with questions, expressions of disbelief, arm waving. Only Noah sat quietly, clearly puzzled. Marianne explained what Ambassador Smith—impossible name!—had told her. When she got to the part about the race that had taken humans to "World" also leaving titanium tablets engraved with astronomical diagrams, Elizabeth exploded. "Come on, Mom, this fandango makes no sense!"

"The Denebs are *here*," Marianne pointed out. "They did find us. And the Denebs are going to give tissue samples. Under our strict human supervision. They're expanding the *Embassy* and allowing in humans. Lots of humans, to examine their biology and to work with our scientists."

"Work on what?" Ryan said gently. "Mom, this can't be good. They're an invasive species."

"Didn't you hear a word I said?" Marianne said. God, if Ryan, the scientist, could not accept truth, how would humanity as a whole? "They're not 'invasive,' or at least not if our testing confirms the ambassador's story. They're native to Earth."

"An invasive species is native to Earth. It's just not in the ecological niche it evolved for."

Elizabeth said, "Ryan, if you bring up purple loosestrife, I swear I'm going to clip you one. Mom, did anybody think to ask this ambassador the basic question of why they're here in the first place?"

"Don't talk to me like I'm an idiot. Of course we did. There's a—" She stopped and bit her lip, knowing how this would sound. "You all know what panspermia is?"

"Yes," said Elizabeth.

"Of course." Ryan.

"No." Noah.

"It's the idea that original life in the galaxy—" whatever *that* actually was, all the textbooks would now need to be rewritten "—came from drifting clouds of organic molecules. We know that such molecules exist inside meteors and comets and that they can, under some circumstances, survive entry into atmospheres. Some scientists, like Fred Hoyle and Stephen Hawking, have even endorsed the idea that new biomolecules are still being carried down to Earth. The Denebs say that there is a huge, drifting cloud of spores—well, they're technically not spores, but I'll come to that in a minute—drifting toward Earth. Or, rather, we're speeding toward it, since the solar system rotates around the center of the galaxy and the entire galaxy moves through space relative to the cosmic microwave background. Anyway, in ten months from now, Earth and this spore cloud meet. And the spores are deadly to humans."

Elizabeth said skeptically, "And they know this *how*?"

"Because two of their colony planets lay in the path of the cloud and were already exposed. Both populations were completely destroyed. The Denebs have recordings. Then they sent unmanned probes to capture samples, which they brought with them. They say the samples are a virus, or something like a virus, but encapsulated in a coating that isn't like anything viruses can usually make. Together, aliens and humans are going to find a vaccine or a cure."

More silence. Then all three of her children spoke together, but in such different tones that they might have been discussing entirely different topics.

Ryan: "In ten months? A vaccine or cure for an unknown pathogen in ten months? It took the CDC six months just to fully identify the bacterium in Legionnaires' disease!"

Elizabeth: "If they're so technologically superior, they don't need us to develop any sort of 'cure'!"

Noah: "What do the spores do to people?"

Marianne answered Noah first, because his question was the simplest. "They act like viruses, taking over cellular machinery to reproduce. They invade the lungs and multiply and then . . . then victims can't breathe. It only takes a few days." A terrible, painful death. A sudden horror came into her mind: her three children gasping for breath as their lungs were swamped with fluid, until they literally drowned. All of them.

"Mom," Ryan said gently, "are you all right? Elizabeth, do you have any wine or anything?"

"No," said Elizabeth, who didn't drink. Marianne suddenly, ridiculously, clung to that fact, as if it could right the world: her two-fisted cop daughter, whose martial arts training enabled her to take down a two-hundred-fifty-pound attacker, had a Victorian lady's fastidiousness about alcohol. Stereotypes didn't hold. The world was more complicated than that. The unexpected existed—a Border Patrol section chief did not drink!—and therefore an unexpected solution could be found to this unexpected problem. Yes.

She wasn't making sense, and knew it, and didn't care. Right now, she needed hope more than sense. The Denebs, with technology an order of magnitude beyond humans, couldn't deal with the spore cloud, but Elizabeth didn't drink and. therefore, together Marianne and Smith and—throw in the president and WHO and the CDC and USAMRIID, why not—could defeat mindless space-floating dormant viruses.

Noah said curiously, "What are you smiling about, Mom?"

"Nothing." She could never explain.

Elizabeth blurted, "So even if all this shit is true, what the fuck makes the Dennies think that *we* can help them?"

Elizabeth didn't drink like a cop, but she swore like one. Marianne said, "They don't know that we can. But their biological sciences aren't much more advanced than ours, unlike their physical sciences. And the spore cloud hits Earth next September. The Denebs have twenty-five years."

"Do you believe that their biological sciences aren't as advanced as their physics and engineering?"

"I have no reason to disbelieve it."

"If it's true, then we're their lab rats! They'll test whatever they come up with on us, and then they'll sit back in orbit or somewhere to see if it works before taking it home to their own planet!"

"That's one way to think of it," Marianne said, knowing that this was exactly how a large part of the media would think of it. "Or you could think of it as a rescue mission. They're trying to help us while there's time, if not much time."

Ryan said, "Why do they want you? You're not a virologist."

"I don't know," Marianne said.

Elizabeth erupted once more, leaping up to pace around the room and punch at the air. "I don't believe it. Not any of it, including the so-called 'cloud.' There are things they aren't telling us. But you, Mom—you just swallow whole anything they say! You're unbelievable!"

Before Marianne could answer, Noah said, "I believe you, Mom," and gave her his absolutely enchanting smile. He had never really become aware of the power of that smile. It conferred acceptance, forgiveness, trust, the sweet sadness of fading sunlight. "All of us believe everything you said.

"We just don't want to."

* * *

MARIANNE

Noah was right. Ryan was right. Elizabeth was wrong.

The spore cloud existed. Although technically not spores, that was the word the Deneb translator gave out, and the word stuck among astronomers because it was a term they already knew. As soon as the clouds' coordinates, composition, and speed were given by the Denebs to the UN, astronomers around the globe found it through spectral analysis and the dimming of stars behind it. Actually, they had known of its existence all along but had assumed it was just another dust cloud too small and too cool to be incubating stars. Its trajectory would bring it in contact with Earth when the Denebs said, in approximately ten months.

Noah was right in saying that people did not want to believe this. The media erupted into three factions. The most radical declared the "spore cloud" to be just harmless dust and the Denebs plotting, in conspiracy with the UN and possibly several governments, to take over Earth for various evil and sometimes inventive purposes. The second faction believed that the spore threat might be real but that, echoing Elizabeth, humanity would become "lab rats" in alien experiments to find some sort of solution, without benefit to Earth. The third group, the most scientifically literate, focused on a more immediate issue: They did not want the spore samples brought to Earth for research, calling them the real danger.

Marianne suspected the samples were already here. NASA had never detected shuttles or other craft going between the ship in orbit around the moon and the *Embassy*. Whatever the aliens wanted here, probably already was.

Teams of scientists descended on New York. Data was presented to the UN, the only body that Smith would deal with directly. Everyone kept saying that time was of the essence. Marianne, prevented from resuming teaching duties by the insistent reporters clinging to her like lint, stayed in Elizabeth's apartment and waited. Smith had given her a private communication device, which no one except the UN Special Mission knew about. Sometimes as she watched TV or cleaned Elizabeth's messy apartment, Marianne pondered this: An alien had given her his phone number and asked her to wait. It was almost like dating again.

Time is of the essence! Time is of the essence! A few weeks went by in negotiations she knew nothing of. Marianne reflected on the word "essence." Elizabeth worked incredible hours; the Border Patrol had been called in to help keep "undesirables" away from the Harbor, assisting the Coast Guard, INS, NYPD, and whoever else the city deemed pertinent. Noah had left again and did not call.

Evan was with her at the apartment when the Deneb communication device rang. "What's that?" he said off-handedly, wiping his mouth. He had brought department gossip and bags of sushi. The kitchen table was littered with tuna tataki, cucumber wraps, and hotategai.

Marianne said, "It's a phone call from the Deneb ambassador."

Evan stopped wiping and, paper napkin suspended, stared at her.

She put the tiny device on the table, as instructed, and spoke the code word. A mechanical voice said, "Dr. Marianne Jenner?"

"Yes."

"This is Ambassador Smith. We have reached an agreement with your UN to proceed, and will be expanding our facilities immediately. I would like you to head one part of the research."

"Ambassador, I am not an epidemiologist, not an immunologist, not a physician. There are many others who—"

"Yes. We don't want you to work on pathogens or with patients. We want you to identify human volunteers who belong to the haplogroup you discovered, L7."

Something icy slid along Marianne's spine. "Why? There hasn't been very much genetic drift between our . . . ah . . . groups of humans in just 150,000 years. And mitochondrial differentiation should play no part in—"

"This is unconnected with the spores."

"What is it connected with?" *Eugenics, master race, Nazis. . . .*

"This is purely a family matter."

Marianne glanced at Evan, who was writing furiously on the white paper bag that sushi had come in: GO! ACCEPT! ARE YOU DAFT? CHANCE OF A LIFETIME!

She said, "A family matter?"

"Yes. Family matters to us very much. Our whole society is organized around ancestral loyalty."

To Marianne's knowledge, this was the first time the ambassador had ever said anything, to anyone, about how Deneb society was organized. Evan, who'd been holding the paper bag six inches from her face, snatched it back and wrote CHANCE OF SIX THOUSAND LIFETIMES!

The number of generations since Mitochondrial Eve.

Smith continued, "I would like you to put together a small team of three or four people. Lab facilities will be provided, and volunteers will provide tissue samples. The UN has been very helpful. Please assemble your team on Tuesday at your current location and someone will come to escort you. Do you accept this post?"

"Tuesday? That's only—"

"Do you accept this post?"

"I . . . yes."

"Good. Good-bye."

Evan said, "Marianne—"

"Yes, of course, you're part of the 'team.' God, none of this real."

"Thank you, thank you!"

"Don't burble, Evan. We need two lab techs. How can they have facilities ready by Tuesday? It isn't possible."

"Or so we think," Evan said.

*　　*　　*

NOAH

It hadn't been possible to stay in the apartment. His mother had the TV on non-stop, every last news show, no matter how demented, that discussed the aliens or their science. Elizabeth burst in and out again, perpetually angry at everything she didn't like in the world, which included the Denebs. The two women argued at the top of their lungs, which didn't seem to bother either of them at anything but an intellectual level, but which left Noah unable to eat anything without nausea or sleep without nightmares or walk around without knots in his guts.

He found a room in a cheap boardinghouse, and a job washing dishes, paid under the counter, in a taco place. Even though the tacos came filmed with grease, he could digest better here than at Elizabeth's, and anyway he didn't eat much. His wages went on sugarcane.

He became in turn an observant child, a tough loner, a pensive loner, a friendly panhandler. Sugarcane made him, variously, mute or extroverted or gloomy or awed or confident. But none of it was as satisfying as it once had been. Even when he was someone else, he was still aware of being Noah. That had not happened before. The door out of himself stayed ajar. Increasing the dose didn't help.

Two weeks after he'd left Elizabeth's, he strolled on his afternoon off down to Battery Park. The late October afternoon was unseasonably warm, lightly overcast, filled with autumn leaves and chrysanthemums and balloon sellers. Tourists strolled the park, sitting on the benches lining the promenade, feeding the pigeons, touring Clinton Castle. Noah stood for a long time leaning on the railing above the harbor, and so witnessed the miracle.

"It's happening! Now!" someone shouted.

What was happening? Noah didn't know, but evidently someone did because people came running from all directions. Noah would have been jostled and squeezed from his place at the railing if he hadn't gripped it with both hands. People stood on the benches; teenagers shimmied up the lamp poles. Figures appeared on top of the Castle. A man began frantically selling telescopes and binoculars evidently hoarded for this occasion. Noah bought a pair with money he'd been going to use for sugarcane.

"Move that damn car!" someone screamed as a Ford honked its way through the crowd, into what was supposed to be a pedestrian area. Shouts, cries, more people rushing from cars to the railings.

Far out in the harbor, the Deneb *Embassy*, its energy shield dull under the cloudy sky, began to glow. Through his binoculars Noah saw the many-faceted dome shudder—not just shake but shudder in a rippling wave, as if alive. *Was it alive? Did his mother know?*

"Aaaahhhhh," the crowd went.

The energy shield began to spread. Either it had thinned or changed composition, because for a long moment—maybe ninety seconds—Noah could almost see through it. A suggestion of floor, walls, machinery . . . then opaque again. But the "floor" was growing, reaching out to cover more territory, sprouting tentacles of material and energy.

Someone on the bridge screamed, "They're taking over!"

All at once, signs were hauled out, people leaped onto the roofs of cars that should not have been in the park, chanting began. But not much chanting or many people. Most crowded the railings, peering out to sea.

In ten minutes, the *Embassy* grew and grew laterally, silently spreading across the calm water like a speeded-up version of an algae bloom. When it hardened again—that's how it looked to Noah, like molten glass hardening as it cooled—the structure was six times its previous size. The tentacles had become docks, a huge one toward the city and several smaller ones to one side. By now even the chanters had fallen silent, absorbed in the silent, aweing, monstrous feat of unimaginable construction. When it was finished, no one spoke.

Then an outraged voice demanded, "Did those bastards get a city permit for that?"

It broke the silence. Chanting, argument, exclaiming, pushing all resumed. A few motorists gunned their engine, futilely, since it was impossible to move vehicles. The first of the motorcycle cops arrived: NYPD, then Special Border Patrol, then chaos.

Noah slipped deftly through the mess, back toward the streets north of the Battery. He had to be at work in an hour. The *Embassy* had nothing to do with him.

* * *

MARIANNE

A spore cloud doesn't look like anything at all.

A darker patch in dark space, or the slightest of veils barely dimming starlight shining behind it. Earth's astronomers could not accurately say how large it was, or how deep. They relied on Deneb measurements, except for the one fact that mattered most, which human satellites in deep space and human ingenuity at a hundred observatories was able to verify: The cloud was coming. The path of its closest edge would intersect Earth's path through space at the time the Denebs had said: early September.

Marianne knew that almost immediately following the UN announcement, madness and stupidity raged across the planet. Shelters were dug or sold or built, none of which would be effective. If air could get in, so could spores. In

Kentucky, some company began equipping deep caves with air circulation, food for a year, and high-priced sleeping berths: reverting to Paleolithic caveman. She paid no more attention to this entrepreneurial survivalism than to the televised protests, destructive mobs, peaceful marches, or lurid artist depictions of the cloud and its presumed effects. She had a job to do.

On Tuesday she, Evan, and two lab assistants were taken to the submarine bay at UN Special Mission Headquarters. In the sub, Max and Gina huddled in front of the porthole, or maybe it was a porthole-like viewscreen, watching underwater fish. Maybe fish were what calmed them. Although they probably didn't need calming: Marianne, who had worked with both before, had chosen them as much for their even temperaments as for their competence. Government authorities had vetted Max and Gina for, presumably, both crime-free backgrounds and pro-alien attitudes. Max, only twenty-nine, was the computer whiz. Gina, in her mid-thirties and the despair of her Italian mother because Gina hadn't yet married, made the fewest errors Marianne had ever seen in sample preparation, amplification, and sequencing.

Evan said to Marianne, "Children all sorted out?"

"Never. Elizabeth won't leave New York, of course." ("Leave? Don't you realize I have a job to do, protecting citizens from your aliens?" Somehow they had become Marianne's aliens.) "Ryan took Connie to her parents' place in Vermont and he went back to his purple loosestrife in Canada."

"And Noah?" Evan said gently. He knew all about Noah; why, Marianne wondered yet again, did she confide in this twenty-eight-year-old gay man as if he were her age, and not Noah's? Never mind; she needed Evan.

She shook her head. Noah had again disappeared.

"He'll be fine, then, Marianne. He always is."

"I know."

"Look, we're docking."

They disembarked from the sub to the underside of the *Embassy*. Whatever the structure's new docks topside were for, it wasn't transfer of medical personnel. Evan said admiringly, "Shipping above us hasn't even been disrupted. Dead easy."

"Oh, those considerate aliens," Marianne murmured, too low for the sub captain, still in full-dress uniform, to hear. Her and Evan's usual semi-sarcastic banter helped to steady her: the real toad in the hallucinatory garden.

The chamber beyond the airlock had not changed, although this time they were met by a different alien. Female, she wore the same faint shimmer of energy-shield protection over her plain tunic and pants. Tall, coppery-skinned, with those preternaturally huge dark eyes, she looked about thirty, but how could you tell? Did the Denebs have plastic surgery? Why not? They had everything else.

Except a cure for spore disease.

The Deneb introduced herself ("Scientist Jones"), went through the so-glad-you're-here speech coming disconcertingly from the ceiling. She conducted them to the lab, then left immediately. Plastic surgery or no, Marianne was grateful for alien technology when she saw her lab. Nothing in it was unfamiliar, but all of it was state-of-the-art. Did they create it as they had created the *Embassy*, or order it wholesale? Must be the latter—the state-of-the-art gene sequencer still bore the label ILLUMINA. The equipment must have been ordered, shipped, paid for (with what?) either over the previous months of negotiation, or as the world's fastest rush shipping.

Beside it sat a rack of vials with blood samples, all neatly labeled.

Max immediately went to the computer and turned it on. "No Internet," he said, disappointed. "Just a LAN, and . . . wow, this is heavily shielded."

"You realize," Marianne said, "that this is a minor part of the science going on aboard the *Embassy*. All we do is process mitochondrial DNA to identify L7 haplogroup members. We're a backwater on the larger map."

"Hey, we're *here*," Max said. He grinned at her. "Too bad, though, about no World of Warcraft. This thing has no games at all. What do I do in my spare time?"

"Work," Marianne said, just as the door opened and two people entered. Marianne recognized one of them, although she had never met him before. Unsmiling, dark-suited, he was Security. The woman was harder to place. Middle-aged, wearing jeans and a sweater, her hair held back by a too-girlish headband. But her smile was warm, and it reached her eyes. She held out her hand.

"Dr. Jenner? I'm Lisa Guiterrez, the genetics counselor. I'll be your liaison with the volunteers. We probably won't be seeing each other again, but I wanted to say hello. And you're Dr. Blanford?"

"Yes," Evan said.

Marianne frowned. "Why do we need a genetic counselor? I was told our job is to simply process blood samples to identify members of the L7 haplogroup."

"It is," Lisa said, "and then I take it from there."

"Take *what* from there?"

Lisa studied her. "You know, of course, that the Denebs would like to identify those surviving human members of their own haplogroup. They consider them family. The concept of family is pivotal to them."

Marianne said, "You're not a genetic counselor. You're a xenopsychologist."

"That, too."

"And what happens after the long-lost family members are identified?"

"I tell them that they are long-lost family members." Her smile never wavered.

"And then?"

"And then they get to meet Ambassador Smith."

"And *then?*"

"No more 'then.' The Ambassador just wants to meet his six-thousand-times-removed cousins. Exchange family gossip, invent some in-jokes, confer about impossible Uncle Harry."

So she had a sense of humor. Maybe it was a qualification for billing oneself a 'xenopsychologist,' a profession that until a few months ago had not existed.

"Nice to meet you both," Lisa said, widened her smile another fraction of an inch, and left.

Evan murmured, "My, people come and go so quickly here."

But Marianne was suddenly not in the mood, not even for quoted humor from such an appropriate source as *The Wizard of Oz*. She sent a level gaze at Evan, Max, Gina.

"Okay, team. Let's get to work."

II: S minus 9.5 months

MARIANNE

There were four other scientific teams aboard the *Embassy*, none of which were interested in Marianne's backwater. The other teams consisted of scientists from the World Health Organization, the Centers for Disease Control, the United States Army Research Institute for Infectious Diseases, the Institute of Molecular Medicine at Oxford, the Beijing Genomics Institute, Kyushu University, and the Scripps Clinic and Research Foundation, perhaps the top immunology center in the world. Some of the most famous names in the scientific and medical worlds were here, including a dozen Nobel winners. Marianne had no knowledge of, but could easily imagine, the political and scientific competition to get aboard the *Embassy*. The Americans had an edge because the ship sat in New York Harbor and that, too, must have engendered political threats and counter threats, bargaining and compromise.

The most elite group, and by far the largest, worked on the spores: germinating, sequencing, investigating this virus that could create a worldwide human die-off. They worked in negative-pressure, biosafety-level-four chambers. Previously the United States had had only two BSL4 facilities, at the CDC in Atlanta and at USAMRIID in Maryland. Now there was a third, dazzling in its newness and in the completeness of its equipment. The Spore Team had the impossible task of creating some sort of vaccine or other method of neutralizing, world-wide, a pathogen not native to Earth, within ten months.

The Biology Team investigated alien tissues and genes. The Denebs gave freely of whatever was asked: blood, epithelial cells, sperm, biopsy samples. "Might even give us a kidney, if we asked nicely enough," Evan said. "We know they have two."

Marianne said, "*You* ask, then."

"Not me. Too frightful to think what they might ask in exchange."

"So far, they've asked nothing."

Almost immediately the Biology Team verified the Denebs as human. Then began the long process of finding and charting the genetic and evolutionary differences between the aliens and Terrans. The first, announced after just a few weeks, was that all of the seventeen aliens in the Embassy carried the same percentage as Terrans of Neanderthal genes: from one to four percent.

"They're us," Evan said.

"Did you doubt it?" Marianne asked.

"No. But more interesting, I think, are the preliminary findings that the Denebs show so much less genetic diversity than we do. That wanker Wilcox must be weeping in his ale."

Patrick Wells Wilcox was the current champion of the Toba Catastrophe Theory, which went in and out of scientific fashion. Seventy thousand years ago the Toba supervolcano in Indonesia had erupted. This had triggered such major environmental change, according to theory proponents, that a "bottleneck event" had occurred, reducing the human population to perhaps 10,000 individuals. The result had been a great reduction in human genetic diversity. Backing for the idea came from geology as well as coalescence evidence of some genes, including mitochondrial, Y-chromosome, and nuclear. Unfortunately, there was also evidence that the bottleneck event had never occurred. If the Denebs, removed from Earth well before the supervolcano, showed less diversity than Terrans, then Terran diversity couldn't have been reduced all that much.

Marianne said, "Wilcox shouldn't weep too soon."

"Actually, he never weeps at all. Gray sort of wanker. Holes up in his lab at Cambridge and glowers at the world through medieval arrow slits."

"Dumps boiling oil on dissenting paleontologists," Marianne suggested.

"Actually, Wilcox may not even be human. Possibly an advance scout for the Denebs. Nobody at Cambridge has noticed it so far."

"Or so we think." Marianne smiled. She and Evan never censored their bantering, which helped lower the hushed, pervasive anxiety they shared with everyone else on the *Embassy*. It was an anxious ship.

The third scientific team aboard was much smaller. Physicists, they worked with "Scientist Jones" on the astronomy of the coming collision with the spore cloud.

The fourth team she never saw at all. Nonetheless, she suspected they were there, monitoring the others, shadowy underground non-scientists unknown even to the huge contingent of visible security.

Marianne looked at the routine work on her lab bench: polymerase chain reaction to amplify DNA samples, sequencing, analyzing data, writing reports on the genetic inheritance of each human volunteer who showed up at the Deneb "collection site" in Manhattan. A lot of people showed up. So far, only two of them belonged to Ambassador Smith's haplogroup. "Evan, we're not really needed, you and I. Gina and Max can handle anything our expensive brains are being asked to do."

Evan said, "Right, then. So let's have a go at exploring. Until we're stopped, anyway."

She stared at him. "Okay. Yes. Let's explore."

*   *   *

NOAH

Noah emerged from the men's room at the restaurant. During the mid-afternoon lull they had no customers except for a pair of men slumped over one table in the back. "Look at this!" the waitress said to him. She and the cook were both huddled over her phone, strange enough since they hated each other. But Cindy's eyes were wide from something other than her usual drugs, and Noah took a look at the screen of the sophisticated phone, mysteriously acquired and gifted by Cindy's current boyfriend before he'd been dragged off to Riker's for assault with intent.

VOLUNTEERS WANTED TO DONATE BLOOD

PAYMENT: $100

HUMAN NURSES TO COLLECT SMALL BLOOD SAMPLES

DENEB EMBASSY PIER, NEW YORK HARBOR

"Demonios del Diablo," Miguel muttered. "Vampiros!" He crossed himself.

Noah said dryly, "I don't think they're going to drink the blood, Miguel." The dryness was false. His heart had begun to thud. People like his mother got to see the *Embassy* up close, not people like Noah. Did the ad mean that the Denebs were going to take human blood samples on the large dock he had just seen form out of nothing?

Cindy had lost interest. "No fucking customers except those two sorry asses in the corner, and they never tip. I shoulda stood in bed."

"Miguel," Noah said, "can I have the afternoon off?"

*   *   *

Noah stood patiently in line at the blood-collection site. If any of the would-be volunteers had hoped to see aliens, they had been disappointed. Noah was not disappointed; after all, the ad on Cindy's phone had said HUMAN NURSES TO COLLECT SMALL BLOOD SAMPLES.

He was, however, disappointed that the collection site was not on the large dock jutting out from the *Embassy* under its glittering energy shield. Instead, he waited to enter what had once been a warehouse at the land end of a pier on the Manhattan waterfront. The line, huddled against November drizzle, snaked in loops and ox-bows for several blocks, and he was fascinated by the sheer diversity of people. A woman in a fur-lined Burberry raincoat and high, polished boots. A bum in jeans with an indecent tear on the ass. Several giggling teenage girls under flowered umbrellas. An old man in a winter parka. A nerdy-looking boy with an iPad protected by flexible plastic. Two tired-looking middle-aged women. One of those said to the other, "I could pay all that back rent if I get this alien money, and—"

Noah tapped her arm. "Excuse me, ma'am—what 'alien money'?" The $100 fee for blood donation didn't seem enough to pay *all that back rent*.

She turned. "If they find out you're part of their blood group, you get a share of their fortune. You know, like the Indians with their casino money. If you can prove you're descended from their tribe."

"No, that's not it," the old man in the parka said impatiently. "You get a free energy shield like theirs to protect you when the spore cloud hits. They take care of family."

The bum muttered, "Ain't no spore cloud."

The boy said with earnest contempt, "You're all wrong. This is just—the Denebs are the most significant thing to happen to Earth, ever! Don't you get it? We're not alone in the universe!"

The bum laughed.

Eventually Noah reached Building A. Made of concrete and steel, the building's walls were discolored, its high-set windows grimy. Only the security machines looked new, and they made high-tech examinations of Noah's person inside and out. His wallet, cell, jacket, and even shoes were left in a locker before he shuffled in paper slippers along the enclosed corridor to Building B, farther out on the pier. Someone was very worried about terrorism.

"Please fill out this form," said a pretty, grim-faced young woman. Not a nurse: security. She looked like a faded version of his sister, bleached of Elizabeth's angry command. Noah filled out the form, gave his small vial of blood, and filed back to Building B. He felt flooded with anti-climactic let-down. When he had reclaimed his belongings, a guard handed him a hundred dollars and a small round object the size and feel of a quarter.

"Keep this with you," a guard said. "It's a one-use, one-way communication device. In the unlikely event that it rings, press the center. That means that we'd like to see you again."

"If you do, does that mean I'm in the alien's haplogroup?"

He didn't seem to know the word. "If it rings, press the center."

"How many people have had their devices ring?"

The guard's face changed, and Noah glimpsed the person behind the job. He shrugged. "I never heard of even one."

"Is it—"

"Move along, please." The job mask was back.

Noah put on his shoes, balancing first on one foot and then on the other to avoid touching the grimy floor. It was like being in an airport. He started for the door.

"Noah!" Elizabeth sailed toward him across a sea of stained concrete. "What the hell are you doing here?"

"Hi, Lizzie. Is this part of the New York State border?"

"I'm on special assignment."

God, she must hate that. Her scowl threatened to create permanent furrows in her tanned skin. But Elizabeth always obeyed the chain of command.

"Noah, how can you—"

A bomb went off.

A white light blinded Noah. His hearing went dead, killed by the sheer onslaught of sound. His legs wobbled as his stomach lurched. Then Elizabeth knocked him to the ground and hurled herself on top of him. A few seconds later she was up and running and Noah could hear her again: "Fucking flashbang!"

He stumbled to his feet, his eyes still painful from the light. People screamed and a few writhed on the floor near a pile of clothes that had ignited. Black smoke billowed from the clothing, setting the closest people to coughing, but no one seemed dead. Guards leaped at a young man shouting something lost in the din.

Noah picked up his shoes and slipped outside, where sirens screamed, honing in from nearby streets. The salt-tanged breeze touched him like a benediction.

A flashbang. You could buy a twelve-pack of them on the Internet for fifty bucks, although those weren't supposed to ignite fires. Whatever that protestor had hoped to accomplish, it was ineffective. Just like this whole dumb blood-donation expedition.

But he had a hundred dollars he hadn't had this morning, which would buy a few good hits of sugarcane. And in his pocket, his fingers closed involuntarily on the circular alien coin.

* * *

MARIANNE

Marianne was surprised at how few areas of the *Embassy* were restricted.

The BSL4 areas, of course. The aliens' personal quarters, not very far from the BSL4 labs. But her and Evan's badges let them roam pretty much everywhere else. Humans rushed passed them on their own errands, some nodding in greeting but others too preoccupied to even notice they were there.

"Of course there are doors we don't even see," Evan said. "Weird alien cameras we don't see. Denebs we don't see. They know where we are, where everyone is, every minute. Dead easy."

The interior of the *Embassy* was a strange mixture of materials and styles. Many corridors were exactly what you'd expect in a scientific research facility: unadorned, clean, lined with doors. The walls seemed to be made of something that was a cross between metal and plastic, and did not dent. Walls in the personal quarters and lounges, on the other hand, were often made of something that reminded her of Japanese rice paper, but soundproof. She had the feeling that she could have put her fist through them, but when she actually tried this, the wall only gave slightly, like a very tough piece of plastic. Some of these walls could be slid open, to change the size or shapes of rooms. Still other walls were actually giant screens that played constantly shifting patterns of subtle color. Finally, there were odd small lounges that seemed to have been furnished from upscale mail-order catalogues by someone who thought anything Terran must go with anything else: earth-tone sisal carpeting with a Victorian camelback sofa, Picasso prints with low Moroccan tables inlaid with silver and copper, a Navaho blanket hung on the wall above Japanese zabutons.

Marianne was tired. They'd come to one such sitting area outside the main dining hall, and she sank into an English club chair beside a small table of swooping purple glass. "Evan—do you really believe we are all going to die a year from now?"

"No." He sat in an adjoining chair, appreciatively patting its wide and upholstered arms. "But only because my mind refuses to entertain the thought of my own death in any meaningful way. Intellectually, though, yes. Or rather, nearly all of us will die."

"A vaccine to save the rest?"

"No, there is simply not enough time to get all the necessary bits and pieces sorted out. But the Denebs will save some Terrans."

"How?"

"Take a selected few back with them to that big ship in the sky."

Immediately she felt stupid that she hadn't thought of this before. Stupidity gave way to the queasy, jumpy feeling of desperate hope. "Take us *Embassy* personnel? To continue joint work on the spores?" Her children, somehow she would have to find a way to include Elizabeth, Noah, Ryan and Connie and the baby! But everyone here had family—

"No," Evan said. "Too many of us. My guess is just the Terran members of their haplogroup. Why else bother to identify them? And everything I've heard reinforces their emphasis on blood relationships."

"Heard from whom? We're in the lab sixteen hours a day—"

"I don't need much sleep. Not like you, Marianne. I talk to the Biology Group, who talk more than anybody else to the aliens. Also I chat with Lisa Guiterrez, the genetic counselor."

"And the Denebs told somebody they're taking their haplogroup members with them before the spore cloud hits?"

"No, of course not. When do the Denebs tell Terrans anything directly? It's all smiling evasion, heartfelt reassurances. They're like Philippine houseboys."

Startled, Marianne gazed at him. The vaguely racist reference was uncharacteristic of Evan, and had been said with some bitterness. She realized all over again how little Evan gave away about his past. When had he lived in the Philippines? What had happened between him and some apparently not forgiven houseboy? A former lover? Evan's sexual orientation was also something they never discussed, although of course she was aware of it. From his grim face, he wasn't going to discuss it now, either.

She said, "I'm going to ask Smith what the Denebs intend."

Evan's smooth grin had returned. "Good luck. The UN can't get information from him, the project's chief scientists can't get information from him, and you and I never see him. Just minor roadblocks to your plan."

"We really are lab rats," she said. And then, abruptly, "Let's go. We need to get back to work."

"Evan said slowly, "I've been thinking about something."

"What?"

"The origin of viruses. How they didn't evolve from a single entity and don't have a common ancestor. About the theory that their individual origins were pieces of DNA or RNA that broke off from cells and learned to spread to other cells."

Marianne frowned. "I don't see how that's relevant."

"I don't either, actually."

"Then—"

"I don't know," Evan said. And again, "I just don't know."

*   *   *

NOAH

Noah was somebody else.

He'd spent his blood-for-the-Denebs money on sugarcane, and it turned out to be one of the really good transformations. He was a nameless soldier from a nameless army: brave and commanding and sure of himself. Underneath he knew it was an illusion (but he never used to know that!). However, it didn't matter. He stood on a big rock at the south end of Central Park, rain and discarded plastic bags blowing around him, and felt completely, if temporarily, happy. He was on top of the world, or at least seven feet above it, and nothing seemed impossible.

The alien token in his pocket began to chime, a strange syncopated rhythm, atonal as no iPhone ever sounded. Without a second's hesitation—he could face anything!—Noah pulled it from his pocket and pressed its center.

A woman's voice said, "Noah Richard Jenner?"

"Yes, ma'am!"

"This is Dr. Lisa Guiterrez at the Deneb embassy. We would like to see you, please. Can you come as soon as possible to the UN Special Mission Headquarters at its pier?"

Noah drew a deep breath. Then full realization crashed around him, loud and blinding as last week's flashbang. Oh my God—why hadn't he seen it before? Maybe because he hadn't been a warrior before. His mother had—*son of a bitch*—

"Noah?"

He said, "I'll be there."

*   *   *

The submarine surfaced in an undersea chamber. A middle-aged woman in jeans and blazer, presumably Dr. Guiterrez, awaited Noah in the featureless room. He didn't much notice woman or room. Striding across the gangway, he said, "I want to see my mother. Now. She's Dr. Marianne Jenner, working here someplace."

Dr. Guiterrez didn't react as if this were news, or strange. She said, "You seem agitated." Hers was the human voice Noah had heard coming from the alien token.

"I am agitated! Where is my mother?"

"She's here. But first, someone else wants to meet you."

"I demand to see my mother!"

A door in the wall slid open, and a tall man with coppery skin and bare feet stepped through. Noah looked at him, and it happened again.

Shock, bewilderment, totally unjustified recognition—he knew this man, just as he had known the nurse who washed tear gas from his and a child's eyes during the West Side demonstration. Yet he'd never seen him before, and he was an *alien*. But the sense of kinship was powerful, disorienting, ridiculous.

"Hello, Noah Jenner," the ceiling said. "I am Ambassador Smith. Welcome to the *Embassy*."

"I—"

"I wanted to welcome you personally, but I cannot visit now. I have a meeting. Lisa will help you get settled here, should you choose to stay with us for a while. She will explain everything. Let me just say—"

Impossible to deny this man's sincerity, he meant every incredible word—

"—that I'm very glad you are here."

* * *

After the alien left, Noah stood staring at the door through which he'd vanished. "What is it?" Dr. Guiterrez said. "You look a bit shocked."

Noah blurted, "I know that man!" A second later he realized how dumb that sounded.

She said gently, "Let's go somewhere to talk, Noah. Somewhere less . . . wet."

Water dripped from the sides of the submarine, and some had sloshed onto the floor. Sailors and officers crossed the gangway, talking quietly. Noah followed Lisa from the sub bay, down a side corridor, and into an office cluttered with charts, print-outs, coffee mugs, a laptop—such an ordinary looking place that it only heightened Noah's sense of unreality. She sat in an upholstered chair and motioned him to another. He remained standing.

She said, "I've seen this before, Noah. What you're experiencing, I mean, although usually it isn't as strong as you seem to be feeling it."

"Seen what? And who are you, anyway? I want to talk to my mother!"

She studied him, and Noah had the impression she saw more than he wanted her to. She said, "I'm Dr. Lisa Guiterrez, as Ambassador Smith said. Call me Lisa. I'm a genetics counselor serving as the liaison between the ambassador and those people identified as belonging to his haplotype, L7, the one identified by your mother's research. Before this post, I worked with Dr. Barbara Formisano at Oxford, where I also introduced people who share the same haplotype. Over and over again I've seen a milder version of what you seem to be experiencing now—an unexpected sense of connection between those with an unbroken line of mothers and grandmothers and great-grandmothers back to their haplogroup clan mother. It—"

"That sounds like bullshit!"

"—is important to remember that the connection is purely symbolic. Similar cell metabolisms don't cause shared emotions. But—an important 'but!'—symbols have a powerful effect on the human mind. Which in turn causes emotion."

Noah said, "I had this feeling once before. About a strange woman, and I had no way of knowing if she's my 'haplotype'!"

Lisa's gaze sharpened. She stood. "What woman? Where?"

"I don't know her name. Listen, I want to talk to my mother!"

"Talk to me first. Are you a sugarcane user, Noah?"

"What the hell does that have to do with anything?"

"Habitual use of sugarcane heightens certain imaginative and perceptual pathways in the brain. Ambassador Smith—well, let's set that aside for a moment. I think I know why you want to see your mother."

Noah said, "Look, I don't want to be ruder than I've already been, but this isn't your business. Anything you want to say to me can wait until I see my mother."

"All right. I can take you to her lab."

It was a long walk. Noah took in very little of what they passed, but then, there was very little to take in. Endless white corridors, endless white doors. When they entered a lab, two people that Noah didn't know looked up curiously. Lisa said, "Dr. Jenner—"

The other woman gestured at a far door. Before she could speak, Noah flung the door open. His mother sat at a small table, hands wrapped around a cup of coffee she wasn't drinking. Her eyes widened.

Noah said, "Mom—why the fuck didn't you ever tell me I was adopted?"

*   *   *

MARIANNE

Evan and Marianne sat in his room, drinking sixteen-year-old single-malt Scotch. She seldom drank but knew that Evan often did. Nor had she ever gone before to his quarters in the Embassy, which were identical to hers: ten-foot square room with a bed, chest of drawers, small table, and two chairs. She sat on one of the straight-backed, utilitarian chairs while Evan lounged on the bed. Most of the scientists had brought with them a few items from home, but Evan's room was completely impersonal. No art, no framed family photos, no decorative pillows, not even a coffee mug or extra doughnut carried off from the cafeteria.

"You live like a monk," Marianne said, immediately realizing how drunk she must be to say that. She took another sip of Scotch.

"Why didn't you ever tell him?" Evan said.

She put down her glass and pulled at the skin on her face. The skin felt distant, as if it belonged to somebody else.

"Oh, Evan, how to answer that? First Noah was too little to understand. Kyle and I adopted him in some sort of stupid effort to save the marriage. I wasn't thinking straight—living with an alcoholic will do that, you know. If there was one stupid B-movie scene of alcoholic and wife that we missed, I don't know what it was. Shouting, pleading, pouring away all the liquor in the house, looking for Kyle in bars at two a.m. . . . anyway. Then Kyle died and I was trying to deal with that and the kids and chasing tenure and there was just too much chaos and fragility to add another big revelation. Then somehow it got too late, because Noah would have asked why he hadn't been told before, and then somehow . . . it all just got away from me."

"And Elizabeth and Ryan never told him?"

"Evidently not. We yell a lot about politics and such but on a personal level, we're a pretty reticent family." She waved her hand vaguely at the room. "Although not as reticent as you."

Evan smiled. "I'm British of a certain class."

"You're an enigma."

"No, that was the Russians. Enigmas wrapped in riddles." But a shadow passed suddenly behind his eyes.

"What do you—"

"Marianne, let me fill you in on the bits and pieces of news that came in while you were with Noah. First, from the Denebs: they're bringing aboard the *Embassy* any members of their 'clan'—that's what the translator is calling the L7 haplogroup—who want to come. But you already know that. Second, the—"

"How many?"

"How many have we identified or how many want to come here?"

"Both." The number of L7 haplotypes had jumped exponentially once they had the first few and could trace family trees through the female line.

"Sixty-three identified, including the three that Gina flew to Georgia to test. Most of the haplogroup may still be in Africa, or it may have largely died out. Ten of those want to visit the *Embassy*." He hesitated. "So far, only Noah wants to stay."

Marianne's hand paused, glass halfway to her mouth. "To *stay*? He didn't tell me that. How do you know?"

"After Noah . . . left you this afternoon, Smith came to the lab with that message."

"I see." She didn't. She had been in her room, pulling herself together after the harrowing interview with her son. Her adopted son. She hadn't been able to tell Noah anything about his parentage because she hadn't known anything: sealed adoption records. Was Noah the way he was because of his genes? Or because of the way she'd raised him? Because of his peer group? His astrological sign? Theories went in and out of fashion, and none of them explained personality.

She said, "What is Noah going to *do* here? He's not a scientist, not security, not an administrator . . ." *Not anything*. It hurt her to even think it. Her baby, her lost one.

Evan said, "I have no idea. I imagine he'll either sort himself out or leave. The other news is that the Biology Team has made progress in matching Terran and Deneb immune system components. There were a lot of graphs and charts and details, but the bottom line is that ours and theirs match pretty well. Remarkably little genetic drift. Different antibodies, of course for different pathogens, and quite a lot of those, so no chance we'll be touching skin without their wearing their energy shields."

"So cancel the orgy."

Evan laughed. Emboldened by this as much as by the drink, Marianne said, "Are you gay?"

"You know I am, Marianne."

"I wanted to be sure. We've never discussed it. I'm a scientist, after all."

"You're an American. Leave nothing unsaid that can be shouted from rooftops."

Her fuzzy mind had gone back to Noah. "I failed my son, Evan."

"Rubbish. I told you, he'll sort himself out eventually. Just be prepared for the idea that it may take a direction you don't fancy."

Again that shadow in Evan's eyes. She didn't ask; he obviously didn't want to discuss it, and she'd snooped enough. Carefully she rose to leave, but Evan's next words stopped her.

"Also, Elizabeth is coming aboard tomorrow."

"*Elizabeth*? Why?"

"A talk with Smith about shore-side security. Someone tried a second attack at the sample collection site shore-side."

"Oh my God. Anybody hurt?"

"No. This time."

"Elizabeth is going to ask the Denebs to give her the energy-shield technology. She's been panting for it for border patrol ever since the *Embassy* first landed in the harbor. Evan, that would be a *disaster*. She's so focused on her job that she can't see what will happen if—no, when—the street finds its own uses for the tech, and it always does—" Who had said that? Some writer. She couldn't remember.

"Well, don't get your knickers in a twist. Elizabeth can ask, but that doesn't mean that Smith will agree."

"But he's so eager to find his 'clan'—God, it's so stupid! That Korean mitochondrial sequence, to take just one example, that turns up regularly in Norwegian fisherman, or that engineer in Minnesota who'd traced his ancestry back three hundred years without being able to account for the Polynesian mitochondrial signature he carries—*nobody* has a cure 'plan.' I mean, 'clan.'"

"Nobody on Earth, anyway."

"And even if they did," she barreled on, although all at once her words seem to have become slippery in her mouth, like raw oysters, "There's no sig . . . sif . . . significant connection between two people with the same mitochondrial DNA than between any other two strangers!"

"Not to us," Evan said. "Marianne, go to bed. You're too tipsy, and we have work to do in the morning."

"It's not work that matters to protection against the shore cloud. Spore cloud. *Spore cloud.*"

"Nonetheless, it's work. Now go."

* * *

NOAH

Noah stood in a corner of the conference room, which held eleven people and two aliens. Someone had tried to make the room festive with a red paper tablecloth, flowers, and plates of tiny cupcakes. This had not worked. It was still a utilitarian, corporate-looking conference room, filled with people who otherwise would have no conceivable reason to be together at either a conference or a party. Lisa Guiterrez circulated among them: smiling, chatting, trying to put people at ease. It wasn't working.

Two young women, standing close together for emotional support. A middle-aged man in an Armani suit and Italian leather shoes. An unshaven man, hair in a dirty ponytail, who looked homeless but maybe only because he stood next to Well-Shod Armani. A woman carrying a plastic tote bag with a hole in one corner. And so on and so on. It was the sort of wildly mixed group that made Noah, standing apart with his back to a wall, think of worshippers in an Italian cathedral.

The thought brought him a strained smile. A man nearby, perhaps emboldened by the smile, sidled closer and whispered, "They *will* let us go back to New York, won't they?"

Noah blinked. "Why wouldn't they, if that's what you want?"

"I want them to offer us shields for the spore cloud! To take back with us to the city! Why else would I come here?"

"I don't know."

The man grimaced and moved away. But—why had he even come, if he suspected alien abduction or imprisonment or whatever? And why didn't he feel what Noah did? Every single one of the people in this room had caused in him the same shock of recognition as had Ambassador Smith. Every single one. And apparently no one else had felt it at all.

But the nervous man needn't have worried. When the party and its ceiling-delivered speeches of kinship and the invitation to make a longer visit aboard the *Embassy* were all over, everyone else left. They left looking relieved or still curious or satisfied or uneasy or disappointed (no energy shield offered! No riches!), but they all left, Lisa still chattering reassuringly. All except Noah.

Ambassador Smith came over to him. The Deneb said nothing, merely silently waited. He looked as if he were capable of waiting forever.

Noah's hands felt clammy. All those brief, temporary lives on sugarcane, each one shed like a snake skin when the drug wore off. No, not snake skins; that wasn't the right analogy. More like breadcrumbs tossed by Hansel and Gretel, starting in hope but vanishing before they could lead anywhere. The man with the dirty pony tail wasn't the only homeless one.

Noah said, "I want to know who and what you are."

The ceiling above Smith said, "Come with me to a genuine celebration."

*   *   *

A circular room, very small. Noah and Smith faced each other. The ceiling said, "This is an airlock. Beyond this space, the environment will be ours, not yours. It is not very different, but you are not used to our microbes and so must wear the energy suit. It filters air, but you may have some trouble breathing at first because the oxygen content of World is like Earth's at an altitude of 12,000 feet. If you feel nausea in the airlock, where we will stay for a few minutes, you may go back. The light will seem dim to you, the smells strange, and the gravity less than you are accustomed to by one-tenth. There are no built-in translators beyond this point, and we will speak our own language, so you will not be able to talk to us. Are you sure you wish to come?"

"Yes," Noah said.

"Is there anything you wish to say before you join your birthright clan?"

Noah said, "What is your name?"

Smith smiled. He made a noise that sounded like a trilled version of *meehao*, with a click on the end.

Noah imitated it.

Smith said, in trilling English decorated with a click, "Brother mine."

*   *   *

MARIANNE

Marianne was not present at the meeting between Elizabeth and Smith, but Elizabeth came to see her afterward. Marianne and Max were bent over the computer, trying to account for what was a mitochondrial anomaly or a sample contamination or a lab error or a program glitch. Or maybe something else entirely. Marianne straightened and said, "Elizabeth! How nice to—"

"You have to talk to him," Elizabeth demanded. "The man's an idiot!"

Marianne glanced at the security officer who had escorted Elizabeth to the lab. He nodded and went outside. Max said, "I'll just . . . uh . . . this can wait." He practically bolted, a male fleeing mother-daughter drama. Evan was getting some much-needed sleep; Gina had gone ashore to Brooklyn to see her parents for the first time in weeks.

"I assume," Marianne said, "you mean Ambassador Smith."

"I do. Does he know what's going on in New York? Does he even care?"

"What's going on in New York?"

Elizabeth instantly turned professional, calmer but no less intense. "We are less than nine months from passing through the spore cloud."

At least, Marianne thought, *she now accepts that much*.

"In the last month alone, the five boroughs have had triple the usual rate of arsons, ten demonstrations with city permits of which three turned violent, twenty-three homicides, and one mass religious suicide at the Church of the Next Step Forward in Tribeca. Wall Street has plunged. The Federal Reserve Bank on Liberty Street was occupied from Tuesday night until Thursday dawn by terrorists. Upstate, the governor's mansion has been attacked, unsuccessfully. The same thing is happening everywhere else. Parts of Beijing have been on fire for a week now. Thirty-six percent of Americans believe the Denebs brought the spore cloud with them, despite what astronomers say. If the ambassador gave us the energy shield, that might help sway the numbers in their favor. Don't you think the president and the UN have said all this to Smith?"

"I have no idea what the president and the UN have said, and neither do you."

"Mom—"

"Elizabeth, do you suppose that if what you just said is true and the ambassador said no to the president, that my intervention would do any good?"

"I don't know. You scientists stick together."

Long ago, Marianne had observed the many different ways people responded to unthinkable catastrophe. Some panicked. Some bargained. Some joked. Some denied. Some blamed. Some destroyed. Some prayed. Some drank. Some thrilled, as if they had secretly awaited such drama their entire lives. Evidently, nothing had changed.

The people aboard the *Embassy* met the unthinkable with work, and then more work. Elizabeth was right that the artificial island had become its own self-contained, self-referential universe, every moment devoted to the search for something, anything, to counteract the effect of the spore cloud on mammalian brains. The Denebs, understanding how good hackers could be, blocked all Internet, television, and radio from the Embassy. Outside news came from newspapers or letters, both dying media, brought in the twice-daily mail sack and by the vendors and scientists and diplomats who came and went. Marianne had not paid attention.

She said to her enraged daughter, "The Denebs are not going to give you their energy shield."

"We cannot protect the UN without it. Let alone the rest of the harbor area."

"Then send all the ambassadors and translators home, because it's not going to happen. I'm sorry, but it's not."

"You're not sorry. You're on their side."

"It isn't a question of sides. In the wrong hands, those shields—"

"Law enforcement is the right hands!"

"Elizabeth, we've been over and over this. Let's not do it again. You know I have no power to get you an energy shield, and I haven't seen you in so long. Let's not quarrel." Marianne heard the pleading note in her own voice. When, in the long and complicated road of parenthood, had she started courting her daughter's agreement, instead of the other way around?

"Okay, *okay*. How are you, Mom?"

"Overworked and harried. How are you?"

"Overworked and harried." A reluctant half-smile. "I can't stay long. How about a tour?"

"Sure. This is my lab."

"I meant of the *Embassy*. I've never been inside before, you know, and your ambassador—" somehow Smith had become Marianne's special burden "—just met with me in a room by the submarine bay. Can I see more? Or are you lab types kept close to your cages?"

The challenge, intended or not, worked. Marianne showed Elizabeth all over the Terran part of the Embassy, accompanied by a security officer whom Elizabeth ignored. Her eyes darted everywhere, noted everything. Finally she said, "Where do the Denebs live?"

"Behind these doors here. No one has ever been in there."

"Interesting. It's pretty close to the high-risk labs. And where is Noah?"

Yesterday's bitter scene with Noah, when he'd been so angry because she'd never told him he was adopted, still felt like an open wound. Marianne didn't want to admit to Elizabeth that she didn't know where he'd gone. "He stays in the Terran visitors' quarters," she said, hoping there was such a place.

Elizabeth nodded. "I have to report back. Thanks for the Cook's tour, Mom."

Marianne wanted to hug her daughter, but Elizabeth had already moved off, heading toward the submarine bay, security at her side. Memory stabbed Marianne: a tiny Elizabeth, five years old, lips set as she walked for the first time toward the school bus she must board alone. It all went by so fast, and when the spore cloud hit, not even memory would be left.

She dashed away the stupid tears and headed back to work.

III: S minus 8.5 months

MARIANNE

The auditorium on the *Embassy* had the same thin, rice-paper-like walls as some of the other non-lab rooms, but these shifted colors like some of the more substantial walls. Slow, complex, subtle patterns in pale colors that reminded Marianne of dissolving oil slicks. Forty seats in rising semi-circles faced a dais, looking exactly like a lecture room at her college. She had an insane desire to regress to undergraduate, pull out a notebook, and doodle in the margin. The seats were filled not with students chewing gum and texting each other, but with some of the planet's most eminent scientists. This was the first all-hands meeting of the scientists aboard. The dais was empty.

Three Denebs entered from a side door.

Marianne had never seen so many of them together at once. Oddly, the effect was to make them seem more alien, as if their minor differences from

Terrans—the larger eyes, spindlier limbs, greater height—increased exponentially as their presence increased arithmetically. Was that Ambassador Smith and Scientist Jones? Yes. The third alien, shorter than the other two and somehow softer, said through the translator in the ceiling, "Thank you all for coming. We have three reports today, two from Terran teams and one from World. First, Dr. Manning." All three aliens smiled.

Terrence Manning, head of the Spore Team, took the stage. Marianne had never met him, Nobel Prize winners being as far above her scientific level as the sun above mayflies. A small man, he had exactly three strands of hair left on his head, which he tried to coax into a comb-over. Intelligence shone through his diffident, unusually formal manner. Manning had a deep, authoritative voice, a welcome contrast to the mechanical monotony of the ceiling.

From the aliens' bright-eyed demeanor, Marianne had half expected good news, despite the growing body of data on the ship's LAN. She was wrong.

"We have not," Manning said, "been able to grow the virus in cell cultures. As you all know, some viruses simply will not grow in vitro, and this seems to be one of them. Nor have we been able to infect monkeys—any breed of monkey—with spore disease. We will, of course, keep trying. The better news, however, is that we have succeeded in infecting mice."

Good and bad, Marianne thought. Often, keeping a mouse alive was actually easier than keeping a cell culture growing. But a culture would have given them a more precise measure of the virus's cytopathic effect on animal tissue, and monkeys were genetically closer to humans than were mice. On the other hand, monkeys were notoriously difficult to work with. They bit, they fought, they injured themselves, they traded parasites and diseases, and they died of things they were not supposed to die from.

Manning continued, "We now have a lot of infected mice and our aerosol expert, Dr. Belsky, has made a determination of how much exposure is needed to cause spore disease in mice under laboratory conditions."

A graph flashed onto the wall behind Manning: exposure time plotted versus parts per million of spore. Beside Marianne, Evan's manicured fingers balled into a sudden fist. Infection was fast, and required a shockingly small concentration of virus, even for an airborne pathogen.

"Despite the infected mice," Manning went on, and now the strain in his voice was palpable, "we still have not been able to isolate the virus. It's an elusive little bugger."

No one laughed. Marianne, although this was not her field, knew how difficult it could be to find a virus even after you'd identified the host. They were so tiny; they disappeared into cells or organs; they mutated.

"Basically," Manning said, running his hand over his head and disarranging his three hairs, "we know almost nothing about this pathogen. Not the *r nought*—for you astronomers, that is the number of cases that one case generates on average over the course of its infectious period—nor the incubation period nor the genome nor the morphology. What we do know are the composition of the coating encapsulating the virus, the transmission vector, and the resulting pathology in mice."

Ten minutes of data on the weird, unique coating on the "spores," a term even the scientists, who knew better, now used. Then Dr. Jessica Yu took Manning's place on the dais. Marianne had met her in the cafeteria and felt intimidated. The former head of the Special Pathogens branch of the National Center for Infectious Diseases in Atlanta, Jessica Yu was diminutive, fifty-ish, and beautiful in a severe, don't-mess-with-me way. Nobody ever did.

She said, "We are, of course, hoping that gaining insight into the mechanism of the disease in animals will help us figure out how to treat it in humans. These mice were infected three days ago. An hour ago they began to show symptoms, which we wanted all of you to see before . . . well, before."

The wall behind Jessica Yu de-opaqued, taking the exposure graphic with it. Or some sort of viewscreen now overlay the wall and the three mice now revealed were someplace else in the *Embassy*. The mice occupied a large glass cage in what Marianne recognized as a BSL4 lab.

Two of the mice lay flat, twitching and making short whooshing sounds, much amplified by the audio system. No, not amplified—those were desperate gasps as the creatures fought for air. Their tails lashed and their front paws scrambled. They were, Marianne realized, trying to *swim* away from whatever was downing them.

"In humans," Yu continued, "we would call this ARDS—Adult Respiratory Distress Syndrome, a catch-all diagnosis used when we don't know what the problem is. The mouse lung tissue is becoming heavier and heavier as fluid from the blood seeps into the lungs and each breath takes more and more effort. X-rays of lung tissue show 'white-out'—so much fluid in the lungs increasing the radiological density that the image looks like a snow storm. The viral incubation period in mice is three days. The time from onset of symptoms until death averages 2.6 hours."

The third mouse began to twitch.

Yu continued, her whole tiny body rigid, "As determined thus far, the infection rate in mice is about seventy-five percent. We can't, of course, make any assumptions that it would be the same in humans. Nor do we have any idea why mice are infected but monkeys are not. The medical data made available from the Deneb colonies do indicate similar metabolic pathways to those of the mice. Those colonies had no survivors. Autopsies on the mice further indicate—"

A deep nausea took Marianne, reaching all the way from throat to rectum. She was surprised; her training was supposed to inure her. It did not. Before her body could disgrace her by retching or even vomiting, she squeezed past Evan with a push on his shoulder to indicate he should stay and hear the rest. In the corridor outside the auditorium she leaned against the wall, lowered her head between her knees, breathed deeply, and let shame overcome horror.

No way for a scientist to react to data—

The shame was not strong enough. It was her children that the horror brought: Elizabeth and Ryan and Noah, mouths open as they tried to force air into their lungs, wheezing and gasping, drowning where they lay . . . and Connie and the as-yet-unborn baby, her first grandchild. . . .

Stop. It's no worse for you than for anybody else.

Marianne stood. She dug the nails of her right hand into the palm of her left. But she could not make herself go back into the auditorium. Evan would have to tell her what other monstrosities were revealed. She made her way back to her lab.

Max sat at the computer, crunching data. Gina looked up from her bench. "Marianne—we found two more L7 donors."

"Good," Marianne said, went through the lab to her tiny office behind, and closed the door firmly. What did it matter how many L7s she found for Smith? Earth was finished. Eight-and-a-half months left, and the finest medical and scientific brains on the planet had not even begun to find any way to mitigate the horror to come.

Gina knocked on the office door. "Marianne? Are you all right?"

Gina was the same age as Ryan, a young woman with her whole life still ahead of her. If she got that life. Meanwhile, there was no point in making the present even worse. Marianne forced cheerfulness into her voice. "Yes, fine. I'll be right out. Put on a fresh pot of coffee, would you please?"

* * *

NOAH

Noah stood with his clan and prepared to *Lllathil*.

There was no word for it in English. Part dance, part religious ceremony, part frat kegger, and it went on for two days. Ten L7s stood in a circle, all in various stages of drunkenness. When the weird, atonal music (but after two months aboard the *Embassy* it no longer sounded weird or atonal to his ears) began, they weaved in and out, making precise figures on the floor with the red paint on their feet. Once the figures had been sacred, part of a primitive religion that had faded with the rapid growth of science nurtured by their planet's lush and easy environment. The ritual remained. It affirmed family, always matrilineal on World. It affirmed connection, obligation, identity. Whenever the larger of World's moons was lined up in a certain way with the smaller, Worlders came together with their families and joyously made Lllathil. Circles always held ten, and as many circles were made as a family needed. It didn't matter where you were on World, or what you were doing, when Lllathil came, you were there.

His mother would never have understood.

The third morning, after everyone had slept off the celebration, came the second part of Lllathil, which Marianne would have understood even less. Each person gave away one-fifth of everything he had earned or made since the last Lllathil. He gave it, this "thumb" as it was jokingly called, to someone in his circle. Different clans gave different percentages and handled that in different ways, but some version of the custom mostly held over mostly monocultural World. The Denebs were a sophisticated race; such a gift involved transfers of the Terran equivalent of bank accounts, stock holdings, real estate. The Denebs were also human, and so sometimes the gift was made grudgingly, or with anger at a cousin's laziness, or resignedly, or with cheating. But it was made, and there wasn't very much cheating. Or so said Mee^haoɪ, formerly known to Noah as Smith, who'd told him so in the trilling and clicking language that Noah was trying so hard to master. "We teach our children very intensively to follow our ways," Smith said wryly. "Of course, some do not. Some always are different."

"You said it, brother," Noah said in English, to Smith's total incomprehension.

Noah loved Lllathil. He had very little—nothing, really—to give, but his net gain was not the reason he loved it. Nor was that the reason he studied the Worldese for hours every day, aided by his natural ear for languages. Once, in his brief and abortive attempted at college, Noah had heard a famous poet say that factual truth and emotional truth were not the same. "You have to understand with your belly," she'd said.

He did. For the first time in his life, he did.

His feet made a mistake, leaving a red toe print on the floor in the wrong place. No one chided him. Cliclimi, her old face wrinkling into crevasses and hills and dales, a whole topography of kinship, just laughed at him and reached out her skinny arm to fondly touch his.

Noah, not like that. Color in the lines!

Noah, this isn't the report card I expect of you.

Noah, you can't come with me and my friends! You're too little!

Noah, can't you do anything right? When he'd danced until he could no longer stand (Cliclimi was still going at it, but she hadn't drunk as much as Noah had), he dropped onto a large cushion beside "Jones," whose real name he still couldn't pronounce. It had more trills than most, and a strange tongue sound he could not reproduce at all. She was flushed, her hair unbound from its usual tight arrangement. Smaller than he was but stockier, her caramel-colored flesh glowed with exertion. The hair, rich dark brown, glinted in the rosy light. Her red tunic—everybody wore red for lllanthil—had hiked high on her thighs.

Noah heard his mother's voice say, "A hundred fifty thousand years is not enough time for a species to diverge." To his horror, he felt himself blush.

She didn't notice, or else she took it as warmth from the dancing. She said, "Do you have trouble with our gravity?"

Proud of himself that he understood the words, he said, "No. It small amount big of Earth." At least, he hoped that's what he'd said.

Apparently it was. She smiled and said something he didn't understand. She stretched luxuriously, and the tunic rode up another two inches.

What were the kinship taboos on sex? What were any of the taboos on sex? Not that Noah could have touched her skin-to-skin, anyway. He was encased, so unobtrusively that he usually forgot it was there, in the "energy suit" that protected him from alien microbes.

Microbes. Spores. How much time was left before the cloud hit Earth? At the moment it didn't seem important. (*Noah, you can't just pretend problems don't exist!* That had usually been Elizabeth.)

He said, "Can—yes, no?—make my—" Damn it, what was the word for microbes? "—my inside like you? My inside spores?"

IV: S minus 6.5 months

MARIANNE

Gina had not returned from Brooklyn on the day's last submarine run. Marianne was redoing an entire batch of DNA amplification that had somehow become contaminated. Evan picked up the mail sack and the news dispatches. When he came into the lab, where Marianne was cursing at a row of beakers, he uncharacteristically put both hands on her shoulders. She looked at his face.

"What is it? Tell me quickly."

"Gina is dead."

She put a hand onto the lab bench to steady herself. "How?"

"A mob. They were frighteningly well armed, almost a small army. End-of-the-world rioters."

"Was Gina . . . did she . . . ?"

"A bullet, very quick. She didn't suffer, Marianne. Do you want a drink? I have some rather good Scotch."

"No. Thank you, but no."

Gina. Marianne could picture her so clearly, as if she still stood in the lab in the wrinkled white coat she always wore even though the rest of them did not. Her dark hair just touched with gray, her ruddy face calm. Brisk, pleasant, competent. . . . What else? Marianne hadn't known Gina very well. All at once, she wondered if she knew anyone, really knew them. Two of her children baffled her: Elizabeth's endemic anger, Noah's drifty aimlessness. Had she ever known Kyle, the man he was under the charming and lying surface, under the alcoholism? Evan's personal life was kept personal, and she'd assumed it was his British reticence, but maybe she knew so little about him because of her limitations, not his. With everyone else aboard the *Embassy*, as with her university department back home, she exchanged only scientific information or meaningless pleasantries. She hadn't seen her brother, to whom she'd never been close, in nearly two years. Her last close female friendship had been over a decade ago.

Thinking this way felt strange, frightening. She was glad when Evan said, "Where's Max? I'll tell him about Gina."

"Gone to bed with a cold. It can wait until morning. What's that?"

Evan gave her a letter, addressed by hand. Marianne tore it open. "It's from

Ryan. The baby was born, a month early but he's fine and so is she. Six pounds two ounces. They're naming him Jason William Jenner."

"Congratulations. You're a nan."

"A what?"

"Grand-mum." He kissed her cheek.

She turned to cling to him, without passion, in sudden need of the simple comfort of human touch. Evan smelled of damp wool and some cool, minty lotion. He patted her back. "What's all this, then?"

"I'm sorry, I—"

"Don't be sorry." He held her until she was ready to pull away.

"I think I should write to Gina's parents."

"Yes, that's right."

"I want to make them understand—" Understand what? That sometimes children were lost, and the reasons didn't necessarily make sense. But this reason did make sense, didn't it? Gina had died because she'd been aboard the *Embassy*, died as a result of the work she did, and right now this was the most necessary work in the entire world.

She had a sudden memory of Noah, fifteen, shouting at her: "You're never home! Work is all you care about!" And she, like so many beleaguered parents, had shouted back, "If it weren't for my work, we'd all starve!"

And yet, when the kids had all left home and she could work as much as she wanted or needed without guilt, she'd missed them dreadfully. She'd missed the harried driving schedules—*I have to be at Jennifer's at eight* and *Soccer practice is moved up an hour Saturday*! She'd missed their electronics, cells and iPods and tablets and laptops, plugged in all of the old house's inadequate outlets. She'd missed the rainbow laundry in the basement, Ryan's red soccer shirts and Elizabeth's white jeans catastrophically dyed pink and Noah's yellow-and-black bumblebee costume for the second-grade play. All gone. When your children were small you worried that they would die and you would lose them, and then they grew up and you ended up losing the children they'd been, anyway.

Marianne pulled at the skin on her face and steeled herself to write to Gina's parents.

* * *

NOAH

There were three of them now. Noah Jenner, Jacqui Young, Oliver Pardo. But only Noah was undergoing the change.

They lounged this afternoon in the World garden aboard the *Embassy*, where the ceiling seemed to be open to an alien sky. A strange orange shone, larger than Sol and yet not shedding as much light, creating a dim glow over the three Terrans. The garden plants were all dark in hue ("To gather as much light as possible," Mee^haoį had said), lush leaves in olive drab and pine and asparagus. Water trickled over rocks or fell in high, thin streams. Warmth enveloped Noah even though his energy suit, and he felt light on the ground in the lesser gravity. Some nearby flower sent out a strange, musky, heady fragrance on the slight breeze.

Jacqui, an energetic and enormously intelligent graduate student, had chosen to move into the alien section of the *Embassy* in order to do research. She was frank, with both Terrans and Denebs, that she was not going to stay after she had gathered the unique data on Deneb culture that would ensure her academic career. Smith said that was all right, she was clan and so welcome for as long as she chose. Noah wondered how she planned on even having an academic career after the spore cloud hit.

Oliver Pardo would have been given the part of geek by any film casting department with no imagination. Overweight, computer-savvy, fan of super-heroes, he quoted obscure science fiction books sixty years old and drew endless pictures of girls in improbable costumes slaying dragons or frost giants. Socially inept, he was nonetheless gentle and sweet-natured, and Noah preferred his company to Jacqui's, who asked too many questions.

"Why?" she said.

"Why what?" Noah said, even though he knew perfectly well what she meant. He lounged back on the comfortable moss and closed his eyes.

"Why are you undergoing this punishing regime of shots just so you can take off your shield?"

"They're not shots," Noah said. Whatever the Denebs were doing to him, they did it by having him apply patches to himself when he was out of his energy suit and in an isolation chamber. This had happened once a week for a while now. The treatments left him nauseated, dizzy, sometimes with diarrhea, and always elated. There was only one more to go.

Jacqui said, "Shots or whatever, why do it?"

Oliver looked up from his drawing of a barbarian girl riding a lion. "Isn't it obvious?"

Jacqui said, "Not to me."

Oliver said, "Noah wants to become an alien."

"No," Noah said. "I was an alien. Now I'm becoming . . . not one."

Jacqui's pitying look said *You need help.* Oliver shaded in the lion's mane. Noah wondered why, of all the Terrans of L7 mitochondrial haplotype, he was stuck with these two. He stood. "I have to study."

"I wish I had your fluency in Worldese," Jacqui said. "It would help my work so much."

So study it. But Noah knew she wouldn't, not the way he was doing. She wanted the quick harvest of startling data, not . . . whatever it was he wanted.

Becoming an alien. Oliver was more correct than Noah's flip answer. And yet Noah had been right, too, which was something he could never explain to anyone, least of all his mother. Whom he was supposed to visit this morning, since she could not come to him.

All at once Noah knew that he was not going to keep that appointment. Although he flinched at the thought of hurting Marianne, he was not going to leave the World section of the *Embassy.* Not now, not ever. He couldn't account for this feeling, so strong that it seemed to infuse his entire being, like oxygen in the blood. But he had to stay here, where he belonged. Irrational, but— as Evan would have said—there it was, mustn't grumble, at least it made a change, no use going on about it.

He had never liked Evan.

In his room, Noah took pen and a pad of paper to write a note to his mother. The words did not come easy. All his life he had disappointed her, but not like this.

Dear Mom—I know we were going to get together this afternoon but—

Dear Mom—I wish I could see you as we planned but—

Dear Mom—We need to postpone our visit because Ambassador Smith has asked me if this afternoon I would—

Noah pulled at the skin on his face, realized that was his mother's gesture, and stopped. He looked longingly at the little cubes that held his language lessons. As the cube spoke Worldese, holofigures in the cube acted out the meaning. After Noah repeated each phrase, it corrected his pronunciation until he got it right.

"My two brothers live with my mother and me in this dwelling," a smiling girl said in the holocube, in Worldese. Two boys, one younger than she and one much older, appeared beside her with a much older woman behind them, all four with similar features, a shimmering dome behind them.

"My two brothers live with my mother and me in this dwelling," Noah repeated. The Worldese tenses were tricky; these verbs were the ones for things that not only could change, but could change without the speaker's having much say about events. A mother could die. The family could be chosen for a space colony. The older brother could marry and move in with his wife's family.

Sometimes things were beyond your control and you had no real choice.

Dear Mom—I can't come. I'm sorry. I love you. Noah

* * *

MARIANNE

The work—anybody's work—was not going well.

It seemed to be proceeding at an astonishing pace, but Marianne—and everyone else—knew that was an illusion. She sat in the auditorium for the monthly report, Evan beside her. This time, no Denebs were present—why not? She listened to Terence Manning enumerate what under any other circumstances would have been incredibly rapid triumphs.

"We have succeeded in isolating the virus," Manning said, "although not in growing it in vitro. After isolation, we amplified it with the usual polymerase processes. The virus has been sequenced and—only a few days ago!—captured on an electromicrograph image, which, as most of you know, can be notoriously difficult. Here it is."

A graphic appeared on the wall behind Manning: fuzzy concentric circles blending into each other in shades of gray. Manning ran his hand over his head, now completely bald. Had he shaved his last three hairs, Marianne wondered irrelevantly. Or had they just given up and fallen out from stress?

"The virion appears to be related to known paramyxoviruses, although the gene sequence, which we now have, does not exactly match any of them. It is a negative-sense single-stranded RNA viruses. Paramyxoviruses, to which it may or may not be directly related, are responsible for a number of human and animal diseases, including parainfluenza, mumps, measles, pneumonia, and canine distemper. This family of viruses jumps species more easily than any other. From what we have determined so far, it most closely resembles both Hendra and Nipah viruses, which are highly contagious and highly virulent.

"The genome follows the paramyxovirus 'Rule of Six,' in that the total length of the genome is almost always a multiple of six. The spore virus consists of twenty-one genes with 21,645 base pairs. That makes it a large virus, but by no means the largest we know. Details of sequence, structure, envelope proteins, etc. can be found on the LAN. I want to especially thank Drs. Yu, Sedley, and Lapka for their valuable work in identifying *Respirovirus sporii*."

Applause. Marianne still stared at the simple, deadly image behind Manning. An unwelcome thought had seized her: the viral image looked not unlike a fuzzy picture of a not-too-well-preserved trilobite. Trilobites had been the dominant life form on Earth for 300 million years and comprised more than 10,000 species. All gone now. Humans could be gone, too, after a much briefer reign.

But we survived so much! The Ice Age, terrible predators, the "bottleneck event" of 70,000 years ago that reduced *Homo sapiens* to mere thousands. . . .

Manning was continuing. This was the bad news. "However, we have made little progress in figuring out how to combat *R. sporii*. Blood from the infected mice has been checked against known viruses and yielded no seriological positives. None of our small number of anti-viral drugs were effective, although there was a slight reaction to ribavirin. That raises a further puzzle, since ribavirin is mostly effective against Lassa fever, which is caused by an arenavirus, not a paramyxovirus." Manning tried to smile; it was not a success. "So, the mystery deepens. I wish we had more to report."

Someone asked, "Are the infected mice making antibodies?"

"Yes," Manning said, "and if we can't manage to develop a vaccine, this is our best possible path to a post-exposure treatment, following the MB-003 model developed for Ebola. For you astronomers—and please forgive me if I am telling you things you already know—a successful post-exposure treatment for Ebola in nonhuman primates was developed two years ago, using a cocktail of monoclonal antibodies. It was the work of a partnership between American industry and government agencies. When administered an hour after infection, MB-003 yields a one hundred percent survival rate. At forty-eight hours, the survival rate is two-thirds. MB-003 was initially developed in a mouse model and then produced in plants. The work took ten years. It has not, of course, been tested in humans."

Ten years. The *Embassy* scientists had less than five months left. Ebola had previously been studied since its first outbreak in 1976. And the biggie: *It has not, of course, been tested in humans.* In whom it might, for all anyone knew, not even work.

Maybe the Denebs knew faster ways to produce a vaccine from antibodies, exponentially increase production, and distribute the results. But the aliens weren't even at this meeting. They had surely been given all this information already, but even so—

—Where the hell were the aliens that was more important than this?

U: S minus 3.5 months

MARIANNE

Marianne felt ridiculous. She and Evan leaned close over the sink in the lab. Water gushed full-strength from the tap, making noise that, she hoped, covered their words. The autoclave hummed; a Bach concerto played tinnily on the computer's inadequate speaker. The whole thing felt like a parody of a bad spy movie.

They had never been able to decide if the labs, if everywhere on the *Embassy*, were bugged. Evan had said yes, of course, don't be daft. Max, with the hubris of the young, had said no because his computer skills would have been able to detect any surveillance. Marianne and Gina had said it was irrelevant since both their work and their personal lives were so transparent. In addition, Marianne had disliked the implication that the Denebs were not their full and open partners. Gina had said—

Gina. Shot down, her life ended just as Jason William Jenner's had begun. And for how long? Would Marianne even get to see her grandson before everything was as over as Gina's life?

Dangerous to think this way. Their work on the *Embassy* was a thin bridge laid across a pit of despair, the same despair that had undoubtedly fueled Gina's killers.

"You know what has to happen," Marianne whispered. "Nobody's saying it aloud, but without virus replication in human bodies, we just can't understand the effect on the immune system and we're working blindly. Mice aren't enough. Even if we could have infected monkeys, it wouldn't be enough. We have to infect volunteers."

Evan stuck his finger into the flow of water, which spattered in bright drops against the side of the sink. "I know. *Everyone* knows. The request has been made to the powers that be."

"How do you know that?"

"I talk to people on the other teams. You know the laws against experimentation on humans unless there have first been proper clinical trials that—"

"Oh, fuck proper trials, this is a crisis situation!"

"Not enough people in power are completely convinced of that. You haven't been paying attention to the bigger picture, Marianne. The Public Health Service isn't even gearing up for mass inoculation or protection—Robinson is fighting it with claw and tusk. FEMA is divided and there's almost anarchy in the ranks. Congress just filibusters on the whole topic. And the president just doesn't have the votes to get much of anything done. Meanwhile, the masses riot or flee or just pretend the whole thing is some sort of hoax. The farther one gets from New York, the more the conspiracy theorists don't even believe there are aliens on Earth at all."

Marianne, still standing, pulled at the skin on her face. "It's all so frustrating. And the work we're doing here—you and I and Max and Gina—" her voice faltered "—is pointless. It really is. Identifying members of Smith's so-called clan? Who cares? I'm going to volunteer myself to be infected."

"They won't take you."

"If—"

"The only way that could happen is in secret. If a subgroup on the Spore Team decided the situation was desperate enough to conduct an unauthorized experiment."

She studied his face. In the biology department at the university, Evan had always been the one who knew how to obtain travel money for a conference, interviews with Nobel Prize winners, an immediate appointment with the dean. He had the knack, as she did not, for useful connections. She said, "You know something."

"No. I don't. Not yet."

"Find out."

He nodded and turned off the water. The music crescendoed: Brandenburg Concerto ***2, that had gone out into space on the "golden record" inside *Voyager 1*.

*   *   *

The secret experiment turned out to be not all that secret.

Evan followed the rumors. Within a day he had found a lab tech in the Biology Group who knew a scientist in the Spore Group who referred him, so obliquely that Evan almost missed it, to a security officer. Evan came to Marianne in her room, where she'd gone instead of eating lunch. He stood close to her and murmured in her ear, ending with, "They'll let us observe. You—what's that, then?"

The last sentence was said in a normal voice. Evan gazed at the piece of paper in Marianne's hands. She had been looking at it since she found it under her door.

"Another note from Noah. He isn't . . . he can't . . . Evan, I need to go ashore to see my new grandchild."

Evan blinked. "Your new grandchild?"

"Yes. He's three months old already and I haven't even seen him."

"It's not safe to leave the *Embassy* now. You know that."

"Yes. But I need to go."

Gently Evan took the note from her and read it. Marianne saw that he didn't really understand. Young, childless, orphaned . . . how could he? Noah had not forgiven her for never telling him that he was adopted. That must be why he said he might not ever see her again; no other reason made sense. Although maybe he would change his mind. Maybe in time he would forgive her, maybe he would not, maybe the world would end first. Before any of those things happened, Marianne had to see little Jason. She had to affirm what family ties she had, no matter how long she had them. Or anyone had them.

She said, "I need to talk to Ambassador Smith. How do I do that?"

He said, "Do you want me to arrange it?"

"Yes. Please. For today."

He didn't mention the backlog of samples in the lab. No one had replaced Gina. As family trees of the L7 haplogroup were traced in the matrilineal line, more and more of Smith's "clan" were coming aboard the *Embassy*. Marianne suspected they hoped to be shielded or transported when the spore cloud hit. She also suspected they were right. The Denebs were . . .

. . . were just as insistent on family connections as she was, risking her life to see Ryan, Connie, and the baby.

Well.

*   *   *

A helicopter flew her directly from the large pier outside the *Embassy* (so that's what it was for). When Marianne had last been outside, autumn was just ending. Now it was spring, the reluctant Northern spring of tulips and late frosts, cherry blossoms and noisy frogs. The Vermont town where Connie's parents lived, and to which Ryan had moved his family for safety, was less than twenty miles from the Canadian border. The house was a pleasant brick faux-Colonial set amid bare fields. Marianne noted, but did not comment on, the spiked chain-link fence around the small property, the electronic-surveillance sticker on the front door, and the large Doberman whose collar Ryan held in restraint. He had hastened home from his field work when she phoned that she was coming.

"Mom! Welcome!"

"We're so glad you're here, Marianne," Connie said warmly. "Even though I suspect it isn't us you came to see!" She grinned and handed over the tiny wrapped bundle.

The baby was asleep. Light-brown fuzz on the top of his head, silky skin lightly flushed with pink, tiny pursed mouth sucking away in an infant dream. He looked so much as Ryan had that tears pricked Marianne's eyes. Immediately she banished them: no sorrow, neither nostalgic nor catastrophic, was going to mar this occasion.

"He's beautiful," she said, inadequately.

"Yes!" Connie was not one of those mothers who felt obliged to disclaim praise of her child.

Marianne held the sleeping baby while coffee was produced. Connie's parents were away, helping Connie's sister, whose husband had just left her and whose three-year-old was ill. This was touched on only lightly. Connie kept the conversation superficial, prattling in her pretty voice about Jason, about the dog's antics, about the weather. Marianne followed suit, keeping to herself the thought that, after all, she had never heard Connie talk about anything but light and cheerful topics. She must have more to her than that, but not in front of her mother-in-law. Ryan said almost nothing, sipping his coffee, listening to his wife.

Finally Connie said, "Oh, I've just been monopolizing the conversation! Tell us about life aboard the *Embassy*. It must be so fascinating!"

Ryan looked directly at Marianne.

She interpreted the look as a request to keep up the superficial tone. Ryan had always been as protective of Connie as of a pretty kitten. Had he deliberately chosen a woman so opposite to his mother because Marianne had always put her work front and center? Had Ryan resented her for that as much as Noah had?

Pushing aside these disturbing thoughts, she chatted about the aliens. Connie asked her to describe them, their clothes, her life there. Did she have her own room? Had she been able to decorate it? Where did the humans eat?

"We're *all* humans, Terrans and Denebs," Marianne said.

"Of course," Connie said, smiling brilliantly. "Is the food good?"

Talking, talking, talking, but not one question about her work. Nor about the spore cloud, progress toward a vaccine, anything to indicate the size and terror of the coming catastrophe. Ryan did ask about the *Embassy*, but only polite questions about its least important aspects: how big it was, how it was laid out, what was the routine. Safe topics.

Just before a sense of unreality overwhelmed Marianne, Ryan's cell rang, and the ringing woke the baby, who promptly threw up all over Marianne.

"Oh, I'm sorry!" Connie said. "Here, give him to me!"

Ryan, making gestures of apology, took his cell into the kitchen and closed the door. Connie reached for a box of Wet Ones and began to wipe Jason's face. She said, "The bathroom is upstairs to the left, Marianne. If you need to, I can loan you something else to wear."

"It would have to be one of your maternity dresses," Marianne said. It came out more sour than she'd intended.

She went upstairs and cleaned baby vomit off her shirt and jeans with a wet towel. The bathroom was decorated in a seaside motif, with hand towels embroidered with sailboats, soap shaped like shells, blue walls painted with green waves and smiling dolphins. On top of the toilet tank, a crocheted cylinder decorated like a buoy held a spare roll of toilet paper.

Keeping chaos at bay with cute domesticity. Good plan. And then: *Stop it, Marianne.*

Using the toilet, she leafed idly through magazines stacked in a rustic basket. *Good Housekeeping*, *Time*, a Macy's catalogue. She pulled out a loose paper with full-color drawings:

HOW TO TELL PURPLE LOOSESTRIFE FROM NATIVE PLANTS

DON'T BE FOOLED BY LOOK-ALIKES!

Purple loosestrife leaves are downy with smooth edges. Although usually arranged opposite each other in pairs which alternate down the stalk at 90-degree angles, the leaves may sometimes appear in groups of three. The leaves lack teeth. The flowers, which appear in mid- to late summer, form a showy spike of rose-purple, each with five to seven petals. The stem is stiff, four-sided, and may appear woody at the base of larger plants, which can reach ten feet tall. Average height is four feet. Purple loosestrife can be distinguished from the native winged loosestrife (*Lythrum alatum*), which it most closely resembles, by its generally larger size, opposite leaves, and more closely placed flowers. It may also be confused with blue vervain (pictured below), which has . . .

At the bottom of the page, someone—presumably Ryan—had hand-drawn in purple ink three stylized versions of a loosestrife spike, then circled one. To Marianne it looked like a violet rocket ship unaccountably sprouting leaves.

Downstairs, Jason had been cleaned up and changed. Marianne played with him the limited games available for three-month-old babies: peek-a-boo, feetsies go up and down, where did the finger go? When he started to fuss and Connie excused herself to nurse him, Marianne said her good-byes and went out to the helicopter waiting in a nearby field. Neighbors had gathered around it, and Ryan was telling them—what? The neighbors looked harmless, but how could you tell? Always, Gina was on her mind. She hugged Ryan fiercely.

As the copter lifted and the house, the town, the countryside got smaller and smaller, Marianne tried not to think of what a failure the visit had been. Yes, she had seen her grandchild. But whatever comfort or connection that had been supposed to bring her, it hadn't. It seemed to her, perhaps irrationally, that never had she felt so alone.

* * *

NOAH

When Noah woke, he instantly remembered what day it was. For a long moment, he lay still, savoring the knowledge like rich chocolate on the tongue. Then he said good-bye to his room. He would never sleep here, out of his energy suit, again.

Over the months, he had made the room as World as he could. A sleeping mat, thin but with as much give as a mattress, rolled itself tightly as soon as he sprang up and into the tiny shower. On the support wall he had hung one of Oliver's pictures—not a half-dressed barbarian princess this time, but a black-and-white drawing of plants in the World garden. The other walls, which seemed thin as rice paper but somehow kept out sound, had been programmed, at Noah's request, with the subtly shifting colors that the Worlders favored for everything except family gatherings. Color was extremely important to Worlders, and so to Noah. He was learning to discern shades that had once seemed all the same. *This* blue for mourning; *this* blue for adventure; *this* blue for loyalty. He had discarded all his Terran clothes. How had he ever stood the yellow polo shirt, the red hoodie? Wrong, wrong.

Drying his body, he rehearsed his request to Mee^hao¡ (rising inflection in the middle, click at the end—Noah loved saying his name).

Breakfast, like all World meals, was communal, a time to affirm ties. Noah had already eaten in his room; the energy suit did not permit the intake of food. Nonetheless, he took his place in the hierarchy at the long table, above Oliver and Jacqui and below everyone else. That was just. Family solidarity rested on three supports: inclusion, rank, and empathy. A triangle was the strongest of all geometrical figures.

"G'morning," Oliver said, yawning. He was not a morning person, and resented getting up for a breakfast he would not eat until much later.

"I greet you," Noah said in World. Oliver blinked.

Jacqui, quicker, said, "Oh, today is the day, is it? Can I be there?"

"At the ceremony? No, of course not!" Noah said. She should have known better than to even make the request.

"Just asking," Jacqui said. "Doesn't hurt to ask."

Yes, it does. It showed a lack of respect for all three supports in the triangle. Although Noah had not expected any more of Jacqui.

He did expect it of the three Terrans who took their places below Oliver.

Isabelle Rhinehart; her younger sister, Kayla; and Kayla's son had come into the World section of the Embassy only a week ago, but already the two women were trying to speak Worldese. The child, Austin, was only three—young enough to grow up trilling and clicking Worldese like a native. Noah gazed with envy at the little boy, who smiled shyly and then crawled onto his mother's lap.

But they could not hold Noah's interest long. This was the day!

His stomach growled. He'd been too excited to eat much of the food delivered earlier to his room. And truthfully, the vegetarian World diet was not exciting. But he would learn to like it. And what a small price to pay for . . . *everything*.

The ceremony took place in the same room, right after breakfast. The other Terrans had left. Mee^hao¡ changed the wall program. Now instead of subtly shifting greens, the thin room dividers pulsed with the blue of loyalty alternating with the color of the clan of Mee^hao¡.

Noah knelt in the middle of the circle of Worlders, facing Mee^hao¡, who held a long blue rod. *Now I dub thee Sir Noah.* . . . Noah hated, completely hated, that his mind threw up that stupid thought. This was nothing like a feudal knighting. It was more like a baptism, washing him clean of his old self.

Mee^hao¡ sang a verse of what he had been told was the family inclusion song, with everyone else echoing the chorus. Noah didn't catch all the trilling and clicking words, but he didn't have to. Tears pricked his eyes. It seemed to him that he had never wanted anything this much in life, had never really wanted anything at all.

"Stand, brother mine," Mee^hao¡ said.

Noah stood. Mee^hao¡ did something with the rod, and the energy shield dissolved around Noah.

Not only a baptism—an operation.

The first breath of World air almost made him vomit. No, the queasiness was excitement, not the air. It tasted strange, and with the second panicky breath he felt he wasn't getting enough of it. But he knew that was just the lower oxygen content. The *Embassy* was at sea level; the O_2 concentration of World matched that at 12,000 feet. His lungs would adapt. His marrow would produce more red corpuscles. The Worlders had evolved for this; Noah would evolve, too.

The air smelled strange.

His legs buckled slightly, but before Llaa^moh¡, whom he had once known as Jones, could step toward him, Noah braced himself and smiled. He was all right. He was here. He was—

"Brother mine" went around the circle, and then the formalities were over and they all hugged him, and for the first time in 150,000 years, Terran skin touched the skin of humans from the stars.

* * *

MARIANNE

The security officer met Marianne and Evan in their lab and conducted them to a euchre game in the observation area outside the BSL4 lab.

From the first time she'd come here, Marianne had been appalled by the amateurishness of the entire setup. Granted, this was a bunch of scientists, not the CIA. Still, the Denebs had to wonder why euchre—or backgammon or chess or Monopoly, it varied—was being played here instead of at one of the comfortable Commons or cafeterias. Why two scientists were constantly at work in the negative-pressure lab even when they seemed to have nothing to do. Why the euchre players paid more attention to the screens monitoring the scientists' vitals than to the card game.

Dr. Julia Namechek and Dr. Trevor Lloyd. Both young, strong, and self-infected with spore disease. They moved around the BSL4 lab in full space suits, breathing tubes attached to the air supply in the ceiling. Surely the Denebs' energy suits would be better for this kind of work, but the suits had not been offered to the Terrans.

"When?" Marianne murmured, playing the nine of clubs.

"Three days ago," said a physician whose name Marianne had not caught.

Spoor disease (the name deliberately unimaginative, non-inflammatory) had turned up in mice after three days. Marianne was not a physician, but she could read a vitals screen. Neither Namechek nor Lloyd, busily working in their space suits behind glass, showed the slightest signs of infection. This was, in fact, the third time that the two had tried to infect themselves by breathing in the spores. Each occasion had been preceded by weeks of preparation. Those times, nothing had happened, either, and no one knew why.

Physicians experimenting on themselves were not unknown in research medicine. Edward Jenner had infected himself—and the eight-year-old son of his gardener—with cowpox to develop the smallpox vaccine. Jesse William Lazear infected himself with yellow fever from mosquitoes, in order to confirm that mosquitoes were indeed the transmission vector. Julio Barrera gave himself Argentine hemorrhagic fever; Barry Marshall drank a solution *H. pylori* to prove the bacterium caused peptic ulcers; Pradeep Seth injected himself with an experimental vaccine for HIV.

Marianne understood the reasons for the supposed secrecy of this experiment. The newspapers that came in on the mail runs glowed luridly with speculations about human experimentation aboard the *Embassy*. Journalists ignited their pages with "Goebbels," "Guatemalan syphilis trials," "Japanese Unit 731." And those were the mainstream journalists. The tabloids and fringe papers invented so many details about Deneb atrocities on humans that the newsprint practically dripped with blood and body parts. The online news sources were, if anything, even worse. No, such "journalists" would never believe that Drs. Namechek and Lloyd had given spore disease to themselves and without the aliens' knowing it.

Actually, Marianne didn't believe that, either. The Denebs were too intelligent, too technologically advanced, too careful. They *had* to know this experiment was going on. They had to be permitting it. No matter how benign and peaceful their culture, they were human. Their lack of interference was a way of ensuring CYA deniability.

"Your turn, Dr. Jenner," said Syed Sharma, a very formal microbiologist from Mumbai. He was the only player wearing a suit.

"Oh, sorry," Marianne said. "What's trump again?"

Evan, her partner, said, "Spades. Don't trump my ace again."

"No table talk, please," Sharma said.

Marianne studied her hand, trying to remember what had been played. She had never been a good card player. She didn't like cards. And there was nothing to see here, anyway. Evan could bring her the results, if any, of the clandestine experiment. It was possible that the two scientists had not been infected, after all—not this time nor the previous two. It was possible that the pathogen had mutated, or just hadn't taken hold in these two particular people, or was being administered with the wrong vector. Stubbins Firth, despite heroic and disgusting measures, had never succeeded in infecting himself with yellow fever because he never understood how it was transmitted. Pathogen research was still part art, part luck.

"I fold," she said, before she remembered that "folding" was poker, not euchre. She tried a weak smile. "I'm very tired."

"Go to bed, Dr. Jenner," said Seyd Sharma. Marianne gave him a grateful look, which he did not see as he frowned at his cards. She left.

Just as she reached the end of the long corridor leading to the labs, the door opened and a security guard hurried through, face twisted with some strong emotion. Her heart stopped. What fresh disaster now? She said, "Did anything—" but before she could finish the question he had pushed past her and hurried on.

Marianne hesitated. Follow him to hear the news or wait until—

The lab exploded.

Marianne was hurled to the floor. Walls around her, the tough but thin membrane-like walls favored by the Denebs, tore. People screamed, sirens sounded, pulsing pain tore through Marianne's head like a dark, viscous tsunami.

Then everything went black.

*   *   *

She woke alone in a room. Small, white, windowless, with one clear wall, two doors, a pass-through compartment. Immediately, she knew, even before she detected the faint hum of blown air: a quarantine room with negative pressure. The second door, locked, led to a BSL4 operating room for emergency procedures and autopsies. The explosion had exposed her to spores from the experimental lab.

Bandages wreathed her head; she must have hit it when she fell, got a concussion, and needed stitches. Nothing else on her seemed damaged. Gingerly she sat up, aware of the IV tube and catheter and pulse oximeter, and waiting for the headache. It was there, but very faint. Her movement set off a faint gong somewhere and Dr. Ann Potter, a physician whom Marianne knew slightly, appeared on the other side of the clear glass wall.

The doctor said, her voice coming from the ceiling as if she were just one more alien, "You're awake. What do you feel?"

"Headache. Not terrible. What . . . what happened?"

"Let me ask you some questions first." She was asked her name, the date, her location, the name of the president—

"Enough!" Marianne said. "I'm fine! *What happened?*" But she already knew. Hers was the only bed in the quarantine room.

Dr. Potter paid her the compliment of truth. "It was a suicide bomber. He—"

"The others? Evan Blanford?"

"They're all dead. I'm sorry, Dr. Jenner."

Evan. Dead.

Seyd Sharma, with his formal, lilting diction. Julia Namechek, engaged to be married. Trevor Lloyd, whom everyone said would win a Nobel someday. The fourth euchre player, lab tech Alyssa Rosert—all dead.

Evan. Dead.

Marianne couldn't process that, not now. She managed to say, "Tell me. All of it."

Ann Potter's face creased with emotion, but she had herself under control. "The bomber was dressed as a security guard. He had the explosive—I haven't heard yet what it was—in his stomach or rectum, presumably cased to protect it from body fluids. Autopsy showed that the detonator, ceramic so that it got through all our metal detectors, was probably embedded in a tooth, or at least somewhere in his mouth that could be tongued to go off."

Marianne pictured it. Her stomach twisted.

Dr. Potter continued., "His name was Michael Wendl and he was new but legitimately aboard, a sort of mole, I guess you'd call it. A manifesto was all over the Internet an hour after the explosion and this morning—"

"This morning? How long have I been out?"

"Ten hours. You had only a mild concussion but you were sedated to stitch up head lacerations, which of course we wouldn't ordinarily do but this was complicated because—"

"I know," Marianne said, and marveled at the calm in her voice. "I may have been exposed to the spores."

"You *have* been exposed, Marianne. Samples were taken. You're infected."

Marianne set that aside, too, for the moment. She said, "Tell me about the manifesto. What organization?"

"Nobody has claimed credit. The manifesto was about what you'd expect: Denebs planning to kill everyone on Earth, all that shit. Wendl vetted okay when he was hired, so speculation is that he was a new recruit to their cause. He was from somewhere upstate and there's a lot of dissent going on up there. But the thing is, he got it wrong. He was supposed to explode just outside the Deneb section of the *Embassy*, not the research labs. His organization, whatever it was, knew something about the layout of the *Embassy* but not enough. Wendl was supposed to be restricted to sub-bay duty. It's like someone who'd had just a brief tour had told him where to go, but either they remembered wrong or he did."

Marianne's spine went cold. *Someone who'd had just a brief tour* . . .

"You had some cranial swelling after the concussion, Marianne, but it's well under control now."

Elizabeth.

No, not possible. Not thinkable.

"You're presently on a steroid administered intravenously, which may have some side effects I'd like you to be aware of, including wakefulness and—"

Elizabeth, studying everything during her visit aboard the *Embassy*: *"Where do the Denebs live?" "Behind these doors here. No one has ever been in there." "Interesting. It's pretty close the high-risk labs. "*

"Marianne, are you listening to me?"

Elizabeth, furiously punching the air months ago: *"I don't believe it, not any of it. There are things they aren't telling us!"*

"Marianne?"

Elizabeth, grudgingly doing her duty to protect the aliens but against her own inclinations. Commanding a critical section of the Border Patrol, a member of the joint task force that had access to military-grade weapons. In an ideal position to get an infiltrator aboard the floating island.

"Marianne! *Are* you listening to me?"

"No," Marianne said. "I have to talk to Ambassador Smith!"

"Wait, you can't just—"

Marianne had started to heave herself off the bed, which was ridiculous because she couldn't leave the quarantine chamber anyway. A figure appeared on the other side of the glass barrier, behind Dr. Potter. The doctor, following Marianne's gaze, turned, and gasped.

Noah pressed close to the glass. An energy shield shimmered around him. Beneath it he wore a long tunic like Smith's. His once-pale skin now shone coppery under his black hair. But most startling were his eyes: Noah's eyes, and yet not. Bigger, altered to remove as much of the skin and expose as much of the white as possible. Within that large, alien-sized expanse of white, his irises were still the same color as her own, an un-alien light gray flecked with gold.

"Mom," he said tenderly. "Are you all right?"

"Noah—"

"I came as soon as I heard. I'm sorry it's been so long. Things have been . . . happening."

It was still Noah's voice, coming through the energy shield and out of the ceiling with no alien inflection, no trill or click. Marianne's mind refused to work logically. All she could focus on was his voice: He was too old. He would never speak English as anything but a Middle Atlantic American, and he would never speak Worldese without an accent.

"Mom?"

"I'm fine," she managed.

"I'm so sorry to hear about Evan."

She clasped her hands tightly together on top of the hospital blanket. "You're going. With the aliens. When they leave Earth."

"Yes."

One simple word. No more than that, and Marianne's son became an extraterrestrial. She knew that Noah was not doing this in order to save his life. Or hers, or anyone's. She didn't know why he had done it. As a child, Noah had been fascinated by superheroes, aliens, robots, even of the more ridiculous kind where the science made zero sense. Comic books, movies, TV shows—he would sit transfixed for hours by some improbable human transformed into a spider or a hulk or a sentient hunk of metal. Did Noah remember that childish fascination? She didn't understand what this adopted child, this beloved boy she had not borne, remembered or thought or desired. She never had.

He said, "I'm sorry."

She said, "Don't be," and neither of them knew exactly what he was apologizing for in the first place, nor what she was excusing him from. After that, Marianne could find nothing else to say. Of the thousands of things she could have said to Noah, absolutely none of them rose to her lips. So finally she nodded.

Noah blew her a kiss. Marianne did not watch him go. She couldn't have borne it. Instead she shifted her weight on the bed and got out of it, holding on to the bedstead, ignoring Ann Potter's strenuous objections on the other side of the glass.

She had to see Ambassador Smith, to tell him about Elizabeth. The terrorist organization could strike again.

As soon as she told Smith, Elizabeth would be arrested. *Two children lost—*

No, don't think of it. Tell Smith.

But—*wait*. Maybe it hadn't been Elizabeth. Surely others had had an unauthorized tour of the ship? And now, as a result of the attack, security would be tightened. Probably no other saboteur could get through. Perhaps there would be no more supply runs by submarine, no more helicopters coming and going on the wide pier. Time was so short—maybe there were enough supplies aboard already. And perhaps the Denebs would use their unknowable technology to keep the *Embassy* safer until the spore cloud hit, by which time, of course, the aliens would have left. There were only three months left. Surely a second attack inside the Embassy couldn't be organized in such a brief time! Maybe there was no need to name Elizabeth at all.

The room swayed as she clutched the side of the bed.

Ann Potter said, "If you don't get back into bed right now, Marianne, I'm calling security."

"Nothing is secure, don't you know that, you silly woman?" Marianne snapped.

Noah was lost to her. Evan was dead. Elizabeth was guilty.

"I'm sorry," she said. "I'll get back in bed." What was she even doing, standing up? She couldn't leave. She carried the infection inside her body. "But I . . . I need to see Ambassador Smith. Right now, here. Please have someone tell him it's the highest possible priority. Please."

*   *   *

NOAH

The visit to his mother upset Noah more than he'd expected. She'd looked so small, so fragile in her bed behind the quarantine glass. Always, his whole life, he'd thought of her as large, towering over the landscape like some stone fortress, both safe and formidable. But she was just a small, frightened woman who was going to die.

As were Elizabeth, Ryan and Connie and their baby, Noah's last girlfriend Emily, his childhood buddies Sam and Davey, Cindy and Miguel at the restaurant—all going to die when the spore cloud hit. Why hadn't Noah been thinking about this before? How could he be so selfish about concentrating on his delight in his new clan that he had put the rest of humanity out of his mind?

He had always been selfish. He'd known that about himself. Only before now, he'd called it "independent."

It was a relief to leave the Terran part of the *Embassy,* with its too-heavy gravity and glaring light. The extra rods and cones that had been inserted into Noah's eyes made them sensitive to such terrible brightness. In the World quarters, Kayla's little boy Austin was chasing a ball along the corridor, his energy suit a faint glimmer in the low light. He stopped to watch Noah shed his own suit.

Austin said, "I wanna do that."

"You will, some day. Maybe soon. Where's your mother?"

"She comes right back. I stay right here!"

"Good boy. Have you—hi, Kayla. Do you know where Mee^hao¡ is?"

"No. Oh, wait, yes—he left the sanctuary."

That, Noah remembered, was what both Kayla and her sister called the World section of the *Embassy.* "Sanctuary"—the term made him wonder what their life had been before they came aboard. Both, although pleasant enough, were close-mouthed about their pasts to the point of lock-jaw.

Kayla added, "I think Mee^hao¡ said it was about the attack."

It would be, of course. Noah knew he should wait until Mee^hao¡ was free. But he couldn't wait.

"Where's Llaa^moh¡?"

Kayla looked blank; her Worldese was not yet fluent.

"Officer Jones."

"Oh. I just saw her in the garden."

Noah strode to the garden. Llaa^moh¡ sat on a bench, watching water fall in a thin stream from the ceiling to a pool below. Delicately she fingered a llo flower, without picking it, coaxing the broad dark leaf to release its spicy scent. Noah and Llaa^moh¡ had avoided each other ever since Noah's welcome ceremony, and he knew why. Still, right now his need overrode awkward desire.

"Llaa^moh¡—may we speak together?" He hoped he had the verb tense right: urgency coupled with supplication.

"Yes, of course." She made room for him on the bench. "Your Worldese progresses well."

"Thank you. I am troubled in my liver." The correct idiom, he was certain. Almost.

"What troubles your liver, brother mine?"

"My mother." The word meant not only female parent but matriarchal clan leader, which Noah supposed that Marianne was, since both his grandmothers were dead. Although perhaps not his biological grandmothers, and to World, biology was all. There were no out-of-family adoptions.

"Yes?"

"She is Dr. Marianne Jenner, as you know, working aboard the *Embassy*. My brother and sister live ashore. What will happen to my family when the spore cloud comes? Does my mother go with us to World? Do my birth-siblings?"

But . . . how could they, unaltered? Also, they were not of his haplotype and so would belong to a different clan for lllathil, clans not represented aboard ship. Also, all three of them would hate everything about World. But otherwise they would die. All of them, dead.

Llaa^moh¡ said nothing. Noah gave her the space and time to think; one thing World humans hated about Terrans was that they replied so quickly, without careful thought, sometimes even interrupting each other and thereby dishonoring the speaker. Noah watched a small insect with multi-colored wings, whose name did not come to his fevered mind, cross the llo leaf, and forced his body to stay still.

Finally Llaa^moh¡ said, "Mee^hao¡ and I have discussed this. He has left this decision to me. You are one of us now. I will tell you what will happen when the spore cloud comes."

"I thank you for your trust." The ritual response, but Noah meant it.

"However, you are under obligation—" she used the most serious degree for a word of promise "—to say nothing to anyone else, World or Terran. Do you accept this obligation?"

Noah hesitated, and not from courtesy. Shouldn't he use the information, whatever it was, to try to ensure what safety was possible for his family? But if he did not promise, Llaa^moh¡ would tell him nothing.

"I accept the obligation."

She told him.

Noah's jaw dropped. He couldn't help it, even though it was very rude. Llaa^moh¡ was carefully not looking at him; perhaps she had anticipated this reaction.

Noah stood and walked out of the garden.

*   *   *

MARIANNE

"Thought," a famous poet—Marianne couldn't remember which one—had once said, "is an infection. In the case of certain thoughts, it becomes an epidemic." Lying in her bed in the quarantine chamber, Marianne felt an epidemic in her brain. What Elizabeth had done, what she herself harbored now in her body, Noah's transformation, Evan's death—the thoughts fed on her cells, fevered her mind.

Elizabeth, studying the complex layout of the Embassy: *"Where do the Denebs live?" "Behind these doors here."*

Noah, with his huge alien eyes.

Evan, urging her to meet the aliens by scribbling block letters on a paper sushi bag: CHANCE OF SIX THOUSAND LIFETIMES! The number of generations since Mitochondrial Eve.

Herself, carrying the deadly infection. Elizabeth, Noah, Evan, spores—it was almost a relief when Ambassador Smith appeared beyond the glass.

"Dr. Jenner," the ceiling said in uninflected translation. "I am so sorry you were injured in this attack. You said you want to see me now."

She hadn't been sure what she was going to say to him. How did you name your own child a possible terrorist, condemn her to whatever unknown form justice took among aliens? What if that meant something like drawing and quartering, as it once had on Earth? Marianne opened her mouth, and what came out were words she had not planned at all.

"Why did you permit Drs. Namechek and Lloyd to infect themselves three times when it violates both our medical code and yours?"

His face, both Terran and alien, that visage that now and forever would remind her of what Noah had done to his own face, did not change expression. "You know why, Dr. Jenner. It was necessary for the research. There is no other way to fully assess immune system response in ways useful to developing antidotes."

"You could have used your own people!"

"There are not enough of us to put anyone into quarantine."

"You could have run the experiment yourself with human volunteers. You'd have gotten volunteers, given what Earth is facing. And then the experiment could have had the advantage of your greater expertise."

"It is not much greater than yours, as you know. Our scientific knowledges have moved in different directions. But if we had sponsored experiments on Terrans, what would have been the Terran response?"

Marianne was silent. She knew the answer. They both knew the answer.

He said, "You are infected, I am told. We did not cause this. But now our two peoples can work more openly on developing medicines or vaccines. Both Earth and World will owe you an enormous debt."

Which she would never collect. In roughly two more days she would be dead of spore disease .

And she still had to tell him about Elizabeth.

"Ambassador Smith—"

"I must show you something, Dr. Jenner. If you had not sent for me, I would have come to you as soon as I was informed that you were awake. Your physician performed an autopsy on the terrorist. That is, by the way, a useful word, which does not exist on World. We shall appropriate it. The doctors found this in the mass of body tissues. It is engraved titanium, possibly created to survive the blast. Secretary General Desai suggests that it is a means to claim credit, a 'logo.' Other Terrans have agreed, but none know what it means. Can you aid us? Is it possibly related to one of the victims? You were a close friend of Dr. Blanford."

He held up something close to the glass: a flat piece of metal about three inches square. Whatever was pictured on it was too small for Marianne to see from her bed.

Smith said, "I will have Dr. Potter bring it to you."

"No, don't." Ann would have to put on a space suit and maneuver through the double airlock with respirator. The fever in Marianne's brain could not wait that long. She pulled out her catheter tube, giving a small shriek at the unexpected pain. Then she heaved herself out of bed and dragged the IV pole over to the clear barrier. Ann began to sputter. Marianne ignored her.

On the square of metal was etched a stylized purple rocket ship, sprouting leaves.

Not Elizabeth. Ryan.

"Dr. Jenner?"

"They're an invasive species," Ryan had said.

"Didn't you hear a word I said?" Marianne said. "They're not 'invasive,' or at least not if our testing bears out the ambassador's story. They're native to Earth."

"An invasive species is native to Earth. It's just not in the ecological niche it evolved for."

"Dr. Jenner?" the Ambassador repeated. "Are you all right?"

Ryan, his passion about purple loosestrife a family joke. Ryan, interested in the *Embassy*, as Connie was not, asking questions about the facilities and the layout while Marianne cuddled her new grandson. Ryan, important enough in this terrorist organization to have selected its emblem from a sheet of drawings in a kitschy bathroom.

Ryan, her son.

"Dr. Jenner, I must insist—"

"Yes. *Yes.* I recognize that thing. I know who—what group—you should look for." Her heart shattered.

Smith studied her through the glass. The large, calm eyes—Noah's eyes now, except for the color—held compassion.

"Someone you know."

"Yes."

"It doesn't matter. We shall not look for them."

The words didn't process. "Not . . . not look for them?"

"No. It will not happen again. The embassy has been sealed and the Terrans removed except for a handful of scientists directly involved in immunology, all of whom have chosen to stay, and all of whom we trust."

"But—"

"And, of course, those of our clan members who wish to stay."

Marianne stared at Smith through the glass, the impermeable barrier. Never had he seemed more alien. Why would this intelligent man believe that just because a handful of Terrans shared a mitochondrial haplotype with him, they could not be terrorists, too? Was it a cultural blind spot, similar to the Terran millennia-long belief in the divine right of kings? Was it some form of perception, the product of divergent evolution, that let his brain perceive things she could not? Or did he simply have in place such heavy surveillance and protective devices that people like Noah, sequestered in a different part of the *Embassy*, presented no threat?

Then the rest of what he had said struck her. "Immunologists?"

"Time is short, Dr. Jenner. The spore cloud will envelop Earth in merely a few months. We must perform intensive tests on you and the other infected people."

"*Other?*"

"Dr. Ahmed Rafat and two lab technicians, Penelope Hodgson and Robert

Chavez. They are, of course, all volunteers. They will be joining you soon in quarantine."

Rage tore through her, all the rage held back, pent up, about Evan's death, about Ryan's deceit, about Noah's defection. "Why not any of your own people? No, don't tell me that you're all too valuable—so are we! Why only Terrans? If we take this risk, why don't you? And what the fuck happens when the cloud does hit? Do you take off two days before, keeping yourselves safe and leaving Earth to die? You know very well that there is no chance of developing a real vaccine in the time left, let alone manufacturing and distributing it! What then? How can you just—"

But Ambassador Smith was already moving away from her, behind the shatterproof glass. The ceiling said, without inflection or emotion, "I am sorry."

*　　*　　*

NOAH

Noah stood in the middle of the circle of Terrans. Fifty, sixty—they had all come aboard the *Embassy* in the last few days, as time shortened. Not all were L7s; some were families of clan brothers, and these too had been welcomed, since they'd had had the defiance to ask for asylum when the directives said explicitly that only L7s would be taken in. *There was something wrong with this system*, Noah thought, but he did not think hard about what it might be.

The room, large and bare, was in neither the World quarters nor the now-sealed part of the *Embassy* where the Terran scientists worked. The few scientists left aboard, anyway. The room's air, gravity, and light were all Terran, and Noah again wore an energy suit. He could see its faint shimmer along his arms as he raised them in welcome. He hadn't realized how much he was going to hate having to don the suit again.

"I am Noah," he said.

The people pressed against the walls of the bare room or huddled in small groups or sat as close to Noah as they could, cross-legged on the hard floor. They looked terrified or hopeful or defiant or already grieving for what might be lost. They all, even the ones who, like Kayla and Isabelle, had been here for a while, expected to die if they were left behind on Earth.

"I will be your leader and teacher. But first, I will explain the choice you must all make, now. You can choose to leave with the people of World, when we return to the home world. Or you can stay here, on Earth."

"To die!" someone shouted. "Some choice!"

Noah found the shouter: a young man standing close behind him, fists clenched at his side. He wore ripped jeans, a pin through his eyebrow, and a scowl. Noah felt the shock of recognition that had only thrilled through him twice before: with the nurse on the Upper West Side of New York and when he'd met Mee^hao¡. Not even Llaa^moh¡, who was a geneticist, could explain that shock, although she seemed to think it had to do with certain genetically determined pathways in Noah's L7 brain coupled with the faint electromagnetic field surrounding every human skull. She was fascinated by it.

Lisa Guiterrez, Noah remembered, had also attributed it to neurological pathways, changed by his heavy use of sugarcane.

Noah said to the scowler, "What is your name?"

He said, "Why?"

"I'd like to know it. We are clan brothers."

"I'm not your fucking brother. I'm here because it's my only option to not die."

A child on its mother's lap started to cry. People murmured to each other, most not taking their eyes off Noah. Waiting, to see what Noah did about the young man. Answer him? Let it go? Have him put off the *Embassy*?

Noah knew it would not take much to ignite these desperate people into attacking him, the alien-looking stand-in for the Worlders they had no way to reach.

He said gently to the young man, to all of them, to his absent and injured and courageous mother: "I'm going to explain your real choices. Please listen."

* * *

MARIANNE

Something was wrong.

One day passed, then another, then another. Marianne did not get sick. Nor did Ahmed Rafat and Penny Hodgson. Robbie Chavez did, but not very.

The lead immunologist left aboard the *Embassy*, Harrison Rice, stood with Ann Potter in front of Marianne's glass quarantine cage, known as a "slammer." He was updating Marianne on the latest lab reports. In identical slammers, two across a narrow corridor and one beside her, Marianne could see the three other infected people. The rooms had been created, as if by alchemy, by a Deneb that Marianne had not seen before—presumably an engineer of some unknowable building methods. Ahmed stood close to his glass, listening. Penny was asleep. Robbie, his face filmed with sweat, lay in bed, listening.

Ann Potter said, "You're not initially viremic but—"

"What does that mean?" Marianne interrupted.

Dr. Rice answered. He was a big, bluff Canadian who looked more like a truck driver who hunted moose than like a Nobel Prize winner. In his sixties, still strong as a mountain, he had worked with Ebola, Marburg, Lassa fever, and Nipah, both in the field and in the lab.

He said, "It means lab tests show that as with Namechek and Lloyd, the spores were detectable in the first samples taken from your respiratory tract. So the virus should be present in your bloodstream and so have access to the rest of your body. However, we can't find it. Well, that can happen. Viruses are elusive. But as far as we can tell, you aren't developing antibodies against the virus, as the infected mice did. That may mean that we just haven't isolated the antibodies yet. *Or* that your body doesn't consider the virus a foreign invader, which seems unlikely. *Or* that in humans but not in mice, the virus has dived into an organ to multiply until its offspring burst out again. Malaria does that. *Or* that the virus samples in the lab, grown artificially, have mutated into harmlessness, differing from their wild cousins in the approaching cloud. *Or* it's possible that none of us know what the hell we're doing with this crazy pathogen."

Marianne said, "What do the Denebs think?" Supposedly Rice was co-lead with Deneb Scientist Jones.

He said, his anger palpable even through the glass wall of the slammer, "I have no idea what they think. None of us have seen any of them."

"Not seen them?"

"No. We share all our data and samples, of course. Half of the samples go into an airlock for them, and the data over the LAN. But all we get in return is a thank-you on screen. Maybe they're not making progress, either, but at least they could tell us what they haven't discovered."

"Do we know . . . this may sound weird, but do we know that they're still here at all? Is it possible they all left Earth already?" *Noah.*

He said, "It's possible, I suppose. We have no news from the outside world, of course, so it's possible they pre-recorded all those thank-yous, blew up New

York, and took off for the stars. But I don't think so. If they had, they'd have least unsealed us from this floating plastic bubble. Which, incidentally, has become completely opaque, even on the observation deck."

Marianne hadn't known there was an observation deck. She and Evan had not found it during their one exploration of the Embassy.

Dr. Rice continued. "Your cells are not making an interferon response, either. That's a small protein molecule that can be produced in any cell in response to the presence of viral nucleic acid. You're not making it."

"Which means . . ."

"Probably it means that there is no viral nucleic acid in your cells."

"Are Robbie's cells making interferon?"

"Yes. Also antibodies. Plus immune responses like—Ann, what does your chart on Chavez show for this morning?"

Ann said, "Fever of 101, not at all dangerous. Chest congestion, also not at dangerous levels, some sinus involvement. He has the equivalent of mild bronchitis."

Marianne said, "But why is Robbie sick when the rest of us aren't?"

"Ah," Harrison Rice said, and for the first time she heard the trace of a Canadian accent, "that's the big question, isn't it? In immunology, it always is. Sometimes genetic differences between infected hosts are the critical piece of the puzzle in understanding why an identical virus causes serious disease or death in one individual—or one group—and little reaction or none at all in other people. Is Robbie sick and you not because of your respective genes? We don't know."

"But you can use Robbie's antibodies to maybe develop a vaccine?"

He didn't answer. She knew the second the words left her mouth how stupid they were. Rice might have antibodies, but he had no time. None of them had enough time.

Yet they all worked on, as if they did. Because that's what humans did.

Instead of answering her question, he said, "I need more samples, Marianne."

"Yes."

Fifteen minutes later he entered her slammer, dressed in full space suit and sounding as if speaking through a vacuum cleaner. "Blood samples plus a tissue biopsy, just lie back down and hold still, please . . ."

During a previous visit, he had told her of an old joke among immunologists working with lethal diseases: "The first person to isolate a virus in the lab by getting infected is a hero. The second is a fool." Well, that made Marianne a fool. So be it.

She said to Rice, "And the aliens haven't . . . Ow!"

"Baby." He withdrew the biopsy needle and slapped a bandage over the site.

She tried again. "And the aliens haven't commented at all on Robbie's diagnosis? Not a word?"

"Not a word."

Marianne frowned. "Something isn't right here."

"No," Rice said, bagging his samples, "it certainly is not."

*   *   *

NOAH

Nothing, Noah thought, had ever felt more right, not in his entire life.

He raised himself on one elbow and looked down at Llaa^moh¡. She still slept, her naked body and long legs tangled in the light blanket made of some substance he could not name. Her wiry dark hair smelled of something like cinnamon, although it probably wasn't. The blanket smelled of sex.

He knew now why he had not felt the same shock of recognition at their first meeting that he had felt with Mee^hao¡ and the unnamed New York nurse and surly young Tony Schrupp. After the World geneticists had done their work, Mee^hao¡ had explained it to him. Noah felt profound relief. He and Llaa^moh¡ shared a mitochondrial DNA group, but not a nuclear DNA one. They were not too genetically close to mate.

Of course, they could have had sex anyway; World had early, and without cultural shame or religious prejudice, discovered birth control. But for the first time in his life, Noah did not want just sex. He wanted to mate.

The miracle was that she did, too. Initially he feared that for her it was mere novelty: be the first Worlder to sleep with a Terran! But it was not. Just yesterday they had signed a five-year mating contract, followed by a lovely ceremony in the garden to which every single Worlder had come. Noah had never known exactly how many were aboard the Embassy; now he did. They had all danced with him, every single one, and also with her. Mee^hao¡ himself had pierced their right ears and hung from them the wedding silver, shaped like stylized versions of the small flowers that had once, very long ago, been the real thing.

"Is better," Noah had said in his accented, still clumsy World. "We want not bunch of dead vegetation dangle from our ears." At least, that's what he hoped he'd said. Everyone had laughed.

Noah reached out one finger to stroke Llaa^mohᵢ's hair. A miracle, yes. A whole skyful of miracles, but none as much as this: Now he knew who he was and where he belonged and what he was going to do with his life.

His only regret was that his mother had not been at the mating ceremony. And—yes, forgiveness was in order here!—Elizabeth and Ryan, too. They had disparaged him his entire life and he would never see them again, but they were still his first family. Just not the one that any longer mattered.

Llaa^mohᵢ stirred, woke, and reached for him.

*   *   *

MARIANNE

Robbie Chavez, recovered from *Respirovirus sporii*, gave so many blood and tissue samples that he joked he'd lost ten pounds without dieting. It wasn't much of a joke, but everyone laughed. Some of the laughter held hysteria.

Twenty-two people left aboard the *Embassy*. Why, Marianne sometimes wondered, had these twenty-two chosen to stay and work until the last possible second? Because the odds of finding anything that would affect the coming die-off were very low. They all knew that. Yet here they were, knowing they would die in this fantastically equipped, cut-off-from-the-world lab instead of with their families. Didn't any of them have families? Why were they still here?

Why was she?

No one discussed this. They discussed only work, which went on eighteen hours a day. Brief breaks for microwaved meals from the freezer. Briefer—not in actuality, but that's how it felt—for sleep.

The four people exposed to *R. sporii* worked outside the slammers; maintaining biosafety no longer seemed important. No one else became ill. Marianne relearned lab procedures she had not performed since grad school. Theoretical evolutionary biologists did not work as immunologists. She did now.

Every day, the team sent samples data to the Denebs. Every day, the Denebs gave thanks, and nothing else.

In July, eight-and-a-half months after they'd first been given the spores to work with, the scientists finally succeeded in growing the virus in a culture. There was a celebration of sorts. Harrison Rice produced a hoarded bottle of champagne.

"We'll be too drunk to work," Marianne joked. She'd come to admire Harrison's unflagging cheerfulness.

"On one twenty-second of one bottle?" he said. "I don't think so."

"Well, maybe not everyone drinks."

Almost no one did. Marianne, Harrison, and Robbie Chavez drank the bottle. Culturing the virus, which should have been a victory, seemed to turn the irritable more irritable, the dour more dour. The tiny triumph underlined how little they had actually achieved. People began to turn strange. The unrelenting work, broken sleep, and constant tension created neuroses.

Penny Hodgson turned compulsive about the autoclave: It must be loaded just so, in just this order, and only odd numbers of tubes could be placed in the rack at one time. She flew into a rage when she discovered eight tubes, or twelve.

William Parker, Nobel Laureate in medicine, began to hum as he worked. Eighteen hours a day of humming. If told to stop, he did, and then unknowingly resumed a few minutes later. He could not carry a tune, and he liked lugubrious country and western tunes.

Marianne began to notice feet. Every few seconds, she glanced at the feet of others in the lab, checking that they still had them. Harrison's work boots, as if he tramped the forests of Hudson's Bay. Mark Wu's black oxfords. Penny's Nikes—did she think she'd be going for a run? Robbie's sandals. Ann's—

Stop it, Marianne!

She couldn't.

They stopped sending samples and data to the Denebs and held their collective breath, waiting to see what would happen. Nothing did.

Workboots, Oxfords, Nikes, sandals—

"I think," Harrison said, "that I've found something."

It was an unfamiliar protein in Marianne's blood. Did it have anything to do with the virus? They didn't know. Feverishly they set to work culturing it, sequencing it, photographing it, looking forward in everyone else. The protein was all they had.

It was August.

The outside world, with which they had no contact, had ceased to exist for them, even as they raced to save it.

Workboots—

Oxfords—

Sandals—

*   *   *

NOAH

Rain fell in the garden. Noah tilted his head to the artificial sky. He loved rainy afternoons, even if this was not really rain, nor afternoon. Soon he would experience the real thing.

Llaa^moh¡ came toward him through the dark, lush leaves open as welcoming hands. Noah was surprised; these important days she rarely left the lab. Too much to do.

She said, "Should not you be teaching?"

He wanted to say *I'm playing hooky* but had no idea what the idiom would be in Worldese. Instead he said, hoping he had the tenses right, "My students I will return at soon. Why you here? Something is wrong?"

"All is right." She moved into his arms. Again Noah was surprised; Worlders did not touch sexually in public places, even public places temporarily empty. Others might come by, unmated others, and it was just as rude to display physical affection in front of those without it as to eat in front of anyone hungry.

"Llaa^moh¡—"

She whispered into his ear. Her words blended with the rain, with the rich flower scents, with the odor of wet dirt. Noah clutched her and began to cry.

*   *   *

VI: S minus two weeks

MARIANNE

The Commons outside the lab was littered with frozen food trays, with discarded sterile wrappings, with an empty disinfectant bottle. Harrison slumped in a chair and said the obvious.

"We've failed, Marianne."

"Yes," she said. "I know." And then, fiercely, "Do you think the Denebs know more than we do? And aren't sharing?"

"Who knows?"

"Fucking bastards," Marianne said. Weeks ago she had crossed the line from defending the aliens to blaming them. How much of humanity had been ahead of her in that? By now, maybe all of it.

They had discovered nothing useful about the anomalous protein in Marianne's blood. The human body contained so many proteins whose identities were not understood. But that wouldn't make any difference, not now. There wasn't enough time.

"Harrison," she began, and didn't get to finish her sentence.

Between one breath and the next, Harrison Rice and the lab, along with everything else, disappeared.

* * *

NOAH

Nine, not counting him. The rest had been put ashore, to face whatever would happen to them on Earth. Noah would have much preferred to be with Llaa^moh¡, but she of course had duties. Even unannounced, departure was dangerous. Too many countries had too many formidable weapons.

So instead of standing beside Llaa^moh¡, Noah sat in his energy suit in the Terran compartment of the shuttle. Around him, strapped into chairs, sat the nine Terrans going to World. The straps were unnecessary; Llaa^moh¡ had told him that the acceleration would feel mild, due to the same gravity-altering machinery that had made the World section of the Embassy so comfortable. But Terrans were used to straps in moving vehicles, so there were straps.

Kayla Rhinehart and her little son.

Her sister, Isabelle.

The surly Tony Schrupp, a surprise. Noah had been sure Tony would change his mind.

A young woman, five months pregnant, who "wanted to give my baby a better life." She did not say what her previous life had been, but there were bruises on her arms and legs.

A pair of thirty-something brothers with restless, eager-for-adventure eyes.

A middle-aged journalist with a sun-leathered face and impressive byline, recorders in her extensive luggage.

And, most unexpected, a Terran physicist, Dr. Nathan Beyon of Massachusetts Institute of Technology.

Nine Terrans willing to go to the stars.

A slight jolt. Noah smiled at the people under his leadership—he, who had never led anything before, not even his own life—and said, "Here we go."

That seemed inadequate, so he said, "We are off to the stars!"

That seemed dumb. Tony sneered. The journalist looked amused. Austin clutched his mother.

Noah said, "Your new life will be wonderful. Believe it."

Kayla gave him a wobbly smile.

*　　*　　*

MARIANNE

She could not imagine where she was.

Cool darkness, with the sky above her brightening every second. It had been so long since she'd seen a dawn sky, or any sky. Silver-gray, then pearl, and now the first flush of pink. The floor rocked gently. Then the last of the knock-out gas left her brain and she sat up. A kind of glorified barge, flat and wide with a single square rod jutting from the middle. The barge floated gently on New York Harbor. The sea was smooth as polished gray wood. In one direction rose the skyline of Manhattan; in the other, the *Embassy*. All around her lay her colleagues: Dr. Rafat, Harrison Rice and Ann Potter, lab techs Penny and Robbie, all the rest of the twenty-two people who'd still been aboard the *Embassy*. They wore their daily clothing. In her jeans and tee, Marianne shivered in a sudden breeze.

Nearby lay a pile of blankets. She took a yellow one and wrapped it around her shoulders. It felt warm and silky, although clearly not made of silk. Other people began to stir. Pink tinged the east.

Harrison came to her side. "Marianne?"

Automatically she said, because she'd been saying so many times each day, "I feel fine." And then, "What the *fuck?*"

He said something just as pointless: "But we have two more weeks!"

"Oh my God!" someone cried, pointing, and Marianne looked up. The eastern horizon turned gold. Against it, a ship, dark and small, shot from the Embassy and climbed the sky. Higher and higher, while everyone on the barge shaded their eyes against the rising sun and watched it fly out of sight.

"They're going," someone said quietly.

They. The Denebs. *Noah.*

Before the tears that stung her eyes could fall, the *Embassy* vanished. One moment it was there, huge and solid and gray in the pre-dawn, and the next it was just gone. The water didn't even ripple.

The metal rod in the center of the ship spoke. Marianne, along with everyone else, turned sharply. Shoulder-high, three feet on a side, the rod had become four screens, each filled with the same alien/human image and mechanical voice.

"This is Ambassador Smith. A short time from now, this recording will go to everyone on Earth, but we wanted you, who have helped us so much, to hear it first. We of World are deeply in your debt. I would like to explain why, and to leave you a gift.

"Your astronomers' calculations were very slightly mistaken, and we did not correct them. In a few hours the spore cloud will envelop your planet. We do not think it will harm you because—"

Someone in the crowd around the screen cried, "*What?*"

"—because you are genetically immune to this virus. We suspected as much before we arrived, although we could not be sure. *Homo sapiens* acquired immunity when Earth passed through the cloud the first time, about seventy thousand years ago."

A graphic replaced Smith's face: the Milky Way galaxy, a long dark splotch overlapping it, and a glowing blue dot for Earth. "The rotation of the galaxy plus its movement through space-time will bring you back into contact with the cloud's opposite edge from where it touched you before. Your physicists were able to see the approaching cloud, but your instruments were not advanced enough to understand its shape or depth. Earth will be passing through the edge of the cloud for two-point-six years. On its first contact, the cloud killed every *homo sapiens* that did not come with this genetic mutation."

A gene sequence of base pairs flashed across the screen, too fast to be noted. "This sequence will appear again later, in a form you can record. It is found in what you call 'junk DNA.' The sequence is a transposon and you will find it complementary to the spores' genetic code. Your bodies made no antibodies against the spores because it does not consider them invaders. Seventy thousand years ago our people had already been taken from Earth or we, too, would have died. We are without this sequence, which appeared in mutation later than our removal."

Marianne's mind raced. Seventy thousand years ago. The "bottleneck event" that had shrunk the human population on Earth to a mere few thousand. It had not been caused by the Toba volcano or ferocious predators or climate changes, but by the spore cloud. As for the gene sequence—one theory said that much of the human genome consisted of inactive and fossilized viruses absorbed into the DNA. Fossilized and inactive—almost she could hear Evan's voice: *"Or so we thought. . . ."*

Smith continued. "You will find that in Marianne Jenner, Ahmed Rafat, and Penelope Hodgson this sequence has already activated, producing the protein already identified in Dr. Jenner's blood, a protein that this recording will detail for you. The protein attaches to the outside of cells and prevents the virus from entering. Soon the genetic sequence will do so in the rest of humanity. Some may become mildly ill, like Robert Chavez, due to faulty protein production. We estimate this will comprise perhaps twenty percent of you. There may be fatalities among the old or already sick, but most of you are genetically protected. Some of your rodents do not seem to be, which we admit was a great surprise to us, and we cannot say for certain what other Terran species may be susceptible.

"We know that we are fatally susceptible. We cannot alter our own genome, at least not for the living, but we have learned much from you. By the time the spore cloud reaches World, we will have developed a vaccine. This would not have been possible without your full cooperation and your bodily samples. We—"

"If this is true," Penny Hodgson shouted, "why didn't they *tell* us?"

"—did not tell you the complete truth because we believe that had you known Earth was in no critical danger, you would not have allocated so many resources, so much scientific talent, or such urgency into the work on the *Embassy*. We are all human, but your evolutionary history and present culture are very different from ours. You do not build identity on family. You permit much of Earth's population to suffer from lack of food, water, and medical care. We didn't think you would help us as much as we needed unless we withheld from you certain truths. If we were mistaken in our assessment, please forgive us."

They weren't mistaken, Marianne thought.

"We are grateful for your help," Smith said, "even if obtained fraudulently. We leave you a gift in return. This recording contains what you call the 'engineering specs' for a star drive. We have already given you the equations describing the principles. Now you may build a ship. In generations to come, both branches of humanity will profit from more open and truthful exchanges. We will become true brothers.

"Until then, ten Terrans accompany us home. They have chosen to do this, for their own reasons. All were told that they would not die if they remained on Earth, but chose to come anyway. They will become World, creating further friendship with our clan brothers on Terra.

"Again—thank you."

Pandemonium erupted on the barge: talking, arguing, shouting. The sun was above the horizon now. Three Coast Guard ships barreled across the harbor toward the barge. As Marianne clutched her yellow blanket closer against the morning breeze, something vibrated in the pocket of her jeans.

She pulled it out: a flat metal square with Noah's face on it. As soon as her gaze fell on his, the face began to speak. "I'm going with them, Mom. I want you to know that I am completely happy. This is where I belong. I've mated with Llaa^moh¡—Dr. Jones—and she is pregnant. Your grandchild will be born among the stars. I love you."

Noah's face faded from the small square.

Rage filled her, red sparks burning. Her son, and she would never see him again! Her grandchild, and she would never see him or her at all. She was being robbed, being deprived of what was hers by *right*, the aliens should never have come—

She stopped. Realization slammed into her, and she gripped the rail of the barge so tightly that her nails pierced the wood.

The aliens *had* made a mistake. A huge, colossal, monumental mistake.

Her rage, however irrational, was going to be echoed and amplified across the entire planet. The Denebs had understood that Terrans would work really hard only if their own survival were at stake. But they did not understand the rest of it. The Deneb presence on Earth had caused riots, diversion of resources, deaths, panic, fear. The "mild illness" of the twenty percent like Robbie, happening all at once starting today, was enough to upset every economy on the planet. The aliens had swept like a storm through the world, and as in the aftermath of a superstorm, everything in the landscape had shifted. In addition, the Denebs had carried off ten humans, which could be seen as brainwashing them in order to procure prospective lab rats for future experimentation.

Brothers, yes—but Castor and Pollux, whose bond reached across the stars, or Cain and Abel?

Humans did not forgive easily, and they resented being bought off, even with a star drive. Smith should have left a different gift, one that would not let Terrans come to World, that peaceful and rich planet so unaccustomed to revenge or war.

But on the other hand—she could be wrong. Look how often had she been wrong already: about Elizabeth, about Ryan, about Smith. Maybe, when the Terran disruptions were over and starships actually built, humanity would become so entranced with the Deneb gift that we would indeed go to World in friendship. Maybe the prospect of going to the stars would even soften American isolationism and draw countries together to share the necessary resources. It could happen. The cooperative genes that had shaped Smith and Jones were also found in the Terran genome.

But—it would happen only if those who wanted it worked hard to convince the rest. Worked, in fact, as hard at urging friendship as they had at ensuring survival. Was that possible? Could it be done?

Why are you here?

To make contact with World. A peace mission.

She gazed up at the multi-colored dawn sky, but the ship was already out of sight. Only its after-image remained in her sight.

"Harrison," Marianne said, and felt her own words steady her, "We have a lot of work to do."

NEBULA AWARD WINNER
BEST NOVEL

EXCERPT FROM
ANNIHILATION

JEFF VANDERMEER

Jeff VanderMeer's most recent work is the New York Times–bestselling Southern Reach trilogy (Annihilation, Authority, and Acceptance), all released in 2014. A three-time World Fantasy Award winner and thirteen-time nominee, VanderMeer has been a finalist for the Nebula, Philip K. Dick, and Shirley Jackson Awards, among others. Annihilation was published by FSG Originals.

CHAPTER ONE

The tower, which was not supposed to be there, plunges into the earth in a place just before the black pine forest begins to give way to swamp and then the reeds and wind-gnarled trees of the marsh flats. Beyond the marsh flats and the natural canals lies the ocean and, a little farther down the coast, a derelict lighthouse. All of this part of the country had been abandoned for decades, for reasons that are not easy to relate. Our expedition was the first to enter Area X for more than two years, and much of our predecessors' equipment had rusted, their tents and sheds little more than husks. Looking out over that untroubled landscape, I do not believe any of us could yet see the threat.

There were four of us: a biologist, an anthropologist, a surveyor, and a psychologist. I was the biologist. All of us were women this time, chosen as part of the complex set of variables that governed sending the expeditions. The psychologist, who was older than the rest of us, served as the expedition's leader. She had put us all under hypnosis to cross the border, to make sure we remained calm. It took four days of hard hiking after crossing the border to reach the coast.

Our mission was simple: to continue the government's investigation into the mysteries of Area X, slowly working our way out from base camp.

The expedition could last days, months, or even years, depending on various stimuli and conditions. We had supplies with us for six months, and another two years' worth of supplies had already been stored at the base camp. We had also been assured that it was safe to live off the land if necessary. All of our foodstuffs were smoked or canned or in packets. Our most outlandish equipment consisted of a measuring device that had been issued to each of us, which hung from a strap on our belts: a small rectangle of black metal with a glass-covered hole in the middle. If the hole glowed red, we had thirty minutes to remove ourselves to "a safe place." We were not told what the device measured or why we should be afraid should it glow red. After the first few hours, I had grown so used to it that I hadn't looked at it again. We had been forbidden watches and compasses.

When we reached the camp, we set about replacing obsolete or damaged equipment with what we had brought and putting up our own tents. We would rebuild the sheds later, once we were sure that Area X had not affected us. The members of the last expedition had eventually drifted off, one by one. Over time, they had returned to their families, so strictly speaking they did not vanish. They simply disappeared from Area X and, by unknown means, reappeared back in the world beyond the border. They could not relate the specifics of that journey. This *transference* had taken place across a period of eighteen months, and it was not something that had been experienced by prior expeditions. But other phenomena could also result in "premature dissolution of expeditions," as our superiors put it, so we needed to test our stamina for that place.

We also needed to acclimate ourselves to the environment. In the forest near base camp one might encounter black bears or coyotes. You might hear a sudden croak and watch a night heron startle from a tree branch and, distracted, step on a venomous snake, of which there were at least six varieties. Bogs and streams hid huge aquatic reptiles, and so we were careful not to wade too deep to collect our water samples. Still, these aspects of the ecosystem did not really concern any of us. Other elements had the ability to unsettle, however. Long ago, towns had existed here, and we encountered eerie signs of human habitation: rotting cabins with sunken, red-tinged roofs, rusted wagon-wheel spokes half-buried in the dirt, and the barely seen outlines of what used to be enclosures for livestock, now mere ornament for layers of pine-needle loam.

Far worse, though, was a low, powerful moaning at dusk. The wind off the sea and the odd interior stillness dulled our ability to gauge direction, so that the sound seemed to infiltrate the black water that soaked the cypress trees. This water was so dark we could see our faces in it, and it never stirred, set like glass, reflecting the beards of gray moss that smothered the cypress trees. If you looked out through these areas, toward the ocean, all you saw was the black water, the gray of the cypress trunks, and the constant, motionless rain of moss flowing down. All you heard was the low moaning. The effect of this cannot be understood without being there. The beauty of it cannot be understood, either, and when you see beauty in desolation it changes something inside you. Desolation tries to colonize you.

As noted, we found the tower in a place just before the forest became waterlogged and then turned to salt marsh. This occurred on our fourth day after reaching base camp, by which time we had almost gotten our bearings. We did not expect to find anything there, based on both the maps that we brought with us and the water-stained, pine-dust-smeared documents our predecessors had left behind. But there it was, surrounded by a fringe of scrub grass, half-hidden by fallen moss off to the left of the trail: a circular block of some grayish stone seeming to mix cement and ground-up seashells. It measured roughly sixty feet in diameter, this circular block, and was raised from ground level by about eight inches. Nothing had been etched into or written on its surface that could in any way reveal its purpose or the identity of its makers. Starting at due north, a rectangular opening set into the surface of the block revealed stairs spiraling down into darkness. The entrance was obscured by the webs of banana spiders and debris from storms, but a cool draft came from below.

*   *   *

At first, only I saw it as a tower. I don't know why the word *tower* came to me, given that it tunneled into the ground. I could as easily have considered it a bunker or a submerged building. Yet as soon as I saw the staircase, I remembered the lighthouse on the coast and had a sudden vision of the last expedition drifting off, one by one, and sometime thereafter the ground shifting in a uniform and preplanned way to leave the lighthouse standing where it had always been but depositing this underground part of it inland. I saw this in vast and intricate detail as we all stood there, and, looking back, I mark it as the first irrational thought I had once we had reached our destination.

"This is impossible," said the surveyor, staring at her maps. The solid shade of late afternoon cast her in cool darkness and lent the words more urgency than they would have had otherwise. The sun was telling us soon we'd have to use our flashlights to interrogate the impossible, although I'd have been perfectly happy doing it in the dark.

"And yet there it is," I said. "Unless we are having a mass hallucination."

"The architectural model is hard to identify," the anthropologist said. "The materials are ambiguous, indicating local origin but not necessarily local construction. Without going inside, we will not know if it is primitive or modern, or something in between. I'm not sure I would want to guess at how old it is, either."

We had no way to inform our superiors about this discovery. One rule for an expedition into Area X was that we were to attempt no outside contact, for fear of some irrevocable contamination. We also took little with us that matched our current level of technology. We had no cell or satellite phones, no computers, no camcorders, no complex measuring instruments except for those strange black boxes hanging from our belts. Our cameras required a makeshift darkroom. The absence of cell phones in particular made the real world seem very far away to the others, but I had always preferred to live without them. For weapons, we had knives, a locked container of antique handguns, and one assault rifle, this last a reluctant concession to current security standards.

It was expected simply that we would keep a record, like this one, in a journal, like this one: lightweight but nearly indestructible, with waterproof paper, a flexible black-and-white cover, and the blue horizontal lines for writing and the red line to the left to mark the margin. These journals would either return with us or be recovered by the next expedition. We had been cautioned to provide maximum context, so that anyone ignorant of Area X could understand our accounts. We had also been ordered not to share our journal entries with one another. Too much shared information could skew our observations, our superiors believed. But I knew from experience how hopeless this pursuit, this attempt to weed out bias, was. Nothing that lived and breathed was truly objective—even in a vacuum, even if all that possessed the brain was a self-immolating desire for the truth.

"I'm excited by this discovery," the psychologist interjected before we had discussed the tower much further. "Are you excited, too?" She had not asked us that particular question before. During training, she had tended to ask questions more like "How calm do you think you might be in an emergency?" Back then, I had felt as if she were a bad actor, playing a role. Now it seemed even more apparent, as if being our leader somehow made her nervous.

"It is definitely exciting . . . and unexpected," I said, trying not to mock her and failing, a little. I was surprised to feel a sense of growing unease, mostly because in my imagination, my dreams, this discovery would have been among the more banal. In my head, before we had crossed the border, I had seen so many things: vast cities, peculiar animals, and, once, during a period of illness, an enormous monster that rose from the waves to bear down on our camp.

The surveyor, meanwhile, just shrugged and would not answer the psychologist's question. The anthropologist nodded as if she agreed with me. The entrance to the tower leading down exerted a kind of presence, a blank surface that let us write so many things upon it. This presence manifested like a low-grade fever, pressing down on all of us.

I would tell you the names of the other three, if it mattered, but only the surveyor would last more than the next day or two. Besides, we were always strongly discouraged from using names: We were meant to be focused on our purpose, and "anything personal should be left behind." Names belonged to where we had come from, not to who we were while embedded in Area X.

*　　*　　*

Originally our expedition had numbered five and included a linguist. To reach the border, we each had to enter a separate bright white room with a door at the far end and a single metal chair in the corner. The chair had holes along the sides for straps; the implications of this raised a prickle of alarm, but by then I was set in my determination to reach Area X. The facility that housed these rooms was under the control of the Southern Reach, the clandestine government agency that dealt with all matters connected to Area X.

There we waited while innumerable readings were taken and various blasts of air, some cool, some hot, pressed down on us from vents in the ceiling. At some point, the psychologist visited each of us, although I do not remember what was said. Then we exited through the far door into a central staging area, with double doors at the end of a long hallway.

The psychologist greeted us there, but the linguist never reappeared.

"She had second thoughts," the psychologist told us, meeting our questions with a firm gaze. "She decided to stay behind." This came as a small shock, but there was also relief that it had not been someone else. Of all of our skill sets, linguist seemed at the time most expendable.

After a moment, the psychologist said, "Now, clear your minds." This meant she would begin the process of hypnotizing us so we could cross the border. She would then put herself under a kind of self-hypnosis. It had been explained that we would need to cross the border with precautions to protect against our minds tricking us. Apparently hallucinations were common. At least, this was what they told us. I no longer can be sure it was the truth. The actual nature of the border had been withheld from us for security reasons; we knew only that it was invisible to the naked eye.

So when I "woke up" with the others, it was in full gear, including heavy hiking boots, with the weight of forty-pound backpacks and a multitude of additional supplies hanging from our belts. All three of us lurched, and the anthropologist fell to one knee, while the psychologist patiently waited for us to recover. "I'm sorry," she said. "That was the least startling reentry I could manage."

The surveyor cursed, and glared at her. She had a temper that must have been deemed an asset. The anthropologist, as was her way, got to her feet, uncomplaining. And I, as was my way, was too busy observing to take this rude awakening personally. For example, I noticed the cruelty of the almost imperceptible smile on the psychologist's lips as she watched us struggle to adjust, the anthropologist still floundering and apologizing for floundering. Later I realized I might have misread her expression; it might have been pained or self-pitying.

We were on a dirt trail strewn with pebbles, dead leaves, and pine needles damp to the touch. Velvet ants and tiny emerald beetles crawled over them. The tall pines, with their scaly ridges of bark, rose on both sides, and the shadows of flying birds conjured lines between them. The air was so fresh it buffeted the lungs and we strained to breathe for a few seconds, mostly from surprise. Then, after marking our location with a piece of red cloth tied to a tree, we began to walk forward, into the unknown. If the psychologist somehow became incapacitated and could not lead us across at the end of our mission, we had been told to return to await "extraction." No one ever explained what form "extraction" might take, but the implication was that our superiors could observe the extraction point from afar, even though it was inside the border.

We had been told not to look back upon arrival, but I snuck a glance anyway, while the psychologist's attention was elsewhere. I don't know quite what I saw. It was hazy, indistinct, and already far behind us—perhaps a gate, perhaps a trick of the eye. Just a sudden impression of a fizzing block of light, fast fading.

The reasons I had volunteered were very separate from my qualifications for the expedition. I believe I qualified because I specialized in transitional environments, and this particular location transitioned several times, meaning that it was home to a complexity of ecosystems. In few other places could you still find habitat where, within the space of walking only six or seven miles, you went from forest to swamp to salt marsh to beach. In Area X, I had been told, I would find marine life that had adjusted to the brackish freshwater and which at low tide swam far up the natural canals formed by the reeds, sharing the same environment with otters and deer. If you walked along the beach, riddled through with the holes of fiddler crabs, you would sometimes look out to see one of the giant reptiles, for they, too, had adapted to their habitat.

I understood why no one lived in Area X now, that it was pristine because of that reason, but I kept un-remembering it. I had decided instead to make believe that it was simply a protected wildlife refuge, and we were hikers who happened to be scientists. This made sense on another level: We did not know what had happened here, what was still happening here, and any preformed theories would affect my analysis of the evidence as we encountered it. Besides, for my part it hardly mattered what lies I told myself because my existence back in the world had become at least as empty as Area X. With nothing left to anchor me, I needed to be here. As for the others, I don't know what they told themselves, and I didn't want to know, but I believe they all at least pretended to some level of curiosity. Curiosity could be a powerful distraction.

That night we talked about the tower, although the other three insisted on calling it a tunnel. The responsibility for the thrust of our investigations resided with each individual, the psychologist's authority describing a wider circle around these decisions. Part of the current rationale for sending the expeditions lay in giving each member some autonomy to decide, which helped to increase "the possibility of significant variation."

This vague protocol existed in the context of our separate skill sets. For example, although we had all received basic weapons and survival training, the surveyor had far more medical and firearms experience than the rest of us. The anthropologist had once been an architect; indeed, she had years ago survived a fire in a building she had designed, the only really personal thing I had found out about her. As for the psychologist, we knew the least about her, but I think we all believed she came from some kind of management background.

The discussion of the tower was, in a way, our first opportunity to test the limits of disagreement and of compromise.

"I don't think we should focus on the tunnel," the anthropologist said. "We should explore farther first, and we should come back to it with whatever data we gather from our other investigations—including of the lighthouse."

How predictable, and yet perhaps prescient, for the anthropologist to try to substitute a safer, more comfortable option. Although the idea of mapping seemed perfunctory or repetitive to me, I could not deny the existence of the tower, of which there was no suggestion on any map.

Then the surveyor spoke. "In this case I feel that we should rule out the tunnel as something invasive or threatening. Before we explore farther. It's like an enemy at our backs otherwise, if we press forward." She had come to us from the military, and I could see already the value of that experience. I had thought a surveyor would always side with the idea of further exploration, so this opinion carried weight.

"I'm impatient to explore the habitats here," I said. "But in a sense, given that it is not noted on any map, the 'tunnel' . . . or tower . . . seems important. It is either a deliberate exclusion from our maps and thus known . . . and that is a message of sorts . . . or it is something new that wasn't here when the last expedition arrived."

The surveyor gave me a look of thanks for the support, but my position had nothing to do with helping her. Something about the idea of a tower that headed straight down played with a twinned sensation of vertigo and a fascination with structure. I could not tell which part I craved and which I feared, and I kept seeing the inside of nautilus shells and other naturally occurring patterns balanced against a sudden leap off a cliff into the unknown.

The psychologist nodded, appeared to consider these opinions, and asked, "Does anyone yet have even an inkling of a sensation of wanting to leave?" It was a legitimate question, but jarring nonetheless.

All three of us shook our heads.

"What about you?" the surveyor asked the psychologist. "What is your opinion?"

The psychologist grinned, which seemed odd. But she must have known any one of us might have been tasked with observing her own reactions to stimuli. Perhaps the idea that a surveyor, an expert in the surface of things, might have been chosen, rather than a biologist or anthropologist, amused her. "I must admit to feeling a great deal of unease at the moment. But I am unsure whether it is because of the effect of the overall environment or the presence of the tunnel. Personally, I would like to rule out the tunnel."

Tower.

"Three to one, then," the anthropologist said, clearly relieved that the decision had been made for her.

The surveyor just shrugged.

Perhaps I'd been wrong about curiosity. The surveyor didn't seem curious about anything.

"Bored?" I asked.

"Eager to get on with it," she said, to the group, as if I'd asked the question for all of us.

We were in the communal tent for our talk. It had become dark by then and there came soon after the strange mournful call in the night that we knew must have natural causes but created a little shiver regardless. As if that was the signal to disband, we went back to our own quarters to be alone with our thoughts. I lay awake in my tent for a while trying to turn the tower into a tunnel, or even a shaft, but with no success. Instead, my mind kept returning to a question: What lies hidden at its base?

* * *

During our hike from the border to the base camp near the coast, we had experienced almost nothing out of the ordinary. The birds sang as they should; the deer took flight, their white tails exclamation points against the green and brown of the underbrush; the raccoons, bowlegged, swayed about their business, ignoring us. As a group, we felt almost giddy, I think, to be free after so many confining months of training and preparation. While we were in that corridor, in that transitional space, nothing could touch us. We were neither what we had been nor what we would become once we reached our destination.

The day before we arrived at the camp, this mood was briefly shattered by the appearance of an enormous wild boar some distance ahead of us on the trail.

It was so far from us that even with our binoculars we could barely identify it at first. But despite poor eyesight, wild pigs have prodigious powers of smell, and it began charging us from one hundred yards away. Thundering down the trail toward us . . . yet we still had time to think about what we might do, had drawn our long knives, and in the surveyor's case her assault rifle. Bullets would probably stop a seven-hundred-pound pig, or perhaps not. We did not feel confident taking our attention from the boar to untie the container of handguns from our gear and open its triple locks.

There was no time for the psychologist to prepare any hypnotic suggestion designed to keep us focused and in control; in fact, all she could offer was "Don't get close to it! Don't let it touch you!" while the boar continued to charge. The anthropologist was giggling a bit out of nervousness and the absurdity of experiencing an emergency situation that was taking so long to develop. Only the surveyor had taken direct action: She had dropped to one knee to get a better shot; our orders included the helpful directive to "kill only if you are under threat of being killed."

I was continuing to watch through the binoculars, and as the boar came closer, its face became stranger and stranger. Its features were somehow contorted, as if the beast was dealing with an extreme of inner torment. Nothing about its muzzle or broad, long face looked at all extraordinary, and yet I had the startling impression of some presence in the way its gaze seemed turned inward and its head willfully pulled to the left as if there were an invisible bridle. A kind of electricity sparked in its eyes that I could not credit as real. I thought instead it must be a by-product of my now slightly shaky hand on the binoculars.

Whatever was consuming the boar also soon consumed its desire to charge. It veered abruptly leftward, with what I can only describe as a great cry of anguish, into the underbrush. By the time we reached that spot, the boar was gone, leaving behind a thoroughly thrashed trail.

For several hours, my thoughts turned inward toward explanations for what I had seen: parasites and other hitchhikers of a neurological nature. I was searching for entirely rational biological theories. Then, after a time, the boar faded into the backdrop like all else that we had passed on our way from the border, and I was staring into the future again.

*   *   *

The morning after we discovered the tower we rose early, ate our breakfast, and doused our fire. There was a crisp chill to the air common for the season. The surveyor broke open the weapons stash and gave us each a handgun. She herself continued to hold on to the assault rifle; it had the added benefit of a flashlight under the barrel. We had not expected to have to open that particular container so soon, and although none of us protested, I felt a new tension between us. We knew that members of the second expedition to Area X had committed suicide by gunshot and members of the third had shot each other. Not until several subsequent expeditions had suffered zero casualties had our superiors issued firearms again. We were the twelfth expedition.

*   *   *

So we returned to the tower, all four of us. Sunlight came down dappled through the moss and leaves, created archipelagos of light on the flat surface of the entrance. It remained unremarkable, inert, in no way ominous . . . and yet it took an act of will to stand there, staring at the entry point. I noticed the anthropologist checking her black box, was relieved to see it did not display a glowing red light. If it had, we would have had to abort our exploration, move on to other things. I did not want that, despite the touch of fear.

"How deep do you think it goes down?" the anthropologist asked.

"Remember that we are to put our faith in your measurements," the psychologist answered, with a slight frown. "The measurements do not lie. This structure is 61.4 feet in diameter. It is raised 7.9 inches from the ground. The stairwell appears to have been positioned at or close to due north, which may tell us something about its creation, eventually. It is made of stone and coquina, not of metal or of bricks. These are facts. That it wasn't on the maps means only that a storm may have uncovered the entrance."

I found the psychologist's faith in measurements and her rationalization for the tower's absence from maps oddly . . . endearing? Perhaps she meant merely to reassure us, but I would like to believe she was trying to reassure herself. Her position, to lead and possibly to know more than us, must have been difficult and lonely.

"I hope it's only about six feet deep so we can continue mapping," the surveyor said, trying to be lighthearted, but then she, and we, all recognized the term "six feet under" ghosting through her syntax and a silence settled over us.

"I want you to know that I cannot stop thinking of it as a tower," I confessed. "I can't see it as a tunnel." It seemed important to make the distinction before our descent, even if it influenced their evaluation of my mental state. I saw a tower, plunging into the ground. The thought that we stood at its summit made me a little dizzy.

All three stared at me then, as if I were the strange cry at dusk, and after a moment the psychologist said, grudgingly, "If that helps make you more comfortable, then I don't see the harm."

A silence came over us again, there under the canopy of trees. A beetle spiraled up toward the branches, trailing dust motes. I think we all realized that only now had we truly entered Area X.

"I'll go first and see what's down there," the surveyor said, finally, and we were happy to defer to her.

The initial stairwell curved steeply downward and the steps were narrow, so the surveyor would have to back her way into the tower. We used sticks to clear the spiderwebs as she lowered herself into position on the stairwell. She teetered there, weapon slung across her back, looking up at us. She had tied her hair back and it made the lines of her face seem tight and drawn. Was this the moment when we were supposed to stop her? To come up with some other plan? If so, none of us had the nerve.

With a strange smirk, almost as if judging us, the surveyor descended until we could only see her face framed in the gloom below, and then not even that. She left an empty space that was shocking to me, as if the reverse had actually happened: as if a face had suddenly floated into view out of the darkness. I gasped, which drew a stare from the psychologist. The anthropologist was too busy staring down into the stairwell to notice any of it.

"Is everything okay?" the psychologist called out to the surveyor. Everything had been fine just a second before. Why would anything be different now?

The surveyor made a sharp grunt in answer, as if agreeing with me. For a few moments more, we could still hear the surveyor struggling on those short steps. Then came silence, and then another movement, at a different rhythm, which for a terrifying moment seemed like it might come from a second source.

But then the surveyor called up to us. "Clear to this level!" This level. Something within me thrilled to the fact that my vision of a tower was not yet disproven.

That was the signal for me to descend with the anthropologist, while the psychologist stood watch. "Time to go," the psychologist said, as perfunctorily as if we were in school and a class was letting out.

An emotion that I could not quite identify surged through me, and for a moment I saw dark spots in my field of vision. I followed the anthropologist so eagerly down through the remains of webs and the embalmed husks of insects into the cool brackishness of that place that I almost tripped her. My last view of the world above: the psychologist peering down at me with a slight frown, and behind her the trees, the blue of the sky almost blinding against the darkness of the sides of the stairwell.

Below, shadows spread across the walls. The temperature dropped and sound became muffled, the soft steps absorbing our tread. Approximately twenty feet beneath the surface, the structure opened out into a lower level. The ceiling was about eight feet high, which meant a good twelve feet of stone lay above us. The flashlight of the surveyor's assault rifle illuminated the space, but she was faced away from us, surveying the walls, which were an off-white and devoid of any adornment. A few cracks indicated either the passage of time or some sudden stressor. The level appeared to be the same circumference as the exposed top, which again supported the idea of a single solid structure buried in the earth.

"It goes farther," the surveyor said, and pointed with her rifle to the far corner, directly opposite the opening where we had come out onto that level. A rounded archway stood there, and a darkness that suggested downward steps. A tower, which made this level not so much a floor as a landing or part of the turret. She started to walk toward the archway while I was still engrossed in examining the walls with my flashlight. Their very blankness mesmerized me. I tried to imagine the builder of this place but could not.

I thought again of the silhouette of the lighthouse, as I had seen it during the late afternoon of our first day at base camp. We assumed that the structure in question was a lighthouse because the map showed a lighthouse at that location and because everyone immediately recognized what a lighthouse should look like. In fact, the surveyor and anthropologist had both expressed a kind of relief when they had seen the lighthouse. Its appearance on both the map and in reality reassured them, anchored them. Being familiar with its function further reassured them.

With the tower, we knew none of these things. We could not intuit its full outline. We had no sense of its purpose. And now that we had begun to descend into it, the tower still failed to reveal any hint of these things. The psychologist might recite the measurements of the "top" of the tower, but those numbers meant nothing, had no wider context. Without context, clinging to those numbers was a form of madness.

"There is a regularity to the circle, seen from the inside walls, that suggests precision in the creation of the building," the anthropologist said. The building. Already she had begun to abandon the idea of it being a tunnel.

All of my thoughts came spilling out of my mouth, some final discharge from the state that had overtaken me above. "But what is its purpose? And is it believable that it would not be on the maps? Could one of the prior expeditions have built it and hidden it?" I asked all of this and more, not expecting an answer. Even though no threat had revealed itself, it seemed important to eliminate any possible moment of silence. As if somehow the blankness of the walls fed off of silence, and that something might appear in the spaces between our words if we were not careful. Had I expressed this anxiety to the psychologist, she would have been worried, I know. But I was more attuned to solitude than any of us, and I would have characterized that place in that moment of our exploration as watchful.

A gasp from the surveyor cut me off in mid-question, no doubt much to the anthropologist's relief.

"Look!" the surveyor said, training her flashlight down into the archway. We hurried over and stared past her, adding our own illumination.

A stairway did indeed lead down, this time at a gentle curve with much broader steps, but still made of the same materials. At about shoulder height, perhaps five feet high, clinging to the inner wall of the tower, I saw what I first took to be dimly sparkling green vines progressing down into the darkness. I had a sudden absurd memory of the floral wallpaper treatment that had lined the bathroom of my house when I had shared it with my husband. Then, as I stared, the "vines" resolved further, and I saw that they were words, in cursive, the letters raised about six inches off the wall.

"Hold the light," I said, and pushed past them down the first few steps. Blood was rushing through my head again, a roaring confusion in my ears. It was an act of supreme control to walk those few paces. I couldn't tell you what impulse drove me, except that I was the biologist and this looked oddly organic. If the linguist had been there, perhaps I would have deferred to her.

"Don't touch it, whatever it is," the anthropologist warned.

I nodded, but I was too enthralled with the discovery. If I'd had the impulse to touch the words on the wall, I would not have been able to stop myself.

As I came close, did it surprise me that I could understand the language the words were written in? Yes. Did it fill me with a kind of elation and dread intertwined? Yes. I tried to suppress the thousand new questions rising up inside of me. In as calm a voice as I could manage, aware of the importance of that moment, I read from the beginning, aloud: "Where lies the strangling fruit that came from the hand of the sinner I shall bring forth the seeds of the dead to share with the worms that . . ."

Then the darkness took it. "Words? Words?" the anthropologist said.

Yes, words.

"What are they made of?" the surveyor asked. Did they need to be made of anything?

The illumination cast on the continuing sentence quavered and shook. Where lies the strangling fruit became bathed in shadow and in light, as if a battle raged for its meaning.

"Give me a moment. I need to get closer." Did I? Yes, I needed to get closer.

What are they made of ?

I hadn't even thought of this, though I should have; I was still trying to parse the lingual meaning, had not transitioned to the idea of taking a physical sample. But what relief at the question! Because it helped me fight the compulsion to keep reading, to descend into the greater darkness and keep descending until I had read all there was to read. Already those initial phrases were infiltrating my mind in unexpected ways, finding fertile ground.

So I stepped closer, peered at Where lies the strangling fruit. I saw that the letters, connected by their cursive script, were made from what would have looked to the layperson like rich green fernlike moss but in fact was probably a type of fungi or other eukaryotic organism. The curling filaments were all packed very close together and rising out from the wall. A loamy smell came from the words along with an underlying hint of rotting honey. This miniature forest swayed, almost imperceptibly, like sea grass in a gentle ocean current.

Other things existed in this miniature ecosystem. Half-hidden by the green filaments, most of these creatures were translucent and shaped like tiny hands embedded by the base of the palm. Golden nodules capped the fingers on these "hands." I leaned in closer, like a fool, like someone who had not had months of survival training or ever studied biology. Someone tricked into thinking that words should be read.

I was unlucky—or was I lucky? Triggered by a disturbance in the flow of air, a nodule in the W chose that moment to burst open and a tiny spray of golden spores spewed out. I pulled back, but I thought I had felt something enter my nose, experienced a pinprick of escalation in the smell of rotting honey.

Unnerved, I stepped back even farther, borrowing some of the surveyor's best curses, but only in my head. My natural instinct was always for concealment. Already I was imagining the psychologist's reaction to my contamination, if revealed to the group.

"Some sort of fungi," I said finally, taking a deep breath so I could control my voice. "The letters are made from fruiting bodies." Who knew if it were actually true? It was just the closest thing to an answer.

My voice must have seemed calmer than my actual thoughts because there was no hesitation in their response. No hint in their tone of having seen the spores erupt into my face. I had been so close. The spores had been so tiny, so insignificant. I shall bring forth the seeds of the dead.

"Words? Made of fungi?" the surveyor said, stupidly echoing me.

"There is no recorded human language that uses this method of writing," the anthropologist said. "Is there any animal that communicates in this way?"

I had to laugh. "No, there is no animal that communicates in this way." Or, if there were, I could not recall its name, and never did later, either.

"Are you joking? This is a joke, right?" the surveyor said. She looked poised to come down and prove me wrong, but didn't move from her position.

"Fruiting bodies," I replied, almost as if in a trance. "Forming words."

PAST NEBULA AWARD WINNERS

1965

Novel: *Dune* by Frank Herbert
Novella: "He Who Shapes" by Roger Zelazny and "The Saliva Tree" by Brian Aldiss (tie)
Novelette: "The Doors of His Face, the Lamps of His Mouth" by Roger Zelazny
Short Story: "'Repent, Harlequin!' Said the Ticktockman" by Harlan Ellison

1966

Novel: *Babel-17* by Samuel R. Delany and *Flowers for Algernon* by Daniel Keyes (tie)
Novella: "The Last Castle" by Jack Vance
Novelette: "Call Him Lord" by Gordon R. Dickson
Short Story: "The Secret Place" by Richard McKenna

1967

Novel: *The Einstein Intersection* by Samuel R. Delany
Novella: "Behold the Man" by Michael Moorcock
Novelette: "Gonna Roll the Bones" by Fritz Leiber
Short Story: "Aye, and Gomorrah" by Samuel R. Delany

1968

Novel: *Rite of Passage* by Alexei Panshin
Novella: "Dragonrider" by Anne McCaffrey
Novelette: "Mother to the World" by Richard Wilson
Short Story: "The Planners" by Kate Wilhelm

1969

Novel: *The Left Hand of Darkness* by Ursula K. Le Guin
Novella: "A Boy and His Dog" by Harlan Ellison

Novelette: "Time Considered as a Helix of Semi-Precious Stones" by Samuel R. Delany
Short Story: "Passengers" by Robert Silverberg

1970

Novel: *Ringworld* by Larry Niven
Novella: "Ill Met in Lankhmar" by Fritz Leiber
Novelette: "Slow Sculpture" by Theodore Sturgeon
Short Story: No Award

1971

Novel: *A Time of Changes* by Robert Silverberg
Novella: "The Missing Man" by Katherine MacLean
Novelette: "The Queen of Air and Darkness" by Poul Anderson
Short Story: "Good News from the Vatican" by Robert Silverberg

1972

Novel: *The Gods Themselves* by Isaac Asimov
Novella: "A Meeting with Medusa" by Arthur C. Clarke

Novelette: "Goat Song" by Poul Anderson
Short Story: "When It Changed" by Joanna Russ

1973

Novel: *Rendezvous with Rama* by Arthur C. Clarke
Novella: "The Death of Doctor Island" by Gene Wolfe
Novelette: "Of Mist, and Grass, and Sand" by Vonda N. McIntyre
Short Story: "Love Is the Plan, the Plan Is Death" by James Tiptree Jr.
Dramatic Presentation: *Soylent Green*

1974

Novel: *The Dispossessed* by Ursula K. Le Guin
Novella: "Born with the Dead" by Robert Silverberg
Novelette: "If the Stars Are Gods" by Gordon Eklund and Gregory Benford
Short Story: "The Day before the Revolution" by Ursula K. Le Guin
Dramatic Presentation: *Sleeper* by Woody Allen
Grand Master: Robert Heinlein

1975

Novel: *The Forever War* by Joe
  Haldeman
Novella: "Home Is the Hangman" by
  Roger Zelazny
Novelette: "San Diego Lightfoot Sue"
  by Tom Reamy
Short Story: "Catch That Zeppelin"
  by Fritz Leiber
Dramatic Presentation: *Young Fran-
  kenstein* by Mel Brooks and Gene
  Wilder
Grand Master: Jack Williamson

1976

Novel: *Man Plus* by Frederik Pohl
Novella: "Houston, Houston, Do You
  Read?" by James Tiptree Jr.
Novelette: "The Bicentennial Man"
  by Isaac Asimov
Short Story: "A Crowd of Shadows"
  by C. L. Grant
Grand Master: Clifford D. Simak

1977

Novel: *Gateway* by Frederik Pohl
Novella: "Stardance" by Spider and
  Jeanne Robinson
Novelette: "The Screwfly Solution"
  by Racoona Sheldon

Short Story: "Jeffty Is Five" by
  Harlan Ellison

1978

Novel: *Dreamsnake* by Vonda N.
  McIntyre
Novella: "The Persistence of Vision"
  by John Varley
Novelette: "A Glow of Candles, A
  Unicorn's Eye" by C. L. Grant
Short Story: "Stone" by Edward
  Bryant
Grand Master: L. Sprague de Camp

1979

Novel: *The Fountains of Paradise* by
  Arthur C. Clarke
Novella: "Enemy Mine" by Barry B.
  Longyear
Novelette: "Sandkings" by George R.
  R. Martin
Short Story: "GiANTS" by Edward
  Bryant

1980

Novel: *Timescape* by Gregory Benford
Novella: "Unicorn Tapestry" by Suzy
  McKee Charnas
Novelette: "The Ugly Chickens" by
  Howard Waldrop

Short Story: "Grotto of the Dancing Deer" by Clifford D. Simak

Grand Master: Fritz Leiber

Short Story: "The Peacemaker" by Gardner Dozois

Grand Master: Andre Norton

1981

Novel: *The Claw of the Conciliator* by Gene Wolfe

Novella: "The Saturn Game" by Poul Anderson

Novelette: "The Quickening" by Michael Bishop

Short Story: "The Bone Flute" by Lisa Tuttle [declined by author]

1982

Novel: *No Enemy but Time* by Michael Bishop

Novella: "Another Orphan" by John Kessel

Novelette: "Fire Watch" by Connie Willis

Short Story: "A Letter from the Clearys" by Connie Willis

1983

Novel: *Startide Rising* by David Brin

Novella: "Hardfought" by Greg Bear

Novelette: "Blood Music" by Greg Bear

1984

Novel: *Neuromancer* by William Gibson

Novella: "Press Enter []" by John Varley

Novelette: "Blood Child" by Octavia Butler

Short Story: "Morning Child" by Gardner Dozois

1985

Novel: *Ender's Game* by Orson Scott Card

Novella: "Sailing to Byzantium" by Robert Silverberg

Novelette: "Portraits of His Children" by George R. R. Martin

Short Story: "Out of All Them Bright Stars" by Nancy Kress

Grand Master: Arthur C. Clarke

1986

Novel: *Speaker for the Dead* by Orson Scott Card

Novella: "R&R" by Lucius Shepard

Novelette: "The Girl Who Fell into the Sky" by Kate Wilhelm

Short Story: "Tangents" by Greg
  Bear
Grand Master: Isaac Asimov

1987

Novel: *The Falling Woman* by Pat
  Murphy
Novella: "The Blind Geometer" by
  Kim Stanley Robinson
Novelette: "Rachel in Love" by Pat
  Murphy
Short Story: "Forever Yours, Anna"
  by Kate Wilhelm
Grand Master: Alfred Bester

1988

Novel: *Falling Free* by Lois McMaster
  Bujold
Novella: "The Last of the Win-
  nebagos" by Connie Willis
Novelette: "Schrödinger's Kitten" by
  George Alec Effinger
Short Story: "Bible Stories for Adults,
  No. 17: The Deluge" by James
  Morrow
Grand Master: Ray Bradbury

1989

Novel: *The Healer's War* by Elizabeth
  Ann Scarborough

Novella: "The Mountains of
  Mourning" by Lois McMaster
  Bujold
Novelette: "At the Rialto" by Connie
  Willis
Short Story: "Ripples in the Dirac
  Sea" by Geoffrey A. Landis

1990

Novel: *Tehanu: The Last Book of
  Earthsea* by Ursula K. Le Guin
Novella: "The Hemingway Hoax" by
  Joe Haldeman
Novelette: "Tower of Babylon" by
  Ted Chiang
Short Story: "Bears Discover Fire" by
  Terry Bisson
Grand Master: Lester del Rey

1991

Novel: *Stations of the Tide* by Michael
  Swanwick
Novella: "Beggars in Spain" by
  Nancy Kress
Novelette: "Guide Dog" by Mike
  Conner
Short Story: "Ma Qui" by Alan Brennert

1992

Novel: *Doomsday Book* by Connie Willis

Novella: "City Of Truth" by James Morrow

Novelette: "Danny Goes to Mars" by Pamela Sargent

Short Story: "Even the Queen" by Connie Willis

Grand Master: Fred Pohl

1993

Novel: *Red Mars* by Kim Stanley Robinson

Novella: "The Night We Buried Road Dog" by Jack Cady

Novelette: "Georgia on My Mind" by Charles Sheffield

Short Story: "Graves" by Joe Haldeman

1994

The 1994 Nebulas were awarded at a ceremony in New York City in late April 1995.

Novel: *Moving Mars* by Greg Bear

Novella: "Seven Views of Olduvai Gorge" by Mike Resnick

Novelette: "The Martian Child" by David Gerrold

Short Story: "A Defense of the Social Contracts" by Martha Soukup

Grand Master: Damon Knight

Author Emeritus: Emil Petaja

1995

Novel: *The Terminal Experiment* by Robert J. Sawyer

Novella: "Last Summer at Mars Hill" by Elizabeth Hand

Novelette: "Solitude" by Ursula K. Le Guin

Short Story: "Death and the Librarian" by Esther M. Friesner

Grand Master: A. E. van Vogt

Author Emeritus: Wilson "Bob" Tucker

1996

Novel: *Slow River* by Nicola Griffith

Novella: "Da Vinci Rising" by Jack Dann

Novelette: "Lifeboat on a Burning Sea" by Bruce Holland Rogers

Short Story: "A Birthday" by Esther M. Friesner

Grand Master: Jack Vance

Author Emeritus: Judith Merril

1997

Novel: *The Moon and the Sun* by Vonda N. McIntyre
Novella: "Abandon in Place" by Jerry Oltion
Novelette: "Flowers of Aulit Prison" by Nancy Kress
Short Story: "Sister Emily's Lightship" by Jane Yolen
Grand Master: Poul Anderson
Author Emeritus: Nelson Slade Bond

1998

Novel: *Forever Peace* by Joe Haldeman
Novella: "Reading the Bones" by Sheila Finch
Novelette: "Lost Girls" by Jane Yolen
Short Story: "Thirteen Ways to Water" by Bruce Holland Rogers
Grand Master: Hal Clement (Harry Stubbs)
Author Emeritus: William Tenn (Philip Klass)

1999

Novel: *Parable of the Talents* by Octavia E. Butler
Novella: "Story of Your Life" by Ted Chiang

Novelette: "Mars Is No Place for Children" by Mary A. Turzillo
Short Story: "The Cost of Doing Business" by Leslie What
Script: *The Sixth Sense* by M. Night Shyamalan
Grand Master: Brian W. Aldiss
Author Emeritus: Daniel Keyes

2000

Novel: *Darwin's Radio* by Greg Bear
Novella: "Goddesses" by Linda Nagata
Novelette: "Daddy's World" by Walter Jon Williams
Short Story: "macs" by Terry Bisson
Script: *Galaxy Quest* by Robert Gordon and David Howard
Ray Bradbury Award: Yuri Rasovsky and Harlan Ellison
Grand Master: Philip José Farmer
Author Emeritus: Robert Sheckley

2001

Novel: *The Quantum Rose* by Catherine Asaro
Novella: "The Ultimate Earth" by Jack Williamson
Novelette: "Louise's Ghost" by Kelly Link
Short Story: "The Cure for Everything" by Severna Park

Script: *Crouching Tiger, Hidden Dragon*
by James Schamus, Kuo Jung
Tsai, and Hui-Ling Wang
President's Award: Betty Ballantine

2002

Novel: *American Gods* by Neil
Gaiman
Novella: "Bronte's Egg" by Richard
Chwedyk
Novelette: "Hell Is the Absence of
God" by Ted Chiang
Short Story: "Creature" by Carol
Emshwiller
Script: *Lord of the Rings: The Fellow-
ship of the Ring* by Frances Walsh,
Phillipa Boyens, and Peter
Jackson
Grand Master: Ursula K. Le Guin
Author Emeritus: Katherine MacLean

2003

Novel: *Speed of Dark* by Elizabeth Moon
Novella: "Coraline" by Neil Gaiman
Novelette: "The Empire of Ice
Cream" by Jeffrey Ford
Short Story: "What I Didn't See" by
Karen Joy Fowler
Script: *Lord of the Rings: The Two
Towers* by Frances Walsh, Phil-
lipa Boyens, Stephen Sinclair,
and Peter Jackson

Grand Master: Robert Silverberg
Author Emeritus: Charles L. Harness

2004

Novel: *Paladin of Souls* by Lois
McMaster Bujold
Novella: "The Green Leopard
Plague" by Walter Jon Williams
Novelette: "Basement Magic" by
Ellen Klages
Short Story: "Coming to Terms" by
Eileen Gunn
Script: *Lord of the Rings: Return of the
King* by Frances Walsh, Phillipa
Boyens, and Peter Jackson
Grand Master: Anne McCaffrey

2005

Novel: *Camouflage* by Joe Haldeman
Novella: "Magic for Beginners" by
Kelly Link
Novelette: "The Faery Handbag" by
Kelly Link
Short Story: "I Live with You" by
Carol Emshwiller
Script: *Serenity* by Joss Whedon
Grand Master: Harlan Ellison
Author Emeritus: William F. Nolan

2006

Novel: *Seeker* by Jack McDevitt
Novella: "Burn" by James Patrick Kelly
Novelette: "Two Hearts" by Peter S. Beagle
Short Story: "Echo" by Elizabeth Hand
Script: *Howl's Moving Castle* by Hayao Miyazaki, Cindy Davis Hewitt, and Donald H. Hewitt
Andre Norton Award: *Magic or Madness* by Justine Larbalestier
Grand Master: James Gunn
Author Emeritus: D. G. Compton

2007

Novel: *The Yiddish Policemen's Union* by Michael Chabon
Novella: "Fountain of Age" by Nancy Kress
Novelette: "The Merchant and the Alchemist's Gate" by Ted Chiang
Short Story: "Always" by Karen Joy Fowler
Script: *Pan's Labyrinth* by Guillermo del Toro
Andre Norton Award for Young Adult Science Fiction and Fantasy: *Harry Potter and the Deathly Hallows* by J. K. Rowling

Grand Master: Michael Moorcock
Author Emeritus: Ardath Mayhar
SFWA Service Awards: Melisa Michaels and Graham P. Collins

2008

Novel: *Powers* by Ursula K. Le Guin
Novella: "The Spacetime Pool" by Catherine Asaro
Novelette: "Pride and Prometheus" by John Kessel
Short Story: "Trophy Wives" by Nina Kiriki Hoffman
Script: *WALL-E* by Andrew Stanton and Jim Reardon. Original story by Andrew Stanton and Pete Docter
Andre Norton Award: *Flora's Dare: How a Girl of Spirit Gambles All to Expand Her Vocabulary, Confront a Bouncing Boy Terror, and Try to Save Califa from a Shaky Doom (Despite Being Confined to Her Room)* by Ysabeau S. Wilce
Grand Master: Harry Harrison
Author Emeritus: M. J. Engh
Solstice Award: Kate Wilhelm, Martin H. Greenberg, and the late Algis Budrys
SFWA Service Award: Victoria Strauss

2009

Novel: *The Windup Girl* by Paolo Bacigalupi
Novella: "The Women of Nell Gwynne's" by Kage Baker
Novelette: "Sinner, Baker, Fabulist, Priest; Red Mask, Black Mask, Gentleman, Beast" by Eugie Foster
Short Story: "Spar" by Kij Johnson
Ray Bradbury Award: *District 9* by Neill Blomkamp and Terri Tatchell
Andre Norton Award: *The Girl Who Circumnavigated Fairyland in a Ship of Her Own Making* by Catherynne M. Valente
Grand Master: Joe Haldeman
Author Emeritus: Neal Barrett Jr.
Solstice Award: Tom Doherty, Terri Windling, and the late Donald A. Wollheim
SFWA Service Awards: Vonda N. McIntyre and Keith Stokes

2010

Novel: *Blackout/All Clear* by Connie Willis
Novella: "The Lady Who Plucked Red Flowers beneath the Queen's Window" by Rachel Swirsky
Novelette: "That Leviathan Whom Thou Hast Made" by Eric James Stone
Short Story: "Ponies" by Kij Johnson and "How Interesting: A Tiny Man" by Harlan Ellison (tie)
Ray Bradbury Award: *Inception* by Christopher Nolan
Andre Norton Award: *I Shall Wear Midnight*, by Terry Pratchett

2011

Novel: *Among Others*, Jo Walton
Novella: "The Man Who Bridged the Mist," Kij Johnson
Novelette: "What We Found," Geoff Ryman
Short Story: "The Paper Menagerie," Ken Liu
Ray Bradbury Award: *Doctor Who*: "The Doctor's Wife" by Neil Gaiman (writer), Richard Clark (director)
Andre Norton Award: *The Freedom Maze* by Delia Sherman
Damon Knight Grand Master Award: Connie Willis
Solstice Award: Octavia Butler (posthumous) and John Clute
SFWA Service Award: Bud Webster

2012

Novel: *2312* by Kim Stanley Robinson
Novella: *After the Fall, Before the Fall, During the Fall* by Nancy Kress
Novelette: "Close Encounters" by Andy Duncan
Short Story: "Immersion" by Aliette de Bodard
Ray Bradbury Award: *Beasts of the Southern Wild*; Benh Zeitlin, director; Benh Zeitlin & Lucy Abilar, writers
Andre Norton Award: *Fair Coin* by E. C. Myers

2013

Novel: *Ancillary Justice* by Ann Leckie
Novella: "The Weight of the Sunrise" by Vylar Kaftan
Novelette: "The Waiting Stars" by Aliete de Bodard
Short Story: "If You Were a Dinosaur, My Love" by Rachel Swirsky
Ray Bradbury Award: *Gravity*; Alfonso Cuarón, director; Alfonso Cuarón, Jonás Cuarón, writers
Andre Norton Award: *Sister Mine* by Nalo Hopkinson
Damon Knight Grand Master Award: Samuel R. Delany

2013 Distinguished Guest: Frank M. Robinson
Kevin O'Donnell Jr. Service to SFWA Award: Michael Armstrong

2014

Novel: *Annihilation* by Jeff VanderMeer
Novella: *Yesterday's Kin* by Nancy Kress
Novelette: "A Guide to the Fruits of Hawai'i" by Alaya Dawn Johnson
Short Story: "Jackalope Wives" by Ursula Vernon
Ray Bradbury Award: *Guardians of the Galaxy*, James Gunn and Nicole Perlman, writers
Andre Norton Award: *Love Is the Drug,* Alaya Dawn Johnson
Damon Knight Grand Master Award: Larry Niven
Solstice Award: Joanna Russ (posthumous), Stanley Schmidt
Kevin O'Donnell Jr. Service to SFWA Award: Jeffry Dwight

ABOUT THE EDITOR

Mercedes Lackey is a full-time writer and has published numerous novels and works of short fiction, including the bestselling Heralds of Valdemar and Elemental Masters series. She is also a professional lyricist and a licensed wild bird rehabilitator. She lives in Oklahoma with her husband, artist Larry Dixon, and their flock of parrots.

ABOUT THE COVER ARTIST

Reiko Murakami is an illustrator and concept artist who specializes in creature design and surreal horror illustrations. In 2015, she was nominated for a Chesley Award. She is also known as raqmo, and has worked for companies such as Hobby Japan, Square Enix, Capcom, INEI, and Harmonix. Her work has been published in *Exposé 11* and *2DArtist Magazine,* and she has been featured in the Japanese Digital Art Masters Gallery on the 3DTotal Japan website. More of her work can be seen at reikomurakami.com and facebook.com/raqmoful.